*Praise for* The I

'The second book by M. R. Hall, whose debut crime novel, *The Coroner*, made the bestseller list last year, does not disappoint . . . an excellent and compelling detective drama'
**Daily Mail**

'*The Disappeared* is every bit as accomplished and challenging [as *The Coroner*] . . . High-mindedness can be too heavy a burden for some thrillers to carry. They become all intellectual argument and no action. Equally, literary ambitions – Hall has a particular knack for conjuring up landscapes, including the Wye Valley, Cooper's base and his own home – can get in the way of the necessary narrative thrust. But *The Disappeared* avoids both potential traps triumphantly'
**Independent**

'Intelligent and intricate, and grips from beginning to end'
**Woman & Home**

'A substantial and satisfying novel which adroitly combines the personal and the political into an engrossing narrative that is ultimately about international paranoia'
**Daily Express**

# THE DISAPPEARED

**M. R. Hall** is a screenwriter, producer and former criminal barrister. *The Disappeared* is his second novel in the Jenny Cooper series. Educated at Hereford Cathedral School and Worcester College, Oxford, he lives in Monmouthshire with his wife and two sons. Aside from writing, his main passion is the preservation and planting of woodland. In his spare moments, he is mostly to be found amongst trees.

*Also by M. R. Hall*

**The Coroner**

M.R. HALL

# THE DISAPPEARED

PAN BOOKS

First published in Great Britain 2010 by Macmillan

This edition published 2010 by Pan Books
an imprint of Pan Macmillan, a division of Macmillan Publishers Limited
Pan Macmillan, 20 New Wharf Road, London N1 9RR
Basingstoke and Oxford
Associated companies throughout the world
www.panmacmillan.com

ISBN 978-0-330-45837-5

3 5 7 9 8 6 4 2

A CIP catalogue record for this book is available from
the British Library.

Typeset by SetSystems Ltd, Saffron Walden, Essex
Printed in the UK by CPI Mackays, Chatham ME5 8TD

Visit **www.panmacmillan.com** to read more about all our books
and to buy them. You will also find features, author interviews and
news of any author events, and you can sign up for e-newsletters
so that you're always first to hear about our new releases.

For Bob and Romayne

and many brave years

*Veil not thy mirror, sweet Amine,*
*Till night shall also veil each star,*
*Thou seest a twofold marvel there:*
*The only face so fair as thine,*
*The only eyes that, near or far,*
*Can gaze on thine without despair.*

James Clarence Mangan

# ONE

DURING HER SIX MONTHS AS coroner for the Severn Vale District, Jenny Cooper had known only a handful of corpses remain unidentified for more than a day or two. Jane Doe, or JD0110, had been wrapped in her white plastic shroud in the refrigerator at the Vale hospital's mortuary for a little over a week. Owing to the large backlog of bodies awaiting postmortem, she remained unopened and unexamined.

She had been washed up on the English side of the Severn estuary at the mouth of the Avon; sucked in with the tide and deposited naked on a mudbank a little downstream from where the M5 motorway thundered across the river. She was blonde, five feet eight inches tall, had no body hair and had been partially eaten by gulls. There was little left of the soft tissue of her abdomen and breasts, and in common with all corpses left open to the elements for any length of time there were empty sockets where her eyes had once been. For the purposes of identification Jenny had insisted that glass ones be fitted. An unnatural blue, they gave her face a dumb, doll-like quality.

Alison Trent, the coroner's officer, had arranged for a number of potential identifiers to attend the mortuary late on a Friday afternoon, but at the last minute she had been called to a supermarket depot, where the bodies of three young African men had been discovered in a refrigerated trailer amongst a cargo of beef carcasses imported from France. Rather than leave the families in suspense, Jenny reluctantly left the office early to preside at the mortuary herself.

It was the final week of January; freezing sleet slanted from a gunmetal sky. It was not yet four o'clock and daylight had all but bled away. Jenny arrived to find a group of a dozen or so waiting in the unmanned reception area of the mortuary building at the rear of the hospital. The antique radiators were either not switched on or were broken. As the couples amongst them whispered to one another their breath emerged in wispy clouds. Most were middle-aged parents who wore expressions of dread masking deeper feelings of guilt and shame. *How did it come to this?* their grim, lined faces seemed to say.

Since there was no assistant available to help conduct the viewings, Jenny was forced to address the group in the manner of a schoolteacher, instructing them to take it in turns to pass through the slap doors and along the corridor to the refrigerator at the far end. She warned them that the body might not be instantly recognizable and provided the details of a private laboratory which would take their DNA samples and compare them with that of the Jane Doe: it entailed a modest expense but not one her meagre budget would extend to. They dutifully noted down the company's email address and phone number, but one of them, Jenny noticed, did not. Nor did he enter his details onto the list of those wishing to be informed in the event that other uniden-tified bodies surfaced. Instead, the tall, lean man, somewhere in his mid-fifties, stood away from the huddle, his slender, sun-weathered face expressionless, his only sign of anxiety the occasional raising of his hand to smooth his short black hair streaked with grey. Jenny noticed his arresting green eyes and hoped he wasn't the one whose tears would spill onto the tiled floor.

There were always tears.

The building was arranged to maximize the visitors' trauma. Their twenty-yard journey through the mortuary required them to pass an extended row of gurneys, each bearing a corpse wrapped in an envelope of shiny white polythene. The stale air was heavy with the smell of decay, disinfectant and an illicit hint of cigarette smoke. One after another, three separate couples made the walk along the corridor and steeled themselves to look down on the bare head and shoulders of the Jane Doe, her skin now starting to yellow and take on a papery texture. And one after another they shook their heads, their expressions of relief mixed with uncertainty and the fear of similar ordeals to follow.

The man with green eyes did not carry himself like the others. His footsteps approached briskly, his manner was abrupt and businesslike, yet somehow seemed to cover a sadness or uncertainty that Jenny read as regret. Without flinching, he looked down at the Jane Doe's face, studied her for a moment, then shook his head decisively. Curious, Jenny asked him who he was looking for. In a cultured transatlantic accent he explained briefly that his stepdaughter had been travelling in the UK and had failed to make contact for several weeks. Her last email was sent from an internet cafe in Bristol. The police had told him about the body. Before Jenny could find a pretext to extend the conversation, he turned and left as quickly as he had come.

Mr and Mrs Crosby arrived after the main group. He was in his late fifties and dressed in the business suit that befitted a high-level professional or businessman; she was several years younger and had the well-preserved features and softer manner of a woman who had not been ground down by life in the workplace. With them came a young man in his late twenties, also dressed formally in a suit and tie. Mr Crosby introduced him stiffly as Michael Stevens, his daughter's boyfriend. The term seemed to embarrass him: a father not yet ready to surrender the affections of his grown-up daughter. Jenny offered a sympathetic smile and watched them gaze down at the body, take in the contours of the staring, lifeless face, exchange glances and shake their heads.

'No, it's not Anna Rose,' Mrs Crosby said with a trace of doubt. 'Her hair isn't that long.'

The statement seemed to satisfy her husband, but the young man was stealing another glance, wise enough to know, Jenny could tell, that the dead can look deceptively different from the living.

'The eyes are glass,' she said, 'so the colour could be different. There are no distinguishing marks and the body was completely depilated.'

Mr Crosby's eyes flitted questioningly towards her.

'She has no body hair,' his wife explained.

He gave a dismissive grunt.

'It's not her,' Michael Stevens said finally. 'No, it's definitely not her.'

'If you're at all unsure I'd advise you to take a DNA test,' Jenny said to the parents.

'We adopted Anna Rose,' Mrs Crosby said, 'but I expect we can find something of hers. A hairbrush would do, wouldn't it?'

'A hair sample would be fine.'

Mr Crosby offered a terse thank you and placed a hand in the small of his wife's back, but as he made to lead her away she turned to Jenny.

'Anna Rose has been missing for ten days. She's a physics graduate – she works at Maybury with Mike. She didn't have any problems, she seemed perfectly happy with life.' Mrs

4

Crosby paused briefly to collect herself. 'Do you ever come across that?'

Mr Crosby, embarrassed at his wife's naivety, lowered his eyes to the floor. Mike Stevens glanced uncertainly between his missing girlfriend's parents. There was alarm in his eyes. He was out of his depth.

'No. Not often,' Jenny said. 'In my experience, suicide – if that is what's in your mind – is invariably preceded by depression. If you were close to the person, I think you would know.'

'Thank you,' Mrs Crosby said. 'Thank you.'

Her husband steered her away.

Mike Stevens glanced briefly at Jenny in such a way that she assumed he had a question of his own, but whether from shyness or family protocol, he kept it to himself and followed the Crosbys out.

As they disappeared from view, Jenny vaguely recalled an item she had heard on the radio about a young woman who had gone missing from her home in Bristol – a trainee at Maybury, the decommissioned nuclear power station that sat three miles east of the Severn Bridge. Maybury and the other three retired stations on the estuary had been much discussed in the local media lately: a new generation of scientists was being recruited to decommission the fifty-year-old reactors and build the new ones that had been given the go-ahead by the government. Listening to the heated phone-in debates, Jenny had felt a stirring of her teenage idealism, evoking memories of weekend trips with fellow students to peace camps outside American airbases. It seemed strange to her that a generation later a young woman would embark on a career in an industry which she had spent her formative years believing represented all that was corrupt and dangerous in the world.

Jenny slipped on a latex glove, pulled the fold of plastic over the Jane Doe's face and pushed the heavy drawer shut.

After five months of the mortuary being staffed exclusively by a string of unreliable locums, a new full-time pathologist was arriving on Monday. Jenny looked forward to prompt post-mortem reports and not having to waste her afternoons with tasks that his staff should have been assigned to. Professional dignity had been hard to maintain in a cash-strapped coroner's office and, though she had now seen many hundreds of corpses in every conceivable state of dismemberment and decay, being close to dead bodies still terrified her.

She disposed of the spent glove and hurried as quickly as she could on her narrow heels out into the sharp air. She had an appointment to keep.

Death, and her uneasy relationship with it, occupied most of the time she had spent with Dr Allen. In the consulting room at Chepstow hospital during their fortnightly early evening meetings progress had been slow and insights limited, but Jenny had managed to keep to the regime of anti-depressants and beta blockers, and had largely respected his injunction forbidding alcohol and tranquillizers. Though by no means cured, her generalized anxiety disorder had, for the previous five months, been chemically contained.

The fresh-faced Dr Allen, as punctilious as ever, reached for the thick black notebook he reserved exclusively for her sessions. He turned to the previous entry and carefully read it through. Jenny waited patiently, prepared with polite replies to the questions about her son, Ross, with which he usually opened. After a short while she began to sense that something was different today. Dr Allen seemed engrossed, distracted.

'Dreams . . .' he said. 'I don't often put a lot of store by them. They're usually just reprocessed garbage from the day, but I confess I've been doing some reading on the subject.' His eyes remained firmly on the book.

'Really?'

'Yes. I dabbled in Jungian analysis when I was at college, but it wasn't really encouraged; something of a cul-de-sac, I remember my professor saying. Never known a patient who'd been cured by understanding the meaning of his dreams.'

'Does this mean I've driven you to despair?'

'Not at all.' He flicked back through his notes, searching for an earlier entry. 'It's just I remember that before the medication you used to have some quite vivid ones. Yes . . .' He found what he was looking for. 'An ominous crack opening in the wall of your childhood bedroom to a dark forbidding space beyond. A terrifying presence lurking in there that you could never see or even fully visualize . . . an unspeakable horror of some description.'

Jenny felt the vessels of her heart enlarge, a pulse of heat cross her face, a flutter of anxiety in her solar plexus. She tried to keep her voice steady. *Act calm, stay calm*, she repeated silently to herself.

'You're right. I used to have those dreams.'

'How old were you when you first had them?' He turned back to a blank page, ready and alert.

'I was in my early thirties, I suppose.'

'A time of stress, juggling work and motherhood?'

'Yes.'

'And how old are you, as the dreamer, in your dream?'

'I'm a child.'

'You're certain about that?'

'I don't ever *see* myself . . . I suppose I just assume.'

'And as a child you feel helpless? Terrified of a threat you have no power to control?'

She nodded. 'And I think I know what you're going to say next.'

'What's that?'

'That it's nothing to do with childhood. That the dream merely reflects my state of fear and paralysis.'

'That's one interpretation.' His face fell slightly at having his theory anticipated so easily.

'I agree. But I still have no memory between the ages of four and five. And don't tell me I've imagined that.' She fixed him with a look that gave him pause.

'There is one school of thought which says that a memory gap is a subconscious defence mechanism,' he said, 'a buffer if you like, a void into which the conscious mind can project a credible reason, a logical explanation for its distress. An intelligent, rational mind like yours – so the theory goes – would head for the answer most likely to satisfy it: hence while the pain persists, your mind has to satisfy itself with the notion that the cause remains undiscovered—'

She interrupted. 'It does.'

'But what if we're looking for the wrong cause? What if the cause is utterly simple and straightforward – mere stress, for example?'

Jenny allowed herself to consider the possibility, though she remained aware that he might merely be attempting to blindside her, to distract her with one novel thought before firing the penetrating question while she was off guard. She waited for his follow-up, but it didn't come.

'So what do you think?' he said, his eyes alight with the ingenious simplicity of his diagnosis.

'You'll be telling me to take a long holiday next, or to change my job.'

A sterner note entered his voice. 'To be fair, you have stubbornly resisted trying either of those tried and tested methods.'

Jenny smoothed out the creases in her skirt as a way of hiding her despondency. 'Is this a polite way of telling me we've exhausted what you can usefully do for me?'

'I'm only trying to rule out the obvious.'

'And having done so?'

'An extended holiday, at least—'

'I'll tell you what happens to me on holidays: everything comes flooding back. The anxiety, the unwanted thoughts, irrational fears, dreams . . .' She paused, her tongue feeling thick in her mouth – a recent addition to her ever-increasing palette of symptoms.

'What, Jenny?'

She saw the tears land in her lap even before she felt them flood her eyes.

'What's making you cry?'

There was no immediate reason, just a vague, familiar sense of dread that was slowly tightening its grip, like vast, suffocating hands around her mind. 'I don't know—'

'The last word you said was *dreams*.'

Another river of tears and the inchoate fear became sharper; a shudder passed through her body and left her hands trembling as she reached for the ever-ready box of tissues.

'Tell me about your dreams.'

She began to shake her head – the medication had blocked, or saved, her from dreams – but then the image flashed behind her eyes, a single frame that connected with her fear, causing a further tremor, like a dull electric shock, to pass through her.

'You've had a dream?'

'I had one . . . the same one—' Her words stuttered out between stifled sobs.

'When?'

'Years ago . . . I was nineteen, twenty . . .'

'Tell me.'

'It's a garden.' The image held fast in her mind. 'There are lots of children, young girls in skirts and pigtails . . . They're following each other in groups of three, holding each others' hands and skipping, it's joyful. And then . . .' She pressed the soggy Kleenex to her eyes. 'They stop. And in their groups of three two girls hold a skipping rope and the third jumps . . . and as the ropes pass over their heads, they *vanish*.'

'Who vanishes?'

'The girls in the middle.'

Dr Allen wrote in his notebook. 'Where do they go?'

'Where? I don't . . . I don't know . . . It's just *nothingness*.'

'And the girls left behind?'

'They don't seem to notice.'

'And that's it?'

'Yes.' Jenny sucked in a breath, the tide of fear slowly washing out, leaving her beached and numb. She stared out of the window at the sodium light catching the rain falling on the barren patch of garden.

'How old were you when you had this dream?'

'I was at university . . . It kept coming. I remember it lingering on throughout days that should have been carefree.'

'What does it represent to you?'

She shook her head, pretending to herself that she didn't know, but words were forming by themselves and spilled out almost against her conscious will. 'For every something there is a nothing. For every object an absence . . . It's not death I'm afraid of, it's *emptiness*.'

'You fear being disappeared?'

'No . . .' She struggled to put her mental state into words. 'It's of being where there is nothing . . . and of not being where there is everything.'

Dr Allen's face registered his struggle to understand. 'Like being trapped on the wrong side of the looking glass? Out of time, out of place, out of context.'

'I suppose.'

There was silence as the doctor scanned his notes, then

rubbed his eyes, straining with a thought his expression said he found troublesome but necessary to express. He looked up and studied her face for a moment before deciding to voice it. 'Are you a woman of faith, Mrs Cooper?' His use of her surname confirmed his unease.

'Why do you ask?'

'The trinity is a powerful Christian symbol. Father, Son and Holy Ghost . . .'

'Lots of things come in threes: mother, father, child. Good, bad, indifferent. Heaven, earth, hell.'

'An apt example. You were brought up in faith, as I remember. The concepts are vivid to you.'

'We were sort of Anglican, I suppose. And there was Sunday school.'

Dr Allen looked thoughtful. 'You know, I think you're right. There is a piece missing – the girl, the space beyond the room. Whether it is emotional, or physical, or spiritual I couldn't yet say. But sometimes what we fear most is what we need. The most powerful stories are often those about strange saviours, demons who become an inspiration . . . like St Paul, or—'

'Darth Vader?'

He smiled. 'Why not?'

'This is sounding like a good old-fashioned diagnosis of suppression. Believe me, I've tried letting it all hang out; it wasn't a happy experience.'

'Would you do one thing for me?' He was suddenly earnest. 'I really would like to have one big push to crack this open.'

'Fire away.'

'For the next fortnight, keep a journal. Write down your feelings, your impulses, your extremes, no matter how bizarre or irrational.'

'In the hope of finding what, exactly?'

'We'll know when we see it.'

'You can be honest. Is this a last throw of the dice?'

He shook his head and smiled gently. 'I wouldn't still be here if I didn't think I could help you.'

Jenny pretended to be comforted, but couldn't help feeling that psychiatry was a slow road to nowhere. She had a small grain of faith that somehow, some day she would look up into a clear sky and feel nothing but undiluted happiness, but how that would come to pass was something she couldn't yet begin to answer. Perhaps her discussions with Dr Allen were worthwhile; at the very least he stirred her up from time to time, made her look into the corners she would otherwise avoid.

Later, as she drove home through the starless night, a single phrase of his kept repeating itself: *strange saviours*. It was a new idea to her. She liked it.

# TWO

JENNY HAD BECOME USED TO living with the noise of a sixteen-year-old in the house, and part of her missed it when Ross spent the weekend with his father in Bristol. She would have phoned Steve, the infuriatingly free spirit she described as her 'occasional boyfriend', but he hadn't called her for nearly a fortnight, even though he had been forced to acquire a phone; the architects' practice he was articled to during his final year of study had insisted on it. She had encouraged him to break out from his self-imposed exile on the small farm above Tintern, where, for ten years, he had tried to live out a self-sufficient fantasy. Now that he went to work in the city and spent his nights at a draughtsman's desk they scarcely saw each other.

She didn't like to admit to loneliness – escaping from a suffocating marriage to live in the country was meant to be a liberation – but driving south along the twisting Wye valley early on Monday morning through the dense, leafless woods, she was glad that she'd shortly be relieved of her own company. A workaday week awaited: hospital and road deaths, industrial accidents and suicides. She drew a certain comfort from dealing with others' unimaginable traumas with professional detachment. Being a coroner had given her an illusion of control and immortality. While Jenny Cooper the forty-two-year-old woman was still struggling to stay sane and sober, Jenny Cooper the coroner had come to enjoy her job.

With a take-out coffee in one hand and her briefcase in the other, Jenny shouldered open the door to her two-room office suite on the ground floor of the eighteenth-century terrace off Whiteladies Road. While her small domain had been made over, the common parts of the building remained tatty and the boards in the hallway still creaked under the threadbare carpet. The landlord's refusal to pay for so much as a coat of paint irked her each time she crossed the threshold. Alison, her officer, was pleased with the compromise, however. Having spent most of her adult life in the police force, she was comfortable in down-to-earth surroundings and suspicious of outward show. She liked things simple and homely. The stylish kidney-shaped desk at which she now sat, sorting through the pile of documents that had arrived in the overnight DX, was home to a selection of pot plants, and her state-of-the-art computer monitor was decorated with inspirational message cards bought at the church bookshop: *Shine as a Light in the World*, encircled with childlike angels.

'Hi, Alison.'

'Good morning, Mrs Cooper. Fifteen death reports over the weekend, I'm afraid.' She pushed a heap of papers across the desk. 'And there's a lady coming in to see you in about five minutes. I told her she'd have to make an appointment, but—'

'Who?' Jenny interrupted, running through a mental list of the several persistent obsessives she'd had to fend off lately.

Alison checked her message pad. 'Mrs Amira Jamal.'

'Never heard of her.' Jenny reached for a spiral-bound folder of police photographs sitting in her mail tray and

flicked through several pictures of the frozen corpses in the supermarket lorry. 'What did she want?'

'I couldn't quite make it out – she was gabbling.'

'Great.' Scooping up the reports, Jenny noticed that Alison was wearing a gold cross outside her chunky polo neck. Not yet fifty-five, she wasn't unattractive – she had curves and kept her thick bob of hair dyed a natural shade of blonde – but a hint of staidness had recently crept into her appearance. Ever since she'd become involved with an evangelical church.

'It was a baptism present,' Alison said, a challenging edge to her voice as she scrolled through her emails.

'Right . . .' Jenny wasn't sure how to respond. 'Was this a recent event?'

'Yesterday.'

'Oh. Congratulations.'

'You don't have a problem with me wearing it at work?' Alison said.

'Feel free.' Jenny gave a neutral smile and pushed through the heavy oak door into her office, wondering if she'd go the same way at Alison's age. Organized religion and late-onset lesbianism seemed to be what hit most frequently. She couldn't decide which she'd opt for given the choice. Maybe she'd try both.

Amira Jamal was a small, round woman barely more than five feet tall and somewhere in her fifties. She wore a smart black suit with a large, elaborate silk scarf, which she lowered from her head and draped around her shoulders as she took her seat. From a small pull-along suitcase she produced a box file containing a mass of notes, documents, statements and newspaper articles. She was clearly an educated woman, but emotional and overwrought: she spoke in short excited bursts about a missing son, as if assuming Jenny was already familiar with her case.

'Seven years it's taken,' Mrs Jamal said, '*Seven years*. I went to the High Court in London last week, the Family Court, I can't tell you how hard it was to get there. I had to sack the solicitor, and three others before him – none of them would believe me. They're all fools. But I knew the judge would listen. I don't care what anyone says, I have always believed in British justice. Look at these papers . . .' She reached for the box.

'Hold on a moment, Mrs Jamal,' Jenny said patiently, feeling anything but. 'I'm afraid we'll have to rewind for a moment.'

'What's the matter?' Mrs Jamal flashed uncomprehending deep brown eyes at her, her lashes thick with mascara and her lids heavily pencilled.

'This is the first I've heard of your case. We'll need to take it a step at a time.'

'But the judge said to come to you,' Mrs Jamal said with a note of panic.

'Yes, but the coroner is an independent officer. When I look into a case I have to start afresh. So, please, perhaps you could explain briefly what's happened.'

Mrs Jamal rifled through her disorganized documents and thrust a photocopy of a court order at her. 'Here.'

Jenny saw that it was dated the previous Friday: 23 January. Mrs Justice Haines of the High Court Family Division had made a declaration that Nazim Jamal, born 5 May 1982, and having been registered as a missing person on 1 July 2002, and having remained missing for seven years, was presumed to be dead.

'Nazim Jamal is your son?'

'My only son. My only child . . . All I had.' She wrung her hands and rocked to and fro in a way which Jenny could see would eventually have caused her lawyers to feel more irritation than sympathy. But she had spent enough years in the company of distressed mothers – fifteen years as a family lawyer employed by the legal department of a hard-pressed local authority – to tell melodrama from the real thing, and it was genuine torment she saw in the woman's eyes. Against all her better instincts she decided to hear Mrs Jamal's story.

'Perhaps you could tell me what happened, from the beginning?'

Mrs Jamal looked at her as if she had briefly forgotten why she was there.

'Can we get you some tea?' Jenny said.

Armed with a cup of Alison's strong, thick, builder's tea, Mrs Jamal started falteringly into the story she had told countless times to sceptical police officers and lawyers. She appeared mistrustful at first, but once she saw that Jenny was listening carefully and taking detailed chronological notes, she slowly relaxed and became more fluent, pausing only to wipe away tears and apologize for her displays of emotion. She was a highly strung but proud woman, Jenny realized; a woman who, given different chances in life, might have been sitting on her side of the desk.

And the more Jenny heard, the more troubled she became.

Amira Jamal and her husband Zachariah had both been brought to Britain as children in the 1960s. Their marriage was arranged by their families when they were in their early twenties, but fortunately for them they fell in love. Zachariah trained as a dentist and they moved from London to Bristol for him to join his uncle's practice in early 1980. They had been married for three years before Amira fell pregnant. The pregnancy came as a huge relief: she was becoming frightened that her husband's very conservative family might put pressure on him to divorce her, or even to take another wife. It was a moment of great joy when she gave birth to a healthy boy.

With all the love and attention his doting parents lavished on him, Nazim sailed through primary school and won a scholarship to the exclusive Clifton College. And as their son became absorbed into mainstream British culture, so Amira and Zachariah adapted themselves to their new social milieu of private school parents. Nazim went from strength to strength, scoring highly in exams and playing tennis and badminton for the school.

The family's first major convulsion occurred when Nazim was seventeen, at the start of his final year. Having spent so much time mixing with other mothers, Amira had come to appreciate what she had been missing cooped up at home. Against Zachariah's wishes she insisted on going out to work. The only position she could find was that of a sales assistant in a respectable women's outfitters, but it was still too much for her husband's pride to stand. He made her choose between him and the job. She called his bluff and chose the job. That evening she came home to find her two brothers-in-law waiting with the news that he was divorcing her and that she was to leave the house immediately.

Nazim gave in to irresistible family pressure and continued to live with his father, who shortly afterwards took a younger wife, with whom he was to have a further three children. Amira was forced out to a rented flat. Nazim loyally visited her several evenings each week, and rather than leave her isolated refused an offer from Imperial College London, and instead took up a place at Bristol University to study physics.

He started at university in the autumn of 2001 in the weeks when the world was still reeling and the word 'Muslim' had become synonymous with atrocity. Uninterested in politics, Nazim barely mentioned events in America and went off happily to college; and in his first act of rebellion against his father he decided to live on campus.

'I didn't see much of him that year,' Mrs Jamal said with a touch of sadness tinged with pride. 'He got so busy with his work and playing tennis – he was trying to get on the university team. When I did see him he looked so well, so happy. He wasn't a boy any more, I saw him change into a man.' A trace of emotion re-entered her voice and she paused for a moment. 'It was in the second term, after the Christmas holidays, that he became more distant. I only saw him three or four times. The thing I noticed was that he'd grown a beard and sometimes he wore the prayer cap, the taqiyah. I was shocked. Even my husband wore Western dress. One time he came to my flat wearing full traditional dress: a white robe and sirwal like the Arabs. When I asked him why, he said a lot of his Muslim friends dressed that way.'

'He was becoming religious?'

'We were always a religious family, but peaceful. My husband and I followed Sheikh Abd al-Latif: our religion was between us and God. No politics. That's how Nazim was brought up, to respect his fellow man, no matter who.' A look of incomprehension settled on her face. 'Later they said he'd been going to the Al Rahma mosque, and to meetings . . .'

'What sort of meetings?'

'With radicals, Hizb ut-Tahrir, the police said. They told me he went to a halaqah.'

'*Halaqah*?'

'A small group. A cell, they called it.'

'Let's stop there. When did he start going to these meetings?'

'I don't know exactly. Some time after Christmas.'

'OK . . .' Jenny made a note to the effect that whatever had happened to Nazim was linked to people he met in the winter of 2001–2. 'You noticed a change in your son in early 2002. What then?'

'He was much the same in the Easter vacation. His father didn't speak to me so I didn't know how he behaved at his house, but I was worried.'

'Why?'

'Nazim didn't talk about religion in my presence, but I'd heard things. We all had. These Hizb, followers of that criminal Omar Bakri, it's all politics with them: telling our young men they have to fight for their people, for a khalifah – an Islamic state. It's poison for young minds.'

'Do you know for certain your son was involved with radicals?'

'I knew nothing. I still don't, only what the police tell me.' She motioned towards the file of papers. 'They say they saw him going in and out of a house in St Pauls every Wednesday night for halaqah. Him and Rafi Hassan, a friend from university.'

'Tell me about Rafi.'

'He was in Nazim's year. He studied law. They had rooms in the same building, Manor Hall. His family comes from Birmingham.'

'Did you meet him?'

'No. Nazim hardly mentioned him. I got all this from the police . . . afterwards.' She pulled a fresh handkerchief from her pocket and dabbed her eyes, rocking back and forth in her chair.

'After what?' Jenny said, tentatively.

'I saw Nazim only once in May. He came on a Saturday, my birthday. His aunties were there and cousins. It was a wonderful day, he was himself again . . . And then once more in June, the 22nd, another Saturday.' All the dates were etched on her memory. 'He arrived in the morning looking pale. He told me he wasn't feeling well, a fever and headache. He lay in the spare bed and slept all afternoon and evening. He ate a little soup but said he was still too tired to go back to college, so he stayed the night. I woke at dawn and heard him praying: with perfect tajwid – reciting from the Koran like he'd learned as a boy.' She took a shaky breath and closed her eyes. 'I must have fallen asleep again. When I got up to make breakfast he'd gone. He left me a note. *Thanks, Mum. Bye. Naz.* It's there in the papers . . . I never saw him again.' Tears ran down her cheeks. She pressed her mascara-stained handkerchief to them and tried to steady herself. 'The police said . . . they said they saw him come out of the halaqah at ten-thirty on the night of Friday, 28 June 2002. That was in Marlowes Road in St Pauls. He walked to the bus stop with Rafi Hassan and that was it. He didn't go to tennis the next morning and neither of them was at class on Monday. The police spoke to all the students in the hall, but no one saw them over the weekend, or ever again.'

For the first time in their interview Mrs Jamal was overcome. Jenny let her weep uninterrupted. She had learned that the best response to grieving relatives was to observe a respectful silence, to offer a sympathetic smile but to say as little as possible. However well meant, words seldom eased the pain of grief.

When her tears eventually subsided, Mrs Jamal described how the college authorities had telephoned her husband, who then called her when Nazim failed to attend his tutorial the following Wednesday. He had been due to hand in an important dissertation. Zachariah and several of his nephews scoured the campus, but no one had seen Nazim or Rafi since the previous week, and neither boy seemed to have any close friends apart from one another. Even the students who lived in adjoining rooms could claim only a nodding acquaintance.

Initially the police responded with their usual indifference to reports of missing persons. A liaison officer even went so far as to suggest that the two young men might have fallen into a sexual relationship and run away together. Mrs Jamal knew her son well enough to know this wasn't likely. Then it emerged that both boys' laptop computers and mobile phones were missing. The police sergeant who had searched their rooms found evidence that their doors had been forced with a similar implement, probably a wide screwdriver. And then, nearly a week later, a girl who had a room in a neighbouring building, Dani James, came forward to tell police that she'd seen a man in a puffy anorak with a baseball cap pulled down over his face walking quickly out of Manor Hall at around midnight on the night of 28 June. She thought he had a large rucksack or a holdall over his shoulder.

Despite protests from both families, the police remained reluctant to investigate. Mrs Jamal was writing to her local councillor and MP, desperate for help, when she had a visit at home from two young men, one white, one Asian, who said they worked for the Security Services. They said they suspected that Nazim and Rafi had become involved with Hizb ut-Tahrir and that they had been observed by the police attending a radical halaqah.

'It was the first I'd heard of it, although I'd suspected something like this,' Mrs Jamal said, 'but I didn't want it to be true. I put those thoughts out of my mind. They kept asking me questions. They wouldn't believe I didn't know about what he got up to at college. They virtually accused me of lying to protect him.'

'What did they think had happened to him?'

'They kept asking whether he'd mentioned going to Afghanistan, whether he'd talked about al-Qaeda. I told them he'd never said anything like that. Never, never.'

'They thought he and Rafi might have gone abroad to train with extremists?'

'That's what they said. But his passport was still at his father's house.'

'And Rafi's?

'He didn't even have one. And they went through all their bank records – there was nothing suspicious.'

'Did either of them use their bank accounts or credit cards after the 28th?'

'No. They just vanished. Disappeared.'

Jenny felt a jolt of anxiety pass through her, the feeling of mental constriction that was the first stage of panic. She took a breath, relaxed her limbs, trying to let the sensation drain away. 'Did you ever find out anything more?'

'Two weeks later, a man named Simon Donovan gave a statement to the police saying that he was on a train to London on the morning of the 29th and saw two young Asian men who met their description. Both with beards and traditional dress, he said. His statement's in the file. This made the police think they had gone abroad, so they spoke again to all the students at the hall. A girl called Sarah Levin claimed she'd once heard Rafi say something in the canteen about "brothers" who were going to Afghanistan.' Mrs Jamal shook her head adamantly. 'He wouldn't have done that, Mrs Cooper. I know my own son. He wouldn't have done that.'

Jenny thought of Ross, of having to fetch him from school last summer when he was high on cannabis; of his unpredictable moods and occasional outbursts of staggering hurtfulness. She thought she knew the sensitive boy underneath, but sometimes she wondered; sometimes it occurred to her that we can't truly know even those closest to us.

'What did the police do with this information?' Jenny said.

'They looked for evidence, but the didn't find any. They said they would have left the country on false papers, gone to Pakistan.'

'Did they check passenger lists? It's not easy to get through an airport unnoticed.'

'They told us they checked everything. They even said they could have gone through another European country, or

Africa or the Middle East . . . I don't know.' The energy had drained from her. She seemed a smaller, more fragile figure than before.

'How did it end?'

'We had a letter in December 2002. The police said they had done everything they could and that the most likely explanation was that they had gone abroad with an Islamist group. That was all. Nothing more. Nothing.'

'What about the mosque and the halaqah?'

'The police told us that the mosque had closed in August that year and the halaqah as well. They said that the Security Services had been following their activities, but nothing else had been learned about Nazim or Rafi. They promised us they would tell us if anything became known.'

'Did these people from the Security Services ever contact you again?'

Mrs Jamal shook her head.

'You mentioned lawyers . . .'

'Yes. I tried to get them to ask questions, to speak to the Security Services and police, but all they did was take my money. It was left to me. I found out for myself that after seven years a missing person can be declared dead.' She met Jenny's gaze. 'And I also read that the coroner must find out how a person died. His father's address, Nazim's official residence at the time, is in your district, so that is why I am here.'

From the moment she had seen the judge's declaration Jenny had assumed that Mrs Jamal had come seeking an inquest, but the prospect threw up a raft of problems, not least the fact that there was no body and only a presumption of death. In such circumstances Section 15 of the Coroner's Act required her to get the Home Secretary's permission to hold one. That would only be granted where holding an inquest was judged to be in the public interest, which was as much a political as a legal decision. And even if that hurdle were cleared, it would be no easy task so many years after the event to cajole reluctant police officers and government officials to dust down their files and release whatever information wasn't deemed a threat to national security. Broad as they were, the coroner's powers would, in this instance, struggle against the powerful machinery of the state.

'Mrs Jamal,' Jenny said, with what she hoped was an appropriate balance of caution and concern, 'I will gladly look into your son's case, but all I can do is write a report to the Home Secretary requesting—'

'I know that. The judge told me.'

'Then you'll know that the chance of getting as far as holding an inquest is slim, probably non-existent. It's extremely unusual in cases where is there no actual proof of death.'

Mrs Jamal shook her head, her expression hardening with disappointment, 'What are you telling me – that I should give up after all this struggle?'

If she were being completely honest, Jenny would have told her that in the absence of a body, and after the passage of seven years, the best thing she could do would be to treat the court order as final proof that Nazim was dead, allow herself to grieve, and then move on. She would have told her that the main obstacle to her happiness was her obsession with her son's fate, and that an inquest was unlikely to satisfy or cure it.

'It would be wrong of me to hold out any hope of finding out what happened to your son,' Jenny said. 'I think perhaps you should ask yourself what purpose you think an inquest might serve. It won't bring him back.'

Mrs Jamal started to gather her jumble of papers. 'I'm sorry I wasted your time.'

'I'm not refusing to investigate—'

'You're obviously not a mother, Mrs Cooper, otherwise you would understand I have no choice. My life is nothing compared with my son's. I would rather die trying to find out what happened to him than live in ignorance.'

Mrs Jamal stood up from her chair as if ready to march out without another word, but seemed suddenly to lose energy and falter. She slowly placed the file back on the desk and folded her hands across her middle, her head dipping forwards as if she hadn't the strength to hold it up. 'I apologize, Mrs Cooper. I expected too much of you. I don't hope for miracles ... I know that Nazim is dead. When he came to my flat that afternoon with a fever, I had a feeling. Yes ... when I think of waking and hearing him reciting the tajwid the next morning, I still can't be sure if it was him or his ghost.' She looked up with dry, desolate eyes. 'Maybe you are right. Too much time has passed.'

Jenny had recoiled in the face of what she had perceived as Mrs Jamal's all-encompassing self-pity, but not for the first time in their meeting she saw beyond to the deep and profound grief of a mother in search of her lost child. The last thing she needed was another fraught and time-consuming case, but her emotions were already churning, the faces of the missing boys were already vivid, their spectres already haunting her.

'Leave the file with me,' Jenny said. 'I'll look through it this afternoon and get back to you.'

'Thank you, Mrs Cooper,' Mrs Jamal replied quietly. She reached for the scarf lying across her shoulders and raised it over her hair.

'What about Rafi Hassan – are his family seeking a declaration?' Jenny asked.

'We don't speak. They were very hostile to me. They chose

to believe that Nazim was responsible for what happened to their son.'

'And your husband?'

'He gave up long ago.'

Jenny detected a frostiness in Alison's demeanour as she showed Mrs Jamal out. During six months of working together she had learned to read every slight shift in her officer's mood. Alison was one of those women with an uncanny ability to let you know precisely what she was feeling without ever saying a word. What Jenny read in her reaction to Mrs Jamal was suspicion bordering on outright disapproval. When, several minutes later, she returned to the doorway to report that the police were agitating to see the post-mortem reports on the bodies in the refrigerated trailer, Jenny remarked that she seemed irritated by Mrs Jamal.

Alison crossed her arms. 'I remember her son's case. I was in CID at the time. Everyone knew he and the other lad had gone off to fight abroad.'

Another trait that Jenny had noticed: Alison's stubborn adherence to the consensus amongst her former police colleagues.

Jenny said, '*Everyone* being . . . ?'

'The squad who were on the obbo for five months. The extremists were operating freely back then.'

Jenny felt a twinge of annoyance. 'His mother still has the right to know what happened to him, insofar as that's possible.'

'If I was her, I'm not sure I'd want to know. We can't exactly call witnesses from Afghanistan.'

'No. You don't happen to remember who was in charge of the observation?'

'I can probably find out. Just don't expect to get very far –

the spooks are all over this sort of thing.' Alison changed the subject: 'What about these bodies in the lorry – do you want me to have a look? I expect the police will want that one for themselves as well.'

'It might be as well for you to make your own report,' Jenny said, and couldn't resist adding, 'we know how our friends in blue can see one thing and write down another.'

'I'm only telling you what I heard at the time, Mrs Cooper,' Alison retorted. 'And back then we still gave Muslims the benefit of the doubt.'

Jenny held her tongue, sensing in Alison's reaction that Mrs Jamal had stirred complicated emotions. Six months on, Jenny knew that Alison was still privately grieving for the man she'd been in love with: the late Harry Marshall, her predecessor as coroner. They had been close. The messy circumstances of his sudden and unexpected passing had left a mess of unresolved feelings which she was attempting to clear up with a dose of full-strength Christianity. When insecure, Alison cleaved to institutions – the police, the church – and resisted anything that threatened them. It was irrational, but who was Jenny to pass judgement? Without her medication she was beset by irrational fears too.

'Her son's been declared dead.' Jenny said. 'She's entitled to an investigation, however limited. I doubt very much it'll amount to anything.'

Alison's hostility hung in the air like an unwelcome presence long after she'd left the office. Jenny felt almost guilty as she arranged Mrs Jamal's papers into a semblance of order. She hadn't felt like this again since the first case she and Alison had worked on together – that of the fourteen-year-old Danny Wills, who'd been found dead in his cell at a privately run prison. Perhaps, as an ex-policewoman, Alison sensed trouble more keenly than she did.

Although numerous, Mrs Jamal's documents cast little light. There were lists of students who lived in the halls of residence at the time; statements from members of both families; statements from police officers who had searched the campus; copies of ineffective correspondence with various councillors and politicians. There was a copy of the original identification statement given by Simon Donovan, in which he described the two young men on the train, and statements from students Dani James and Sarah Levin, describing the mysterious intruder and Rafi's overheard remark about Muslim brothers heading for Afghanistan. There was a sketchy photocopy of Nazim's UK passport, confirmation from the Passport Office that Rafi Hassan had never possessed or applied for one, and a dry letter written by a DC Sarah Owens, Family Liaison Officer, explaining in patronizing tones that the police had decided to suspend their investigation until such time as further evidence came to light. The final document was a 'missing' poster put together on a home computer displaying various head shots of the young men. Jenny was struck by how handsome they both were: keen-eyed and slender featured. She stared at them for a long moment, then felt an unexpected wave of almost unbearable sadness: they weren't even dead. It was worse than that: they had simply *disappeared*.

She pushed the file aside, fighting against the irrational connections her mind was already making with her discussions with Dr Allen. People vanished without trace all the time. It was purely coincidental that this case had arrived on her desk when it had. Technically it could also have been handled by the Bristol coroner as Jamal was last seen in his jurisdiction. Jenny needn't take it at all . . . but yet she knew she had no choice.

The telephone rang in the empty outer office and was

automatically diverted to the phone on her desk. She answered in her most businesslike voice. 'Severn Vale Coroner's office. Jenny Cooper speaking.'

'Good morning. Andrew Kerr. New pathologist at the Vale.' He sounded chatty and energetic. 'I've just had a look at this Jane Doe of yours. I think perhaps we ought to meet.'

# THREE

SHE WAS BUZZED INTO THE mortuary building by one of the monosyllabic assistants – a taciturn breed whom she'd only ever heard laughing from a distance and between themselves – and stepped carefully over the newly mopped reception floor, becoming aware of the sound of raised voices on the other side of the slap doors. She pushed through to find a muscular young man wearing surgical scrubs, who she took to be the new pathologist, doing his best to fend off a bellicose Scotsman. Dressed in a dark suit and coat, the visitor had a threatening tone and an aura of unpredictable menace which hit her like a minor shock wave as he jabbed his finger at the pathologist's chest.

'Listen, son – my client's wee girl has been gone six months and not a trace. The poor sod's lost every hair on his head. I wouldn't be surprised if he got the cancer if he doesn't find her soon.'

'You'll have to come back with the police. You can't walk in here and simply demand to see a body.'

'I'm his lawyer for Christ's sake, his legal agent. I know the education's all to cock these days, but they must've taught you what that means.' He pushed his unruly, sandy hair back from his forehead revealing once attractive features now lined and lived in.

The pathologist set his hands on his hips and stood his

ground, showing off a thick pair of gym-pumped shoulders. 'All right, that's enough. I've told you how it is. You've got the detective's number – call him. I've got a job to do here.' He looked past the man to Jenny. 'Sorry, madam. How can I help you?'

Not about to back down, the angry Scotsman said, 'What in the hell difference does it make to you if I've got a copper holding my hand?'

Jenny stepped forward and addressed him. 'Jenny Cooper. Severn Vale District Coroner. The body's in my charge at the moment.' She had both men's full attention now. 'Dr Kerr?'

'Yes.'

She turned to the visitor. 'And you are?'

'Alec McAvoy. O'Donnagh & Drew.' He looked her up and down with startling blue eyes that belonged to a much younger face. 'Any chance of giving this young laddie a law lesson?'

Ignoring the remark, she said, 'Perhaps if you could tell me exactly who you're representing I might be able to help.'

'Client's name's Stewart Galbraith. My firm's represented the family since God was a boy. It was the police who told him about this body in the first place.'

'Which police?'

'Now *you're* being funny. You tried calling the cop station lately? If it's not Bangalore it's a fuckin' robot.'

Jenny saw Dr Kerr bristle, but she remained calm. Lawyers were paid to be awkward. Despite his bluster, the mischief in McAvoy's eyes told her there was no personal animosity intended.

'Have you got a business card?'

McAvoy grunted, fished in his coat pocket and came out with a card:

*Alec McAvoy LLB, Legal Executive, O'Donnagh & Drew, Solicitors.* She scanned it twice, wondering why a man with a law degree was a mere legal executive and not a qualified solicitor.

He saw that she'd noticed.

'There's a story behind that. I'll tell you sometime,' McAvoy said.

'Do you mind if I give your office a call?'

'Go ahead.'

She reached for her phone, then thought better of it. It felt petty to question his credentials. She knew the name of O'Donnagh & Drew from her days in practice. They were a long-established firm chiefly known for having cornered Bristol's market in major criminal litigation.

She turned to Dr Kerr. 'Would you mind if we have a quick look? It won't take a minute.'

'It's your body, Mrs Cooper. I'll be in my office.' He turned and walked swiftly across the corridor, pulling the door hard shut behind him.

'You're sure he's old enough to be doing this job?' McAvoy said. 'He's hardly out of short trousers.'

'Shall we get this done?'

She led the way to the refrigerator, passing half a dozen bodies parked on trolleys, aware of McAvoy's eyes on her as he followed. He was one of those men who didn't even try to pretend they weren't looking.

She took a latex glove from a dispenser screwed to the wall. 'Have you got a photograph of your client's daughter? It can sometimes be hard—'

'No need. I've known her from a baby.'

'What's her name?'

'Abigail.'

She opened the fridge door – a heavy hunk of metal eight feet by four – and pulled out the drawer. She observed McAvoy instinctively cross himself as she reached down to pull the plastic back from the face. They both started at the sight that met them: the face staring up with empty eye sockets.

'Dear God,' McAvoy whispered.

Jenny flinched and looked away. 'Sorry about that. She did have glass ones. Someone must have removed them.'

He leaned down for a closer examination. With her peripheral vision Jenny watched him examining every detail of the face, then tug back the plastic a little further to reveal the top portion of the torso.

'No. It's not Abigail,' he said, straightening up. 'She'd a dimple in her chin and a wee birthmark on the side of her neck. Thanks anyway.'

Jenny nodded, hesitating to look down again and cover the face.

'Let me,' McAvoy said, and pulled the sheet across before she could reach out a hand. 'Nothing but dust once the soul's departed – that's what you've got to tell yourself.' He pushed the drawer back into the cabinet. 'Another torment the godless majority have to live with – thinking flesh and blood are all there is.' He pulled the fridge door shut and glanced at the bodies lined up on trolleys along the corridor. 'Leave an unbeliever down here for the night, he'd soon be crying out for his Maker.' He flashed her a wicked smile. 'I've not seen you before, have I?'

'No.' She pulled off the glove and dropped it in the bin.

'New?'

'Relatively.'

'Some job for a woman.' He studied her for a moment then nodded, as if having satisfied his curiosity. 'Yes, I can see it now.' His smile became kinder: a window to a gentler side of him, perhaps. 'Oh well, don't spend too much time with these fellas. See you around.' He turned and walked away, tossing his hair away from his eyes, hands pushed deep into his coat pockets.

She stood and watched him until he'd gone, half-expecting him to steal something on the way out.

Jenny entered Dr Kerr's office to find him busy at his computer, his scrubs replaced with a T-shirt that hugged his pecs. She guessed he was thirty or so and still single, with plenty of time to spend on himself.

'Have we got rid of him yet?' he said, firing off an email.

'Yes. She wasn't the one he was looking for.'

Dr Kerr swivelled on his chair to face her. She noticed he'd rearranged the furniture, and replaced the shelving and carpet. The row of textbooks on the shelf behind his desk looked new and unthumbed; next to them were a number of *Men's Health* and *Muscle and Fitness* magazines.

'Pleased to meet you, Mrs Cooper.'

He extended his hand. She tried and failed to match his powerful grip.

'And you. I've had just about all I can take of dealing with locums.'

'Then you'll be glad to know I type my own post-mortem reports and like to get them out of the way before I go home each night.'

'I see you've been got at already.'

'No comment,' he said, smiling.

Jenny realized the trace of accent she'd detected in his voice was Ulster. For some reason she found it reassuring: solid, reliable.

Dr Kerr said, 'I noticed that your Jane Doe had been sitting around for a while, so I had a look at her this morning.' He handed her a three-page report. 'I wasn't sure whether it was you or the police I should speak to first, but I saw on the file that you've opened an inquest.'

'Opened and adjourned while I try to find out who she is.'

'Aren't the police interested?'

35

'They will be if anything incriminating turns up. Till then they're more than happy to farm out the legwork.'

He nodded, though his expression was one of surprise. Jenny hoped his pathology was better than his grasp of professional politics.

'From an initial examination it's impossible to say what killed her. Most of the internal organs were missing – seagulls, I read.'

'Apparently so.'

'There was some lung tissue left, enough to give a suggestion that the bronchi were distended . . .'

'Meaning?'

'Drowning is a possibility, but I couldn't prove it. One thing that does interest me, though, is two nicks in the stomach side of the lumbar vertebrae. They could have been caused by the gulls, but equally I couldn't rule out stab wounds.'

'Is there no way of telling?'

'Afraid not.' He continued a little less confidently. 'Two other things. Firstly, her teeth: no decay, no fillings, so dental records probably won't help. And, secondly, I dissected her neck looking for evidence of strangulation. I didn't find that, but she has an early-stage tumour on her thyroid gland. It was large enough that she may have begun to feel it. She might have gone to the doctor complaining of pressure on her windpipe.'

'Thyroid cancer? What would have caused that?'

'What causes any kind of cancer? Unless she had a dose of radiation or something it's impossible to say.'

'Radiation?' She remembered the Crosby family and their daughter who worked at the decommissioned power station. 'There's a young woman missing who works at the Maybury nuclear plant, out on the Severn.'

'Right. I was going to say that it's the kind of tumour that's most common in Eastern Europe, in the Chernobyl footprint. Her cheekbones have a touch of that Slavic look.'

'The family's arranging a DNA test. If that doesn't turn up anything we could try something more sophisticated – geographical mineral analysis or whatever.'

'Not on my budget, we can't.'

'We'll see,' Jenny said, with a half-smile. 'We might persuade the police to pay for it.'

'I guess I could rustle up a radiometer from somewhere – there's some pretty accurate radiological data I could match her with. If she is from Eastern Europe, I might be able to get a rough location.'

'Anything would be helpful.' Jenny got up from her chair. 'The sooner we ID her, the sooner you free up your fridge space.'

'About that: couldn't the body be moved to an undertaker's or—'

Jenny cut in. 'You're on a permanent contract, right?'

'Yes . . .'

'Then you can afford to flex your muscles. If you don't start making demands first they'll bleed you dry – you'll be stealing cutlery from the canteen to conduct your postmortems.'

'It feels a bit early to start rocking the boat.'

She felt an almost maternal concern for him – not yet thirty and in charge of the repository of the hospital's darkest secrets. 'Listen, Andrew – can I call you that?'

'Sure.'

'They'll give you a week, then the consultants will be on the phone trying to lean on you to cover up their mistakes and the management will be suggesting you do anything but record hospital infection as cause of death. Get corrupted once and you're stuck with it for all time. Ask your predecessor.'

'Right,' he said uncertainly. 'I'll bear it in mind.'

The rain had passed and given way to a hard frost, which glinted on the tarmac as Jenny drove back towards home across the vast span of the Severn Bridge. The lights of the factories of Avonmouth to the left and Maybury to the right reflected off the flat water on a windless night. Reaching the far side and entering Wales, she waited for the tensions of the day to leave her as she slipped past Chepstow and plunged into the forest. The knots loosened a little, but somehow the sense of release wasn't as profound tonight. Meeting Mrs Jamal and the ordeal of dealing with the Jane Doe had roused a stubborn anxiety that refused to let her enjoy the glimpses of a crescent moon through the skeletal trees.

She tried to analyse her feelings. Random, unjust and terrifying were the inadequate words which came to mind. Why, for the last three years of her life, she had been haunted and occasionally overwhelmed by such deep and unsettling forces she was scarcely closer to knowing than when they had first made themselves felt. She had made some modest progress. Only six months before, she was limping through the days only with the help of handfuls of tranquillizers and bottles of wine. Dr Allen had helped her break both habits. She was medicated, but holding herself together: she functioned. And she had proved that the mask she hid behind was not as flimsy as she feared. In six months it hadn't slipped. No one who didn't know her history would ever guess.

Her pocket-sized stone cottage, Melin Bach, had lights at every window, meaning Ross was in. He'd taken to getting a lift home most evenings from a recently qualified English lecturer at his sixth-form college who lived further up the valley. From what she could tell, they passed their journey smoking cigarettes and listening to indie tracks they'd download and swap with each other. The teacher was as much of a kid as Ross.

'Do we have to have *every* light on?' she called up the stairs. Music pounded from his room: raw guitars and vocals that sounded like a weak mimic of the Stones. 'What about the planet?'

'It's already screwed,' Ross shouted back from behind the door.

Great. She hung up her coat. 'Don't suppose you thought about dinner?'

'Nope'. The music got louder. Jenny retreated into the living room, slamming the door behind her.

She scooped up the plates covered with toast crumbs, dirty cups and glasses, and kicked aside the discarded trainers in the middle of the flagstone floor as she carried them into the tiny unmodernized kitchen at the back of the house. Her ex-husband had laughed when he'd seen it – his had cost £80,000 and been installed by a team of German craftsmen who had arrived in a Winnebago – which was precisely why she clung to her ancient Welsh dresser and the erratic coke-fired range which dated back, neighbours told her, to the early 1940s.

As usual, there wasn't a scrap of food in the house. Ross had eaten everything except a jar of dried lentils and a packet of sugarless muesli some self-improving and misplaced instinct had urged her to buy the previous summer. She rooted around in the back of the cupboard and found only a can of evaporated milk and a mouldering jar of curry paste.

Ross thumped through the door wearing a combat jacket. He stood over six feet tall; her eyes were on a level with the underside of his chin.

39

'You should shop online, get a home delivery. You must be the only person who doesn't,' Ross said and dropped an empty Pepsi can in the bin.

'Hey – recycling.'

'Yeah, right. Like that's going to save us all.' He headed back for the door. 'I'm going out.'

'Where?'

'Karen's. Her mum actually feeds her in the evenings.'

'There's nothing to stop you—'

'Cooking? You have a panic attack every time I come in here.'

'You never clean up after yourself.'

'You wanted to live with a teenager. Reality check.' He shrugged, gave a sarcastic smile, and left the room.

Jenny went after him. 'How are you going to get there at this time of night?'

'Walk.'

'It's freezing.'

'So's this place.' He crashed through the door into the hall. 'Steve called.'

'What did he want?'

'Didn't say.'

Slam. He was out of the front door and off into the night.

Jenny let him go. She was feeling too fragile to face another verbal assault. She understood that pushing her away was part of his growing up, but that didn't make it any easier to bear.

She contemplated her options: driving out to find a supermarket or sitting down hungry to clear her backlog of death reports before an early night. Neither appealed. She dropped into an armchair and tried to work out how she could organize her domestic life to keep Ross happy for the remaining eighteen months before he took off to university. She needed a system to replace the ad hoc trips to petrol station convenience stores. She needed to make the cottage more comfortable: it was all wood and stone; Ross preferred his friends' charmless, carpeted, centrally heated homes. She needed to behave like a proper mother.

She had forced herself upstairs to tidy his tip of a bedroom when the doorbell rang. She peered cautiously around the curtain and felt a flood of relief: it wasn't Ross returning to berate her, it was Steve.

She opened the door to find him standing on the doorstep in walking boots and thick coat, carrying a flashlight. Alfie, his sheepdog, was sniffing around the front lawn.

'Haven't seen you in a while,' Jenny said, with an involuntary trace of reproachfulness.

He gave an apologetic smile. 'I thought it was about time.'

'You want to come in?'

'I'm walking Alfie – he's been cooped up all day. Thought you might want to come along. It's a beautiful evening.'

They walked briskly up the steep, narrow lane with its high, enclosing hedges, and turned right onto the dirt track that led into a thousand acres of forest. Alfie skirted ahead of them, nose to ground, making forays into the undergrowth. Jenny stayed close to Steve, their arms brushing together but neither of them willing to reach for the other's hand. Since they'd met the previous June they'd spent no more than half a dozen nights together and had only once discussed their 'relationship'. They had come to no conclusion except that after ten years in the wilderness Steve was ready to go back and take his final exams to qualify as an architect. To make ends meet he'd rented his farmhouse to some weekenders from London and moved into a makeshift one-room apartment he'd cobbled together in the upper storey of the barn. He'd never suggested moving in with her and she'd never invited him to, but she couldn't pretend she hadn't thought about it. Living alone was manageable, but co-existing with a moody teenage son could be painfully lonely. There had been times when she'd longed for a man's solid energy to dissolve the tension.

The frozen mud crunched beneath their feet. A tawny owl hooted and from deep in the trees another screeched in response.

Steve said, 'You know what I love about coming out here at night – you never see a soul. Everyone's stuck in front of the TV not realizing all this is outside their back door.'

It was a point of pride that he didn't own a television and never had. Jenny had once told him that for a dogged anti-materialist he managed to find plenty of things to get competitive about it. He hadn't got the joke.

'Is that your idea of happiness, not seeing other human beings?' she said.

'I like the peace.'

'Being alone frightens the hell out of most people.'

'They must be frightened of themselves.'

'Aren't you ever? I am.'

'No. Never.'

Another thing that changed about him: since he'd quit smoking grass he had a keener edge. He'd give straight answers where once he'd just shrugged or smiled. She liked the new attitude.

'You don't mind being in an office full of people all day?'

'I survive. Most of us have a lot in common.'

'I thought idealists always fell out with each other.'

'Haven't yet.'

Despite her cynicism she liked the idea of Steve and his self-styled 'ecotect' colleagues spending their days trying to make the world a more beautiful and harmonious place. Her work had always been one long fight and it showed no sign of letting up.

'You don't regret renting out the farm?'

'I hate it, but it won't last. Give it a year or two and I'll take it all over again.'

'You might like a change, or to build something from scratch.'

'Who knows?'

His response surprised her. He had always talked about the farm as the one thing that gave meaning and stability to his life. The woods he worked and the vegetables he grew were his reality; everything else was a means of allowing him to remain there immersed in nature. She felt for a moment as if she didn't know him, yet she'd prompted him: on some level she must have suspected.

'You'd really consider moving?'

'I'm open to change.'

'Wow.'

He glanced at her. 'You were the one who started it for me.'

'Maybe I was just the excuse you needed?'

He looked away. 'You never take a compliment.'

They walked on in silence: Steve retreating into private thoughts and Jenny trying to fathom them. She wasn't used to him being touchy. He was always easy-going, taking whatever she said lightly. Her disquiet at his brooding turned to unease. She realized how badly she wanted them to get on, how much she'd like to spend the night with him, to push aside the images of the dead and the missing which were never far from her thoughts.

She slid her arm beneath his, squeezing it close to her body. She felt for his hand and threaded her cold fingers between his. They slowly relaxed. They were warm and softer than she remembered, an architect's hands not an artisan's.

'Sorry it's been so long,' she said quietly. 'It's not that I haven't been thinking about you.'

'It's OK.'

'It's not . . . I get caught up in myself. Work, Ross . . .'

Steve hesitated, then said, 'Are you still seeing the psychiatrist?'

'Yes. I'm doing all right.'

'Sure?'

'Why? Do I seem strange?'

'No . . . not at all.' There was a trace of uncertainty in his voice.

'Then what's the matter?' Jenny said. 'You're not yourself.'

'Nothing . . .'

She gripped his hand tighter, determined to get it out of him. 'Tell me.'

'Really it's nothing . . .' He sighed. 'It's just that my ex, Sarah-Jane, showed up the other day—'

'Oh.' Jenny felt a knot of jealousy form in her stomach. She had always thought of Sarah-Jane as belonging to the distant past. The few times Steve had mentioned her he had painted her as a monster: artistic, emotional, erratic, and not at all ashamed of having put him through years of hell before taking off to sleep her way around the world.

'Mad as ever . . . said I owed her money. Left screaming when I told her to get lost, then turned up in the middle of the night wanting to share my bed.'

'Did you?'

'What do you think?'

'Sorry.' She wished she hadn't asked. 'I didn't mean—'

'I know.' Steve let go of her hand. God, he was tetchy. 'I don't even know why I'm telling you . . . I thought I'd got rid of her. She's like some sort of succubus. You know what it's like – the one person in the world who can cut you down with a single word.'

Jenny had never known him like this, shaken up, absorbed in himself, but she could understand. She'd met women like

Sarah-Jane: emotional parasites who passed off their selfishness and violent moods as creativity. Steve was methodical, a planner and, Jenny had come to realize, quite delicate in many ways. Her instinct was to take him home, comfort him and build him up, but at the same time she was frightened of smothering him and pushing him further away.

She wanted to say something kind and insightful, but what came out was, 'I guess the last thing you need is another complicated woman to deal with.' She realized how needy that sounded even as she said it.

Steve said, 'It's cold. I should be getting you home.'

He walked her as far as the gate and headed off without pausing for the customary moment in which she might have invited him in. She was confused. He had come calling for her, but at some point during their walk she had come to feel as if she were imposing on him. She thought she'd learned how to read him, how to lift him from his occasional melancholy and make him laugh. Nothing had worked tonight.

Ross wasn't yet home and the house was cold and still. Standing in the silence, she could hear its ancient fabric creak and contract, noises that even now, in her fifth decade of life, her imagination turned to ghosts. A faint tapping in the hotwater pipes became the lost spirit of the Jane Doe, wandering listlessly, looking for an earthly soul to tug at and whisper her secrets to.

She retreated to the smallest, most secure room – her study at the foot of the stairs – and closed the door securely behind her. She switched on a fan heater, as much for its reassuring rattle as its feeble heat, and fetched the legal pad from the bottom drawer of her desk which was to serve as the journal Dr Allen had asked her to keep. She closed her eyes for a moment, allowing her emotions to rise as fully into consciousness as she could safely let them, then wrote:

M. R. HALL

*Monday, 26 January*

*You asked me if I had faith. I'm not sure what that means. Do I have a religion? No. Do I believe in good and evil? Yes. Heaven and hell? I think so. Why? Because I know about the place in between, I know about limbo. That's the place I'm frightened of. The empty space, oblivion, where souls wait, and wait, unable to feel, not knowing how or why. I hate the fact that I know. I wish I could draw everything back to the here and now, live in the present, be happy and ignorant. But for some reason I've been allowed a glimpse beyond, and I wish I could shut the door.*

# FOUR

ALISON PUT DOWN THE PHONE abruptly as Jenny entered the office. She seemed edgy.

'Everything all right?' Jenny said.

'Fine.'

She could tell that it wasn't and knew that Alison wouldn't welcome her probing any further. From snatches of overheard phone calls, Jenny had gathered that Alison and her husband, Terry, were going through a difficult patch. Also a retired detective, he bumped between temporary jobs that always seemed to disappoint. Most recently he'd been working for a private investigator contracting for an insurance company. His task was to spy on personal-injury litigants. Alison thought it tacky, following a man with a video camera to try to catch him out playing football with his kids when he was signed off sick, but Terry had aspirations to a condo on a Spanish golf course and didn't much care how he paid for it.

'Mrs Jamal left you some messages,' Alison said tersely. 'Five actually.'

'Oh? What about?'

'The police mostly – how they're all liars and criminals and like to intimidate defenceless women. If she wasn't Muslim, I'd say she'd had a few.'

Ignoring Alison's snipe, Jenny went through to her office

and played them back. They were each preceded by a time code. Mrs Jamal had first called at ten p.m. and had left her last message after midnight sounding tired and tearful. Jenny didn't think she sounded irrational, just lonely, grief-stricken, and needing to share her tormented thoughts. At the heart of her anguish was a belief that the police knew far more about her son's disappearance than they were prepared to reveal. Jenny sympathized, but her instinct was that Mrs Jamal's suspicions were ungrounded. It was difficult enough to get the police to investigate a missing persons case thoroughly at the best of times. Two Asian boys who'd flirted with extremism and left the country were two potential problems off their hands. After a cursory search, their files could have been shelved marked 'No Further Action', and with no suggestion that more should have been done.

Jenny prevaricated about whether to phone back then decided she ought to, if only to lay down some ground rules.

She dialled Mrs Jamal's number and reached an answerphone. She started to leave a message: 'Mrs Jamal, this is Jenny Cooper, Severn Vale District Coroner. Thank you for your calls. I can assure you your son's case will get my full attention, but if you could bear in mind the fact—'

The receiver was snatched up at the other end. Mrs Jamal spoke in an urgent whisper. 'They've been watching me, Mrs Cooper. I know they have. They can see my flat from over the road. There are men in a car. One of them tried to break in last night. I heard them trying the door.'

'I know this is a very anxious time for you, Mrs Jamal, but you really will have to trust me to—'

'No, Mrs Cooper, it's true. They went away for years, and now they're back. I can see them from my window. Two of them. They're out there now.'

Dismissing her would do no good and probably provoke another flurry of calls. Jenny decided to humour her. 'OK.

48

Maybe you could go to the window and tell me what they look like, or what kind of car they're driving.'

She heard the receiver being set down and the sound of feet shuffling across the room, a curtain sliding back, then an exclamation of mild surprise.

Mrs Jamal returned to the phone. 'They've gone. They must have heard us.'

'I see,' Jenny said patiently. 'This is what I want you to do. By all means contact me with any piece of evidence that you think I should have which you haven't already given me, and as soon as I've carried out a few inquiries I'll open an inquest.'

'When?'

'I can't say exactly. Soon. In a week or two. But in the meantime, if there's anything else that's bothering or frightening you, you must call the police.'

'Huh! Do you think I haven't? I call them all the time, and always the same answer: name, address, crime number. What good is it calling the criminals?'

Jenny held the phone away from her ear while Mrs Jamal launched into a lengthy tirade. When, after some time, she showed no sign of letting up, Jenny spoke calmly over her, promising to be in touch as soon as she had anything to report.

Alison came through from the outer office wearing a wry smile. 'I'll screen her out if you like.'

'She'll calm down.'

'Are you sure you want to take this one on, Mrs Cooper? It's not that I'm unsympathetic, but there are some you just get a feeling about.'

'And what is your feeling?'

Alison wore a pained expression. 'We're both mothers, you know what it's like – if someone told you something you didn't want to believe about your child, how would you feel?'

It was one of the few times Alison had mentioned Bethan, her daughter and only child. All Jenny knew about her was that she was twenty-three and lived in Cardiff. Sensing that she was speaking from personal experience, Jenny said, 'I'll catch her in a lucid moment and try to explain that a coroner's inquiry is impartial, not there to validate her theories.'

'Good luck.' Alison handed her a note containing a name and telephone number.

'What's this?'

'DI Dave Pironi, an old friend and colleague of mine,' Alison said, implying that it was a relationship not to be sullied or betrayed. 'He was heading up the obbo at the Al Rahma mosque.'

'Thanks. Anything I should know about him?'

'He's a good man, lost his wife to breast cancer a couple of years ago. His boy's a corporal in the Rifles. Just started his third tour in Afghanistan.'

Jenny nodded. She got the message.

They arranged to meet on neutral territory – a coffee chain halfway between the office and New Bridewell, the police station at which Pironi was currently based. Jenny arrived first and found a table as far away as possible from the stereo speakers that were pumping out an old Fleetwood Mac number.

From his abrupt telephone manner, she had expected DI Pironi to be gruff and taciturn with a detective's jowly face and dead, unshockable eyes. The man who wandered over with an espresso and a tumbler of water looked more like a businessman who'd just signed off an unexpectedly lucrative deal. He was in his early fifties and trim. His smart-casual clothes looked Italian and stylish: black knitted polo shirt beneath a wool blazer. She noticed his nails – filed and buffed.

'Mrs Cooper?' He had a light Welsh accent.

'Yes.' She half-rose from her chair and shook his hand.

'I've only got a few minutes, I'm afraid.'

'No problem. Anything exciting?'

'I'm giving evidence at Short Street. Heard of Marek Stich? He's Czech. Shot one of the uniform lads late last year. Real piece of work.'

'I know. Owns a nightclub?'

'That's one of his interests. Our boy was fresh out of training college – pulled him over for jumping a light, and *pop*.'

'Is he going down?'

'I'd like to think so. All on forensics, though – not one single decent witness with the balls to come forward.' He shook his head as he stirred a sweetener into his coffee. 'You know what really turned the public off the police? Roadside cameras. Machine as judge, jury and executioner, no discretion involved. Makes people despise all authority.'

'You're a benefit-of-the-doubt man?'

'Always have been.' He smiled as he raised his cup to his lips.

Jenny tried to marry the smart-dressing modern detective with what little she knew of the reality of life in the force. What did it say about a policeman near the end of his career that he'd maintained such studied self-control? What was he hiding?

She cut to business. 'Alison tells me you were in charge of the observation on the Al Rahma mosque.'

'Uh-huh.' He set his cup back on its saucer with measured precision.

'Can you tell me what you were looking at?'

'We had some intelligence that extremists were operating inside it, setting up cells to try to recruit young men to Hizb ut-Tahrir and other organizations. We weren't tooled up with informers at the time; we had to sit and watch for three months, get to know names, times and places.'

'Are you allowed to say where this information was coming from?'

'Let's say we were one of the partners in the operation.'

'With the Security Services?'

'I'm just a humble DI, Mrs Cooper. I'd get into all sorts of trouble for giving straight answers to questions like that.'

That was more like a policeman: letting her know but pretending he wasn't, thinking the way he did it was clever.

'Let's imagine a hypothetical situation,' Jenny said. 'Say MI5 had a tip-off and wanted a mosque looked into. They'd hook up with the local force and get them to do the sitting around in cars, right?'

'They've taken on a lot more staff in recent years. These days they might run it all themselves.'

'But back then?'

'We were all a lot greener, weren't we?'

'Meaning what – that things were missed that shouldn't have been?'

'I'm just saying – we'd do it differently now. We'd have insiders, hook onto things more quickly. Pre-empt trouble before it happened.'

Jenny pushed her hair back from her face and held him in an innocent gaze she thought might pique his interest, throw him off guard a little. 'Nazim Jamal and Rafi Hassan were two of the young men you were watching, presumably?'

'Yes.' His eyes traced her neck down to the open top of her blouse.

'How long for?'

'A number of weeks as far as I recall.'

'Have you any idea what happened to them on the night of 28 June 2002?'

'After they left their meeting? No.'

'Nobody followed them?'

'My officers saw them leave, but their job was to stay put and watch who came and went from the building, not to follow those two across the city.'

'Do you think they went back to their rooms in the hall of residence that night?'

'I'm sure you've seen my team's reports, Mrs Cooper. We don't know for sure, but they were seen on the London train the next morning.'

'Any idea where they went after that?'

'The CCTV tapes at Paddington had been overwritten by the time we got to them. The trail went cold. We got as far as finding out that there were rat-runs through France, Italy and the Balkans, but there was no positive sighting. If they made it to Turkey, they could have caught a flight out to Kabul, Islamabad, wherever.'

He swallowed the last drops of his coffee and carefully dabbed his lips with the paper napkin.

Jenny said, 'Am I right in assuming that your partners took the lead role once it was known they'd disappeared?'

'We did what we could, within our resources. Whether others looked further, I wouldn't know. We didn't receive any more information.'

'There are very few police statements in the papers Mrs Jamal handed me. I presume your officers made detailed observation logs.'

'We did the job we were asked to,' he said and glanced at his expensive gold watch. Jenny imagined him letting villains see it across the interview table, showing them that a cop didn't have to go without.

'So how about some names – people who knew these

boys? They must have had friends and associates you were looking at.'

Pironi glanced out through the window. She knew he was treading a fine line. While conducting a joint operation with the Security Services he and his officers would have been warned time and again that secrecy was paramount, but she sensed his vanity wouldn't let him leave her with nothing.

Pironi said, 'You know the form. All I can tell you is which of the names in the statements we made at the time we considered the most important. There was a mullah, Sayeed Faruq – must've been about thirty at the time – disappeared to Pakistan a couple of weeks later. Never spoke to us. Never came back. And there was another guy, a radical we think set up this halaqah. His name was Anwar Ali. He was a regular at the mosque, and held smaller meetings at his flat. I investigated him myself, couldn't pin a thing on him, but I had a hunch he was drawing kids in and passing them on to others. He was a post-grad at the university . . . politics and sociology, something like that.'

'Any idea what happened to him?'

Pironi studied his well-kept hands. 'I agreed to meet you this morning because Alison's a good friend of mine. We worked out of the same station for fifteen years. She took her fair share of risks and this isn't the time of life for her to be taking on any more. I'd be grateful if you didn't send her out to talk to these people.'

'I wouldn't make her do anything she's uncomfortable with.'

'That's not what I asked.'

He looked into her eyes. She felt like a suspect.

'Fine. Understood.'

'Good.'

He reached a scrap of paper out from his pocket and tucked it under his saucer.

'Nice meeting you, Jenny.' He got up from the table.

'One more thing,' Jenny said. 'Is this case still of any interest to anyone?'

'You won't have to scratch far to find out.'

He moved off towards the door.

She watched him jog across the road and jump into an unmarked squad car that was parked opposite, a junior detective at the wheel. She reached the folded message out from under his saucer and opened it. Printed on it was the name Anwar Ali and an address in Morfa, south Wales.

It was late in the afternoon before she had processed the most urgent files on her desk. Among the mountain of paper had been Dr Kerr's report on the Africans in the refrigerated trailer. He'd found traces of paint under their nails, suggesting they'd tried to scratch their way out before succumbing to the cold. The youngest of the three was a fifteen-year-old boy dressed only in a Manchester United football shirt. None had any papers or documents to identify them by. They too would now be stored in the mortuary until the police, at some indeterminate time, decided they had exhausted their inquiries.

She chose her moment – while Alison was caught up in another tense, whispered phone call with her husband – and slipped out of the office. Alison still coveted her role as the investigator in their professional partnership, treating any attempt by Jenny to speak to potential witnesses without her as an act of trespass on her territory. It was true that most coroners chose to operate largely from their desks, preferring to send their officers to collect statements and gather evidence on the ground, but there was no reason – apart from a misplaced sense of propriety – why they couldn't pursue their search for the truth as far as they were able. According to centuries-old law, the coroner's duty was to determine the who, when, where and how of a death. Jenny had never understood how that was possible without getting your hands dirty.

Morfa was a 1960s housing estate on the outskirts of Newport, thirty miles to the north-west of Bristol on the Welsh side of the Severn; a neglected corner of a largely forgotten city. Conceived at a time when coal mines and steel works still employed the bulk of men in south Wales, the estate was a sprawl of identical prefabricated concrete boxes built to house the workers and their families. It now housed the non-workers. Groups of shaven-headed boys and pasty-faced, overweight girls stood at corners; broken-down cars sat wheel-less on bricks; a stray dog scavenged on a patch of litter-strewn wasteland that had once been a park. It wasn't a neighbourhood, it was a holding pen.

To add to the estate's problems, it had also become a dumping ground for asylum seekers. Here and there, as she drove through a disorientating network of similar streets, Jenny saw Middle Eastern, Asian and occasional African faces. In an arcade of shops there was an Indian takeaway protected by heavy steel shutters, and next to it a burned-out and boarded up former off-licence.

She drew up outside the address in Raglan Way, which, being near the end of a terrace, at least had the benefit of a view of distant mountains. In contrast with the neighbouring houses, the path and patch of grass at the front were clean and swept and the front door had been recently painted. A small oasis of pride in a sea of apathy.

She rang the bell. There was no answer, though she thought she heard sounds of movement from inside. She tried again and was met with silence. She looked for a letter box to call through and found that it had been screwed shut. Resigned to having to return later, she was turning to leave when she noticed a twitch of one of the heavy net curtains in the upstairs windows. A veiled woman retreated quickly behind it. Jenny returned to the front door and called through. 'Is that Mrs Ali? My name's Jenny Cooper – I'm a coroner. I'd like to speak to your husband. He's not in trouble, it's just a routine inquiry.'

She waited for a response and thought she heard hesitant footsteps on the stairs.

'What do you want?' a frightened female voice said from behind the door.

'I'm investigating the disappearance of a young man in 2002. His name was Nazim Jamal. I understand Mr Ali knew him.'

'He's not here. He's still at work.' She sounded young, her accent a fusion of northern British and Pakistani.

'When will he be home?'

'I don't know. He's got a meeting.'

'Is this his wife I'm talking to?' There was no reply. Jenny took a visiting card out of her wallet and fed it under the door. 'Look, this is my card. You can see who I am. I'm not a police officer, but you are obliged by law to cooperate with my inquiry. All I need to know is where I can find your husband to talk to him.'

She could feel the woman's panic and indecision. Eventually the card was pushed back out again, a phone number written on it.

The refugee centre was housed in a two-storey concrete building in the centre of the estate. It had once been a pub. Foot-high letters had been unscrewed from the front, leaving their ghostly impression in a lighter shade of grey: The Chartists' Arms. Through the partially closed blinds covering the ground-floor window, she could see a stick-thin Asian man with a wife and two small children in tow gesticulating across the desk at a tired-looking white woman. Oblivious to his remonstrations, the woman was straining to make sense of a large envelope stuffed with papers he had handed her. The walls were lined with ex-civil service filing cabinets, and there were steel bars at the windows to protect the few shabby computers and an elderly photocopying machine.

Anwar Ali answered the door himself. She placed him in his early thirties, though his full beard and suit and tie made him look older. He uttered a brief greeting and ushered her upstairs to a small, tidy office. Directly across the narrow corridor was a classroom in which a language class was taking place, the students chanting, 'Pleased-to-meet-you.' She glanced at the tidy shelves and noticed a collection of books both in English and what she assumed was Urdu. Among them were several political biographies of Middle Eastern figures whose names she didn't recognize.

'How can I help you, Mrs Cooper?' Ali said, his anger at her presence covered by only a thin veneer of politeness.

'Your name was given to me as someone who was associated with Nazim Jamal and Rafi Hassan before their disappearance.'

'By whom?' He spoke precisely, his bearing that of a man with a sharp analytical mind: the kind of person who made Jenny feel anxious. Ali was prickly and she'd have to tread carefully.

'The police. Apparently you went to Al Rahma mosque with Jamal and Hassan in the months beforehand and ran a halaqah at your flat in Marlowes Road – I hope I pronounced that correctly.'

'Your pronunciation is fine. The police are still peddling this story?'

'They certainly had you marked down as a radical at the time. How they feel about you now I've no idea.'

'Thankfully we've had very little to do with each other. My brief spell in unlawful custody was sufficient. I still don't know if it was the police or the Security Services holding me. I was punched, kicked, deprived of food and sleep, not permitted to wash, disturbed at prayers, forced to urinate on the floor. They found no evidence against me, I was not charged, nor have I ever been.' He leaned forward in his chair. 'I should be extremely wary of taking notice of what people who behave in this way tell you, Mrs Cooper. They were not concerned with guilt or innocence, or even with the truth. All they wanted was to put Muslims behind bars.'

'They told Mrs Jamal you were a member of Hizb ut-Tahrir.'

'You're sounding very much like them. I thought the coroner's functions were separate from the police?'

He sat back, regarding her calmly, waiting for her explanation.

'Nazim Jamal has been pronounced legally dead. My function is to find out how that happened.'

'I thought he was only *presumed* dead? That's not sufficient grounds for an inquest.'

'This is a preliminary inquiry. Mrs Jamal has spent many years in limbo; I feel it's the least I can do for her.' She affected what she hoped would appear a genuine smile. 'I presume that you were close to the two of them, friendly even?'

'Yes, for a while.'

'Is there anything you'd like their families to know?'

'There's nothing to tell. We went to mosque, studied a little together. That's it.'

'Would you mind telling me what you studied?'

'Facets of our religion.'

She nodded towards his bookshelf. 'Would these discussions have had a political slant?'

'We were students. We discussed all sorts of things.'

'Seven years is a long time. I expect you've changed.'

He shook his head. 'You really have missed your vocation,

Mrs Cooper. I am not – ' he paused for emphasis – 'nor have I ever been, an advocate of violence.'

'Do you know where they went, Mr Ali?'

He held her gaze, unblinking. 'Do you honestly think I would not have told their families if I did?'

'Did they ever they mention going abroad to you, to Afghanistan perhaps?'

'No.'

'You know they were allegedly seen on a London train the next morning.'

'If that was so, I knew nothing about it.'

'The police think you were some sort of recruiter, that you hooked in idealistic young men and passed them down the line to dangerous fanatics.'

'They think a lot of things, but understand very few.'

'So tell me. You must have a theory.'

He glanced down for a moment, considering his response carefully. 'I've had many years to think, and I can conclude only two things. Firstly, that even those we believe we know we may not; and secondly, that even in this country a Muslim life is cheap.'

'Are you telling me the whole truth, Mr Ali?'

'Those two young men weren't just friends to me, they were my *brothers*. Why would I lie?'

For all sorts of reasons, she thought, but knew there was little point in forcing the issue. The best she could do was appeal to his conscience and leave it with him. 'I'll ask just one thing of you,' she said, 'that you'll think about Mrs Jamal. Nazim was her only child.' She took out a business card and placed it on his desk. 'She has a right to know even if the public doesn't.'

He didn't get up to show her out. As she laid a hand on the door, he said, 'Be careful whom you trust, Mrs Cooper – when a friend cuts your throat, you don't see him coming.'

\*

Ali's parting words remained with her. She hadn't known what to make of him, except that he inhabited a world she didn't understand and that he had made her slightly nervous. She could believe that he had been a young radical, a fanatic even, but she struggled with the thought that a Muslim mother would not have been told by someone on the inside, even anonymously, if her devout son had volunteered to fight for a religious cause. And if Nazim and Rafi hadn't gone to fight or train with the mujahedin, where else could they have gone? They were scarcely more than schoolboys, only nine months into their university careers. Several dark scenarios presented themselves to her: perhaps they were lured to London and press-ganged into an organization against their will? Perhaps they were still very much alive, zealous and fanatical; or perhaps they were fugitives, living underground, running scared.

Only one thing was now certain: if Ali was connected with their disappearance, whoever he was involved with would already know about her and her investigation. Common sense told her to pull back now while she still could, but every time she entertained the thought something deep inside her rebelled.

She had felt like this before. It was as if she had no choice.

# FIVE

IN ORDER TO OBTAIN THE Home Secretary's permission to hold an inquest into the case of a missing person presumed dead, Jenny needed to convince him that there was at least a strong likelihood that Nazim Jamal was in fact deceased. Strictly speaking, she also needed reason to believe that the death had occurred in or near her district – which could be impossible to prove – but she hoped to argue by analogy with bodies flown home from abroad, that if the body were ever to be repatriated it would be to within her jurisdiction. It was a weak argument, and viewed in the cold light of day the arguments against holding an inquest seemed even flimsier. It was clearly within the public interest to know why two bright young British citizens had vanished. To refuse to inquire would smack of official cover up, and the one-and-a-half million British Muslims were too big a constituency for any government to risk alienating.

Held steady by her morning combination of beta blockers to calm her physical symptoms of anxiety and anti-depressants to level her mood, she was ready to face the world again. She wanted to write her report to the Home Office as soon as possible, but first needed to carry out the two most logical lines of inquiry: to discover what, if anything, was known about the missing boys at the university, and what other documents the police still held from their original investigation.

She called through to the university offices during her morning commute while Ross slouched half asleep in the passenger seat plugged into his iPod. She was passed on to the office of Professor Rhydian Brightman, head of the department of physics. His none-too-helpful secretary claimed he was booked solid for the next week, but Jenny stood her ground and calmly reminded her that failure to assist with a coroner's inquiry could land the obstructing party in jail.

Ross looked round during this exchange and pulled out one of his headphones to catch the result: a meeting was swiftly arranged for late morning.

He said, 'Wow. Is that true? Can you really throw people in prison?'

'If I have to.'

'Have you ever?'

'Last summer. Two witnesses in the same inquest. Caused quite a stir.' She glanced over with a smile, but he was already plugged back in, his head bouncing to the music.

Alison greeted her with the usual stack of paperwork and a clutch of requests from other families with missing daughters wanting to look at the Jane Doe.

'What about the lab tests from the last lot? Shouldn't we rule them out first?' Jenny said.

'If I know anything they'll take at least a fortnight. Don't worry, I'll fix a viewing for later in the week. Probably have them queuing round the block by then.'

Jenny skimmed through the list of requests. It was unbelievable how many apparently well-adjusted young people there were who had vanished from their previous lives. Where did they go? Alison assured her there were hundreds if not thousands of cases every year, mostly people who'd had breakdowns or who were escaping from debts or bad relationships. The good news was that all but a fraction turned up eventually.

Jenny handed Alison a letter she had written to the Bristol and Avon Chief Constable. It requested that she be given access to all their archived files relating to the boys' disappearance and their observation of the Al Rahma mosque and Marlowes Road halaqah.

Alison glanced at it dismissively. 'You'll be wasting your time, Mrs Cooper. They haven't got them any more.'

How do you know?'

'I spoke to Dave Pironi last night. A couple of suits came up from London yesterday afternoon with a certificate from the Minister and took them away.'

'Do we know who these people were?'

'He can't tell me that.'

'He must have given you some idea.'

Guardedly Alison said, 'I didn't get the impression they were police.'

'Then they'll have been MI5.' Jenny clicked onto her internet browser and started to search for a phone number.

Alison stood watching her from the doorway.

'What?' Jenny said.

'I wouldn't normally say anything like this, Mrs Cooper, but Dave doesn't think you should get involved.'

'Oh, really?' She found the number for MI5's central switchboard and scribbled it down. 'What's he got to hide?'

'Nothing. The fact is the police got pushed aside more or less straight after they went missing. The people who do know, if there are any, are so far up the food chain it's pointless even trying to go after them. All you'll do is make trouble for yourself.'

'He told you this?'

'Not in so many words, but if he says don't go there, it's for a reason.'

'Maybe he'd like to share that with my inquest.'

Alison sighed in frustration. 'I'll grant you there wasn't much sympathy around for those two boys, but even in CID they weren't happy with the way the investigation ended. I know you think all the police are closet racists, but as far as they were concerned they had a major investigation stepped on. For all they knew at the time, those lads could have disappeared to a safe house to strap bombs to themselves. They weren't even allowed to put pictures—' She stopped herself mid-sentence, realizing that she had said too much.

'They weren't allowed to put pictures where?'

'It doesn't matter. Just canteen gossip.'

'Are you telling me that Pironi's people were ordered not to carry out a normal missing persons investigation?'

'He's never said that.'

'Maybe you should be giving a statement. What else were they saying in the canteen?'

'I wish I hadn't said a word. You won't even be allowed to hold this inquest anyway.'

Jenny looked up from her computer screen and sensed in Alison something approaching mild panic. 'Pironi's asked you to try to steer me away from this, hasn't he?'

'He would never ask me to do such a thing. But we all know how blame gets shifted downwards, and Dave's a year away from retirement. He paid for his wife's treatment out of his own pocket and he needs his pension. If you have to get into this, I'd at least ask you to accept my word that he would never have done anything wrong.'

Alison had a history of putting men other than her husband on a pedestal – Harry Marshall, the previous coroner, eight months dead, had been one of them. Jenny didn't doubt that Dave Pironi could be perfectly charming, but she was equally aware that when it came to men she found attractive, her officer had no judgement.

Jenny said, 'I'm sure you're right, but I'd be grateful if you sent the letter anyway.' She grabbed a legal pad and dropped it into her briefcase. 'I'll see you later. I've got a meeting at the university.'

Rhydian Brightman was a tall, fidgety man with a permanently distracted expression. He could only have been a year or two older than Jenny, but had already embraced middle age and wore thick glasses that balanced in a groove halfway down his nose. They met in a busy canteen on the physics department's ground floor, Brightman claiming his office was being used by a colleague for a meeting. She assumed the real reason was that her presence had unnerved him. He looked to her like a highly strung man who was comfortable only in his own world among his own kind. That did not include prying coroners.

They sat at a small, sticky table and drank foul-tasting cups of tea purchased from a vending machine. At the next table several boisterous undergraduates were exchanging lurid stories of drunken sexual exploits, but the professor didn't seem to notice. He had one eye on Jenny and the other on the door.

'You remember Nazim Jamal – he started as an undergraduate in the autumn of 2001,' Jenny said.

'A little. He would have been to my lectures. We probably met in the seminar room once or twice.'

'You do remember his disappearance?'

'Yes, of course. We all remember that. Terrible.'

'I assume the police must have asked you a lot of questions at the time.'

'They were very busy here for a week or two. I didn't get the impression they found much to enlighten them. It all seemed to remain rather mysterious.' He gave an awkward, apologetic smile. 'The thing is, there's not that much connection between staff and undergraduates, not on a personal level. I could recognize most of our first years, but I couldn't tell you what they got up to outside the department.'

'Who was the main point of contact for the police while they were investigating?'

'Me, I suppose. I was technically responsible for our undergraduates at the time. We had a number of meetings. As I say, not a lot transpired.' He became aware of his restless fingers drumming on the table and thrust his hands self-consciously into his lap.

'*Technically*?'

'In an academic sense. Of course, if they wanted to come to me with a personal problem . . . But we do have other avenues for those sorts of things.'

'What I really want to know at this stage is what was being said amongst the students or staff. There must have been endless speculation; others who were closer to him must have had theories.'

'Surprisingly few, actually. That's what seemed so odd. The police spoke to a lot of undergraduates, but the other chap—'

'Hassan.'

'Yes. He seemed to be the only one Jamal was really close to. Even those in his seminar group knew very little about him.'

'His mother gave me the impression he was sociable – came from Clifton College, played tennis—'

'You would have thought there would have been more to go on, wouldn't you?'

Jenny recalled the student noticeboards she had passed on the way in covered with flyers and announcements for societies and political meetings. There were several from Muslim groups organizing speaker meetings, and debates on US foreign policy and the future of Palestine.

'Was there much in the way of Islamic activity on campus at the time?'

'So the police said, but I can't say that I was aware of it as a live issue. Science students tend to be rather less politicized than others – too busy working, I assume.' He let out a burst of nervous laughter and cast an apprehensive glance at two colleagues who had seated themselves at a nearby table.

Jenny lowered her voice, attempting to bring him into her confidence. 'I'll be straight with you. I doubt there's much you could contribute to an inquest; I probably won't even have to call you as a witness – ' the muscles in his forehead relaxed, smoothing the creases from his brow – 'but I do need more than this.' She paused, fixing him with a look, trying to reach the man underneath. 'Can I assume that it wasn't just the police who interviewed you and others here at the time?'

'It would be a logical assumption.'

'In which case, you were doubtless told to keep the content of your discussions secret.'

'Believe me, Mrs Cooper, there really isn't much to tell.'

'I'm not asking you to breach a confidence, but if you could just tell me whether Nazim Jamal was believed to be a member of an extremist group – Hizb ut-Tahrir, for example?'

'It may have been mentioned.'

'This one may be harder for you: were any other students, apart from Rafi Hassan, also suspected of being members?'

Brightman hurriedly shook his head. 'No one said anything to me.'

'Did you make a formal statement at the time?'

'No. There was nothing like that. Just a few "chats".'

She studied him closely for a moment, wondering what reason a professor of physics might have for withholding information. She reasoned that the university would have been the subject of close attention by the Security Services for a considerable period, that members of staff would have been issued with directives to report any students they suspected of having extremist leanings to a senior manager, that effectively all tutors were recruited as spies. And once a spy, always a spy. Professor Brightman probably still had a number in his address book that he was tempted to call periodically, if only to cover his own back. To reveal all of this to Jenny would be compromising to say the least. His MI5 contact would have stressed the vital importance of discretion: to identify radicals the university would necessarily have to tolerate a certain amount of their activity. If it was known that all staff were potential informers, the extremists would be driven underground.

She said, 'I appreciate the delicacy of your position, but perhaps you could help me make contact with some of Jamal's contemporaries. You never know, someone might remember something that didn't seem relevant at the time.'

'I can certainly put you in touch with the university offices,' he said. 'They'd have a record of that year group. Actually, one of our junior staff here was one of them, but I'm afraid she's at a conference in Germany for the next couple of days – her team discovered a new particle.' He smiled, relieved at the prospect of their interview drawing to an end.

'Great. What's her name?'

'Sarah Levin, or *Dr* Levin should I say. One of our rising stars.'

The name was familiar. 'Didn't she give a statement to the police at the time?'

'Quite possibly. I'm sure she would have done whatever she could to help.'

Professor Brightman called through to the university offices to arrange for Jenny to meet one of the administrators, who printed a list of alumni and their contact details from Nazim and Rafi's year. Jenny took a hard copy and had the file emailed through to her office so Alison could start making phone calls straight away.

She walked back across the campus, taking the opportunity to observe the students and absorb the atmosphere. The first group she passed were dressed in stylish casual clothes, carried laptops and had cellphones pressed to their ears. Young men and women seemed to mix easily with one another and the political meetings advertised on the student noticeboards were far outweighed by announcements for parties and happy hours at local bars. Hedonism, not idealism, was the order of the day. She couldn't pretend that things had been that different during her time at Birmingham. She'd marched for the striking miners and CND, but in truth had been more interested in her guitar-playing boyfriend and cadging drinks in the student union. She and her friends had been a little less hung up about money, career and possessions perhaps, but apart from the odd spell of pre-exam cramming, it had been three years of more or less non-stop partying.

Then she saw something which made her change her mind. A group of ten or so young women, all wearing identical niqabs – the black robes and veils which revealed only their eyes – crossed the quadrangle in a tight huddle. When they passed a group of boys, they looked away or at the ground. Their separateness was absolute. Masked and impenetrable, they had cut themselves off from the public realm. When Jenny was a student she'd had lots of Muslim friends, girls who came from strict orthodox families but who were only too keen to cut loose and behave and dress like everyone else. Twenty years on, the next generation were adopting clothing more conservative than their grandmothers'. Faced with a bewildering and hostile world they had chosen religion as their crutch. They weren't being made to do it: it was a choice.

A black hybrid saloon drew up silently behind her and slid into a space as she approached the front door of her office. She was reaching for her keys when a suited woman and a male colleague, both barely over thirty, climbed out and stepped towards her.

'Mrs Cooper?' the woman said.

'Yes?'

The woman, dark, attractive, but tired around the eyes, offered her hand. 'Gillian Golder. This is my colleague, Alun Rhys.'

Rhys said a polite hello. He was a solid, stocky young man who could have come straight from a college rugby field.

Gillian Golder said, 'This is just a friendly visit. We're intelligence officers with the Security Services. Have you got a moment?'

'Sure,' Jenny said lightly, and led them along the dim hallway.

Jenny couldn't decide if Golder and Rhys's relaxed pre-business chit-chat was reassuring or sinister. She had met enough government officials of various stripes to know that the modern way was to give the appearance of approachability and reasonableness, even if the underlying agenda hadn't changed. Coolness, in the teenage sense, had replaced uprightness as the common virtue. Body language was to remain open, language euphemistic and non-confrontational. If you played by these rules, you were considered an insider. If you exhibited signs of aloofness or appeared too starchy, you had 'issues' and weren't to be trusted.

'I suppose you've guessed why we're here?' Gillian Golder said, taking the lead, Rhys adopting the role of observer.

Jenny smiled, straining not to appear threatened or defensive. 'I assume it concerns Nazim Jamal.'

'Yeah. We obviously heard about the judge's ruling last week and presumably Mrs Jamal has been to see you about holding an inquest.'

Jenny knew full well that they knew. DI Pironi would have lifted the phone the moment she had asked to meet him. It was all part of the dance, Golder trying to see if Jenny would adopt an attitude.

'She has.'

'Uh-huh. Well, it's hardly surprising. It's got to be tough for her.'

'Sure.'

'So . . . how do you feel about that?'

'How do *I* feel?' Jenny was thrown by the question. 'I'm just doing my job, compiling a report to go the Home Secretary, who has to authorize the holding of an inquest.'

'Do you think it will happen?'

'I've no idea.'

'For what it's worth, we think you'll get the go-ahead. It would only look as if there was something to hide if permission were refused.' Rhys nodded in agreement. 'And we're all obviously trying to do our best to build bridges with the Muslim community.'

There was a pause in which Jenny felt as if she were expected to respond. Growing confused and more than a little irritated by Gillian Golder's obliqueness, she asked, 'Is there something specific you wanted to discuss?'

Golder said, 'Obviously this is a case in which sensitive issues will come up. And we all know the media have a tendency to pounce on stories like this and sensationalize . . .' She glanced at her colleague, 'But from our end we feel that if we could head off any potential mistrust at the outset, we can avoid setting off major hysteria.'

'Mistrust?' Jenny said, pretending to be confused by the notion.

'Yes.' Gillian Golder shifted in her chair. 'Clearly Mrs Jamal is very upset, anyone would be in her position, but she might be tempted to see an inquest as an opportunity to vent her more irrational feelings in public . . . It would be unfortunate if a perfectly proper inquiry were to be hijacked in that way, especially as we've worked so hard to earn the trust of young British Asians in recent years.'

'I can't stop her talking to the press, if that's what you mean.'

'Of course not. The thing is, what we'd like to avoid is her making unwarranted allegations against the Security Services. We'll cooperate as much as we're able, but we might as well tell you now that we know virtually nothing about what happened to Jamal and Hassan. Really, we've looked through all the files – the trail went dead.'

'Will I be able to see them?'

'That'll be decided higher up. Sometimes we'll seek a public interest immunity certificate to cover our working files – to protect our methods and what have you – but we'll certainly provide you with a witness who can speak to the facts of our investigation.'

'What about the police records? I assume you've looked at those, too.'

'Not much of interest in those, either, what's left of them.'

Jenny sat back in her chair and tried to see through the fog. She had the feeling that this was an attempt to gag and control her from the outset, but the messengers seemed so benign she couldn't be sure.

'Just so I've got this straight,' Jenny said, 'you're telling me that if I do get to hold an inquest, you'll provide one witness from the Security Services but I won't get to see your records.'

Gillian Golder nodded. 'Pretty much.'

'And you're asking me not to push for any more documentary evidence or to plant the thought in Mrs Jamal's head that there might be secret information to which I won't have access.'

Rhys cut in. 'We're not trying to clip your wings, Mrs Cooper, we just need to get two things clear. First off, the chances of any of our internal notes or records being released to a public inquest are zero. The most you can hope for is that you'll get to look at them in private. Second, we're asking you to trust us when we say we have absolutely no clue what happened to Nazim Jamal and Rafi Hassan. Apart from reviewing the papers, we've spoken to the retired officer who was heading up the case at the time. These two just vanished – I mean, off the face of the earth. OK, so the investigation was only live for a month or so, but there wasn't one solid lead after the sighting on the train.'

'So what do you people think happened to them?'

'We assume they went abroad. Plenty of others did at the time.'

'No other theories?'

'None that stand up. They were just a couple of Muslim boys flirting with radicals, who were most likely shipped off to be fighters.'

'Is it really that easy to escape the country undetected? I don't buy it.'

Both officers smiled at once. 'You'd be amazed,' Rhys said. 'Just because you've got CCTV doesn't mean the picture's any good, or that some klutz hasn't taped over it.'

'I hear the army have routinely taken DNA from dead insurgents in Iraq and Afghanistan. Has any attempt been made to trace them that way?'

'They're both on a database. We'd have been told if anything had turned up.'

Jenny sighed. Something niggled. 'One more question: why

was the police inquiry so short-lived? I've heard some officers felt it was closed down prematurely.'

Gillian Golder fielded the question without hesitating. 'Because they vanished so completely it was felt they might be in hiding. A decision was taken to tone things down and concentrate on picking up intelligence. It was thought that if we smoked them out too soon we might miss out on being led to something bigger.'

Jenny nodded, but if the meeting was intended to dispel her mistrust it hadn't succeeded. Golder and Rhys were young, but knew how to go about their business.

They had dangled the possibility of an inquest in front of her, but on condition that she played by their rules. They wanted it low key, not to ask too many questions of the Security Services, to appear to appease the Muslim community and above all to avoid inflaming it.

She considered her dilemma, then decided on the only course she could square with her conscience. 'I don't want my inquest descending into a media circus any more than you do,' she said, 'and I've no intention of providing a platform for wild, unfounded allegations. But as you've driven all this way to see me, you ought to know that I won't tolerate any outside interference in my inquiry. If it's done, it's done properly, thoroughly and independently and in accordance with the law. '

Gillian Golder said, 'We wouldn't expect any less. Honestly, Mrs Cooper, we're as keen to find out what happened as you are.'

Jenny couldn't tell if she had won or lost the encounter; whether she had guaranteed that an inquest would never happen or whether her display of honesty had marked her down as sufficiently naive to be trusted. Nor could she decide if she had been brazenly lied to or if there was more than a grain of truth in Golder and Rhys's claim that the Security Services were clueless as to what had happened to Rafi and Nazim. All she could be certain about was that she was entering a world of which she had no experience.

Fending off Alison's attempts to extract a verbatim account of her conversation with the two intelligence officers, she locked herself away for the rest of the afternoon to write her report to the Home Secretary. She kept it tight and uncontroversial, cited case law sparingly and strove to give every impression of reasonableness. Her conclusion was a model of restraint, arguing that while legally the Home Secretary would be perfectly entitled to conclude there were insufficient reasons to hold an inquest – not least the absence of a body – the interests of justice tipped in favour of a formal inquiry.

'Finally,' she wrote, allowing herself one rhetorical flourish,

> *while other agencies of the Crown are frequently accused by the deceased's relatives of pursuing self, or political interest, the coroner is a truly independent judicial officer whose only duty is to unearth truth. Although in this case the chances of that occurring are slim, a non-finding is surely preferable to no attempt having been made at all.*

She had the report sent to London by motorcycle courier. As it went, she found herself mouthing a silent prayer.

# SIX

Mrs Jamal had somehow managed to get hold of Jenny's home number. She arrived back to Ross's announcement that a mad woman had been calling every ten minutes. The answerphone was jammed with messages. In ascending degrees of hysteria, they all rehearsed the same allegations: that she was being watched, followed in the street, that her post was being intercepted and that secret cameras had been placed in her apartment. 'I am a prisoner in my home,' was a phrase she repeated many times. The final call was so tearful Jenny could barely make it out.

Personal contact with the next of kin should be kept on a formal footing: to enter into a relationship with surviving family members could only lead to trouble. Relatives seldom understood that the coroner was acting purely in the public interest, and that any appearance of friendliness was out of courtesy and a desire to make the process as painless as possible for those left behind. The correct way to deal with Mrs Jamal would have been to write her a letter politely explaining that it was inappropriate for her to behave in this way and asking her to desist. To respond to such behaviour by phoning back would risk creating expectations she could never fulfil. But what sort of person could ignore such desperate pleas for help?

Mrs Jamal snatched up the phone on the first ring. 'Yes. Who is it?' She sounded fraught.

'Mrs Jamal, this is Mrs Cooper, the—'

'Oh, thank goodness,' she cut in. 'I knew I could trust you. You were sent by God, I know you were. No one else understands, no one else.' She continued without drawing breath. 'These people are hounding me day and night, Mrs Cooper, they won't leave me alone. They're watching my flat, they follow me in the street. They've been in here at night, I know they have. They've moved things. They've put bugs in the flat, that's what they've done. They're listening to this now. I've got to leave, I have to go—'

'Hold on a moment. Calm down. Let me speak.'

'Yes, yes, of course, but you have to believe—'

'*Listen* to me.'

Finally, Mrs Jamal stopped talking.

'Now keep calm. Getting worked up is going to achieve nothing.'

'No, you're right. I'm so grateful—'

'Tell me who you think is watching you.'

'I don't know who they are. They're *men*. White men. I don't know what they want with me. I don't know anything. I'm just a mother . . .' She sniffed back tears.

'Remember last time we spoke – you went to the window and there was no one there.'

'They listen to me. They know when to disappear. That's why I have to go somewhere they can't find me.'

'Mrs Jamal, you're upset. You're going through one of the most stressful experiences anyone can imagine. You've lost your son and you're desperate to know where he went. Now think about this: you don't know where he went, that's why you want an inquest. No one has any reason to follow or listen to you. I know it may be hard to understand, but I think your mind may be playing tricks.'

'No . . .' Mrs Jamal said, but without much conviction.

'What I want you to do is go to your doctor and talk

78

about how you're feeling. This won't get better by itself and I want you to feel calm enough to sit through an inquest if we can hold one.'

'I'm not insane, Mrs Cooper, I know what I see. I can't stay here. They'll come in the night—'

'*Trust me*. Please. I know enough about how people react to understand exactly how you're feeling.' She paused and sensed that, now she had got the attention she craved, Mrs Jamal was actually listening. 'You're feeling very alone, very exposed and very uncertain,' she continued, 'but once you start to see some progress these feelings will pass. You'll have to take my word on that.'

'But I'm frightened, Mrs Cooper.'

'That's perfectly natural. You've lived with an unanswered question for seven years. You're frightened of what the next few weeks might bring.'

Mrs Jamal spoke through quiet sobs. 'I know he wouldn't leave me. He was a good son. He always came to see me, even when his father tried to stop him. Nazim wouldn't leave me.'

Jenny said, 'I'll make you a deal. I'll get on and do my job the best I can, and you get yourself some help to see you through the next few weeks. Can we agree on that?'

'Yes . . .' came the feeble reply. 'Thank you.'

Ross spent the evening locked in his room talking to friends over the internet and listening to music, anything rather than come downstairs to spend time with his mother. To stave off the pangs of rejection Jenny retreated to her study and tried to make an impression on her ever-increasing pile of untended paperwork. Corpses were a good indicator of social trends. In recent weeks she'd had two women under twenty-five who had died following sudden and catastrophic alcohol-related liver failure, and a third who had collapsed and died in a nightclub toilet from alcohol poisoning; two depressed fifteen-year-old boys who had committed suicide after meeting in a chat room; and a married father of thirty-five who had jumped from a motorway bridge when his mortgage company foreclosed. If the young seemed unhappy, the old were scarcely better off. In front of her lay a photograph of an eighty-year-old widower who had rigged up the bedroom in his tiny flat as a makeshift gas chamber. He had left a note explaining that the struggle of making ends meet was too much to bear.

Depressed, Jenny dumped her papers into her briefcase and picked up the phone to call Steve, hoping he might welcome an hour or two away from his draughty barn. There was no reply, not even a machine on which to leave a message. And he didn't have a mobile. She supposed he was out walking his dog, who was now confined to a chicken-wire pound during the weekdays, but when she tried again later, and again and again until midnight, she accepted he wasn't at home. There were any number of explanations why he would be out late on a Wednesday evening, she told herself: he was probably with friends, or staying over with a colleague in Bristol. He wouldn't be with another woman. He couldn't be. Their relationship, however tenuous, was too significant to be betrayed by the temptation of casual sex. And she had never turned him away when she sensed he wanted to spend the night.

Too restless for once to write in her journal, she took two pills and lay in the darkness listening to freezing rain beating on the window. The leaded panes rattled in their shrunken frames and the wind moaned fitfully under the eaves, conjuring ghosts and darker spirits, as she dipped in and out of consciousness. Her last sensation before being pulled into a deep, uneasy sleep was of the ground shifting beneath her, a groaning of the earth, and a sense that something had changed profoundly.

\*

Preoccupied and disturbed as she was, she clung to a semblance of normality throughout the morning routine, making Ross breakfast and keeping up light conversation until she had dropped him at college. Only when he merged into the stream of kids pushing through the school gates did she succumb to the mild attack of panic which had been bubbling under since she had stood under the shower and barely felt the water on her skin. Dr Allen had convinced her that the worst symptoms of her disorder had been confined to the past. He'd drawn her graphs explaining how the medicated brain retrained itself, returning the fight-or-flight response triggered deep in the amygdala to normal levels. He had *promised* her she wouldn't go back to where she had once been. Yet six months later, trapped in rush-hour traffic, her heart felt twice its normal size and a band was tightening around her diaphragm.

She railed against the symptoms. She shouted and swore at them, drawing stares from other drivers. How dare they return to pollute her life? She fought through each diminishing wave, refusing to pull over and succumb, until the adrenalin at last subsided and left her feeling tired, heavy and hollow. She stopped at lights and pulled down the vanity mirror to look at herself. Her pupils were wide and staring, her face pale: both classic signs of acute anxiety. Fury gave way to despair. Why? Why on an ordinary morning, with nothing to threaten her, was she terrified? What was stirring in her? And why now, when she needed more than ever to be in control, had it chosen to resurface?

Her mobile rang as she pulled into a parking space opposite her office. She nudged the car behind as she fished it out of her handbag. There was a crunch of plastic. She pretended she hadn't heard.

An agitated voice said, 'Mrs Cooper? It's Andy Kerr at the

Vale. I wondered if you had signed release for the removal of the Jane Doe.'

'I beg your pardon?'

'I thought perhaps you might have authorized its removal . . . it's gone.'

'*What?*'

'The body was here yesterday evening and it's missing now.'

'You're serious? Who was on duty?'

'There was only one person on last night. I guess it's possible if someone managed to break in . . .'

She could hear the alarm in his voice. She could already imagine the newspaper headlines: *Unidentified Body Stolen from Morgue.*

'It's not here, Mrs Cooper. It was in your custody. What should we do?'

'I'll be right there.'

Dr Kerr looked even more ashen than she felt. She followed him along the corridor and stared down at the empty drawer. He explained that the assistant who'd been on night duty was more of a watchman, a Filipino who worked a cleaning shift in the day and sometimes remained overnight. Chances were he would have spent most of his time asleep in the staff rest room, which was around the corner, at least thirty feet from the refrigerator. Intruders could either have come through the door opening onto the car park or along the underground tunnel which led over from the sub-basement level of the main hospital building. There were no signs of forced entry, but the locks were hardly sophisticated.

Jenny said, 'You're sure there hasn't been a mix up? It's not unknown for undertakers to take the wrong body.'

Andy Kerr shook his head. 'We've got thirty-six here at the moment. Every one accounted for.'

Jenny's mind raced over the possibilities, but there was

only one logical conclusion: the Jane Doe had been stolen. But why would anyone steal a body?

Nervous, Andy said, 'There's one other thing. You know you mentioned the missing girl who worked at Maybury?'

'Yes?'

'I couldn't get hold of any sophisticated kit, but I did manage to borrow a basic dosimeter from the radiology department . . . The body was emitting low levels of beta and gamma radiation. I couldn't say what isotope, but she'd definitely been exposed to a significant source at some point.'

'So what are we talking about – nuclear accident?'

'No. Nothing like that. But more than double what you'd expect to find, even in someone who works at a plant. It's not that uncommon in East Europeans.'

'Enough to cause a thyroid tumour?'

'Maybe. But exposure probably took place some time ago, years possibly.'

'Still, I think it's time we called the police, don't you?'

The detective sergeant's name was Sean Murphy. A man of no more than thirty-three in a crumpled suit with a shirt open at the collar, tousled hair and a thin beard that ran along his jaw-line to hide the first signs of sag under his chin. And when he turned to the side, Jenny saw he was wearing a miniature diamond stud at the top of his left ear.

They stood around the empty drawer in the refrigerator as if it might yield some clue. Murphy said, 'How do you know which is which?'

'They're all toe-tagged,' Andy said. 'And we keep a separate record on the whiteboard over there.'

'Ever get mix-ups?'

'I couldn't say – it's only my fourth day here.'

Murphy said, 'Oh,' and nodded, as if that might explain what had happened.

Jenny said, 'It's very rare. Dr Kerr is adamant that the body went missing overnight. There's no record of any undertaker having been here during that time or having signed for a body. I think we can assume it's been stolen.'

'Any idea who might have done it?' Murphy said.

'None at all,' Jenny said. 'We've had maybe twenty-five groups of relatives through here in the past week, all of whom have missing daughters. None of them ID'd her. We've got more who were meant to be coming in tomorrow.'

'And you've no idea who she is?'

Andy shook his head.

Jenny said, 'The families have all been put in touch with a lab who are running DNA tests.'

'Uh-huh.' Murphy reached out with his foot and nudged the drawer shut with the toe of his loafer. 'Have we got any pictures of this body?'

Andy said, 'I can email some over to you.'

'It'd be good.' He glanced up and down the corridor. 'What about this guy who was meant to be looking after the place?'

'He went home at eight. He'll be back on a cleaning shift at midday.'

Murphy rubbed a hand over his mouth and scratched his whiskers while pulling a face. 'What's he like, this bloke?'

'Very reliable, according to the other staff.'

Jenny guessed what was coming next and interjected to save the detective the trouble. 'If you're wondering whether he might have abused the body in some way, I'd say it's unlikely. The eye sockets were empty, most of the abdomen was missing and last time I was here it didn't smell too good. If you have a look around there are plenty more attractive propositions.'

'I'll take your word.' He gave her a leering smile, his eyes still shot through with broken veins from the previous night's excess. 'No cameras or anything, I suppose?'

'Not in here,' Andy said, 'only in the hospital's main reception and maternity unit. It's unlikely they would have passed any.'

'There'll be some out in the street I expect. I guess we ought to get a team down here, see if these body snatchers left any prints behind. Been a lot of people through this morning?'

'Five or six,' Andy said.

Pulling out his phone, Murphy said, 'Shit. There's no fucking reception in here. Where's yours?'

'Wouldn't you like to know more about the body?' Andy said. 'I can't prove it forensically, but there's a chance she could have been a murder victim.'

'We'll do all that stuff later when you write your statements.'

'Could I get on with that now? I've got a busy day.'

Murphy dipped his chin and turned to look at him with raised eyebrows. 'I don't think so, my friend – you're a suspect.'

Jenny said, 'I don't know how much you had to drink last night, Mr Murphy, but I hope you didn't drive here.'

Murphy opened his mouth to answer back, but Jenny caught him with a sharp look and said, 'Ask nicely and Dr Kerr might let you use the phone in his office.'

The detective sniffled and slouched off in search of a signal.

Andy said, 'Is he serious? What would I want with a body?'

'Ignore him. He's hungover.'

A few moments later Murphy reappeared at the end of the corridor and called out to them, 'What's the name of this lab doing the DNA tests?'

Jenny stopped herself from slapping him down again. She'd complain to his superintendent later, get him to teach him some manners. 'Meditect. They're out by Parkway.'

'Interesting. They just burned down.'

It was early afternoon by the time Jenny made it back to the office. She could have cut and run sooner, but Andy had looked so bewildered as a team of forensics officers and several more detectives swarmed over his mortuary that she felt compelled to hold his hand. They had both made statements and Alison had emailed over the details of all those who had viewed the body or had expressed an interest in doing so.

Initial reports had been sketchy, but over the course of the morning it emerged that Meditect, which was housed in a small industrial unit in a business park, had been very skilfully razed to the ground. Alarm cables had been cut and diesel oil pumped through the ventilation system and set alight. Another fire had been started on nearby wasteland, which distracted the fire brigade for vital minutes during which catastrophic damage was caused to the testing lab. Its entire contents had been destroyed.

Jenny and Andy went together to the hospital's histology department to track down the blood and tissue samples from the thyroid tumour he had sent up for analysis, and came upon a scene of unfolding chaos. Several racks of samples appeared to have gone missing from their chill cabinets overnight. Among them were the Jane Doe's. The in/out log on the card-swipe system showed that a junior technician had been present in the lab for seven minutes at four a.m. She swore that she had been in bed at the time. Murphy came up to speak to her in person, but she broke down and asked to speak to a solicitor. The last Jenny saw of her, she was being led away by two constables.

The Jane Doe's DNA had been erased from the record. Even the inside of the refrigerator drawer had been sprayed with industrial bleach. There was no physical trace of her left in existence, and whoever had arranged it had been thorough, well resourced and far cleverer than most criminals.

Alison was completely caught up in the drama. Every five minutes she was on the phone to another of her ex-colleagues, fishing for an update and exchanging excited gossip. Wild and extravagant theories about the identity of the Jane Doe were already proliferating.

Jenny was opening an email sent from the office of the Home Secretary when Alison bustled in with the latest exciting titbit. 'The lab assistant they arrested – she claims she had her pass stolen when she went to the canteen yesterday morning, but it turned up again in the afternoon.'

'What's she saying – that someone cloned it?'

'It's possible. It's just like a credit card – once through a reader and you've got a copy in minutes.'

'Where do you get a reader?'

'A few pounds on the internet. It seems complicated, but it's easy. Anyone with half a brain could do it – happens at petrol stations all the time.'

Jenny said, 'It's not easy working out where the samples in the histology lab are stored, believe me. They knew what they were looking for.'

'Apparently there were several in and outs with her card yesterday afternoon. If she's telling the truth, it looks as if someone was coming and going, getting the lie of the land.'

Jenny was only half listening. The email she had just opened was from the Permanent Secretary informing her that the Home Secretary agreed that it was very much in the public interest that the disappearance of Nazim Jamal be the subject of an inquest:

*with the caveat that the coroner must be advised to exercise*
*particular discretion in matters affecting national security.*
*In this regard the coroner may wish to consider consulting*
*with appropriate persons, contact with whom, it is under-*
*stood, has already been made.*

'It seems Mrs Jamal is going to get her wish,' Jenny said.

'They're not letting you go ahead?' Alison said incredulously.

'After a fashion.'

'It won't achieve anything. They'll make sure of that.'

'You don't have to be involved, Alison.'

'Did I say that? I'm just giving you my opinion, Mrs Cooper. No one will ever find out what happened to those boys. They reined in the police eight years ago, and you'll be treated no differently.'

'We'll see. But if you've got a problem with this case, or with Muslims or whatever it is, can you get it off your chest so we don't run into difficulties later?'

'No, I don't have a lot of sympathy with radical Muslims, Mrs Cooper. It's always struck me as strange that we bend over backwards to be decent to these people when we despise everything they stand for. Their views on women for one thing: if my husband thought like they do he'd be a pariah.'

'Aren't all radicals outcasts?'

'Try being on the receiving end of them – see if you still feel as reasonable.'

'You've had personal experience?' Jenny said, sarcastically.

Alison set her jaw and looked away. 'Mrs Cooper, I'm quite capable of putting personal feelings to one side when I'm at work. I *was* a police officer for twenty-five years.' She turned and walked out of the door, leaving a toxic wake.

# SEVEN

THE INQUEST HAD BEEN ARRANGED for Monday morning, the second day of February. In common with many coroners throughout the country, Jenny was still without a permanent, or even a semi-permanent, courtroom. Alison leaned on her contacts in the Court Service, but was told that none would be available in the Bristol area for several months. Jenny had grown used to this sort of low-level obstruction. She had no objection to the range of village and community halls she had used over the previous months – some coroners had been known to convene in scout huts and the function rooms of unlicensed restaurants (by law inquests could not be held in licensed premises) – but part of her secretly craved the recognition and gravitas a proper court would bring. Alison had suggested the former Methodist chapel in which her New Dawn Church met each Sunday. Jenny politely declined. They had compromised on an unassuming venue at the northern end of the Severn estuary. It was in a village close to the Slimbridge bird sanctuary, of which Alison was a life member and which had an excellent cafe, she said.

Such were the trivialities which competed for Jenny's attention, along with stolen corpses, a steady stream of paranoid text messages (which had replaced the phone calls) from Mrs Jamal, and planning tactics to extract maximum information from the police and Security Services. And all the while she was staving off the symptoms of acute anxiety with extra beta blockers. She had tried emailing Dr Allen for advice, but received an out-of-office reply that said he had gone skiing in the Italian Alps for a week. Lucky him. She had a mobile number for critical emergencies, but feared that the moment she called it he would be forced to sign her off sick, with or without her consent. She had little choice but to manage as best she could.

Ross came home late on Saturday night. Jenny was woken by his and Karen's stifled giggles and two pairs of clumsy footsteps on the stairs. They retreated to his bedroom, and moments later music started. It had been part of their deal that he could have his girlfriend over to stay if her parents agreed, and Jenny had a certain self-satisfaction in being cool enough to suggest it in the first place. The reality was a pain. She resented him wanting to be treated like an adult without being prepared to take an ounce of responsibility. And she was childishly jealous. She was still just about young enough to have the kind of good time they were having next door, but the chances of it ever happening for her seemed increasingly remote.

The teenagers lay in bed until close to midday, then appeared yawning and dishevelled, complaining of being tired. Despite her disturbed night, Jenny had spent a productive morning in her study planning questions for the witnesses at her inquest. A rush of adrenalin had temporarily pushed her subconscious anxieties aside. Focused and purposeful, she carried her energy into the kitchen and set about preparing lunch. Her sense of achievement gave her the tolerance not to be irritated by the sight of the two of them slumped on the sofa with the curtains half drawn to keep the daylight – God forbid – from hitting the TV screen. With forced cheer she fetched and carried cups of tea, even drawing a smile and a thank you from Karen.

The kids were still glued to a movie when Jenny emerged from the kitchen having produced a full-scale Sunday lunch. She gazed on her achievement with pride: she was capable of being a good mother.

Jenny laid the table at the far end of the living room and they sat down to eat, Ross and Karen appearing surprised at the sudden magical appearance of food. She attempted to make uncontroversial conversation. It was tough going. Terrified of being embarrassed in front of his girlfriend, Ross shot her silencing looks each time she opened her mouth. His timidity was baffling. He was being allowed to behave however he wanted – Jenny was doing all in her power to treat him as a grown-up – yet he was cringing like a frightened child.

Tired of treading on eggshells, Jenny said to Karen, 'Did Ross tell you what happened on Friday? A body was stolen from the hospital mortuary. It completely vanished.'

'God. That's awful. Why?'

Ross threw her a glance. She ignored him.

'We're not sure. The best guess is that she was murdered and whoever killed her is trying to dispose of the evidence.'

Ross said, 'Do we have to talk about your gross work all the time?'

'I don't mind,' Karen said. 'It's interesting.'

'Not to me it isn't. Dealing with dead people all day, it's sick.'

Jenny said, 'We have to know how people died.'

'I don't. It gives me the creeps.'

She held up her hands. 'Sorry I mentioned it.'

'I'm only saying – you don't have to get uptight about it.'

She snapped. 'Me uptight? I was trying to make an effort so we wouldn't have to sit here in silence.'

'Well, don't bother.'

'Fine.'

She helped herself to more potatoes, smiled at Karen and ate in silence. What she should have done was tell him to behave properly or leave the table, either to contribute to the household or put up with being treated like the baby he was. Instead she let the silence yawn and open up to a chasm. Her positivity drained away and a sense of rising panic rushed in to take its place. Her stomach began to knot and her hand trembled as she lifted her glass to take a sip of water. God, she wished it was wine. Just a little alcohol would take all the pain away, dissolve the tears that wanted to come and make her relaxed enough to turn the atmosphere with a single light remark.

Jenny gathered the empty plates quickly and offered to heat up some apple pie. Ross refused on Karen's behalf and announced they were going to her house for the afternoon. He made for the door without lifting a finger to help.

Jenny said, 'Ross, could I have a word with you, please?'

'What about?'

'Karen, could you take those dishes out to the kitchen? Thanks.'

Jenny silenced her son's protest with a look that promised a scene way beyond merely embarrassing if he objected. He traipsed sulkily after her into the hall.

'Maybe you can tell me what it is about letting you have your girlfriend stay the night then cooking you both lunch that's so unreasonable that you can't even bring yourself to say a civil word to me,' Jenny said.

'I didn't say anything.'

'No, you just sit there giving me looks as if you wished I'd curl up and die.'

'You're so moody all the time. Why can't you just relax like other people?'

'Dear God, I'm doing my best.'

'Yeah, right.'

'*What?*'

'The atmosphere in this place . . . I don't know what's wrong with you.'

'With me? I've kept my side of the bargain. How could I possibly try any harder – tell me, I'd love to know.'

'You never calm down. Never.'

Jenny opened her mouth to reply, but the words caught in her throat and she felt her eyes welling.

'See what I mean?'

'Ross—'

He shook his head and went back through the door to join his girlfriend.

Jenny hid in her study trying to stifle the tears that wouldn't dry up, wanting desperately to go and make peace but with no way of doing so without appearing red-eyed in front of Karen. Trapped, she listened to them clear the table and load the dishwasher, then leave quietly through the back door so as not to risk meeting her on their way out.

The sky was bluer and sharper than it ever was in summer. The brook at the end of the garden beyond the tumbledown mill was clear and deep. Tiny brown trout gathered in a pool of sunlight to soak up the first warming rays of the year, and along the shale banks fragile crocuses and snowdrops burst through the cold earth. It had been a revelation to her that nature didn't sleep through the winter. When she lived in the city she had only noticed the trees as they came into leaf in April. Living among them during a whole winter, she had seen how even as the last of the leaves fell in late December, new buds were forming. There was no time of stillness. Life was in constant, unstoppable rotation.

She comforted herself with these thoughts as she drifted

around her third of an acre, trying to absorb its peace before returning to her desk. She ran her fingers over soft, deep moss on the mill shed's crumbling stone wall and felt the tenderness of fresh holly leaves on a tiny sapling which had sprung from the decaying lime mortar. Everything old and rotten was fertile ground for something new.

As pricks of hope slowly began to pierce her veil of melancholy, she allowed herself to believe that Ross was merely going through another inevitable and necessary phase; that to grow into an individual in his own right he had to reject her with or without just cause; that if she could only understand, it would be bearable. He'd move away, find his feet, and one day soon would return again as a sure and confident young man. It wasn't her he objected to, or her *atmosphere*; he was tugging against the chains of childhood. She wished him more luck than she had had: heading into middle age and still in mental shackles that seemed to grow tighter the older and rustier they became.

There was a sound of breath and rushing feet behind her. She turned to see Alfie bounding across the grass from the old cart track at the side of the house. He plunged into the stream and snapped at the rushing water as he lapped at it. Steve followed some moments behind, dressed only in T-shirt and jeans, a sweater knotted over his shoulders.

'Beautiful day,' he said, wandering over. 'Am I interrupting?'

'No.'

He came to the stream's edge and stood alongside her. 'Busy week?'

'Yes . . . you?'

'Had to look at a job we're pitching for in Manchester. Hated it. Architect's curse – you want to tear everything down and start again.'

'I wondered where you were.'

'I was going to call you—'

'You don't have to.'

'But maybe I should?' He glanced at her with a smile that seemed somehow expectant.

She shrugged, wishing she could be more expansive, but feeling her delicate equilibrium tip and the emotion which she thought had washed through her rise up again.

'You OK?'

'Yes.' She glanced away over the wall to the three-acre meadow and woodland rising behind it. Several sheep, uncomfortably pregnant, stood in ankle-deep mud.

She felt his warm hand slide over her shoulders, another loop round her waist. He stood behind her and held her close. And as he leaned her weight against him, he touched her hair and face, saying nothing as he felt her tears.

She wiped her eyes with the cuff of her coat. 'I'm sorry.'

'Do you want to talk about it?'

She moved round to face him and shook her head. He leaned forward and kissed her gently.

Later, they sat at the scrub-top table on the lawn, wrapped in sweaters, drinking tea. Steve smoked a skinny roll up and Jenny stole puffs as she grudgingly confessed that her old symptoms had come back to haunt her since her last session with Dr Allen. He listened in silence, letting her talk herself out while he rolled a second cigarette.

When she'd finished, he said, 'You had these dreams when you were what, twenty?'

'About that.'

'Just becoming an adult. Have you ever thought it could be as simple as grief for lost childhood?'

'My childhood wasn't bad. Not blissful, but not particularly sad, either. Not until my mum went at least, and I was nearly a teenager by then.'

'That still fits. It's *innocence* that vanishes in your dream.

95

It's one of the many human tragedies: once you've lost it, there's no way back.'

'So why doesn't everyone feel it?'

'We can all get stuck at a certain point, God knows, I did – ten years hiding in the woods.'

'So where am I stuck, Dr Freud?'

'You married a domineering man when you were still very young.'

'David was *not* a father substitute.'

'I'll bet you've got to know yourself a lot better since you left him.'

'I'll give you that.'

'And for all of your marriage you worked with troubled kids.'

'And your theory is?'

'I'm still working on it.' He lit his cigarette with the antique brass lighter she had given him as a birthday present. 'It all gets on top of you, you break down—'

'Yes . . .' she said, sceptically.

'And then . . . then to recover from all this stored-up crap, you get yourself a career trying to find out how people died.'

'Which means?'

'Part of you died?'

Jenny sighed. It was all territory she'd visited before in one way or another. 'My first psychiatrist, Dr Travis – I know he was convinced someone had abused me. I don't know how many times I've thought about it, but I know it didn't happen. It just didn't.'

'Can I say one more thing? Do you think this job is right for you? I mean, do you think part of you is trying to do the impossible, bring the dead back to life when really you should be letting life move on?'

She fell still. His words were well meant but they landed like a wounding accusation.

'That sounded harsher than it was meant to—'

'Actually, people tell me I'm pretty good at what I do.'

'All I'm saying is maybe there's room for more joy in your life, if you'd just let it in.'

'What was this afternoon?'

'A start.' He smiled. 'But you know, however you're feeling inside, you're looking fine.'

Something inside her sank. She hated being told that. He might as well have said she was making a fuss over nothing.

He reached over and stroked the soft side of her wrist, a gesture which meant he was angling to take her back to bed.

She drew her hands back under her arms and shivered. 'I'd better get on.'

A little hurt, Steve said, 'Sure.' He stood up from the table and whistled to Alfie, who bounded over from where he'd been scratching for mice behind the mill. Pulling on his sweater, Steve looked over at the ash trees silhouetted against the twilit sky, and said, 'I've told you before – you live in a beautiful place. Listen to it, it might be telling you something.' He touched her lightly on the cheek as he passed and left her to her thoughts.

Back at her desk, she took out her journal and tried to put her confusion into words, but they wouldn't come. There was no reasoning it out. She had gone round and round in the same circles for over three years and gained no insight other than a twenty-year-old dream and a few snatches of uncomfortable but far from life-shattering childhood memories. For all her agonizing, and for all her attempts to improve her situation and career, nothing had shone a light into the dark place. Looking into herself only seemed to make it worse. She felt as if she were crossing a marsh: walk quickly and the ground might hold you, but stop for a moment and the mud would suck you under.

All she could think to write was: *Things have got to change. Thinking's got me nowhere. From now on I simply go where my instincts tell me and hope I reach the other side.*

# EIGHT

ROSS NOTICED THE UPTURN IN her mood during their rushed breakfast and managed a semi-apology for his behaviour the day before. Jenny told him to forget about it, just hurry up and get ready – she had an inquest to get to. As he disappeared upstairs to gel his hair and spray on too much deodorant, she dashed to her study to swallow her pills. As the chemicals hit her bloodstream she lost the heightened sense of excitement she had woken with; her heart slowed, her limbs grew heavier and her scattered thoughts drew gradually back towards the centre. She told herself that Friday's panic attack had been a blip, a subconscious way of testing her resolve. She had seen it off and had grown stronger.

And now she had a job to do.

Alison had made limited progress working through the list of Bristol alumni from Nazim and Rafi's year. So far, only Dani James, the girl who had given a statement describing the man hurriedly leaving Manor Hall at midnight, had come forward as a witness. Dr Sarah Levin had agreed to make herself available on the second day of the inquest, but said she had nothing to add to what she had told the police at the time. All the others who had been contacted claimed to have little or no recollection of the two boys, let alone any information to shed light on their disappearance. It left Jenny with a very short list of witnesses for her opening day, but it would ease her gently into day two, when several police officers and a since retired MI5 agent named David Skene were listed to testify.

The room she'd been allocated as an office in Rushton Millennium Hall had an internal window overlooking the main meeting room, which also doubled as a gymnasium. Insofar as it was possible, Alison had arranged the furniture to resemble a court. Jenny took a perverse pleasure in looking down at the arriving lawyers who huddled together and shook their heads in disbelief at their incongruous surroundings. In the foyer there were notices advertising an over-sixties quiz night and photographs from the recent village pantomime.

As she seated herself behind the table at the head of the hall, she was pleased to see that there was only a handful of reporters in the two rows of seats which served as a press gallery. The presence of too much news media tended to frighten – or at the very least excite – witnesses to the point where they were no longer reliable. To their right sat a pool of fifteen jurors, from whom eight would be chosen. Mrs Jamal was sitting unobtrusively in the second row alongside another Asian woman, who looked as though she might be related. Both were dressed in black salwar kameez and head-scarves. The second woman held Mrs Jamal's hand tightly in her lap. A cluster of witnesses including Anwar Ali and a pretty young woman Jenny took to be Dani James sat in the front row. Tucked away discreetly in the right-hand corner of the hall behind the reporters was Alun Rhys, the young MI5 officer.

Once everyone had settled, Jenny introduced herself and invited the lawyers to do the same. Mrs Jamal was represented by Trevor Collins, a balding high street solicitor dressed in a shapeless suit which hung sadly off his narrow shoulders. He spoke in a nervous, faltering voice and gave the impression that he would much rather be spending the morning in his poky office drafting wills. A handsome and urbane criminal barrister, Fraser Havilland, whom Jenny knew to have featured in several recent high-profile inquests in London, had been briefed to represent the Chief Constable of the Bristol and Avon police force, and Martha Denton QC, a spiky, abrupt woman, who was normally to be found in the Old Bailey prosecuting terrorists, represented the Director General of the Security Services. Each barrister had assorted instructing solicitors sitting in the row immediately behind them, armed with textbooks and a battery of laptops: two hefty legal teams determined to put on a show of strength. For her part, Jenny had only a well-thumbed copy of *Jervis on Coroners*, a stack of fresh notebooks and the fountain pen her father had given her as a graduation present. Alison, who sat at a small desk to the right, operated the same cassette recorder that had kept the official record of Severn Vale District inquests since the early 1980s.

With the exception of Havilland, the lawyers were restless and fidgety as, assisted by Alison, Jenny called the pool of jurors forward and asked each in turn whether there was any reason why they couldn't serve. She took pity on two single mothers and released them, then selected eight from the remainder by lot. Those whose names were drawn took their places in two rows of four seats to Jenny's left. They were all white and six of them had grey hair. The one male under thirty wore grubby jeans and a hooded sweat top and already gave the impression of being bored to distraction. The youngest, a girl of nineteen or twenty, wore a bemused, uncomprehending expression that seemed to say, 'Where am I?'

Ignoring the lawyers' impatient sighs, Jenny told the jury to forget about the courtroom dramas they had seen on television and to understand that this wasn't a criminal trial. They would hear evidence about the unexplained disappearance of Nazim Jamal and his friend, Rafi Hassan. If, and only if, the evidence was sufficient to show that Nazim Jamal was dead, their task was to determine when, where and how that had happened. After thirty minutes of careful explanation she was satisfied that they had grasped the basic concepts. She asked if they had any questions. No hands went up.

Explanations complete, Mrs Jamal was making her way forward to the witness chair when the doors at the back of the hall swung open and a group of young Asian men burst in, followed by at least another half-dozen excited journalists. They had a hostile, intimidating air and made no attempt to move quietly, as those that could occupied the spare seats and the remainder lined up against the wall. The room felt suddenly cramped and oppressive. There was an atmosphere of simmering anger.

Jenny noticed Anwar Ali nod in recognition to one of the new arrivals. Alison shot her an anxious look.

'This is a public hearing,' Jenny said, trying to sound reasonable, 'but this room can only hold so many people. I'll allow everyone who's here now to remain for the rest of this session, but I may have to review the situation later.'

'May it please you, ma'am, I appear on behalf of the British Society for Islamic Change.' A Pakistani man in his early thirties approached the lawyers' table clutching a legal pad and several text books. 'Yusuf Khan. I am the society's legal representative.' He set his belongings down and handed Alison a business card. 'If you'll hear me, ma'am, I am instructed to seek the right to examine witnesses in this inquest.'

Jenny glanced at the card Alison had passed to her. Khan

was a solicitor from a firm in Birmingham she had never heard of. 'On what grounds, Mr Khan?'

'Ma'am, rule twenty of the Coroner's Rules gives the coroner a wide discretion to allow any person who in your opinion is properly interested, to be represented. In this case I ask you to extend that privilege to Mr Khalid Miah, president of the society I represent. His organization has five thousand members in the UK, all of whom are young Muslim men and women aged between eighteen and thirty-five. It is the leading advocate for the community and has regular high-level meetings with politicians of all parties. It consults with the Home Office on matters of criminal justice and has representatives on several major think tanks.' He extracted a glossy brochure from between his books. Alison took it from him and handed it to Jenny with a suspicious frown.

Jenny turned through the professionally produced pages. The society called itself 'BRISIC' and had a cheerful logo featuring brown and white hands clasped together. There were photographs of young men standing proudly outside a new mosque, others of their number meeting with cabinet ministers inside the Houses of Parliament, and a reassuring section showing members enjoying a wholesome summer camp in the Yorkshire Dales.

'You clearly represent a respectable and successful organization, Mr Khan, but rights of audience can only be granted to those who have a legitimate and well-grounded interest.'

'Ma'am, as one of the leading organizations of young Muslims in the UK, I would submit we clear that hurdle. It's not just Mr Jamal's case that concerns us; there are tens of others who have disappeared in the years since 2001. The official reason given is invariably that they have gone abroad to train or fight with radical insurgents in Afghanistan or Iraq, but my clients are far from satisfied with what little evidence has been provided. A large part of the coroner's purpose is to determine cause of death so that similar deaths don't occur in the future. I represent a constituency which is suffering from, if not proven deaths, many unexplained and seemingly permanent disappearances.' A murmur of approval travelled around the room. 'The British Society for Islamic Change does not come here with a political or religious agenda. It comes out of concern for tens if not hundreds of young Asian men. Where are they going? Where have they gone? If these are not legitimate questions, I do not know what are.'

Jenny noticed Alun Rhys trying to catch her eye. She deliberately avoided his gaze. She didn't need him to tell her what he was thinking, she could read it from here: let these people in and risk turning the inquest into a political and media circus. Even if their lawyer behaved himself – and she could always exclude him if he didn't – BRISIC could take public offence at or exploit every turn of events. But what was the alternative? If she refused them now, they'd raise a protest, inflame Muslim opinion and convince Mrs Jamal that she was being subjected to yet a further layer of conspiracy.

Rhys was resorting to unsubtle gestures to attract her attention. He'd tell her they were a political front wanting to hijack the inquest and mercilessly exploit the publicity it would bring them. Maybe so, but who was she to take orders from the Security Services? She had a legal duty to make up her own mind. She resolved to disregard him.

'Wait there, Mr Khan,' Jenny said. She addressed the entire assembled company: 'I'm not a coroner who believes in restricting access to my inquiries. In the interests of openness and fairness I'm willing to allow any legitimately interested party the right to cross-examine witnesses, not least because it serves to counter any accusation that important questions have not been put. I am therefore prepared in principle to allow the British Society for Islamic Change to have a representative at the advocates' table, but if there are any objections I will hear them.'

Fraser Havilland glanced round at his instructing solicitor, who gave an indifferent shrug. The portly young man instructing Martha Denton, however, was in a furious, whispered heads-together with Alun Rhys. Jenny gave them a moment to finish conferring and for the red-faced solicitor to pass a message forward to his counsel.

Unfazed by the silent, but palpable enmity which greeted her as she rose, Martha Denton addressed the court in perfunctory tones. 'Ma'am, there is no evidence that Mr Jamal or his surviving relatives had or have anything to do with this amorphous organization. They may claim to represent others who have gone missing for one reason or another, but this is an inquest into the disappearance of one man only. There is therefore no reason why they should be represented. But of course if they wish to observe, they are more than free to do so.'

'Can you point to any facet of their activities which makes them unsuitable to be represented?' Jenny said.

'The question is, ma'am, whether they have any legitimate right to be represented at all.'

'Which is a matter entirely in my discretion.'

'All discretion has to be exercised *reasonably*,' Martha Denton said.

Jenny felt Rhys's threatening glare. She turned to BRISIC's lawyer, her mind made up. 'On condition that all legal representatives behave reasonably, I will allow you rights of audience, Mr Khan.'

'Thank you, ma'am,' Khan said and gave a deferential bow. There were surprised smiles on the faces of the young men in the room.

Pouting, Martha Denton sat back pointedly in her seat. Alun Rhys crossed his arms defensively across his chest.

Jenny said, 'Right. If you could come forward to the witness chair now, Mrs Jamal.'

Her face partially obscured by her veil, Mrs Jamal made her way to the front of the hall and sat on a chair positioned halfway between Jenny and the jury, immediately to the side of which stood a small desk just large enough to carry a bible, a koran and a jug of water. She read her oath in a quiet, but steady voice with only the faintest trace of nervousness. Her demeanour was composed and dignified, in stark and surprising contrast to the woman Jenny had met at her office.

Allowing her to tell her story in her own time, Jenny led Mrs Jamal through Nazim's young life, his scholarship to Clifton College, her divorce and his arrival at Bristol University. She painted a picture of a devoted son and a hardworking student. The first tremor of emotion entered her voice as she described how he had arrived at her flat in traditional dress during his second university term.

'Did you talk to him about his reasons for dressing this way?' Jenny asked.

'Yes. He said lots of Muslims his age were wearing these clothes.'

'Did you ask why?'

Mrs Jamal faltered briefly. 'I did . . . He wouldn't talk about it. He said it was just something he wanted to do.'

'How did you react? Were you concerned?'

'Of course. We all knew what was happening to our sons, that these extremists were coming into mosques and talking to them about jihad and such nonsense.'

'Didn't you then discuss any of this with him?'

She shook her head. 'I didn't like to. It may not make much sense to you, but I didn't want to upset him. And I trusted him ... Young people go through these phases. It's part of growing up. He was a *scientist*, he'd never been that religious. I didn't think it would last.'

'Was there part of you that was frightened of pushing him away if you challenged him too directly?'

'Yes. He was all I had.' She turned to the jury. 'I was alone. He was my only child.'

The faces that looked back at her were more sceptical than sympathetic.

Jenny allowed Mrs Jamal a moment to recompose herself, then led her through her final two meetings with Nazim: the happy occasion of her birthday in May 2002, and his unexpected arrival, pale and feverish, on Saturday, 22 June.

'When Nazim stayed for the night in June, would you say he was different from when you saw him in May?'

'He wasn't well ...' she stopped, as if arrested by another thought.

'Mrs Jamal?'

'There was one difference.'

'Yes?'

'On my birthday he went twice to the spare room to perform his afternoon and evening prayers. He was praying five times a day as you're meant to ... not many do.'

'And in June?'

'He arrived at noon and went to bed at about nine o'clock. He didn't pray. He talked about his work, and tennis – he'd stopped playing for a while and mentioned he was thinking of taking it up again. We talked about family, his cousins ... but I don't think we discussed religion.'

'How was he dressed on that occasion?'

'In normal clothes: jeans, a shirt. His hair and beard were shorter than before.' She glanced anxiously around the room, aware that she was being listened to closely. Most of the Muslims in the hall wore Western clothes, a few traditional dress, nearly all had beards. 'I remember feeling glad about that. In our family we didn't believe that you had to dress as if you live in the desert to be close to God. That's something that's come from outside. It's never been that way with us.'

The young men in the hall traded disapproving glances.

'Did he say anything to indicate that he had changed in some way?'

'No. But when you look at your child you know. Something had changed in him. He wanted me that day. He wanted things the way they used to be before . . . when he was a boy.'

'Do you have any idea what this "change" was about, Mrs Jamal, what had caused it?'

She lowered her head and looked down at the floor, silent for a long moment. 'I remember thinking, *it's over*. I was relieved. And when I heard him at dawn the next morning, praying the way he was taught as a child, I knew.'

'What was over?'

'Whatever ideas those people had put in his head.' She nodded towards Anwar Ali. 'People like him. *Radicals*.' She spat out the word. 'My Nazim was never one of them.'

Anwar Ali held her in a steady, unflinching gaze. His friends and associates in the room stirred restively.

'Mrs Jamal,' Jenny said, 'did your son ever mention Rafi Hassan?'

'Never once.'

'Did he mention any university friends?'

'Not by name.'

'You didn't consider that odd?'

'For eight months, from October to June, I hardly saw him . . . When I did, perhaps I was a little selfish. I wanted him with *me*, not talking about friends.'

'Is the truth more that you didn't want to know?'

'Perhaps . . .'

'Because you knew that groups, such as Hizb ut-Tahrir, had no qualms about prising members away from their families?'

'Yes . . . I had heard that.'

Jenny made a note that from January to June 2002 Mrs Jamal knew full well that her son was radicalized and had buried her head in the sand. Her own painful experience had taught her how easily a mother could deceive herself.

In terms of evidence, Mrs Jamal had little more to offer, but Jenny nevertheless took her through the events of the weeks following Nazim and Rafi's disappearance. She described her sketchy meetings with DC Sarah Owens, the family liaison officer appointed by the Bristol and Avon police, and her interviews with David Skene and Ashok Singh, the MI5 officers who met her three times before the investigation was effectively brought to a halt in December. Mrs Jamal insisted that the last formal contact she had with the police or with the Security Services was the letter from DC Owens dated 19 December 2002, which contained the nonsensical sentence: 'In the absence of any firm evidence concerning the whereabouts of your son or Mr Hassan, it has been decided that the investigation will be suspended until such time as further evidence becomes available.' A detective whose name she couldn't remember had told her several days before that the Security Services had received intelligence suggesting the two young men may have gone abroad, but no one, she claimed, had ever come up with one solid fact to back this up. In the months and years that followed she wrote countless letters to the police and MI5 both personally and through a number of lawyers, but received nothing in return except barely polite acknowledgements, and often there was no response at all.

She had been met with a wall of silence and indifference.

Before handing her over to the waiting lawyers, Jenny leafed through the photocopied documents Mrs Jamal had given her and pulled out a statement made by Detective Sergeant Angus Watkins on 3 July 2003. She passed it to Alison to read aloud to the jury. Watkins stated that he had examined the door frames of both Nazim and Rafi's rooms in Manor Hall and found identical quarter-inch wide depressions in both, consistent with the use of a blunt object to force entry. He also noted that laptops and mobile phones belonging to both students were missing from their rooms, but there was no sign of their other possessions having been disturbed. Valuable objects such as an MP3 player were still in evidence.

'Was this suggestion of forced entry to both rooms ever followed up to your knowledge?' Jenny asked Mrs Jamal.

'I don't know. I didn't even get this statement until my solicitor wrote to them the following year.'

'Did you go to your son's room yourself?'

'Yes, I did.'

'What impression did you form?'

'All his clothes were still there, and his suitcase. His koran – the one his father and I gave him when he won his scholarship – was still on the shelf. His prayer mat was on the floor. All that we could see that was missing were his phone and computer.'

'What about Mr Hassan's room?'

'I spoke to his mother briefly. It was the same. No computer. Everything else was as he would have left it.'

'Was there no burglary investigation? Didn't your solicitor take this up with the police, ask if they searched for fingerprints or DNA samples?'

'My solicitor . . .' She shook her head in exasperation. 'He was working on the case when he was arrested and went to prison. He claims he was innocent . . .'

'Arrested for what?'

'Something to do with evidence in another case.' She shook her head. 'I don't know what to believe about him.'

'What was his name?'

'Mr McAvoy,' she said, as if she could never forget. 'Mr Alec McAvoy.'

From the corner of her eye, Jenny saw Alison look up with a frown of recognition. And then she remembered. McAvoy: the legal executive she'd met at the morgue, whose card she still had in her purse. She turned to Alison, 'Could you request that Mr McAvoy attend, please, Usher? This afternoon if possible.' She would like to hear his side of the story before she called the police witnesses. It was becoming apparent that their investigation had been pursued with far less than the usual rigour and she would expect a full and comprehensive explanation.

Fraser Havilland, counsel for the chief of police, had only a few low-key questions for Mrs Jamal. Did the police respond swiftly when she raised the alarm? Would she accept that they had taken appropriate steps to trace her son? Could she agree that if her son really had left the country, perhaps on false documents, that there was little more the police could have done? He didn't get the answers he would have liked, but neither did Mrs Jamal react angrily or emotionally as Jenny had feared she might. When Havilland asked, quite reasonably, what was her chief complaint against his client's force, she replied that she didn't believe it was the police who were to blame. They were being told what to do by a higher authority, she said. They were merely obeying orders. Why else would they have given up so easily?

Martha Denton, counsel for the Security Services, whom it was now clear were the focus of Mrs Jamal's suspicion, shared none of her colleague's deference. Her first question, more of a statement, was a well-aimed arrow designed to do harm: 'You've been disingenuous, haven't you, Mrs Jamal? You knew your son had become a radical Islamist and you are using these proceedings as an attempt to assuage the guilt you feel at not having taken action to stop him being sucked in as far as he was.'

'I don't understand. Why should I feel guilty? It was your people who stopped the police from finding out what had happened to him.'

'And where did you get that idea?'

'The detective who told me about the intelligence, he almost said as much.'

'The one whose name you can't remember?'

'He was about forty years old. Slim.'

'I see.' Denton struck a sarcastic tone: 'And did he explain to you why the Security Services might be so keen *not* to find two radical Islamists who were known to have been associating with members of Hizb ut-Tahrir, an organization which, although not officially supportive of terrorism, harbours known sympathizers within its ranks?'

Thirty pairs of unforgiving eyes fixed on Martha Denton.

She remained unmoved. 'Did he explain that, Mrs Jamal?'

'No.'

'This is an invention of yours, isn't it? You are desperate to blame someone for the fact you haven't discovered the fate of your son and you have chosen to fixate on my clients.'

Jenny cut in to issue a reproach. 'We may have a jury but this is not a criminal court, Miss Denton. It is a civilized inquiry and will be conducted in that manner. Please moderate your tone.'

Martha Denton raised her eyebrows at her instructing solicitor and continued with mock politeness. 'Mrs Jamal, did your son ever talk to you about his new-found religious conviction?'

'No, he didn't.'

'Did you know that he was meeting regularly with members of Hizb ut-Tahrir, an organization whose aim is to help bring about an international Islamic state?'

'That's what you say. I have no idea.'

'But you did suspect something like that was going on?'

Jenny said, 'What exactly is the point of your question, Miss Denton?'

Martha Denton sighed impatiently. 'What I am attempting to extract from the witness, ma'am, is exactly what she did know about her son's involvement with radicals and extremists.'

Mrs Jamal erupted. 'My son would never do a bad thing. *Never*. Anyone who said he would is a liar.' Her words echoed around the silent hall.

'His father took rather a different attitude, didn't he?' Martha Denton said. 'He resigned himself to the most obvious explanation for your son's disappearance very quickly, didn't he? That's why he isn't here. For him there is no question to be answered.'

'I can't speak for that man. He hasn't even lifted the phone to me in six years. How should I know what he thinks?'

'And Rafi Hassan's family, too?'

'They're frightened. They're all frightened of your people. I'm the only one who won't be intimidated. I've seen them outside my home, following me in the street—'

'Thank you, Mrs Jamal,' Martha Denton said with an amused expression and sat down.

Mrs Jamal scowled at her, all her efforts to appear reasonable unravelling with her final outburst. Several of the jurors exchanged dubious glances. Jenny doodled a row of question marks on her pad. Try as she might, she couldn't take Mrs Jamal at her word.

Yusuf Khan got to his feet with a placatory smile. 'Mrs

Jamal, you said that your son would never have done a bad thing. Do you honestly believe that?'

'He would never have hurt another human being. I swear on my life.'

'Do you believe he went abroad to join a jihadist organization?'

'If he did, it was not of his free will. That was not his way.'

'You told this to the police and Security Services at the time, I presume, but what – they wouldn't believe you?'

She shook her head. 'They believe only what suits them.'

Khan said, 'Did they give you the impression that they believed your son was an extremist, a young man seduced into sympathy with violence against the West?'

'They didn't have to. It was written in their faces – even the Indian one, Singh.'

Jenny glanced at Alun Rhys. He caught her eye, his expression saying: *just wait*.

'And did they even appear to entertain the possibility that your son or Mr Hassan might have been the victims of a crime, even though there were signs of forced entry on both their doors?'

'No. Never.'

Khan turned to the jury. 'Were you made to feel, Mrs Jamal, that your son was one of the *enemy within*?'

Jenny threw him a warning look. She wasn't going to tolerate grandstanding.

To her credit, Mrs Jamal didn't give him the soundbite he was hoping for. 'I was made to feel that nobody cared. But I prayed to God every day, and I still believe there can be justice.'

Khan snapped back: 'You don't think this inquest has been permitted merely to seal your son's reputation as a traitor and a jihadi?'

'Mr Khan,' Jenny said, 'I'll warn you once and not again – this is an inquest, not an opportunity for you to score political points. Next time, you're out.'

The murmur of dissent rose like a wave. Accusing glares turned on her.

Khan said, 'You're quite right, ma'am. Perish the thought that an inquest should ever be used to play politics.'

And as he smiled someone sniggered, then another joined him. A moment later the hall was filled with the sound of mocking laughter. Thrown, Jenny hesitated long enough to lose all face. She felt her cheeks redden and her heart crash against her ribs.

# NINE

THE HALVED BETA BLOCKER JENNY had gulped down on leaving the courtroom had barely got to work when Alison tapped on the door and let herself in before she could answer.

'Mr Rhys would like to talk to you.'

'Tell him he can send me a note.'

'He was insistent.'

'I don't talk to interested parties during the inquest. He should know that.'

Alison gave a dubious nod, turned halfway to the door, then looked back.

'What?' Jenny said, impatiently.

'I think you should clear the gallery, Mrs Cooper. They're not interested. It's just a mob with a few ringleaders. They're already out at the front talking to news cameras.'

'How could I claim to be holding an open and fair inquiry if I shut out the public?'

'Do you think those people care? Nothing will change what they think.'

'And what's that?'

'Their solicitor as good as said it. He thinks this is window dressing. You're just here to prove those two boys ran off to become terrorists, or whatever we're meant to call them.'

'I can handle a few rowdy kids. Tell Rhys to get lost.' She

took a gulp of water from the glass on her desk. Alison watched it shake in her hand but made no comment.

Jenny said, 'Have you got hold of McAvoy yet?'

Alison grimaced. 'His office says he's been in court on a long-running trial, but he'll try to get over this afternoon.'

'Do you know him?'

'Everyone in CID knew McAvoy.'

'Really? What's the story?'

'Whatever he says it is, it isn't.'

She left the room.

Jenny sat back in her chair, closed her eyes and tried to relax. She had conducted stressful inquests in the full public glare before and got through, just. All the morbid, anxious and unwanted thoughts that were assailing her were merely the by-products of stress. They had no meaning. She was in control.

Her limbs were finally starting to feel heavy when her phone bleeped alerting her to a text message. Her eyes started open and she reached for it. It said: *Have it you're way. Your on you're own.* Working for MI5 and he couldn't even spell.

The mood was noticeably more sober when the court reconvened and Anwar Ali took his place in the witness chair. Composed and confident, he seemed to command respect among the young Muslim men. Jenny ran her eyes over the faces in the public gallery and couldn't see Rhys. She felt a flutter of anxiety and realized how quickly his presence had become a safety blanket. She found herself desperately curious about what he might have said had she let him speak to her. A coroner only ever acted alone, she had to remind herself; a coroner was independent and answered only to the Lord Chancellor. She didn't need anyone else.

She began with the uncontroversial questions, establishing that Ali was thirty-two years old and had been part way through a post-graduate MA in politics and sociology when Nazim and Rafi disappeared. He was currently employed by Newport Borough Council as general manager of the refugee centre where Jenny has visited him, and was a part-time doctoral student at the University of Cardiff. His thesis was entitled: 'Anglo-Muslim Identity: Integration or Cohabitation?' He claimed not to be a member of the British Society for Islamic Change although he admitted to having contributed several articles to their website. He described himself as 'a politically engaged British Muslim concerned with promoting peaceful coexistence between communities'.

'During your time at Bristol, Mr Ali, you were a regular at the Al Rahma mosque, were you not?'

'Yes, I prayed there on Fridays.'

'And this was a small mosque in what had once been a private house?'

'It was.'

'What was its purpose? There were other mosques in the city, weren't there?'

'It was progressive. Mullah Sayeed Faruq established it in the mid-1990s to cater for young men and women who had a different vision of their place in the world.'

'How would you describe Sayeed Faruq's theology?'

'Mainstream.'

'His politics?'

'Questioning.'

'Could you enlarge on that?'

Ali thought carefully before responding. 'He questioned to what extent Muslim identity was being diluted by Western influences and values. Many of us wanted to talk about a future that wasn't based on materialism and violence. We wanted to rediscover the essence of our religion.'

'I understand the police believed him to hold radical and extremist views. Did he?'

'If you mean did he personally advocate violence, no, he did not. Persuasion, force of argument, asserting that the Islamic way was better for the spiritual health of mankind, yes.'

'Was Sayeed Faruq a member of Hizb ut-Tahrir?'

'I believe he was,' Ali said. 'I was not, nor to my knowledge were Nazim or Rafi. But you ought to understand, ma'am, Hizb specifically does not advocate violence to promote Islam. Its purpose is to argue and persuade. It has attracted much suspicion, but in the vast majority of free countries it is not an illegal organization.' He turned to the jury. 'The name means party of liberation.'

'Thank you, Mr Ali. I've done a little research myself. I've read that Hizb's methods of persuasion involve inviting young people to meetings – halaqah – such as the ones you held in your flat at Marlowes Road.'

'I hosted discussion groups, but I was never a member of Hizb or any other organization.'

Unflappable, he had a smooth, well-rehearsed answer for everything. Jenny pushed and probed, but he wouldn't budge from his position that at both the mosque and his discussion group only peaceful means of spreading the Islamic message were discussed. Both he and Sayeed Faruq had believed in working towards the establishment of an international caliphate, but violence and terrorism were condemned as sacrilegious except in self-defence.

Interesting as their exchange was, Jenny noticed a number of jurors beginning to yawn. The finer points of Islamic theology weren't holding their attention. It was time to push on into more contentious territory.

'When did Nazim Jamal first come to the Al Rahma mosque?'

'In October '01, I think. I couldn't say exactly. Rafi came first, Nazim a few weeks later.'

'And when did they start attending your discussion groups?'

'About November time.'

'Who else was there apart from you and them?'

'Various people came and went. They were mostly students.' He rattled off half a dozen names but claimed not to have kept in touch with most of them. Jenny made a note. She'd track them down if necessary.

'Can you give us an idea of a typical discussion – the kind of subjects covered?'

Ali shrugged. 'We talked about Palestine, possible solutions to the conflict; the war in Afghanistan; American paranoia and how Muslims should respond to it.'

'How would you describe Nazim's politics?'

Ali glanced over at Mrs Jamal. She met him with a searching gaze. She was looking at a man who had seen a side of her son she knew nothing of.

'At first he was quiet . . . then he became more confident, more inspired. I remember he was a good scholar. He knew his Koran.'

'Inspired to what, exactly?'

'Ideas. To the notion of a society built on religious principles. He had the untainted enthusiasm of youth, you might say.'

'What was his take on the use of political violence?'

'He was against it, as we all were.'

'And Rafi Hassan?'

'He was quieter. More of a listener than Nazim. I didn't feel I knew him as well.'

'Did he hold similar views?'

'As far as I know. Really, you have to understand, no matter what the police or Security Services may have thought, our discussions were no more *radical* than those you would have heard at any of the university's political societies. We were young men grappling with ideas, that's all. I believe we were watched simply because Sayeed Faruq was on a list of Hizb members. He was automatically assumed to be part of a fifth column. Little was known about British Muslims at the time except that they shared a faith with some notorious terrorists.'

Thus far Jenny hadn't learned a single piece of new information from the one witness who had been closer to the two missing boys than anyone else she would be calling. She went in harder, pressing Ali to admit that the subject of fighting the Muslim cause must at least have been discussed, but he wouldn't have it. He denied coming into contact with anyone recruiting potential jihadis to fight abroad and maintained that none of the regulars at Marlowes Road halaqah had ever shown the slightest inclination to take up arms. He insisted that he had no clue as to where Nazim and Rafi had disappeared to and denied even suspecting that they had extremist tendencies. She pressed him as to whether he recalled a change in Nazim's mood the weekend before he disappeared, as Mrs Jamal had described: he claimed not to have. Ali had been close to the members of his halaqah, he said, but not so close that he knew the details of their lives. They held spiritual, intellectual gatherings, not social ones.

It was a masterful performance and Jenny didn't believe half of it.

Growing frustrated, she said, 'You must have some idea where they went. You would have heard rumours, at least?'

'No. I must have spent hundreds of hours answering these questions at the time and my answer hasn't changed. I swear before my God, Allah the most merciful, that I do not know where they went or what became of them.'

The solemnity of his oath was greeted with a respectful and reflective silence. All the young men in the room were still and sombre. Even Alison seemed to be affected by its sincerity.

Jenny said, 'What became of Sayeed Faruq? Where did he go?'

'He went to Pakistan. He was wise enough to know that he would always be under suspicion in this country.'

'You're sure he had nothing to do with their disappearance?'

'Again, I swear it. Whatever happened to them is as mysterious to me as it is to you.' He turned to Mrs Jamal. 'I sincerely wish it wasn't so, ma'am.'

Fraser Havilland and Martha Denton both declined the opportunity to cross-examine. Having failed to open up a single fissure, Jenny sensed they were content not to risk accidentally succeeding. It gave the lie to Gillian Golder's claim that the Security Services were as anxious as she was to find out the truth, but came as no surprise. Jenny was beginning to agree with Yusuf Khan that her inquest had only been allowed to proceed because they were confident it posed no danger other than to project the already diabolical image of young Muslim men. The meaning of Rhys's text message still puzzled her, but perhaps he simply meant that she would have to face the consequences of a non-result alone: it would be she, personally, who would take the blame for failing to unearth the truth.

Pushing these troubling thoughts aside, she asked Yusuf Khan if he wished to cross-examine.

'Only briefly, ma'am.' He turned to the witness. 'Mr Ali, you must have heard the rumours, as I have, that in the pre-emptive war on terror, agents provocateurs have been used to lure potentially radical young men abroad to a fate we can only guess at.'

'Yes, I've heard those rumours.'

'Has anyone ever approached you, or anyone you know, in this way?'

Ali stalled long enough before answering *no* for Jenny not

to believe him. And from the look Yusuf Khan gave him, she could tell he didn't believe him either.

Dani James was twenty-eight years old and now practised in a prosperous solicitor's firm in Bath which specialized in handling the estates of the seriously wealthy. She had an open, attractive face which inspired trust, and spoke with an endearing trace of a Manchester accent. Uncomplicated, was Jenny's first impression: straightforward. Dani had waited patiently all morning and didn't seem to begrudge her enforced absence from a busy professional life.

Jenny established that she had been a law student in the same year as Rafi and Nazim and had occupied a room on the first floor of Manor Hall. She hadn't had much to do with Rafi, she said, apart from attending the same seminars; he was a quiet student and kept mostly to himself. She had seen him talking with other Asians in the common room and had formed the impression that he liked to be among his own. Nazim, on the other hand, was more sociable. She remembered seeing him at a number of parties in the autumn term – he was a good dancer and always full of energy. What she saw of him, she liked.

In the spring term she hadn't recognized him when he passed her in the corridor wearing a beard and a prayer cap. She tried to say hello a few times, but didn't receive much of a response. She noticed that he and Rafi had taken to dressing the same way and had seemed to have withdrawn from student society. They didn't come to parties or hang out in the bar as they had in their first term, even to drink orange juice. She remembered thinking it was a shame, but it had happened to a number of Muslim students. They seemed to develop chips on their shoulders and form cliques. There was a girl on her course who had started out wearing mini-skirts and sleeping with a different man each weekend, who, by the end of the spring term, was teetotal, celibate and fully veiled. Each to his own, had been Dani's attitude. She didn't blame them for being defensive when everyone talked about Muslims as terrorists.

'You made a statement to the police on 8 July 2002,' Jenny said. 'What prompted that?'

'They were coming round the halls knocking on doors, asking everyone what they knew about Nazim and Rafi. What was the last time we saw them? Who were they with?'

'Were you able to help?'

'Not really. I just remember telling them that I'd seen someone strange coming out of Manor Hall on the Friday they were meant to have disappeared.'

'Friday, 28 June?'

'Yes. I'd been out late somewhere. It was about midnight. I was coming through the main door, not exactly sober, and this tall man, fortyish, came rushing down the stairs and shoved past me. He was in a real hurry and didn't seem to care he'd thrown me halfway across the room.'

'What did he look like?'

'Thinnish . . . kind of wiry. He had a baseball cap pulled down over his eyes, so I couldn't see his face. He had a blue puffy anorak on, which seemed odd as it was the middle of summer. I think he had a rucksack over one shoulder.'

'In your statement you said "large rucksack or holdall".'

'I don't remember in detail, just that it seemed strange. I do remember thinking he had a real attitude shoving me like that.'

'Have you any idea what the police did with this information?'

'No. I made a statement, that was it.'

'Do you know if anyone else saw him?'

'Not that I know of. It was late.'

Jenny said, 'My office has made contact with a lot of

students from your year, yet virtually none of them seems to have anything to say. Do you have any idea why that is?'

'Because they didn't know them, I guess.'

Jenny nodded. Her own brief excursion through the university precincts had been enough to convince her that Dani was probably right: devout, politicized Muslims would have occupied a world apart.

She was ready to hand the witness over for cross-examination by the lawyers when she remembered the statement that Sarah Levin – a witness not listed to appear until tomorrow – had given to the police a short while after Dani had spoken to them. She reached for a file and turned up the flagged page. It was brief, only two paragraphs, the first giving her personal details and stating that she was in the same year and faculty as Nazim, and the second detailing a conversation overheard some time in May 2002.

'Do you remember a student in your year called Sarah Levin?' Jenny said.

'Vaguely. I think she lived in a different hall.'

'That's right – Goldney. She gave a statement to the police on 10 July saying that in May 2002 she overheard Nazim talking to some other young Asian men in a canteen on the main campus.' She read aloud. ' "I overheard him saying that some of the "brothers" were volunteering to fight the Americans in Afghanistan. That's all I heard, just a snatch of their conversation, but I got the impression they were talking a lot about other young Muslims who were committed enough to fight for their beliefs. I remember the expression on Nazim's face – he seemed to be in awe of them." Did you ever overhear any conversations like this?'

Dani gave an uncertain shake of her head.

'Are you sure?'

She glanced from Jenny to Mrs Jamal, then back to Jenny again. 'I don't find it surprising – he was quite macho, the way he held himself . . .' Another flick of the eyes to Mrs Jamal. 'But what his mother said about him changing . . .' She paused and swallowed, the colour leaving her face.

'Yes?'

Dani opened her mouth to continue, but stalled, startled, as the door opened at the back of the hall and a tall man dressed in a long coat entered. Jenny recognized McAvoy immediately. He picked her out with those still blue eyes and gave a lawyer's nod before finding standing room among the young men lining the back wall.

Jenny drew her gaze away from him. 'You were about to say, Miss James?'

'I think a lot of it might have been posing,' she said, her voice shaky. 'He wasn't as religious as all that . . . not in late June, anyway.'

'What makes you say that?'

Dani turned her face away from Mrs Jamal. 'It was on the night of 26 June, a Wednesday. Nazim came into the bar and we got talking. He wasn't drinking, obviously, but he was fun, more like his old self . . .' She paused, then lifted her eyes. 'We spent the night together.'

A whisper went around the room. The journalists crouched over their notebooks. Jenny noticed McAvoy give a bemused shake of his head. Mrs Jamal wiped away a bewildered tear. Jenny felt a burst of excitement. At last, a revelation.

'You slept with Nazim on the night of the 26th?'

'Yes, I did.' Dani seemed relieved to have made a public confession. 'There was no relationship or anything, it was just impulsive. Only the one night. He left my room early next morning and that was fine with both of us.'

'Did you talk?'

'Not really.'

'Did you get any insight into his state of mind?'

'He was laughing, cracking jokes . . . like someone who

126

was demob happy. And I was quite far gone, to be honest. I don't think I put up too much resistance. It just sort of happened.'

'Did you see him again?'

'No. Never.'

'And you've no idea why he chose that night to approach you?'

'I was nineteen and partying. It didn't matter enough to ask.'

'Wait there, Miss James.'

Fraser Havilland and Martha Denton had their heads together in animated conversation. Seeming to reach an agreement, Havilland stood and addressed the witness.

Sleek and polished, he gave her a disarming smile. 'You didn't tell the police about this night together at the time?'

She shook her head.

'Because?'

'It didn't seem relevant.' She let out a breath, her face twisted in a frown. 'And I suppose I felt guilty somehow . . . There was no reason to, but I didn't know what was going on in his mind.'

Havilland glanced down at his notes. 'You said he seemed "demob happy"?'

'Yes.'

'Demobbed from what?'

'I don't know. It was just his mood.'

'He wasn't wearing traditional dress at the bar, I take it?'

'No. He'd stopped that. I'd noticed a few weeks before.'

Havilland drummed his fingertips thoughtfully on the table as he searched for a suitable form of words. 'Did it occur to you that this *elation* of his might have had something of the final fling about it?'

'Not at the time. Later, when I heard what was being said—'

'Thank you, Miss James,' Havilland said, cutting her off, and sat down with the look of a man satisfied that he'd made a powerful point.

Martha Denton rose. 'Do you not think it dishonest of you not to have told the police this at the time?'

Dani looked to Jenny. 'Can I please finish what I was going to say?'

'Go ahead,' Jenny said.

Martha Denton rolled her eyes impatiently.

'I've thought about it a lot, again and again . . . I don't believe Nazim was going off somewhere. It felt exactly the opposite – it was as if he was *coming back*.'

'It certainly seems dishonest of you not to have told the police that,' Denton fired back.

'It's not easy to talk about those things, especially when you're that young.'

'It doesn't sound as if you were particularly inhibited.'

Stung, Dani said, 'Believe me, it's easier to go to bed with someone than to talk to the police.'

'Miss James, whether or not you slept with Nazim Jamal, you have no idea whatsoever where he went, do you?'

'No, I just have an instinct. I don't believe he was ever a religious fanatic, not truly.'

'You're in the legal profession, you know an instinct's not evidence.'

Dani's face hardened. 'Devout Muslims don't sleep around. I caught chlamydia from Nazim. I suffered severe inflammation and ended up in hospital a month later. I suffered permanent damage and may not be able to carry a child.' She turned to Jenny. 'You can check my medical records.'

Rattled, Martha Denton said, 'Perhaps you just don't like the idea that he used you.'

Dani didn't answer; Jenny didn't press her to.

'Or perhaps we can't trust your evidence at all. Keeping quiet on such a matter for eight years, then coming forward with a story which you know full well would kick up all sorts of dust—'

'It's the truth.' She looked at Mrs Jamal. 'I'm only sorry I didn't say this before.'

Martha Denton glanced sceptically at the jury. 'I'm sure we all are.'

Yusuf Khan, who had appeared embarrassed at the turn Dani's evidence had taken, offered no cross-examination, and requested only that she give permission for her medical records to be made available to the court. She consented.

Before releasing her, Jenny asked Dani if she'd had other sexual partners before Nazim. She admitted to one, a boy she had slept with during the first term, but insisted they had used condoms. With Nazim she'd taken a chance. There was no doubt in her mind that it was he who had infected her.

Jenny asked Alison in open court to make copies of both Nazim and Rafi's medical records available to the lawyers and told the jury that from what she'd seen there was nothing to suggest Nazim had an STD or any health problems at all. According to his GP's notes he hadn't visited the doctor in three years.

Dani James left the witness chair and walked out of the hall, drawing a mixture of admiring and suspicious looks. Jenny was impressed with her. She was a successful lawyer with a reputation to uphold. It had taken a lot of courage to give the evidence she had.

There was time for one more witness before breaking for lunch. She decided to call Simon Donovan and use the recess to plan her questions for McAvoy. She had a long list accumulating.

Donovan was a fifty-three-year-old managing accountant

for a Ford dealership. He was married and lived in the suburb of Stoke Bishop. A man remarkable only for his overwhelming blandness, he told the court that several weeks after Nazim and Rafi's disappearance he had seen their photographs in the *Bristol Evening Post*. He immediately recognized them as the two young Asian men who had been sitting across the aisle from him on the ten a.m. train from Bristol Parkway to London Paddington on Saturday, 29 June. He had been en route to a football match, as had many of his fellow travellers, and had noticed them mainly because they seemed not to approve of the sometimes boisterous fans. As far as he could recall they were both dressed in smart casual clothes and had only small items of luggage with them.

Jenny said, 'You remembered the faces of two strangers that clearly after three weeks?'

'They were different, I suppose,' Donovan said. 'Maybe it was because they were young lads with beards. And we were all pretty jumpy about terrorists at the time, weren't we? You notice these things on a train.'

'Is this a polite way of saying their presence made you anxious?'

'I'm not a racist,' Donovan said. 'I haven't got a racist bone in my body. But you just can't help wondering, can you? Especially when they're looking so serious.'

Jenny said, 'I see. Thank you, Mr Donovan.'

Havilland asked only a few soft questions designed to shore up Donovan's credibility as a reliable and concerned member of the public with no axe to grind. Martha Denton delved a little further and managed to prompt him into saying that both young men seemed worried or apprehensive. Jenny pointed out that this detail was missing from his statement made three weeks after the event. Donovan replied that the police officer who took his statement had been in a hurry and seemed only to want the bare facts. Jenny wasn't convinced by his explanation.

Yusuf Khan looked at Donovan for a long moment, his head cocked thoughtfully to one side, before asking how many bearded young Asian men he came across in his daily life at that time. Very few, Donovan had to admit.

'But the newspapers at the time were full of them, weren't they? We all remember the hysteria. Every time you caught a train or a plane, the media would have had you believe, you took your life in your hands.'

'What's your question for the witness, Mr Khan?' Jenny said.

'My question, Mr Donovan, is whether you think you could have told one bearded young man with Asian features from another? That's all you recognized, wasn't it – their beards and the colour of their skin?'

'I wouldn't have called the police if I wasn't sure it was them.'

'What was your motivation?'

'I thought it the right thing to do.'

'Do you make a habit of calling the police?'

'No.'

'Were you under the impression they might be terrorist suspects?'

'Well, I . . . I suppose it might have crossed my mind.'

Khan nodded calmly. 'When you first called the police, did you say to them, "I definitely saw the two missing men", or did you say, "I saw two young Asian men who might have been them"?'

Donovan moved uncomfortably in his seat, his thick neck reddening. 'I said I'd seen these two lads . . . They came round to my house with photographs. When I'd seen a few, I was sure it was them. Why would I have made it up?'

Jenny heard a sudden sharp derisive laugh from the back of the hall. She looked up, angry, and saw that it had come from McAvoy.

# TEN

ALISON WAS FRANTICALLY DEALING WITH a hitch in the jury's catering arrangements – the promised sandwich delivery had failed to arrive and she was organizing a convoy to the nearby bird sanctuary's waterside restaurant. Outside, at the front of the hall, clusters of angry young Asian men were courting the media pool gathered incongruously in the quiet village lane. Two television news vans had appeared and make-up girls were busy powdering faces. The lawyers hurried through the melee, refusing to answer any questions, and took off in a posse of expensive cars. A cluster of puzzled locals watched the chaotic scene from a safe distance, wondering what could have brought such madness to their quiet corner of the countryside.

Feeling suddenly drained, Jenny slipped out of the back door and found a damp plastic bench which looked out over a field. A tractor was ploughing, a swarm of assorted birds followed after it, fighting over the worms thrown up in the freshly turned earth. Huddled in her thin raincoat, she ate the chocolate bar Alison had dredged up for her, and sipped coffee tasting vaguely of detergent from a cracked mug.

She attempted to process the morning's events and unravel the various parties' competing agendas. She understood that the police mainly wanted to cover their backs, and she presumed that the Security Services were keen to vindicate their theory that Nazim and Rafi had gone abroad. Yusuf Khan and his friends, who appeared to include Anwar Ali, were harder to fathom. Khan's mention of agents provocateurs entrapping young radicals had caught her attention, but on reflection it struck her as another baseless conspiracy theory. Khan was representing a lobby with a positive message to sell – that young British Muslims were good, responsible citizens – and this didn't sit well with the proven fact that a few of their number had taken up arms against their country.

'Is this the best those stingy bastards can do for you?'

She looked up to see McAvoy rounding the corner of the building. The sound of the tractor had masked his footsteps.

Alarmed, she said, 'You're a witness, Mr McAvoy. I can't talk to you before you give evidence.'

His face creased into a smile that managed to be both boyish and menacing. Trying to avoid the blue eyes which looked straight into her, she noticed his hair was starting to kink at the back where it needed a cut, and that he wore a dark green silk paisley scarf inside his upturned coat collar.

'I don't think you can afford not to talk to me.'

'Look, this really isn't—'

'I'd have got to you before, but you kicked off faster than I expected. I've been up to my neck in a trial.' He brought a battered soft pack of Marlboros out of his pocket and offered it to her. 'Something to warm you up.'

'You know the rules . . .'

'Fuck 'em. Anyway, I thought these things were different from criminal trials. You're a coroner, you can talk to who you like.'

He tapped out a cigarette, struck a match in cupped hands and leaned back against the wall. He took a slow, full draw and slowly exhaled, letting the breeze carry the smoke from his lips.

'Did Mrs Jamal tell you that I was solicitor for both families for four months?'

Annoyed, Jenny said, 'I'd rather you kept what you've got to say for the witness box.'

She got up and tossed her half-eaten chocolate bar into a rusting wire waste bin. The damp on the bench had soaked through to her skin.

'No, you wouldn't. It'd only screw it up, put those bastards so far out of reach you'll never get to the truth.' He took another draw and glanced lazily towards her, 'Maybe you don't care either way.'

'Which bastards are we talking about, precisely?'

'I don't know. They put me away before I got the chance to find out.' He gave a hint of a smile. 'Would you like to hear about it?'

'How about writing a statement and handing it to my officer? That's the usual practice.'

'Screw that. This case has already cost me one marriage and a perfectly good career.' He strolled across the weedy concrete slabs towards the pig-wire fence bordering the field. 'Are those seagulls? We're miles from the bloody sea.'

'The estuary's almost the sea.'

'I suppose . . . Look at them, kicking the other ones out of the way.' He stared out at the field. 'They pecked that poor girl's guts out, didn't they? That's what I read in the paper.'

'Then it must be true.'

'Didn't dare look that far down myself . . . Heard anything about where the body went?'

'Not yet.'

'Madness. What's anyone going to do with it? You always see on the TV – the bad guys dig a hole in the woods. Have you ever tried putting a spade in the ground where there are trees? It's all roots. It'd be as easy to get through concrete.' He sucked hard on the cigarette and flicked the butt over into the field margin. 'It's not as if I don't know villains, but that's a new one on me . . . right out of the morgue.'

He stood and watched the tractor stop at the end of the row, lift its gear and turn around. A sudden change in the wind carried the sound of the birds to them: a raucous, vibrant, strangely beautiful cacophony.

McAvoy smiled. ' "I could scale the blue air, I could plough the high hills, Oh, I could kneel all night in prayer, To heal your many ills . . . My Dark Rosaleen" . . . My God. Where did that come from?' He laughed and shook his head. 'Schoolmaster for a father – drilled all sorts of stuff into me.' He turned, walked several steps towards Jenny and stopped. 'I thought you weren't going to talk to me, Mrs Cooper.'

'Mrs Jamal said you went to prison.'

'I had that pleasure.'

'What was your offence?'

'Being a nuisance. My record says perverting the course of justice. Cops set me up with an undercover wearing a wire. Spliced it all together, made it sound like the alibi she was offering my client was all my idea.' He shrugged. 'Not that it wouldn't've happened eventually. Show them up too may times they'll skewer you in the end.'

'You were a criminal defence solicitor, right?'

'Solicitor *advocate*. I wasn't going to trust any bastard barristers to do my talking for me. Couldn't fight sleep most of them.'

'And Mrs Jamal came to you after her son disappeared?'

'She and the Hassans both. October '02. The cops had stopped answering their calls. Hired me to rattle their cage. Three months later I was behind bars. Didn't even get bail.'

'And you don't want to talk about this in evidence?' Jenny said.

'Look, I applaud your efforts getting this thing on so quickly, but let's be realistic for a moment. You'd think that with all their resources they could have found out the truth by now if they'd wanted to. No offence, Mrs Cooper, but in my humble opinion they're pimping you out. An honest woman like you wouldn't want that, surely?'

'You've a charming way of putting things.'

'Tell you what – why don't you call off this afternoon and talk to me instead?'

She looked at him, astonished. Arrogant prick, telling to tell her how to run her inquest.

'I don't think so. I'll see you inside.'

She headed for the back door of the building.

'You won't. And if you send me a summons I'll stand mute. I've got sod all to lose, and now it's come round again I think I've probably got more interest in finding out what happened than you have.'

'Oh, really?'

'Yes, really. You see, I'm a man with not a few past sins that still need atoning for, Mrs Cooper – my alleged offence not one of them, by the way. So there's no way I'm going to put my hand on the Holy Bible and swear to tell you the whole truth when this inquest you're conducting's a fucking sham.'

She fought an involuntary urge to hit him, hard.

McAvoy said, 'I'm hungry. I'll be down the road at that bird place. Took the ex-wife there once, I recall – pink flamingos.'

'This had better be good.'

She found him in a corner of the restaurant by the floor-to-ceiling window overlooking a large, shallow pond in which a flock of flamingos huddled against the cold. On a dismal February afternoon the large dining room was almost empty.

McAvoy pushed aside his empty plate and reached for his coffee. 'You want something?'

'Just to know what the hell this is about.'

'What d'you tell the jury?'

'That they could have the afternoon off.'

'You'll be popular. How's Mrs Jamal?'

'She followed me all the way to my car insisting that Dani James was a whore who'd been put up to blacken her son's name.'

'Have her arrested for contempt. Can you imagine anyone barracking a Crown Court judge like that?'

'Yeah, right.'

McAvoy said, 'She always was a pain, poor woman. I expect she's right round the bloody bend by now.'

'She has her moments.' Jenny's eyes skipped around the room, checking no one was watching them. The tension of a court day had worn her medication thin. It wasn't yet three o'clock and she was feeling jumpy and raw.

'She should be grateful the poor wee bastard had a shag before he went. She'd have had him hanging off her teat until he was forty.' He nodded out of the window towards a clutch of chilly looking flamingos. 'D'you know they still don't know why those things stand on one leg. One of the great unsolved mysteries of science.'

'I heard it was so they still had one left if they got bitten by a crocodile.' She fetched a legal pad out of her case. 'Can we get on now?'

'I'm not making a statement.'

'Fine, we'll call it notes.' She uncapped her fountain pen. 'But this was your idea, remember?'

He grunted as if he'd rather forget. 'We can deal with Simon Donovan for a start. The cops were all over him from April '02 in a fraud investigation. He was a personal accountant back then: used clients' tax cheques to buy rental property and borrowed off the equity to pay the Inland Revenue. In a rising market it worked like a dream until he bought six flats off plan that never went up. One of my partners was defending his co-defendant, a mortgage broker. It was set down for trial in August. Next thing he knows Donovan's a witness for the prosecution against four of his tax-evading clients and he's made his statement about the missing boys. All the charges against him and the broker were dropped.'

'So he cut a clever deal on his case – why would IDing the boys be part of it?'

'Have you any idea how lazy coppers are? I've known them piss in a pint pot to save a walk to the gents.'

'Donovan just happened to be down at the station in the right frame of mind?'

'More than likely. Plus they'd have been desperate to get it off their patch. Get a statement putting them in London and it was someone else's problem.'

'What about the Security Services?'

'The police hate them – they make them *do* things.'

'You really think they'd give them a false statement?'

McAvoy grinned. 'What are you, born again every morning? I thought you'd bloodied your knuckles as a lawyer.'

'I was mostly involved with childcare proceedings.'

'Then there's nothing you shouldn't know about the shitty side of human nature. What you've got to remember about cops, Mrs Cooper, is that lying gets to be a way of life. They start off gilding the lily when they write up their first arrests and end up framing innocent lawyers.'

Jenny made a note, though she wasn't hopeful that it would be of much help. Neither Donovan nor the police were likely to admit to fabricating evidence, and Donovan's ID statement was disconnected enough from the fraud charges not to be obviously linked.

'Tell me about your involvement in this case,' Jenny said.

McAvoy told her that Mrs Jamal and Mr and Mrs Hassan – shopkeepers from Birmingham – came to see him early in the October. They'd had moderately regular contact with the police in the first few weeks after their son's disappearance, but by early autumn it had tailed off. They'd written to MPs and councillors for help, but were referred back to the police, who wouldn't even pay for a missing poster. They had come to him in desperation. He wrote to the police and four weeks later obtained copies of the witness statements they'd taken. He picked up on Dani James's sighting of the possible intruder and wrote again asking what they were doing to follow it up. He never received a reply.

In December both families received their letters from DS Owens stating that the investigation was being shelved. McAvoy wrote back to protest and got nowhere. Over the Christmas holiday Mrs Jamal took to phoning him all hours of the day and night, obviously having some kind of break-down; then at the start of the new year the Hassans wrote to say they had decided to end their retainer.

'Any idea why?' Jenny said.

'They were conservative people. Their boy had been gone six months. The way they saw it, he'd either deserted his family or he was up to no good.'

'And Mrs Jamal?'

She detected a trace of guilt in McAvoy's expression. 'To be honest, I was trying to avoid her. I like to give the benefit of the doubt, but even I was beginning to think they'd hopped off to a training camp somewhere.' He stared out of the window at the pond, as if confronting a painful memory. 'That's what I told her . . . She threw a fit, accused me of collaborating with all the forces of darkness, so I offered to get a private investigator onto it. She had five hundred pounds. It scarcely bought us two days, but this guy I knew – dead now – knocked on some doors down in St Pauls. He found a little old lady who said she'd spotted a black people carrier sitting outside her house on the night of the 28th. It was right along from the bus stop the boys used to get back to college, about two hundred yards from Anwar Ali's place. There were two white men in the front. From her description it sounded like a Toyota. It was late in the evening and she thought they looked suspicious. She was picking up the phone to call the police when she heard it take off.'

'That's it?'

'More or less. I phoned the bus depot and tried to find out whether the police had spoken to any of their drivers who might have spotted them that night. I was told they couldn't discuss it. I tried to be reasonable, assured them there was no legal reason why they couldn't, but it was a stone wall. I went back to the police to ask them what their problem was and got the same response. A week later a pretty girl came into my office saying she might be able to help out a client of mine who was up for armed robbery at the time. I took her alibi statement. Next morning I was dragged bollock naked from my bed and didn't see the outside of a cell for two-and-a-half years.'

'You believe the two things are connected?'

'I'll admit there were lots of reasons the cops wanted me out of the way. The fact I'd got two guys off a murder charge and had a DI nicked for perjury the previous year were two of them. In fact, for the best part of six months that's what I thought it was all about.'

It was McAvoy's turn to sweep the room with his eyes. Only when he was satisfied that none of their elderly companions were undercover detectives did he turn his gaze back to Jenny.

'Two things changed my mind. First, I remembered something. A couple of nights before I was arrested I'd been out with a client; we were both drunk as hell. I got a call on my mobile, my private number, and this American-sounding voice said, "What do you know?" I was that lashed I could hardly make him out. He said it again, "What do you know, Mr McAvoy?" No threats, nothing. I took him for a crank and rang off.'

'And you remembered this when?'

'Sometime in the middle of '03. Lying on my bunk waiting for my room-mate to finish his business on the potty.'

'Nice. What was the second thing?'

'This phone call starts going round in my mind – you get like that inside. The Law Society's struck me off, my wife's fucking somebody else, I want to know what the hell's going on. I phoned the investigator again – Billy Dean his name was – and said could he have a scout around, try and get a lead on this call or the Toyota. Fine. He tried to trace the call first but had no joy – the incoming number was one of those unregistered pay and gos. He had more luck on the Toyota, though. If you think about it, there are only half a dozen major roads out of Bristol. Two of them go over the Severn. Billy talked to some guys in the toll booths and found a fella on the old Severn crossing who actually remembered seeing a black MPV, two stocky white guys in the front, two Asian boys in the back.'

'A *year* later?'

'It was an unusual sight, the man said. You don't get many dark skins heading over into Monmouthshire. He was from Chepstow – one Chinese takeaway and a French polisher.'

'Haven't they got cameras there that read the number plates?'

'All data's scrubbed after four weeks. The one time Big Brother might have been some use.'

'Did you follow any of this up?'

McAvoy shook his head. 'I put it out of my mind. Billy took a stroke, and the blessed Father O'Riordan helped reconcile me to my fate. The spirit seemed to be moving against it.'

'Mrs Jamal didn't tell me any of this.'

'I didn't trouble her. What would she have done, except go even nuttier? Wasn't even anything solid. To tell you the truth, I'd almost convinced myself it was nothing until I heard about your inquest.'

'What changed your mind?'

'Now you're asking.' He thought for a moment. 'I suppose you could say I felt the spirit moving the other way. My client with the missing daughter for one thing, and thinking back again – whether those poor families wouldn't have found some peace if they hadn't fetched up with an unholy bastard like me.'

'Right.' She glanced over her notes – there weren't many of them. 'Your bid for redemption consists of an untraceable phone call – possibly, possibly not, relevant – and a fleeting glimpse into a car, nearly eight years ago, by a toll booth operator.'

'I still remember the guy's name: Frank Madog.'

Jenny wrote it down. 'I'll see if we can get him along to give evidence.'

'I don't think that's a good idea. Why don't you adjourn for a few days and talk to him, see if it goes anywhere? I can make the approach, if you like.'

'I see.' She closed her notebook. 'Any particular reason you feel entitled to tell me how to run my inquest?'

'Yes,' McAvoy said. 'I had a call at home this weekend. Yesterday morning, ten a.m. – caught me sober. It was like a robot, through one of those voice distorters. I assume it was a man's voice, "Tell me what you know, McAvoy, or you're a dead man."'

'Know about what?' Jenny said, with a note of scepticism.

'That's what I asked. He said, and this is actually what the man said, in this robot voice: "I wouldn't even take a shit in the cheap casket you're going to hell in." "Casket", not "coffin". Who says that this side of the Atlantic?'

'Then what?'

'I hung up.'

She nodded with what she hoped was a neutral expression, an insistent voice in her head telling her to walk away now without a backward glance.

McAvoy said, 'Before you get into any of this, there's something else you should know.'

'I might as well hear it all.'

'Your officer, Alison Trent – she was one of the CID that put me away.' He gave a forgiving shrug. 'So, do you want me to get in touch with Madog?'

She heard Alison's raised voice as she opened the front door to her office. It sounded as if she was on the telephone.

'Of course she's welcome, she's my daughter, I just don't see why she has to bring *her*.'

Jenny stopped outside the outer office door, guilty at eavesdropping, but it didn't feel right to interrupt mid-conversation. And she was curious.

'How many times have I got to say this? It's not her I disapprove of, it's the situation . . . Because I don't believe it's real, that's why. She's had plenty of boyfriends for goodness sake.' Alison sighed loudly. 'Fine. You deal with it your way, I'll cope with it mine. Just don't expect me to welcome her with open arms. Whatever else you might accuse me of, you can't call me a hypocrite.' She slammed down the receiver and thumped over to the kitchenette.

Taken aback, Jenny mulled over what she had heard. Was Alison's daughter in a relationship with another woman? It would explain the scratchy moods and the New Dawn Church. Its slickly produced newsletter, which Alison had taken to leaving out on the coffee table, was full of stories of drunks, junkies and homosexuals who had been brought back to the straight and narrow by the power of prayer. Some of the testimonies, she had to admit, were very moving.

'Hi,' Jenny said, as she came through the door. She went to Alison's desk to check the message tray.

There was a moment of moody silence before Alison came to the kitchenette door.

'Mrs Jamal called – three times. She thinks someone's been in her flat.'

'I've got to speak to her anyway. I'm going to adjourn until next Monday.' Jenny flicked through three death reports that needed immediate attention. A previously healthy man of thirty-two had dropped dead while jogging on the Downs and a van had plunged down a motorway embankment killing both occupants. Neither had been wearing a seat belt. Alison had printed off the emailed police photographs of the wreck: two bloody snowflake shatter-patterns on the windscreen where their heads had impacted.

'Oh? Any particular reason?' Alison asked, disapproving.

'Alec McAvoy, that legal executive, came forward with a few pieces of information. I'd like to follow them up before I call any more live witnesses.'

'I know who McAvoy is. He's one of the most corrupt lawyers this city's ever produced.'

'He mentioned that you were part of the team that brought him to justice.'

'I'm sure that's not how he put it.' Alison scowled. 'He fabricated evidence. It's what he did for a living. I heard it straight from the mouths of his ex-clients. Anything he told you this afternoon I should take with a shovelful of salt, if I were you, Mrs Cooper.'

'I appreciate there's a history. I won't ask you to get

involved.' She tucked the reports under her arm. 'If you wouldn't mind putting the word out that we're reconvening next Monday—'

'Do you mind my asking what this information was?'

Jenny told half the truth. 'It's about a suspicious vehicle that was seen near Anwar Ali's flat the night of the disappearance. It just seems odd the police didn't pick up on it, seeing as they had an observation team nearby.'

'Why not ask Dave Pironi? He'll give you a straight answer.'

'Didn't you tell me that the Security Services were calling the shots?' Jenny said. 'He's not going to want to talk about that, is he?'

Alison didn't respond.

Gently, Jenny said, 'Is everything all right?'

'Perfectly, thank you, Mrs Cooper. I'm just concerned you don't get taken in by a professional conman, that's all.' Alison turned at the sound of the kettle coming to the boil and hurried back to her tea-making.

Jenny retreated to her office and closed the door behind her. A fresh pile of unread post-mortem reports sat on her desk alongside the growing heap of correspondence she had been avoiding for several days. She slumped into her chair and clicked onto her emails, anything rather than start into work. Amidst the trivia and spam there was a message from DS Murphy asking her for further details of some of those who had come to view the Jane Doe, the latest turgid round robin from the Ministry of Justice – this one instructing coroners to refrain from emotive or potentially headline-generating language in court (the duller and more mechanical they could be the better) – and a brief request from Gillian Golder to call her on her direct line.

Jenny bit the bullet and dialled her number.

Gillian Golder answered on the second ring. 'Jenny. Thank you so much for calling.' She sounded delighted.

'No problem. How can I help?'

'Look, obviously we don't want to interfere, but Alun told me that you've allowed the BRISIC lawyer rights of audience.'

'It's a matter in my discretion. I took the view his client has a legitimate interest.'

'Of course. But it's only right you should know that their agenda is far from benign. This is a political Islamist organization that peddles malicious conspiracy theories. Take a look at the message boards on their website – they accuse the British state of everything from black propaganda to murdering its own citizens. I'm afraid I'd have to disagree that their interest is legitimate.'

Refusing to be cowed, Jenny said, 'I'm sure I can keep them under control.'

'I understand you've adjourned already. One of our people was due to give evidence tomorrow . . .'

'It's nothing sinister.'

'Not according to our friends' news interviews. You're already orchestrating a cover-up as far as they're concerned.'

'And how are you suggesting I should be influenced by this information?'

'I'm not suggesting anything,' Gillian Golder said. 'I'm merely forewarning you. Dangerous nonsense can sound very credible, even to a perfectly sound and rational mind.' She drew out this final phrase, giving Jenny a message that needed no further articulation: *embarrass us and we'll rubbish you.*

# ELEVEN

THE WIND CAME UP IN the late evening, a cold northerly that found new cracks and crevices in the fabric of the cottage to penetrate. When it gusted, the back door rattled on its hinges, making Jenny start and long for a drink to soak up the childish fears that the creaking building stirred up in her. Ross was staying over at a friend's in Bristol, and she was too embarrassed to phone Steve to say she was scared of being alone in her own home. She spent the evening locked in her study becoming steadily more jittery. Late in the afternoon the police photographer had emailed more images from inside the wrecked van and they refused to leave her: two men in their early twenties with exploded foreheads, one twisted across the bench seat, the other lying face up in the footwell, his broken features grossly swollen. A partially eaten burger lay on top of the dash. They were tree surgeons, men who earned a living clambering on rotten branches with chainsaws, but it seemed that something as tiny as a faulty tyre valve had sent them into oblivion. Her work was a constant reminder that every day, and without notice, life was snatched away from even the fittest and healthiest. And where did they go, these poor souls catapulted into the afterlife with a mouthful of flame-grilled and onions? To think it could be as simple as switching out the lights would be comforting, but she couldn't believe that for a moment.

Two pills weren't enough to put her under. In what was becoming a routine, she lay in the darkness, the duvet pulled up around her ears, flinching at every sound. Mrs Jamal, the missing boys and the corpses in the van paraded behind her eyes and entered her fitful dreams: she and Mrs Jamal chased through a labyrinth of anonymous streets after a fleeing black van which limped along with a flat tyre. Desperate, breathless and exhausted they eventually rounded a corner and found it crumpled against a tree. Blood dripped out from under the sills onto the pavement. While Mrs Jamal wailed and rent her clothes, Jenny steeled herself with righteous anger and wrenched open the cab door. Inside was a young girl who looked up with blood-soaked hands she had wiped across her face. The child split the air with a cry and Jenny recoiled and fled with legs that turned to stone. As she fought to drag one foot in front of the other, a cold shadow stole over her; she heard the disembodied voice of her son: 'You don't know me. You can never know me.' She tried to call his name, to bring him out from his hiding place, but the landscape changed around her and became the street where she had lived as a child. For a brief second she was elated to be safe, then realized that the buildings were empty shells. There were no curtains at the windows, no people or furniture inside. Utterly and completely alone and bereft, she wept.

Jenny woke to a sensation of wetness on her pillow and with a sense of dread that was almost exquisite in its clarity. She sat upright and reached for the light, trying to shake off the image of the girl with the bloodied face. It was four-thirty a.m. She reminded herself it was only a dream, the product of a churning, restless mind that would soon calm down, but it didn't. The girl's face, somehow familiar, lodged like a bone in her throat. She was impressing herself on her, haunting her, pleading to be seen.

She pulled on her robe and made her way downstairs,

switching on all the lights as she went. She dug her journal out from the drawer of her desk and started to write, then frantically to sketch the face of the child . . .

She took the slip road off the M48 and drew into the car park of the Severn View service station for her early-morning rendezvous with McAvoy. He was leaning against his elderly black Ford smoking a cigarette. She pulled up in the space alongside and climbed out, the cold breeze biting into her cheeks.

He smiled through tired, red eyes that looked as if they'd seen little sleep.

'Will you look at you, fresh and beautiful at this godfor-saken hour.'

'That'd be the three hours in make-up.'

'Modest, too.' He tossed down his cigarette butt and rubbed it out with his toe. 'You truly are one of nature's innocents.' He pushed back his hair with both hands and rolled his stiff shoulders. She could *feel* his hangover.

'Late night?'

'It's the people I have to do business with. They don't tend to keep conventional hours.' He shivered. 'The air con's busted in this heap – any chance I can come with you?'

'Didn't you say Madog was going to meet us here?'

'That's what I suggested. He seemed a little reticent. But I know he was on the early shift this morning. He should be about due his break.'

McAvoy's smell was an aromatic mix of cigarettes, whisky and a hint of perfume. With the heater on full it filled her little car and conjured images of cheap casinos and topless hostesses.

'Swing round onto the northbound carriageway and we'll end up at the canteen block this side of the plaza,' McAvoy said and opened his window a touch. 'Do you mind?'

'I've got some painkillers if you need them.'

'Thank you, but I'm superstitious about treating self-inflicted pain. I worry the devil'd only give it back to me twice over.'

She smiled and drove on in silence for a short while. 'You're serious?'

'Read your gospel of Matthew – nine separate mentions of hell. They can't all have been metaphorical.'

'You sound like my officer. She goes to an evangelical church—'

'Bad luck. No poetry or humility those people,' McAvoy said, interrupting her. 'Try going to confession once a fortnight and spilling your sins out to a celibate priest. There's something to put you in your place.'

'Is that what you do?'

'I try.'

Curious, Jenny said, 'How do you find that squares with your work? I know criminals need defending—'

'When I was in the jail, you know who visited me, gave money to the wife? My clients. From my upstanding colleagues, not a single damn word. We could have both been rotting for all they cared.'

'Maybe they didn't know what to say.'

'The thing about villains, they live with the consequences. Forget your sociology bullshit, no one understands right and wrong like they do. Your lawyers and politicians and businessmen, it's all arm's length with them. They're sipping Chablis while the wee girl's getting her legs blown off in Africa. It's not the robbers and thieves, it's those suited bastards who are the rulers of darkness of this world.'

She glanced across and saw the tension in his face.

'Sorry,' she said.

'Take no notice. I always rant like a madman when I've a sore head.'

'Only then?'

He gave her a pained smile. 'Shut up and drive.'

As they approached the English end of the bridge, McAvoy told her to pull over next to a single-storey building at the edge of the plaza just short of the toll booths. It was commuting time and traffic was heavy in both directions. He told her to sit tight while he found Madog.

She watched him approach a young woman in toll collector's uniform who came out of the building to light a cigarette. She looked uncertain as McAvoy gave his spiel and glanced suspiciously over at Jenny, before pointing to one of the booths in the middle of the plaza. McAvoy thanked her and cadged a light before hopping out between the queues of traffic, giving the finger to the driver of a Range Rover who took exception to being held up for half a second.

She didn't have a clear view, but she could see enough to realize that Madog was reluctant to stop work. She saw McAvoy rap on the glass and gesticulate, then finally step out into the toll lane and block it off with two plastic bollards. The angry chorus of car horns he provoked brought a supervisor hurrying out of the building. Jenny jumped out of the car and intercepted him.

'Excuse me, sir. Jenny Cooper, Severn Vale District Coroner. My colleague and I need to talk to one of your staff, Mr Frank Madog.'

'What?' He pointed to her car. 'Who said you could park there? It's an access lane.' The supervisor was in his early thirties, pasty, overweight and spoiling for a fight.

She thrust a hand in to her coat pocket and dug out a business card. 'I'm on an official investigation. Mr Madog is obliged to cooperate by law. I'd be grateful if you could arrange for him to come over.'

McAvoy's voice carried over the din, colourfully cursing

the driver of the lorry that was nudging aggressively up to his bollards.

Ignoring the card, the supervisor said, 'Who's that bloody lunatic?'

Jenny said, 'I don't know. Why don't you take his registration?'

Judging by the tattoos on the backs of his hands, Frank Madog had a thing for Elvis. He'd swept his thin ginger hair into a semblance of a quiff and there was a hint of finger drapes about his overlong dandruff-scattered blazer, too roomy for his bony shoulders. That wasn't a patch of wall in the module of portable cabins which served as a temporary canteen for the bridge staff that wasn't decorated with a no smoking sign. Deprived of a cigarette, Madog's nicotine-stained fingers fiddled with the frames of his greasy glasses.

'You're not kidding it was a long time ago,' Madog said, 'more 'n eight years.'

'You remember my associate, Billy Dean, coming to talk to you in '03? Big bull of a guy. Bald, red face. Ugly looking.'

'I think so.' He sounded far from certain.

'Come on, Mr Madog, how often does collecting the tolls get you interviewed by a private investigator?'

Madog rubbed his forehead, showing yellow teeth as he grimaced. 'Like I said, I think I remember the man.'

Jenny threw McAvoy a look, urging him to go easy. This was an official visit by the coroner, after all.

He struck a reasonable tone: it was clearly a strain. 'I spoke with Mr Dean at the time, he gave me your details. He said you saw a black Toyota MPV coming through on the night of 28 June 2002. Two stocky-looking white men in the front, two Asian boys in the back. You told him it was an unusual sight – that's why you remembered.'

Madog looked at Jenny with a vague expression, as if this

information only rang the faintest of bells. 'He's got a better memory than I have.'

'Actually he's dead,' McAvoy said, 'otherwise we'd have brought him along. His face would've jogged your memory all right.'

Jenny said, 'I would like you to do your best, Mr Madog. I will be calling you as a witness to my inquest.'

Madog's Adam's apple rose and fell in his crêpy throat. 'Look, I might have told your friend I saw a car, but I've had a lot of nights out since then if you know what I mean.' He tapped his temple. 'The old memory slips a cog now and again.'

Jenny sighed. 'Are you saying you don't remember the four men in the black Toyota? It's very important you tell the truth, Mr Madog.'

Madog looked from Jenny to McAvoy, and back again, his mouth beginning to work but failing to produce a sound.

Admiring Madog's tattoos, McAvoy said, 'It's his gospel stuff I like best. "Peace in the Valley" – you know that one?'

Madog gave a cautious nod.

McAvoy said, 'Do you remember how it goes? I've forgotten.'

Madog and Jenny traded a look.

'Come on, Frank,' McAvoy said, 'You know that one. Let me see now . . . "Well the morning's so bright and the lamb is the light, and the night is as black, as black as the sea."' He began to sing, the words coming back to him in an unbroken stream. ' "And the beasts of the wild will be led by a child, and I'll be changed, changed from this creature that I am, oh yes indeed . . ."' He smiled. 'A beautiful message of hope. We're all going to change, Frank, and if he managed to avoid the hot place, even my friend Mr Dean'll have cheeks sweet enough to kiss by now.'

Jenny felt her face redden with embarrassment, but Mc-Avoy was in full flow and not in any mood to stop.

'You see, the King was a deeply religious man, Frank, which is why I believe he did get to heaven despite all the drugs and girls and what have you. And I'm sure you'll agree that any true fan would hate to sully his precious memory by telling a lie, especially about such a grave and important matter.' He leaned forward across the table and placed his hand on top of Madog's. 'Can you imagine meeting him on the other side and trying to tell him why you didn't tell the whole truth? There's a mother down the road crying for her lost boy, Frank.'

Madog slowly eased his hand out from under McAvoy's.

'So what have you got to tell us?' McAvoy said.

'Who were they?' Madog said. 'What's this all about?'

Jenny said, 'As far as we know, they were just two young university students. They went missing, the police couldn't trace them and it's my job to find out if they're alive or dead. And if they are dead, how they died.'

'Oh. Right.' Madog rubbed his temples.

McAvoy gave him a moment, glanced at Jenny, then said, 'Someone else has spoken to you about this, haven't they? You're among friends now, Frank, we'll start with that, shall we?'

Madog looked up at Jenny. 'What happens with this information?'

'It helps me to find the truth. And if there's criminality involved, it may be used to assist a prosecution.'

'You *are* the coroner?'

'You've seen Mrs Cooper's picture in the *Post*, Frank. Check out her website – she hasn't even had herself airbrushed.'

Madog nodded. 'OK. Only your friend told me he was a

detective. That's the only reason I spoke to him. He threatened to charge me if I didn't.'

McAvoy said, 'I apologize posthumously on his behalf. He was good to his wife and kids.'

Jenny opened the legal pad she had waiting in front of her, 'All right, Mr Madog – when you're ready.'

'It was like I told your man way back when – I saw a black Toyota, two white fellas in the front, about eleven o'clock at night. One of them, the driver, was kind of thickset with a shaved head. The passenger had a ponytail.'

'What age were they?' Jenny said.

'Thirties ... And the two lads in the back were both Asians. Bearded, but young looking – teenagers almost.'

'What made you notice them?'

'I suppose they seemed scared. One of them looked at me with these big brown eyes almost like he was trying to say something.'

'Did anyone in the car speak to you?'

'Nothing. Not a word. That's another thing – you usually get a thank you. I make a point of being cheerful to the customers . . .' He paused to recall. 'No, this fella had a face like thunder. A real tough nut.' He swallowed, anxious. 'But it was the other one who came after me.'

Jenny glanced up. 'What?'

'About a week later. I was leaving the house with my granddaughter. Six years old she was at the time. I was taking her home to her mammy's on a Saturday afternoon. We'd got in the car outside the house and this fella with the ponytail knocked on the passenger window. I wound down the window and he leaned in, smiling, and said, "Anyone asks, you never saw us." Then he brings out this can of orange paint and sprays it all over my granddaughter's hair. She was screaming. He didn't stop . . .' Madog shook his head. 'I had to wash it out with turpentine. Took all morning.'

'You didn't report this to the police?' Jenny said.

Madog said, 'If you'd've been there you wouldn't ask that. I'm telling you, he was spraying that paint and *smiling*.'

'But did you tell all this to Mr Dean?'

'Not the paint bit. I swear to God, to this day even my daughter still doesn't know.'

'This man must have really scared you,' Jenny said.

'Yeah, he was like a . . . like—'

'The devil in disguise?' McAvoy said.

'You shouldn't take that kind of crap from people,' McAvoy said. 'You're the coroner, for God's sake – more powers than a High Court judge.'

'Hardly.'

'Look 'em up. If you'd got the balls you'd use them.'

Jenny glanced across at him as she swung the Golf back up the slip road to the service station. He was good-looking in a battered kind of way, but not a man you'd trust to mind your handbag. There was something of the con artist about him: the suit was good, but you couldn't be sure if that wasn't all there was to him.

'So what are you going to do? This guy with the ponytail sounds like an evil son of a bitch. A real professional, thought all the psychology through. Spray paint on a kiddy's head – sweet Jesus.'

'I'll get my officer to take Madog's statement and call him as a witness.'

'And what are the jury going to do with that? You've got to find this Toyota surely, and the ponytail fella.'

'A black Toyota? There must be thousands of them.'

'You'd be surprised. Probably only a few hundred the

same model. Break them down geographically. There aren't many places you'd be going over the old Severn Bridge to get to – all the road does is head up the border country.' He slammed his hand on the dash for emphasis. 'You've got to find out who these people are, not give them a chance to get away by wheeling Madog into court before you've tracked them down. I'll give you a hand, it's got my blood up again.'

Jenny thought about it. His passion was infectious. 'Maybe it wouldn't hurt. Most of the jury didn't look in any hurry to get back to their day jobs.'

'That's the way.' He grinned. 'Good girl.'

Jenny turned into the near-empty car park, her mind swimming with questions about who the men in the front of the Toyota might have been. But could she even be sure Madog was telling the truth? She glanced at McAvoy again and realized she didn't know what to believe in his presence, he seemed to alter reality around him. She wouldn't be able to think straight until she'd got away. She pulled up next to his car.

'Buy you a coffee?' he said.

'I'd better not. Work, you know—'

'I took you for a free spirit, Mrs Cooper.'

There was suddenly an atmosphere between them. The way he was looking at her with smiling, perceptive eyes, he seemed to know her, to reach under her skin. She felt hot and mildly panicked.

'Another time. I'll be in touch . . . And thanks.'

McAvoy nodded as if he understood the many reasons for her reticence entirely. He reached for the door handle, then paused. 'Oh, I forgot to mention it to you – standing in the inquest yesterday, I remembered Mrs Jamal once saying she suspected Nazim had a girlfriend.'

'She knew about Dani James?'

'No, I think she was talking about earlier, months before that.'

'She hasn't said anything to me.'

'Ask her.' He smiled, said, 'God bless,' and stepped out into the freezing wind.

Alison was still smarting from the premature adjournment of the inquest. Jenny guessed that she'd had Pironi on the phone asking what the hell was going on, and that in the conflict of loyalties Pironi had won. She had evidently spent her first two hours at work tidying: her office was immaculate apart from the overspilling tray on the corner of her desk reserved for Jenny's messages and mail.

Sorting the critical items from the merely urgent, Jenny ignored her officer's frostiness and told her about her trip to the toll plaza with McAvoy. Alison listened, unimpressed, as Jenny announced that she had decided to make finding the Toyota and its occupants a priority before resuming the inquest.

'And when might that happen?' Alison said.

'I thought we'd agreed Monday.'

'Have you any idea how long it takes to get any joy out of the vehicle licensing people at Swansea? It's like Stalin's Kremlin.'

'I was thinking we might go through the police – they're hooked up to the Swansea computers, aren't they?'

'They're snowed under already. Believe me, I've used up all my favours, Mrs Cooper, and more. It's got so even my ex-colleagues are dodging my calls.'

'It's probably best Bristol CID don't know about this one, seeing as they were so closely involved in the original investigation.' She could sense Alison's hackles rising. 'I'll call DS Williams over in Chepstow, see if I can't persuade him to give us a hand.'

'I'm sure he will,' Alison said with feeling. 'He'll leap at any chance to do down the English police.'

'Who said anything about doing them down?'

Alison looked up from her computer screen. 'I told you what I think of Alec McAvoy. He went to prison for fixing witnesses – he made a career out of it. You can't expect me to believe someone he suddenly pulls out of a hat.'

'Madog seemed very sincere to me.'

'Do you really believe he wouldn't have gone to the police if what he told you was true?'

'What possible interest could McAvoy have in interfering with this inquest?'

'Do you want my honest opinion, Mrs Cooper?'

'Fire away.'

Alison unleashed. 'Before he was struck off he was cock of the walk, the flashiest, richest criminal lawyer in town. He didn't only think he was above the law, he thought he *was* the law. When we caught him out he happened to be representing the missing boys' families. It suited his purposes to say his arrest was political – they were his only clients who weren't hardened villains with form longer than a donkey's dick, as we used to say. Now he's using this inquest. Think about it: he'll dredge up evidence to support his claim that he was the victim of a conspiracy, get the media behind him, and before you know it the Law Society will be pressured into letting him back on the roll.' Alison looked at her imploringly. 'He's a clever man, Mrs Cooper, but rotten to the core. He doesn't give a damn what happened to those boys – this is someone who built his reputation representing gangsters, rapists, murderers.'

'All right,' Jenny said. 'Point taken. But I have to check the car story. And I need you to take a formal statement from Madog.'

She retreated to her office with renewed doubts about

McAvoy. Alison's outburst began to explain some of the unease she'd felt in his company. There was something about his powerful aura that frightened her. It wasn't just the uneasy fragility of a disgraced man clinging to tattered shreds of dignity, it was his cast of mind, the unnerving sense that there was a part of his humanity missing. The business with the bollards and the truck: he was reckless, inviting trouble and not giving a damn for the consequences. But when he'd looked at her . . . there'd been an eruption of heat in her chest and a sensation that shot straight down between her legs. It almost shamed her to admit it.

Burying these thoughts, she reached for her address book and turned up the numbers of DS Owen Williams, her contact across the border. She caught him during his mid-morning break. They'd spoken maybe three or four times since the Danny Wills case and on each occasion he'd been delighted to hear from her. He listened carefully as she explained that a witness 'had come to light', neglecting to mention McAvoy, and asked whether he could help trace all black Toyota MPVs that may have been in the vicinity of the Severn Bridge on a June night eight years ago.

'I'd be ab-so-lutely delighted,' Williams said in his exaggerated Welsh lilt. 'Anything to help my favourite coroner, especially – as I presume – you can't trust the Bristol police not to do an honest job for you.'

'Some of the officers involved in the original investigation are still in place.'

'You don't have to tell me any more, Mrs Cooper. You know I'd trust a Bangkok brothel keeper sooner than any one of those English bastards.'

Jenny had barely put the receiver down when the phone rang and Alison came on the line saying she had Mrs Jamal on hold.

'OK, put her through.'

Jenny braced herself. She was greeted by the sound of inconsolable sobs.

'Mrs Jamal? This is Mrs Cooper. What can I do for you?'

The sobbing continued, Mrs Jamal unable to speak except to mumble something that sounded like, 'I don't know . . . I don't know.'

Jenny wanted to ask about McAvoy's memory of her mentioning a girlfriend, but the moment wasn't right. She seemed simply to need to have her grief heard and acknowledged.

Jenny offered what few words of comfort she could and heard herself say, 'I promise, I won't rest until I've lifted every stone to find out what happened to your son.'

With the sharpening of her symptoms over recent days, Jenny was beginning to dread the long hours between office and sleep with no alcohol or tranquillizing drug to soothe the mental sores. As the adrenalin subsided, the intangible fear ascended as surely as if the two were balanced on a pair of old-fashioned scales. Her desire not to let Ross see how she was feeling intensified the pain. She had staked her relationship with him on a promise that she could cope; that what she wanted more than anything else was to have him share her home until he went away to university. It hadn't been easy for him to move out of his father's house – David's disapproval had been largely silent, but all the more crushing for it – and his decision to trust her left her feeling that their cohabitation was a long, drawn-out test of her ability as a mother and of the truth of her recovery from emotional collapse.

She pulled up outside Melin Bach and sat in the darkness summoning strength. She knew she could hold it together, at a push, but she lacked the energy to be light or joyful. Her weakness infuriated her. She'd been better off with tranquil-

THE DISAPPEARED

lizers; at least they'd allowed the illusion of control. Part of
her wished she could just go inside and go straight to bed,
sleep through it and wake to her pills next morning, but there
was dinner to cook, conversations to be had. Suddenly she
felt as if she had an impossible mountain to climb. She
reached for her beta blockers, snapped one in half with her
teeth and swallowed.

Thank God for drugs. Thank God.

The tightness in her chest had already begun to loosen a
little as she entered the house. She opened the living-room
door to find Ross and Steve sitting side by side on the sofa
eating sandwiches.

'Oh, hi.' Steve levered himself to his feet. 'Called by on my
way down to the pub – got waylaid.'

Jenny turned to Ross, whose eyes were glued to the screen.
'I guess you won't be wanting any dinner.'

'No thanks. I'm going to Karen's.'

'On a Tuesday?'

'Why not?'

She couldn't think of a reason that wouldn't make her
sound like the kind of mother she'd already sworn to him she
wasn't. She compromised. 'All right, just make sure you're
back by eleven. You don't want to be exhausted tomorrow.'
She headed for the kitchen.

Steve said, 'Can I do anything?'

Jenny said, 'No. I'm fine.'

She was searching through the dregs in the fridge – it
seemed to empty as soon as she'd filled it – when she heard
Steve come in behind her. He set his empty plate on the
counter and put an arm around her waist.

'Rough day?'

She wished he'd stop touching her. It was one more thing
to deal with. 'No more than usual.'

Ross called out from the living room: 'See you.'

163

Steve was silent for a moment, his hand on the small of her back while she rummaged for a three-day-old lettuce, a tomato and a scrap of cheese. The front door opened and closed. They were alone.

'You're tense,' Steve said.

'Just tired.'

She slipped away from him and grabbed a plate from the cupboard, feeling self-conscious with him watching her fix her meagre supper.

'Ross mentioned you'd been fraught lately.'

'Oh, did he?'

'It's tough on your own.'

There was no answer to that. She tipped the last of a bottle of French dressing onto her plate and looked at the half-dead salad with no enthusiasm. She wasn't even hungry.

Steve stepped up close behind her, brought both hands around her middle and held her until she relaxed enough to lean into him. She felt the hard contours of his body through her clothes.

'You never ask me for anything,' he said quietly. 'You're not on your own, Jenny . . .' He kissed her neck. 'I'm here.'

She turned to face him and let him kiss her face and eyes and mouth, trying to submit to the moment, to let their closeness overwhelm her and push the intruding, chaotic thoughts from her mind. She let him take her hand and lead her upstairs; without speaking a word, she went with him to her bed and for a short while managed to lose herself.

Afterwards, she huddled close to him. The bedroom radiator never managed more than a tepid heat and there was hardness to the cold tonight, their breath almost visible in the frigid air. She slipped in and out of a restless doze, a carousel of faces passing in front of her eyes.

She vaguely heard Steve say, 'Are you awake?'

She forced her eyes open. 'Sorry . . .'

He pushed the hair gently back from her face. 'You were murmuring.'

'Anything interesting?'

'Couldn't make it out.'

In his concerned smile Jenny saw a different man from the one she'd met the previous June. He was gentler, more straightforward, less mysterious. This familiarity made her strangely sad: their bursts of excitement together were still intense, but briefer, his touch wasn't as electric, the heightened thrill had gone. And he wanted to *know* her when she didn't even know herself.

Steve said, 'I think you need a good night's sleep.' He kissed her forehead, slid out from under the duvet and pulled on his clothes.

'I'll call you,' he said and quietly let himself out.

Jenny listened guiltily to his footfalls on the stairs. He was a good man, she was fond of him, yet when they had been making love she had fantasized for a moment that she was with someone else. And it had unsettled her: it was as if the constant tug she felt towards the darker corners of her subconscious had found another weakness to work on. The one pure thing she had was being corrupted.

Frightened by the places her imagination wanted to take her, she summoned the will to haul herself out of bed and find her journal. She would write down the thoughts that were preying on her in the hope that bringing them to light would exorcise them. But as she wrote: *When I felt his touch on my belly, I closed my eyes and let it be Alec McAvoy*, a surge of excitement passed through her.

It was the same sensation she had felt the first time she set eyes on Steve: she had known, profoundly and without question, what would happen next.

# TWELVE

DS WILLIAMS HAD MOVED QUICKLY. Jenny arrived in the office to find an emailed list of nearly five hundred black Toyota MPVs registered in the UK during 2002 together with their owners' addresses. She passed them on to Alison and asked her to pick out any registered either in the Bristol area or a fifty-mile-wide corridor to the north. It was an arbitrary approach, but they had to start somewhere. Also in her inbox was a message from another detective sergeant, Sean Murphy, to let her know that the inquiries into the missing Jane Doe and the fire at the Meditect lab were now being treated as one and the same investigation. Alison said the word inside the force was that there were no leads as yet, but that the CID was working on the theory that the dead girl had been about to inform on an organized criminal gang, possibly people traffickers.

A further email arrived as she was clicking away from Murphy's. It was from Gillian Golder copying a link to an article on BRISIC's website. She signed off, *All best, Gillian.* The piece was written anonymously under the headline, 'Coroner Adjourns Inquest into the Disappeared'. The unnamed writer speculated that government agencies had been panicked by the speed at which the inquest had commenced and had stepped in to bring a halt to proceedings before any compromising evidence came to light. The author cited unsourced rumours alleging the existence of shady agents provocateurs who were said to have induced young British Asian men to go abroad, where they were secretly arrested and imprisoned. The final paragraph ended:

> *Don't expect the coroner's inquest to tell us anything we*
> *don't already know. The small window of opportunity has*
> *closed. Mrs Cooper has given in to pressure and denied the*
> *grieving families and their communities their one chance of*
> *discovering the truth.*

For a brief moment Jenny toyed with the idea of trusting Gillian Golder, even with asking her to help hunt down the Toyota and its occupants. The familiarity of the brief email had disarmed her into believing they were on the same side, that she wasn't alone after all. She checked herself. Golder was a spy for God's sake, a professional deceiver. Her job was to forge false friendships and make the isolated feel loved.

She replied tersely: *Thank you. Contents noted.*

Her immediate task was to review the evidence and decide where to put her limited energies. She fetched out the legal pad on which she'd made a note of the testimony she'd heard on the first day of her inquest and read it through. She had an uneasy feeling about Anwar Ali. He was close to BRISIC and something in his demeanour had suggested that, despite appearances, he was still the Islamist he had been eight years before. Until she'd heard Madog's story, she had assumed Ali's role might have been to hook Nazim and Rafi up with a third party who had helped them to leave the country. Several more outlandish possibilities now presented themselves. One was that Ali was working for the government, spotting and informing on potential radicals. It seemed unlikely, but she was aware she was entering a world where the normal rules didn't apply.

Dani James was less mysterious, but her evidence raised troubling questions. The fact that she had slept with Nazim days before his disappearance chimed with Mrs Jamal's account of the change she'd seen in her son. What didn't fit was McAvoy's memory of Mrs Jamal mentioning her suspicion of a previous relationship. Everything Mrs Jamal had told her to date suggested that Nazim had become pious and outwardly observant during his first term at Bristol. Yet his behaviour late the following June seemed to be that of a young man freshly released from doctrinal bonds.

She needed to talk to Mrs Jamal again. Strictly speaking, the proper course would have been to recall her to the witness box to deal with McAvoy's recollection. In reality, Jenny knew that she was far more likely to open up in private. It would be easy to hide behind the rules and let the law take its course, but the same instinct which had prompted her to take the case in the first instance wouldn't let her. This was one occasion on which the law could take second place to what felt right.

Amira Jamal lived in a modern five-storey building on a leafy, comfortable street north of the city centre. She buzzed Jenny through the main door and met her by the lift on the third floor, dressed soberly in a dark suit and long batik scarf. She led her into a small, tidy apartment, where they sat in the living room surrounded by mementos of Nazim's brief life. In her short career as coroner Jenny had already lost track of the number of homes she had visited that were maintained as private shrines to lost loved ones. The only unusual feature was a shelf lined with neatly labelled box files, all of which related in some way to Nazim's disappearance and the long slog of letter writing that had followed in its wake. A small desk was set up beneath it. On it were a laptop, assorted papers and a book entitled *A Family's Guide to Coroners' Inquests*.

Mrs Jamal had made tea and set out her best china. She poured Jenny a cup with a shaky hand. 'I'm sorry for how I was on the phone, Mrs Cooper. Sometimes I just can't stop myself.'

'I understand.'

'I see his face when he was a little boy. It's as if I'm still holding him . . .'

'You seem better today.'

'I did what you told me, went to the doctor. She gave me some pills.' She shook her head. 'I've never taken drugs in my life.'

Jenny picked up her teacup and placed it down again, finding the situation even more uncomfortable than she'd anticipated. 'Mrs Jamal, there are a couple of questions—'

'I have one first, Mrs Cooper. Why did you stop the inquest – the real reason?'

'It's not stopped, it's adjourned until Monday. Your former solicitor, Mr McAvoy, told me about something I ought to investigate.'

A look of alarm bordering on terror spread across Mrs Jamal's face. 'What?'

'I'm telling you this on the strict understanding that it goes no further than this room. Do I have your word on that?'

'Yes . . .'

'You remember that, before he went to prison, he hired a private investigator who found an old lady who claimed to have seen a black Toyota outside her house along the road from the halaqah?'

'I spoke to that man, Mr Dean – he said she was confused. She might even have got the night wrong.'

'She didn't. Mr Dean was probably trying not to raise your hopes . . . About six months later McAvoy asked him to follow it up. He found a toll collector on the old Severn Bridge. I spoke to him yesterday. A black Toyota came past his booth on the night of 28 June 2002. He remembers two white men in the front, two young Asian men in the back. He said they seemed frightened.'

'Who is this man? Why didn't he say any of this before?' Mrs Jamal asked, breathless with shock.

'It seems he was intimidated. I can't be sure he's telling the truth, but he claims one of the men in the front of the car tracked him down the following week and assaulted his young granddaughter – sprayed her hair with paint.'

Mrs Jamal held her head in her hands. 'I don't understand . . . Why now? Who was driving this car?'

'That's what I'm trying to find out.'

'You say Mr McAvoy knew? I never trusted that man.'

'Only some of it. Mr Dean died when Mr McAvoy was in prison.'

Mrs Jamal reached for a box of tissues.

'I know it's a lot for you to deal with,' Jenny said, 'but Mr McAvoy also remembers you mentioning that Nazim might have had a girlfriend before Dani James.'

'My son never touched her. She's a prostitute. She's staining his memory.'

'Why do you say that?'

'You heard what she said – she had a *disease*.'

'It could be important. Did you tell Mr McAvoy about another girl?'

She fell silent and held a Kleenex to her eyes.

'It's no disgrace, really it isn't. It's what young people do.'

'Not my people.'

'Mrs Jamal, I can't conduct an inquest without all the information . . . You do have a legal duty to assist me.'

'You've come here to threaten me?'

'Of course not.'

Mrs Jamal blew her nose loudly. 'All these questions. What's the point? You don't know who's lying. None of us can.' She lifted her gaze to a portrait photo of Nazim aged sixteen or thereabouts: a boy posing as a man. He had wide, soulful eyes and smooth, dark, unblemished skin. He was almost seraphic.

'I'd have fallen for him, so other girls must have,' Jenny said.

She waited for Mrs Jamal to recover herself.

There was a long, unbroken stretch of silence before Mrs Jamal said, 'I don't know what she was to Nazim. It was near the end of his first term. He'd left his phone here. A girl called and asked for him.'

'Did she say her name?'

'No.'

'What did she sound like?'

'About his age. Well spoken. White.'

'You could tell she was white?'

'Of course.'

'How do you know she wasn't just a friend?'

'When she heard my voice, she sounded guilty, as if I'd caught her out. She ended the call very quickly.'

'Did you ever mention this to Nazim?'

Mrs Jamal shook her head. Jenny saw in her face some-thing almost bleaker than grief – the thought of her son loving another woman more than her.

'I'm going to need to find out more about Nazim's life at that time. Do you think Rafi Hassan might have told his family anything?'

'They won't help you. They blame Nazim. I know they do. The looks his mother gave me, she might as well have spat in my face.'

'I think I'll go there this afternoon. I'll let you know if they have anything to say.'

Mrs Jamal shrugged.

Jenny sensed that the meeting had reached an end. The air

was growing thicker with emotion with every passing second. But there was one more question, ridiculous as it seemed, that she felt obliged to ask. 'When you gave evidence, you claim to have been followed in the street—'

'You don't believe me?'

'Tell me what happened.' Jenny gave a comforting smile. 'Please.'

'It started about two months ago when I filed the case with the County Court to get Nazim declared dead. A car would come and sit across the road. There were two men inside it, sometimes just one. Young men, in suits. I could see their faces from there.' She pointed over her shoulder to the French window that opened onto a small balcony at the side of the building. 'They were there when I left the house. Sometimes they'd follow in their car, sometimes on foot.'

Keeping her scepticism hidden, Jenny said, 'What did they look like?'

'Twenty-five to thirty. White. Both tall and with short hair, shaved at the sides – like the army.'

'Could you tell them apart?'

'Not really.'

'Have you seen them recently?'

Mrs Jamal shook her head. 'Not this week. But I still have phone calls in the night. It rings four, five times, then goes off. If I answer, there's no one there . . . Who do you think they are, Mrs Cooper?'

Imaginary demons, Jenny thought: white devils that look like soldiers.

Instead of the usual battle with rising, claustrophobic anxiety she fought when driving along a motorway, she felt at once removed from herself. Detached. It wasn't just the chemical veil of her medication still lying heavily across her halfway through the day; it was a sense of building unreality. There were so many unanswered questions, so many bizarre and alarming possibilities, that she couldn't make sufficient sense of things to find her way through them. Why would Nazim have been sleeping with a white girl at the height of his religious enthusiasm? Who was the man with the ponytail? Did he even exist? Was Mrs Jamal a fantasist? Was McAvoy? And why did he cast such a long shadow over her, his face hovering constantly at the back of her mind?

What was he *saying* to her?

She didn't have answers to any of it. It was as if she had stepped onto a moving walkway from which there was no exit, only a destination that remained an indistinct pinprick in the far distance. The spirit was moving her, as McAvoy might have said, and she had no choice in the matter.

Hassan's Grocery and Off-Licence had grown into a small supermarket specializing in Asian and West Indian foods. It was housed in what had once been a filling station, the forecourt now a customer car park. The dowdy area of Kings Heath, a sprawl of identical, faintly grubby Victorian terraces, was showing signs of going up-market. Jenny parked next to a shiny Mercedes, out of which climbed an Asian couple in matching his and hers leather jackets. Their infant daughter wore a pink one in the same style.

Jenny approached a teenage employee carting cases of cheap beer and asked him where she could find Mr Hassan. Only once she'd convinced him that she wasn't a tax inspector did he go in search of his boss. He reappeared shortly afterwards with the unconvincing explanation that Mr Hassan had gone out to a meeting and wasn't expected back until much later. Jenny glanced along the aisle to an office at the back, which was shielded from the shoppers by a pane of one-way glass, and told the assistant fine, but insisted he leave her card on Mr Hassan's desk with instructions to call her as soon as he returned. In the meantime she'd see if she couldn't speak to Mrs Hassan at home.

The young man's expression sharpened. 'What's this about exactly?'

'Something that happened eight years ago – his son went missing.'

'You mean Rafi?'

'Did you know him?'

'I'll give Mr Hassan the message,' he said, quickly adding, 'when he gets back.'

She hadn't yet turned the key in the ignition when her phone rang. She waited for several seconds before answering, letting him sweat.

'Hello, Jenny Cooper.'

'Imran Hassan. What can I do for you?'

'Would you rather not talk in front of your staff? If possible, I'd like to speak to your wife, too.'

The Hassans had made money. Their home was a large detached property in the affluent suburb of Solihull with a tarmac drive and electric gates flanked by a pair of stone lions. Mr Hassan, a man in his mid-sixties, drove a Jaguar. Quiet, well spoken and faultlessly polite, he led her inside to meet his wife, a still handsome woman dressed in an elegant black and gold embroidered salwar kameez. After formal introductions they sat in a warm conservatory surrounded by half an acre of formal garden, in the middle of which stood an ornate fountain fringed with palms: a golden carp spewed water into a pool lit with coloured lights.

Mrs Hassan said, 'We've been expecting this, Mrs Cooper, but we have nothing of any use to tell you. We have long ago resigned ourselves to never knowing what became of our son.'

Her husband nodded in uncertain agreement.

'I've no wish to stir up painful memories without good cause,' Jenny said, 'and I appreciate it's not your son's disappearance I'm investigating, but I'd be grateful if you would tolerate a few questions.'

'Certainly,' Mr Hassan said before his wife could protest.

Mrs Hassan glowered. 'The police said Rafi went abroad. I'm happy to take their word. But it was not his idea. He was a good student and a loyal son.'

Jenny said, 'Did you notice any change in him after he went to university? His religious beliefs, his appearance?'

'I'm sure Mrs Jamal has told you all this. It was her son who took him to that mosque. This is a Sufi family. Politics has no place in religion – that's what he was brought up to believe.'

Mr Hassan nodded. Dressed in a dark business suit and clean shaven, he showed no outward signs of observance. His store sold alcohol; they lived in a white neighbourhood.

'When did this change in him occur?' Jenny said. 'Was it during his first term at Bristol?'

'They put ideas in his head,' Mrs Hassan said sharply. 'He was going to be a lawyer—'

'Yes,' her husband interjected, 'it was during the first term. We believed it would be a phase. All young men need ideals, mine was creating a business. We hoped it would pass.'

'But it didn't?'

'Whoever these people were he'd been involved with, they poisoned them against their families, Mrs Cooper,' Mrs Hassan said. 'They convinced him our values were wrong. He came home for a week before Christmas and that was it. He stayed at college the rest of the time.'

'Where? Weren't the student halls closed out of term time?'

'With friends was all he'd tell us.'

'You must have been worried.'

'We have six children,' Mr Hassan said. 'We worry about each of them.'

Jenny noticed the couple exchange a glance, which she interpreted as Mr Hassan urging his wife not to let emotion overcome her. There was anger in her face, a need to cast blame.

'What did your son say about Nazim?' Jenny said.

'Until they disappeared, we hadn't even heard his name,' Mr Hassan said.

She aimed her next question directly at his wife. 'So why do you say that he was the one who led your son astray?'

'They were friends – that's what the police found out. They went to mosque together, and these meetings.'

Jenny pushed Mrs Hassan for further explanation but she could offer none. She had it fixed in her mind that Rafi had gravitated towards a fellow Muslim and fallen under his negative spell. Jenny asked for more detail of Rafi's behaviour during his time at university but was met with shrugs and shakes of the head. There had obviously been a confrontation in the early part of the Christmas vacation which still remained painfully unresolved.

'How often did you speak to your son between January and June?' Jenny asked them both.

Mr Hassan stared at the tabletop, leaving his wife to respond.

'I telephoned him a few times,' she said. 'Every week or two, to tell him we loved him, that we were still here for him.'

'It sounds almost as if he'd disowned you.'

'He was simply rebelling. That's what the young do in this country, isn't it? It comes with the luxury of not having to go out to work each day.'

Her husband nodded solemnly in agreement.

'This was new to us, Mrs Cooper,' Mrs Hassan continued. 'We knew he had the right values underneath – we had spent eighteen years giving them to him.' For the first time, her voice cracked. 'We assumed we had simply to wait for him to come back . . .'

'You didn't go to anyone for advice?'

Both shook their heads.

'Did Rafi ever mention any other friends or associates by name, anyone at the mosque, perhaps?'

'No,' Mrs Hassan said. 'He was very secretive on the matter. He talked a little about his studies, and he had a tutor, Tariq Miah, whom he mentioned once or twice.'

Jenny made a note of the name.

'Is there anything else I should know about your son – his hobbies, interests? Was he a sportsman?'

Mrs Hassan looked at her husband, then got up from the table and went into the next room. She came back with a folder which she handed to Jenny. She opened it to find a collection of examination certificates. Rafi Hassan had scored top marks in his A levels: Latin, Greek, Arabic and History.

'He was a gifted scholar,' Mrs Hassan said. 'Since he was eight years old he spent all his spare time studying and reading. He played cricket, but not like his brothers. No, not like them. Rafi was an intellectual.'

'Which must have made the change in him all the more shocking?' Jenny said.

Neither parent replied.

As she was leaving, Jenny overhead Mr Hassan whisper comfortingly to his wife that he would spend the rest of the afternoon at home. Making her way out between the stone lions, Jenny turned left and headed back towards Kings Heath.

Pulling into the forecourt of Mr Hassan's store for the

second time that day, she saw the young assistant carrying a heavy load of shopping to the car of an elderly customer. Her memory was correct – he did look like the photograph of Rafi she had in her files. She caught him on his way back inside.

'Excuse me.' He turned with a polite smile. 'Hello again. Could we have a word?'

He pointed inside. 'I'm due to go on the till.'

'It won't take a minute.'

'I can't—'

'Do you know what a coroner is?' Jenny said. 'You can talk to me now or receive a summons to come to court. Your choice.'

The assistant glanced nervously through the shop window at a colleague who was busy serving a customer. 'I can't talk here.'

'No problem. We'll go to my car.'

His name was Fazad, one of Mr Hassan's many nephews. He was eleven when Rafi went missing and said the family hardly mentioned him after that. He had never heard anything about his cousin's disappearance other than the official explanation that he'd gone abroad, nor had he ever been aware of any of his relations speculating where he had gone to, or with whom. The subject was off-limits, he said, as if it were somehow shameful. He remembered how as a kid Rafi was always held up as the model student, the kind of young man he and his other cousins should aspire to be.

Jenny asked if he knew what had happened during the Christmas vacation.

A queasy look came over Fazad's face. 'I don't want to disrespect my uncle. He's my boss, too.'

'Just between us,' Jenny said. 'It won't go any further.'

With another nervous glance into the shop, Fazad said, 'Rafi gave me a ride in his car when he came back from college, it was a little Audi A3. A few years old but tidy. I asked did his dad buy it for him. He said no, he'd bought it himself with his savings, but he didn't pay insurance or register it in his name because those were all kafir rules that didn't apply to Muslims.'

'Kafirs are non-believers, right?'

'Yeah . . . I thought it sounded kind of cool, but looking back it was strange. He had the beard and the prayer cap, but he was driving like a maniac, seeing how many cameras could flash him because he wouldn't get a ticket.'

'What did his father say?'

'That's what the fight was about.'

'Fight?'

'It's what I heard from my cousins – my uncle didn't like the way he was driving and took the keys away. Rafi beat him up so bad he broke his jaw and busted three of his ribs. His two older brothers took the car down the road that afternoon and set fire to it . . . That was the end of Rafi's car.'

# THIRTEEN

ANNA ROSE CROSBY WAS OFFICIALLY a missing person. Her picture was on page two of the *Post*, together with an article stating that the 'brilliant young nuclear scientist' had been missing for a little over a fortnight. Her mother was described as having been tearful and desperate as she made a moving plea from the front steps of her exclusive Cheltenham home. Jenny found herself unwittingly sucked into the dark, yet somehow thrilling, fantasy the picture editor had created. The colour photograph showed Anna Rose beaming, blonde and innocent: the perfect, unsuspecting bait for a violent sexual predator.

A document landed on her desk. 'The Toyotas,' Alison said. 'Forty-three of them registered in the areas you were interested in. What do you want to do with them?'

'I'll have a look through, tick the ones I'd like you to follow up.'

'The police haven't got anywhere with those poor Africans in the refrigerated trailer. That'll be back here tomorrow needing a full inquest. I can't imagine how I'm going to manage – all the witnesses in Nigeria or wherever they came from.'

'We'll cope. Did you get a statement from Madog yet?'

Alison raised her eyebrows.

'Well, could you do it today?' Jenny said, straining to remain calm.

'I can try, but if you remember I've got a meeting today – I did tell you.'

'You did?'

'Last week. It's a church event.'

'Oh—'

Alison said, 'Don't worry, I'm not deserting you. I'll be back by two.'

Curiosity got the better of her. Once Alison had left the room, Jenny clicked onto a search engine and typed in New Dawn Evangelical Church, Bristol. She followed the link and brought up an expensively produced website complete with a news ticker: 'Over four hundred attend family Eucharist – a new record!' The church proclaimed itself ordained by the Holy Spirit to carry God's word to the people of Bristol. Beneath his grinning photograph, Pastor Matt Mitchell wrote that New Dawn had been newly anointed to perform the ministry of healing. A number of miracles had taken place in recent months: a heroin addict had been made clean, a woman with multiple sclerosis had risen from her wheelchair, a child with leukaemia was in remission and a teenage schizophrenic had been completely cured. Dedicated healing services were being held every Sunday evening and Thursday lunchtime.

At the foot of Pastor Matt's inspiring message was a link to a page on which church members were invited to leave their prayer requests. Jenny clicked. One of the posts leaped out at her the instant the page appeared. It read: 'Please pray for my daughter, who has fallen into a "relationship" with a woman. Her father and I love her very much.'

She heard Alison's footsteps on the other side of the door and fumbled with her mouse to collapse the page. Her cheeks were flushed with embarrassment as her officer reappeared in the doorway.

'Rafi Hassan's law tutor emailed back,' Alison said. 'He's on study leave. He can see you at one.'

Jenny was pulling on her coat and heading out for her appointment at the campus when the phone on Alison's desk rang. She craned round to glance at the caller display on the sleek new console: Mrs Jamal. Jenny hovered in an agony of indecision, struggling with her conscience. Alison had already left for church, so it was down to her. Resolving to make it quick, she was reaching for the receiver when her mobile chimed. An instinctive reflex made her answer it first.

'Hello?'

'Mrs Cooper,' a familiar voice said. 'I was wondering how you were getting on looking for that car.' It was McAvoy.

'Oh, hi,' Jenny said, surprised at the flutter she felt on hearing his voice.

The landline stopped ringing. Relieved, Jenny went out into the hall and locked the door behind her, fielding the call on the move. Mrs Jamal could leave a message.

'We've gathered a list of possibles,' she said.

'Well done. I was worried the cops would stymie you.'

'I've got ways round them.'

'I'd like to hear.'

'Trade secret, I'm afraid.' God, what did she sound like?

As she stepped out onto the pavement she dimly heard the office phone start ringing again: Mrs Jamal refusing to take no for an answer.

McAvoy said, 'I was wondering if you might let me buy you that drink later, toss around a few ideas.'

'Oh? What drink was that?' She couldn't help herself. She was flirting with him like a simpering schoolgirl.

'The coffee you didn't have time for, but come evening it'll be a wee glass of something I shouldn't wonder.'

She got a grip. 'Thanks, but I really shouldn't until you've given evidence.'

'It's a bit late to stand on that rule, isn't it?'

'Alec, you know the issues—'

'I've been reading my law books, come up with a few ideas for you – like how to make those MI5 bastards cough up their files. If you get before the right High Court judge you might just swing it – there are still a few good ones left.'

'Friends of yours, are they?'

'I have my methods too.'

Jenny imagined the brown paper bag passing to the minor official in the Court Service in exchange for a favourable listing. McAvoy would take the credit and doubtless call in the favour. And what would he want in return? she wondered.

She knew she should put him off, have nothing to do with him until after the inquest, but couldn't summon the words to turn him down. Ignoring the chorus of warning voices in her head, she agreed to meet him at five-thirty in a wine bar by the law courts.

'I promise I'll behave myself,' he said.


Tariq Miah met Jenny outside the School of Law and took her behind the building into a formal garden – stark and bare in early February with a hint of frost still hanging in the air – but free from prying eyes. He was in his late thirties, the first threads of grey showing in his black hair and closely trimmed beard. His features were Middle Eastern: copper skin and dark eyes. From a brief glance at the faculty's website Jenny had learned that he was working his way steadily through the hierarchy. A specialist in constitutional law, he had joined as a junior research fellow in the late 1990s.

As they strolled along the narrow gravel paths, she explained that she was looking for an insight, anything to shed light on who or what Rafi Hassan and Nazim Jamal had become involved with. She mentioned Anwar Ali and the elusive mullah at the Al Rahma mosque, Sayeed Faruq, and asked if he knew them.

'Only by reputation,' he said, speaking in the overly precise manner of academic lawyers shieldeded from the day-to-day stresses of practice.

'And what was that?'

'I heard it said the mosque was a recruiting ground for Hizb ut-Tahrir. You're familiar with that organization?'

'I've read a little, but I'm still confused. The Security Services seem to associate it with terrorism, but it claims to be peaceful.'

'It doesn't advocate violence, but individuals within it obviously do.'

'Are you thinking of anyone in particular?'

'No. It's just to say that I wouldn't be surprised if the Al Rahma mosque acted as a conduit to others without a public profile.'

'You think it was a base for recruiters?'

'Perhaps.' He stopped to admire a bank of snowdrops. 'I would be surprised at Jamal and Hassan being assimilated so quickly, however. Hizb tends to indoctrinate new members over several years before asking them to swear an oath of allegiance.'

'Allegiance to what, exactly?'

'The organization. The cause of bringing into existence a global caliphate. It's not a conventional political party working for the short term, it sees itself as doing God's will over as many generations as it takes. It has a three-stage plan: to establish cells and networks of members, to build opinion amongst the Muslim population in favour of an Islamic state, and finally to infiltrate the institutions and governments of target countries to effect a revolution from within.'

Jenny said, 'One thing that puzzles me is why young men, let alone women, are drawn to these ideas. I mean, who'd want to live in Iran?'

'We all fantasize about removing the mess from our lives, cutting a swathe through the chaos and replacing it with certainties,' Miah said. 'What more fearful time is there in life than the threshold of adulthood? If someone were to offer you a free pass to status and security and make you feel morally superior into the bargain, it would be hard to resist, would it not? And if you already believe yourself to be a stranger in your own land it would become almost impossible not to be seduced: all men are conquerors by instinct, it's in our DNA. One's own seed must prevail. All our complex Western political institutions have evolved out of the need to check such impulses.'

'Both these boys came from good families. Integrated, established, English-speaking—'

'The parents were under no illusions about who they were – outsiders. It's their offspring, neither outsiders or insiders who have to fight for their identity.'

'Did you see that in Rafi Hassan?'

Having had his fill of the snowdrops, Miah resumed his meander. 'I had very little to do with him. I make clear to Asian students that I'm there for them if they need me, but he never approached me privately.'

Jenny tried to read him. There was something coded in his careful manner, a vague sense that he was inviting a conclusion that he wasn't prepared to spell out.

'I don't know if you've read about my inquest,' Jenny said. 'I've granted rights of audience to an outfit called the British Society for Islamic Change. I think Anwar Ali's involved with them.'

Miah nodded. 'Essentially the same organization as Hizb ut-Tahrir, or a branch of it. They're very clever. They seduce the government into believing they're moderates providing for the needs of disaffected Asian youth, and inculcate themselves into the Establishment. It becomes racist to question them. But the philosophy remains the same: Islam is the one and only truth and it must prevail.' He gave a slight shake of his head, his eyes suddenly those of an older man, telling the story of long years of fruitless struggle. 'We are at a bad juncture in history, Mrs Cooper. Life has become too fraught and complex for most of us to understand our place in it. The forces of liberal progression offer only more uncertainty, more competition, more casualties. Is it any wonder that fundamentalists emerge, saying we should drop anchor and stop the ship before it dashes on the rocks?'

'I think what you're trying to tell me is that you think those boys went abroad to fight.'

Miah exhaled, his breath a heavy cloud of vapour. He stopped and turned to face her, fixing her with a look that was both pained and profoundly serious. 'When they disappeared I was only beginning to understand the nature of the problem. But now I can tell you, if I were to draw a template for the ideal recruit to the extremist cause, both of them would fit it perfectly. Middle class, highly intelligent, ambitious, culturally displaced and as emotionally vulnerable as any young person. They were there for the taking. Eight years on it's not just one or two or even tens, it's hundreds and thousands.' He was fired by a tortured passion. 'We live in a country that doesn't know itself, Mrs Cooper. We keep moving, but beyond the base struggle for survival we have no idea why.'

Having said his piece, Miah retreated to his academic shell. He told Jenny that both MI5 and police officers had questioned him extensively at the time, but little of note had emerged. He denied that they had been in touch recently. Any faith he once had in the ability of the state to address these problems, he said, had long since evaporated. He no longer sat on policy-making committees or wrote papers to inform government departments; he wrote books and articles and tried his best to inspire the students who passed through his classes with values that would inoculate them against extremism.

'But the fundamentalists do have a point,' he said as they neared the garden gates and the end of their meeting. 'Without a story to explain ourselves, we are nothing.'

Miah's words lodged stubbornly in her mind as she walked back through the thin drizzle to the office. They had pierced her defences and unsettled the waters that her medication struggled to still. Storyless herself, searching for the pieces of her childhood that might explain what lay in her threatening, still unexplored recesses, he had loosened her grip on solid reality a little further. Every face in the street, lined or fresh, bright or dulled, seemed confident in its history, rooted in a certainty she had long since lost.

Walking past a florist's, she glanced at her reflection in the window and for a brief second didn't recognize herself. It was a ghostly, transparent, semi-being that looked back at her. A surge of panic tightened her chest and throat. She quickened her pace, focusing on the strength in her limbs, the breath in her lungs, the life in her. Her state, she realized, was due to being *aware* of the part that was missing. Rafi and Nazim hadn't been. Their voids had been filled before they had even become conscious of them. Darting across the road, dodging the traffic, a phrase surfaced from long-forgotten school days: *nature abhors a vacuum*. If nature forbids an absence to occur, it must, as she had always suspected, be perverted and unnatural forces that opened up fissures in the fabric of reality, and untethered nascent souls from their moorings.

Hurrying past a row of scruffy shops, turning her head

away from their plate-glass fronts, her spiralling thoughts spewed up yet another realization: that the evil she touched in her dreams was such an absence, a nothingness into which innocence was easily seduced.

Nazim and Rafi had passed through the vortex, evaporated with a trace, and it fell to her, to her of all people, to follow them.

Jenny leaned heavily against the reassuringly heavy and cumbersome front door and made for the sanctuary of her office. Her brief interview with Miah had disturbed her to an extent which felt out of all proportion. Here was where she made sense of things, surrounded by her books and the trappings of office, the objects that told her who she was and all that she stood for.

Alison looked up with a start as she entered. She was sitting at her desk in her overcoat, her face drained of colour. An answerphone message was playing: Mrs Jamal pathetically pleading for someone to answer, *please*. She was frightened, she said, there had been more phone calls in the night. Wouldn't somebody help her? She lapsed into sobs and sniffles.

'I thought she was going to stop that,' Jenny said.

'She left three like it. Claimed she was being watched—'

'I'll call her,' Jenny said and started towards her office.

'She's dead, Mrs Cooper.'

Jenny stopped midway across the room. 'What?'

'I called her back,' Alison said, 'just now. A young constable answered. A neighbour found her body in the front garden about fifteen minutes ago. She'd fallen from her balcony.'

Numb, Jenny glanced at her watch. It was a quarter past two. It had been an hour and a half since she had left the office.

'When did she make her last call?'

'Just after one,' Alison said. 'I feel dreadful ... You can never see it coming, can you?'

Jenny left a message on McAvoy's phone telling him she wouldn't be able to meet him, something – she didn't say what – had come up. She replaced the receiver and reached for her pills, shook out one of each and swallowed. She doodled agitatedly on a legal pad while waiting for them to dull the frantic thoughts that were crowding her mind. She felt nauseous with guilt that she hadn't answered Mrs Jamal's call. An irrational part of her blamed McAvoy for phoning when he had. A second later and she would have answered Mrs Jamal's call, and perhaps ... It didn't bear thinking about.

# FOURTEEN

A POLICE CORDON HAD GONE up across the street, attracting a small crowd of onlookers eager for a glimpse of the corpse. Jenny pushed through them and caught sight of DI Pironi leaving the front of the building. It was his patch. New Bridewell police station was less that half a mile away. She caught up with him as he stood on the pavement pulling off latex gloves and the elasticated plastic bags that covered his shoes.

'David—'

'Jenny.' He didn't seem pleased to see her. 'You can't go in, I'm afraid. Forensics have got to sweep it first.'

'What happened?'

'Looks like she fell from the balcony.'

She looked up at the building. 'How could she fall? Those railings must be waist high.'

He balled up the plastic bags and gloves and tossed them into the gutter. 'She could have jumped, I suppose.'

'Why would she do that?'

'No idea. You can take a look at her if you like. She's still there.' He gestured to a female constable who didn't look old enough to be out of school. 'Show the coroner the body, would you? Don't get too close.' He aimed a key fob at a pool car that was double-parked in the street. 'We've booked her in for a post-mortem early this afternoon. I thought you'd appreciate a swift turnaround, what with the inquest and everything. I expect we'll talk in the morning.' He gave her a flat smile and left.

Jenny followed the constable, stepping over the cordon tape and crossing a damp patch of lawn around to the side of the building. Two more uniforms stood guard in front of a temporary screen made from black plastic stretched between two poles. The constable said she was permitted to look around the edge but not to go beyond the barrier. Jenny moved towards it, reminding herself that it was just a body behind there, an empty shell, and took another step forward.

The corpse was naked and the legs soiled. It lay in a contorted heap: bent in the middle, partially kneeling, a dislocated arm twisted under the torso, face planted in the grass. Jenny was surprised at how little shock she felt.

'Did anyone see it happen?' she said.

The constable said, 'No one's come forward yet. A neighbour thinks he might have heard a scream.'

'What happened to her clothes?'

'In a heap on the sitting-room floor – next to a whisky bottle.'

'*Whisky?* She's a Muslim.'

'The man who found her said she reeked of it.'

A sense of loyalty and a large measure of guilt propelled Jenny to the mortuary. Next of kin – her ex-husband and a sister in Leicester – had been informed. According to the detective sergeant she had spoken to, neither had showed any inclination to get involved. Both, apparently, had listened to the news in silence and merely thanked the officer for letting them know. He had gained the impression that Mrs Jamal's apparent suicide hadn't come as a shock to either of them.

Jenny sat and waited by the defunct vending machines in the empty reception area. It was nearly six p.m. and all but one of the technicians had left for the night. The only sound in the building was the whine of the surgical buzz saw, which she pictured Dr Kerr carefully tracing around Mrs Jamal's skull, not forgetting the little v-cut at the back to stop the excised portion slipping when replaced.

In the silent thirty minutes that followed Jenny couldn't help but imagine the procedure being conducted on the other side of the wall. The brain would be lifted free of the skull and cut into slices on the stainless-steel counter. A small sample would be taken for analysis, and the remainder would be stuffed unceremoniously into a polythene bag along with the rest of the carved-up internal organs and pushed back into the abdominal cavity. She could tolerate the dissection of liver and kidneys, even heart and lungs, but there was something about the treatment meted out to the brain that felt sacrilegious.

Andy Kerr came out to meet her already washed and scrubbed. The smell of soap only partially obscured that of sickly disinfectant, which, after a day in the autopsy room lodged deep in a pathologist's pores.

'It's pretty much as per the police report,' he said rapidly, eager to finish up and get home. 'There was a dislocated shoulder, neck fracture and broken ribs. Those alone wouldn't have been fatal – cause of death was cardiac arrest, probably caused by the shock of the fall. Judging from the photographs of the body at the locus I'd say it was pretty much instantaneous. It didn't look as if she moved after impact.'

'What about alcohol?'

'We'll know in the morning, but there seemed to be a large amount of what smelled like whisky in the stomach.'

'Could you tell if she was a regular drinker?' Jenny said.

'Her liver was perfectly healthy. No scarring. I've asked for tests that'll tell us if it was an unusual occurrence or not.

Anyone who consumes alcohol regularly develops certain enzymes to digest it.'

'Was there anything else in her stomach – had she taken any tablets?'

'No. Apart from the alcohol it was virtually empty.'

Jenny nodded, her uneasy sense of being personally responsible for Mrs Jamal's death intensifying. How much had Mrs Jamal drunk after she'd dodged her call? Could anything she might have said stopped her, or would she have snapped at her to calm down and merely hastened the end?

'Are you all right?' Andy said, 'You look—'

'I knew her. Her son—'

'The police told me. I'm sorry. But I don't have to tell you, we see a lot of suicides like this. Drunk, naked. There's always something that's tipped them over the edge. I guess it was the inquest.'

'She fought for it for eight years,' Jenny said.

Andy shrugged. 'Maybe the fight was the one thing that kept her going.'

'Surely she would have waited for a verdict?'

'What if it turned out to be the wrong one?'

The Coroner's Rules obliged the coroner to step aside while the police investigated a suspicious death, but Jenny was in no mood to wait. She knew her motives were partly selfish – the urgent need to absolve herself of blame – but there was also something else, a niggling fear that Mrs Jamal's emotional phone calls weren't entirely the product of delusion after all. Painful experience had taught her how easily irrational thoughts could take hold, but what if she had been far saner than she appeared? What if someone *had* been watching her? Or what if she had been lying and hiding evidence vital to the inquest all along?

By the time she had crossed the hospital car park Jenny

had convinced herself of the need to trespass on police territory. She imagined Pironi's foot soldiers, lumbering and incompetent, knowing nothing of Mrs Jamal's state of mind or history. Whatever they could do, she could do better and faster.

Revving the engine to crank up the sluggish heater, she started to make calls. She checked in with Ross and told him she'd be back late. She caught Alison as she was leaving the office and told her to record Mrs Jamal's surviving messages to tape and pass a copy to the police. She already had. Lastly she called directory enquiries and tried to track down Zachariah Jamal. She got hold of the number of his dental practice: her call was answered by a machine. She tried the emergency number it gave out and reached the off-duty receptionist, who was dealing with a crying baby. The woman refused to give out Mr Jamal's private number and would only agree to pass on her details.

Waiting for his call back, Jenny checked her own messages. There were two from consultants at the Vale asking if death certificates had been issued for their respective deceased patients – second only to being sued, the prospect of their professional competence being scrutinized in a public inquest was the most frightening prospect a doctor could face – and one from McAvoy. Sounding apologetic, he said, 'Sorry you can't make it – I'll have one for you. You know where to find me if you change your mind.' She was fighting the temptation to call him back – but to say what? – when a beep indicated an incoming call.

Zachariah Jamal sounded as if he was phoning from outside his home: there was traffic noise in the background, his voice was brittle and uncertain. She wondered if he had even broken the news of his first wife's death to the new Mrs Jamal and children. Drunk, naked and very publicly dead, they'd know soon enough.

'What is it I can do for you?' he said. 'I've had very little contact with Amira in recent years.'

Jenny said, 'It looks as if she might have taken her own life. Would that surprise you?'

He sighed. 'I don't know. She was a very complicated woman. Emotional, but . . .'

She waited for him to articulate his thoughts.

'. . . determined. Long after I had resigned myself to Nazim's death, she kept on.'

'Why do you say *death*?'

'Of course he died. Probably in Afghanistan. I know my own son. If he were alive he would have made contact.'

'But your wife, your *ex*-wife, didn't want to believe that?'

He paused for a moment. She could feel the force of his suppressed emotion. 'No. She didn't want to believe that.'

'I suppose it's possible that the inquest into your son's disappearance was confronting her with having to accept that.'

'Yes . . .'

'I think we might be having the same thought, Mr Jamal. Maybe you could give me your version?'

'Our contact has been entirely businesslike. I don't know what was in her mind.'

You don't want to get involved, Jenny thought, too many painful memories, guilt layered upon guilt. Shut the door and bolt it. Forget that she or Nazim ever existed.

Jenny said, 'I've met her a few times in the last two weeks. She was emotional, maybe even a little paranoid, but I wouldn't say depressed. Depressed people go into themselves, shut off from the world. She'd forced an inquest, she was being dynamic. Wouldn't she have wanted to hear the jury's verdict?'

'I really can't say.'

'I can imagine a bereaved mother killing herself in the

belief that she might be reunited with her son. Is that possible?'

Mr Jamal didn't answer.

'Was your ex-wife a religious woman?'

'Very much so.'

'Excuse my ignorance, but doesn't Islam consider suicide a serious sin?'

'It does,' he said quietly.

'I wouldn't expect someone who feels suicidal to think logically—'

'She must have been ill,' he said, and then, with a catch in his voice, 'she must have been very ill . . .'

'The post-mortem showed that she'd been drinking whisky shortly before her death. Quite a substantial amount.'

At this Mr Jamal fell completely silent. Jenny could hear the wind over his handset, a car pass by.

'I'm just trying to get a picture of what it would mean. Alcohol, suicide – even if she were ill, certain taboos can be more powerful even than the disease. I was with her yesterday, she wasn't psychotic.'

Faintly, Mr Jamal said, 'I agree with you, Mrs Cooper. I don't know what to say. It doesn't make any sense.'

'I'll let you go now,' Jenny said, 'but there's one more thing. Has your wife ever told you anything about Nazim's disappearance, about his friends, anything she might not have wanted to be publicly known?'

'No. There was nothing. That's what drove her – the need to know.'

The last members of the forensic team were dribbling out of the building and climbing into their minibus. A single constable was winding up the plastic cordon tape. Business appeared to be nearly over for the day. The front door was propped open with an upturned broom. Jenny stepped inside and took the lift up to Mrs Jamal's floor. DI Pironi and a younger plain-clothes officer with patchy stubble and his hair in corn rows were locking up the apartment as she approached along the landing.

Jenny said, 'Hi. Any objection to me having a look around?'

The detectives exchanged a look. 'Mrs Cooper, the coroner,' Pironi said to his subordinate. 'I think we should christen her Mrs Snooper.'

The young guy smiled and ran his eyes over her, thinking – she could read his mind – *just about*.

Jenny snapped angrily, 'Have you got a problem with that or not?'

Pironi looked at his fancy watch and sighed. 'As long as you're quick.'

'Mind if I catch a smoke, boss?' the younger man said. Pironi waved him on and drew out a set of keys, sorting through them laboriously as if she were asking a huge and unreasonable favour of him.

'Have you taken anything away?' Jenny said.

'Some prints, a pile of clothes and a whisky bottle. Looks like she swallowed about half of it – enough to send anyone out the bloody window.' He found the key, unlocked the door and held it open for her. He might as well have said, '*After you, your ladyship*.'

Jenny stepped inside. It looked and smelled just as it had yesterday, a vaguely exotic scent in the air: herbs and spices. She pushed open the bathroom and bedroom doors. Both were spotless and tidy. The bedspread was drawn tight across the single bed, chintz cushions arranged against the headboard. The kitchen, too, was in perfect order. There was a single dirty cup in the sink, breakfast crockery sitting clean on the drainer. A shopping list was stuck to the fridge with a quaint, floral-patterned magnet.

'Mind if I look in the drawers?' she said to Pironi, who was waiting impatiently in the doorway.

'Go ahead.'

She pulled several open: cutlery, tea towels, utensils. Everything clean and in its proper place.

'Any sign of prescription medication?'

'Nope.'

She opened an overhead cupboard and found the source of the smell: bunches of dried thyme and outsize jars of spices. 'No booze in the house apart from the whisky?'

'Not a drop.'

'No note?'

Pironi shook his head.

Jenny stepped past him and went into the sitting room where she had sat yesterday morning. It was precisely as she remembered it, only stiller. There was an inertia about the rooms of the recently deceased, as if the air had ceased moving. She could smell the carpet and the fabric of the furniture: the place, rather than the person who had inhabited it. Her eyes circled the room a second time. Something had changed.

'Has anything been moved in here?' she said.

'Just that chair.' He pointed to the wooden upright chair which yesterday had been at the desk in the corner. It was now on the opposite side of the room next to the French window leading to the balcony. 'It was where you're standing. Her clothes were in a heap next to it with the bottle.'

'With the top screwed on?'

'Who are you trying to be, Miss fucking Marple?'

Jenny let his remark pass without comment. 'Were the curtains open? What about the French window?'

Pironi rolled his eyes. 'The curtains were closed and there was one lamp on in the corner. She sat there drinking, took her clothes off then jumped out of the window.'

'It's only three storeys down.'

'If you're having a brainstorm, you don't fetch out the plumb line and measuring tape,' Pironi said. 'Seen enough? I'm expecting a call from my lad in Helmand.'

'Won't be a moment.' She moved over to the French window and tried to picture a naked Mrs Jamal climbing over the railings. It wouldn't have been a graceful exit. She turned and took one last look around the room. The photographs of Nazim were all arranged as she remembered them, as were the ornaments on the shelf unit: fussy china figurines and several shiny sporting trophies.

She was walking back to the door when she noticed – the two shelves above the desk. The day before they had held half a dozen grey box files. Now there was a stack of magazines on the top shelf and a few paperbacks on the bottom.

'Did you take any files from here?' Jenny said. 'There was a whole row of them on that shelf when I was here yesterday. All her paperwork to do with her son.'

'We didn't take anything.'

'Has anyone else been here? You know who I mean.'

'Straight up. There weren't any files.' He scratched his head. 'I don't know . . . Maybe she put them out with the rubbish?'

Pironi left Jenny to deal with the caretaker, Mr Aldis, an irascible old man irritated at being dragged away from the football match he was watching on television. The communal dustbins were in a locked cupboard on the outside of the building. They hadn't been emptied for five days and he swore that the police hadn't asked for access to them. Jenny borrowed a pair of rubber gloves and spent a cold and unpleasant hour sifting though garbage. There was no sign of any box files.

*

'Why didn't you tell me?' McAvoy said. 'It's a cop in here who tipped me off. Dear God. *Dead* . . .' Glasses clinked in the background. He sounded as if he'd made a night of it.

The hands-free cradle in her car had snapped and she had the phone wedged on her shoulder as she drove homewards, praying she wouldn't meet a police car.

'The police think she jumped,' Jenny said.

'She'd be going straight to hell, then,' McAvoy said. 'Like my crew – no messing. Suicides are roasted in fire "which is easy for Allah", is what it says in the Koran. Guy inside lent it to me one time.'

'Her files were missing. All her papers connected with the case.'

'The cops would have had those, no danger.'

'Pironi denies it.'

'St Peter denied our Lord three times and still got to be Bishop of Rome.'

'He looked me in the eye. I believed him.'

'That's because you're an untainted soul, Mrs Cooper . . . Fucking *dead*. Why?'

'She'd been drinking. Half a bottle of whisky.'

'Poor soul . . . Poor wretched soul.'

She was clear of the bridge and skirting around Chepstow. She'd soon be past the racecourse and into the gorge of the valley out of radio contact.

'I'm about to lose my signal. I'll update you soon as I hear anything.'

McAvoy said, 'I know what you're doing, Jenny. I understand you want to stay above board, but I could help you . . . If you really want to dig down to the shit, you're going to need a man like me.'

It was six steeply winding miles through dark woods between St Arvans and Tintern, the ancient village with its ruined abbey at which she would turn up the narrow lane and climb the hill to Melin Bach. Since the night the previous June, when – in the thick of the Danny Wills case and suffering from acute anxiety – she had pulled up in the forest car park and wrestled with desperate impulses, she dreaded this stretch of her journey. This late in the evening there was little or no traffic. A skin of water lay over the surface of the road and the bends, always sharper and longer than they appeared on approach, forced her to slow to a crawl or risk plunging down the steep embankment. Each year they claimed several lives.

She switched on the radio to distract her imagination from turning shadows into listless ghosts, and tried to lose herself in the gentle classical music. She conjured a pastoral scene of fields and wild flowers, attempting to engage all the senses as Dr Allen had advised her, but the purer she made the image, the sharper the point of her unprompted fear became. It was a cold, menacing, tangible presence, an entity that clung to her.

Go away, go away, she repeated in her head, trying to force herself back to her idyll. Then out loud, 'You're not real. Leave me alone . . . Leave me alone.'

There was a sudden noise, a sniff, a stifled sob of rejection. Jenny's eyes flicked left to the passenger seat. Mrs Jamal's wide, black, desolate eyes looked momentarily back at her then vanished. Jenny forced a long, deep breath against her pounding heart and pushed the throttle down as far as she dared. She had been battered with all manner of symptoms, but she'd never seen things before.

She hurried from the car to the house, rationalizing that her imagination had been playing tricks. The eyes were flickers of reflected light, the face a fleeting shadow. It was only natural for the mind to make pictures out of darkness.

She locked and bolted the front door.

Hostile rap music with a window-shaking bass boomed

out of Ross's room. She called up to say hi, but there was no answer. It was nearly eleven, too late to eat. She needed to calm down. What she would have given for a drink. She stepped into her study, resolving to release her tension onto the page.

She switched on the light and saw that the papers on her desk had been disturbed and that the drawer where she kept her journal wasn't fully closed. She wrenched it open. It was there beneath the jumble of envelopes and writing paper – the black cover clasped shut by the band of elastic – but had she left it that way, with the spine to the left?

'Hi. You're late.'

She spun round to see Ross in the doorway dressed in a hooded sweat top and baggy Indian trousers.

'Have you been touching my things?'

'No . . .'

'Tell me the truth.'

'There was no food in the house. I was looking for money to go down to the pub and get some.'

'Don't lie to me.'

'I didn't touch anything.'

'You must never go through my desk. My personal things are in there.'

'Yeah, a lot of crap.' He turned and went up the stairs.

She chased after him. 'Ross, I'm sorry . . .'

'You're a mess,' he said, more in pity than anger.

'Ross, please—'

He crashed into his bedroom and slammed the door.

# FIFTEEN

SHE WOKE AT FIVE, drained by the fitful dreams that had disturbed her shallow sleep. Her body was exhausted but her brain was firing, making wild connections and hurling itself into crazy speculation: a confusion of police and government agents, secret deals and concealed evidence; and, hovering in the shadows, the faintly smiling figure of McAvoy. Where did he fit in? Was he genuine or was he, as Alison feared, using her? As if in answer, two images presented themselves at once: an angel and a demon. One of them was him, she was sure, but which she couldn't tell. Perhaps he was both.

The initial shock of Mrs Jamal's sudden death had dulled to a low ache that contained within it several different sources of pain. There were guilt and pity, but beneath them a sense of the shame that she must have carried with her in the moments before her death leap. Jenny still couldn't relate the well-dressed woman who had arrived in her office, and who had sat with such quiet dignity in court, with the crumpled remains she had viewed on the grass the previous afternoon. She climbed out of bed, pulled on a jumper over her pyjamas and went downstairs to make a pot of coffee, which she took through to her study. She sifted through the notes and papers she had brought home, now searching for another piece in the jigsaw: the thing that Mrs Jamal hadn't told, the thing that had pushed her over the edge.

She read and reread the original police statements, then picked over every word that had been said in court. Apart from the fact that Mrs Jamal had reacted so violently to Dani James's evidence, there was no clue. She tried to recall the conversation with her at her flat, wishing now she had made notes. Mrs Jamal had been distressed when she heard about Madog's evidence but mistrustful of both McAvoy and his investigator friend: there had been tears, but Madog's story had felt like more mud in the same waters. It was only when Jenny had asked her whether there had been another girl that she had reacted differently and reached a state beyond tears. She had remembered the voice of the girl who telephoned as if it were yesterday – she was Nazim's age, well spoken and white. It couldn't have been Dani James, Mrs Jamal would have noticed her Mancunian accent. Their exchange had been brief, yet it had affected her profoundly. Jenny groped for possible explanations. It was more than mere disapproval. Was there a scandal – had the girl been pregnant? Had Mrs Jamal caught them together in her apartment perhaps? Had she driven the girl away and forced such a rift with her son that he never forgave her? And if that was the case, why had the girl never come forward?

Apart from Dani James, the only young female to have given a formal statement to the police was Sarah Levin, now Dr Levin in the department of physics. She was another pending witness, whom Jenny should not contact before the resumed hearing; her instinct told her it was a further occasion on which the rules should be stretched. Besides, she was in desperate need of a lead, anything to unlock the past.

To much grumbling and protest, Jenny dragged Ross from his bed at seven and dropped him at a café near the sixth-form college, still groaning, before eight. She had planned to apologize for her outburst the previous evening, but he had insisted on sleeping for the entire forty-minute journey. It was becoming a pattern: during their increasingly rare moments together he would do anything but communicate with her.

Sarah Levin's home address, gleaned from a sequence of early-morning phone calls to obstructive university officials, was a second-floor apartment in a large Victorian terraced house close to Bristol Downs: an expensive piece of property for a young woman. The label next to the doorbell said Spencer-Levin, and it was a man's voice that came over the intercom.

Jenny announced herself and said that she needed to speak to Dr Levin immediately.

'She's in the shower. And she's got a class at nine,' he said, with the self-important tone she associated with corporate lawyers or investment bankers.

Irritable following her bad night, Jenny said, 'Didn't I make myself clear? I'm a coroner conducting an official inquiry.'

There was a brief pause.

'Don't you have to have a warrant or something?'

'No. Now are you going to help me out or make this difficult?'

She heard him curse. The buzzer sounded angrily.

He didn't look like a lawyer or any sort of professional for that matter. He was wearing a T-shirt under a canvas jacket and trainers. His shoulder-length hair was tweaked and gelled and his jeans slung just-so across hips that were starting to fill out. Advertising or TV, Jenny guessed, a dress-down business that seems like a good idea when you're twenty-one but becomes embarrassing by forty. Spencer – she assumed that was his surname and he didn't have the manners to introduce himself – showed her into an open-plan kitchen-diner. It was a self-consciously stark affair: a polished wood floor and everything white, a single abstract print on the wall.

'I've got to go. She'll be out in a minute.'

He picked up a designer shoulder bag and headed out to ply his uncertain trade.

Sarah Levin came in towelling her long blonde hair. She was tall and slim, effortlessly attractive in a way Jenny could only describe as refined. Spencer had struck exceptionally lucky.

'Hi. What can I do for you?' she said, guardedly. 'It's Mrs Cooper, isn't it?'

'Yes. Sorry to disturb you at home,' Jenny said, aware Sarah Levin's arresting beauty had temporarily distracted her. 'There are a few questions I'd like to ask you . . .'

'Your office called the other day. I was told the inquest had been adjourned.'

'Only until next week. I'm trying to fill in some detail on Nazim Jamal's first term at Bristol. I understand you and he were both studying physics?'

'We were.' She placed the towel on the counter and pushed her hair back from her face. It reached nearly down to her waist.

'Did you talk? Were you friends?'

'Not particularly. Can I get you some coffee?'

'No thanks. You go ahead.'

Sarah flicked the switch on an electric espresso maker and fetched a stylish white cup and saucer from a glass-fronted cupboard. Jenny watched for a moment, sensing her tension. *Not particularly.* What did that mean?

Jenny said, 'His mother died yesterday.'

'Oh . . .' Sarah turned, unscrewing a jar of coffee, 'I'm sorry.'

'I don't suppose you ever met her?'

'No.'

'She told me that she suspected Nazim had become friendly with a girl towards the end of that first term.'

'I can't say I remember.'

'So you were close enough that you'd have noticed?'

'Not really ... Obviously I've thought more about him since than I did at the time.' She leaned back against the counter waiting for the coffee maker to heat up. She seemed uncomfortable, on edge.

'Did you ever call Nazim on his mobile?'

She shook her head. 'I don't think so.'

'Mrs Jamal answered a call on his phone that December. It was a girl – well spoken, English. She acted as if she'd been caught out, as if she knew Nazim's mother wouldn't approve. Any idea who she might have been?'

'Sounds like half the girls at Bristol. Sorry. Not a clue.'

'How close to him were you?'

'We went to the same lectures and seminars. We partnered up in a few practicals. He was just one of the crowd, not a friend of mine, especially ... or of anyone's for that matter. He was pretty determined to set himself apart, as far as I remember.'

'Because of his faith?'

'The Muslim boys tended to hang out together. Still do.' She turned round to check the machine.

Jenny said, 'So he was in your class, he set himself up as religious, separate – wouldn't you find it odd that he had a white girlfriend?'

'Did his mother see her? There were plenty of Muslim girls who spoke without an Asian accent.' She pressed a button that noisily filled her cup. 'I hardly knew him, but people like me weren't exactly going to throw themselves at a guy with a beard and whatever you call those clothes.'

Jenny watched her tap the spent grains into the waste disposal and wipe up the drips on the counter, thinking she didn't look much like a physicist. Back in her student days the scientists had been mostly lank-haired guys with bad skin. The few women among them were the kind that always looked as if they were about to set off on a hiking trip.

Jenny said, 'What's your specialism, if you don't mind my asking?'

'Particle physics, theoretical stuff. Looking for new forms of energy – that's the Holy Grail.'

'Must be quite a man's world.'

'My family were all scientists. I never thought of it that way.'

But I bet you like the attention, Jenny thought unkindly.

'You gave a statement to the police after Nazim and the other boy disappeared,' Jenny prompted. 'You said you'd once heard him in the canteen talking about "brothers" who'd gone to Afghanistan.'

'That's right . . . He was with a group of friends. It seemed like a bit of bravado at the time. I only heard snatches – boys talking about how cool it would be to fire guns and kill people, that sort of thing. They were laughing, showing off to each other.'

'You don't remember anything more specific?'

'If I had, I would have told the police.' She sipped her coffee with a steady hand. 'It was a hell of a long time ago.'

'No gossip around the department? Rumours, speculation?'

'No.' Sarah Levin frowned and shook her pretty head. 'It seems just as weird now as it did then. He just . . . vanished.'

Alison was in one of her tense, frosty moods, which had been become an increasingly regular feature in recent weeks. Annoyed and refusing to say why, she bustled noisily around her office and banged the cupboard doors in the kitchenette. Jenny had put them down to menopausal mood swings or the usual tussles with her husband – and doubtless the issue with her daughter was part of it – but this morning's atmosphere was unusually thick. The more Jenny tried to ignore her, the heavier Alison's footsteps became. Reading through the latest batch of post-mortem reports she tolerated it for nearly an hour. She was switching her attention to the list of black Toyotas when Alison entered without knocking and dumped a pile of mail on top of the document she was reading.

'Your post. And some of yesterday's, too.'

Holding her temper, Jenny said, 'Is something the matter?'

'I'm sorry, Mrs Cooper?'

'You seem out of sorts.'

Alison forced a tight, patient smile, 'I'll be out of your hair in a minute. I've arranged to take a statement from Mr Madog.'

The game was following its usual pattern: Alison would repeatedly deny anything was wrong until finally, as if she were conceding only to satisfy some irrational need of Jenny's, she would tell her what it was.

'I'll get through all the outstanding files this weekend,' Jenny said. 'If there are consultants at the Vale hassling you for decisions you can tell them Monday at the latest.'

'Last time I checked we were no more behind than normal.'

'Then is there something I've overlooked?'

'I don't think so.'

'Anything I've done?'

Alison's frown hardened.

Jenny said, 'I sense I'm getting warmer.'

Alison sighed. 'It's not for me to tell you how to do your job, Mrs Cooper, but I do sometimes get a little tired of being piggy in the middle.'

'Between whom, exactly?' Jenny said.

'I had Dave Pironi calling me at home last night asking what a coroner was doing interfering with a police investigation.'

'Mrs Jamal's death impacts on my inquest.'

'It's not just him. Gillian Golder has phoned more than once this week demanding to know what on earth is going on during this adjournment.'

'It's none of her business . . . Why didn't you just put her through to me?'

Alison gave her a look which said: *isn't it obvious?*

'She's asking you to spy on me for her?'

'It wasn't expressed in quite those terms.'

'I'll deal with her,' Jenny said.

'That puts me in a rather awkward situation.'

'I won't mention your name.'

Alison looked doubtful.

'Honestly. Trust me. Anything else?'

Alison sucked in her cheeks and agitatedly flicked some imaginary fluff from her lapel. 'You know I wouldn't normally say anything like this . . .'

'Hello? Anybody home?' an unmistakable voice – McAvoy's – called through from the outer office.

Alison flashed Jenny an accusing look. 'What's he doing here?'

Jenny shrugged. 'I've no idea.' She got up from her desk.

Alison stepped between her and the door. 'Please, Mrs Cooper – let me see to this. I told you you shouldn't have anything to do with that man.'

'He's come up with the only new lead we've got.'

'You can't trust him. He's poison. I sat in on his interviews.'

There was a knock on the office door.

'Mrs Cooper?'

Jenny said, 'Hold on a moment.' She turned to Alison. 'At least let me see what he wants.'

She stepped past and out into reception. McAvoy was standing in the waiting area idly leafing through Alison's church newsletter.

'Mr McAvoy—'

'Sorry to arrive unannounced,' he said, with a mock formality imitating hers. 'I wonder if we might have a quick word about Mrs Jamal.'

Alison came to Jenny's shoulder. 'I really wouldn't advise it, Mrs Cooper. Mr McAvoy is a witness. You don't want to run the risk of tainting your inquest.'

'Good to see you again, Mrs Trent,' McAvoy said, with more than a hint of irony. 'It's been a fair wee while.'

Alison took a step forward, squaring up like the detective she had once been. 'You should know that Mr McAvoy was imprisoned for perverting the course of justice. He arranged a false alibi in a violent armed-robbery case – and that was just the time he got caught.'

McAvoy smiled and tossed the newsletter back on the table. 'I've heard that your old boss Dave Pironi claims to have found Jesus. In my humble opinion it may be a little too late. He was one of the dirtiest, most corrupt policemen I ever met. He sent that wee lassie to me, and I think you know that.'

Alison said, 'See what you're dealing with?'

McAvoy said, 'Did you ever ask yourself why my office happened to be bugged on that day? Or why, when any sane person wouldn't touch CID with a shitty stick, that witness couldn't do enough to help them?'

Jenny said, 'Can we stop this now, please?' She turned to McAvoy. 'Should you really be here?'

McAvoy said, 'This case has already cost me my liberty and career—'

Alison gave a dismissive grunt.

He ignored her and continued. 'And if you remember, it was immediately I got on the trail of that Toyota eight years ago that your officer and her colleagues fingered me.'

'That was nothing to do with it,' Alison said.

'With respect,' McAvoy replied, raising his voice, 'as a DS you wouldn't have had a fucking clue, Mrs Trent. Pironi and whoever was working him put me away to stop that car ever being identified. And then this call the other day – the guy asking what did I know, and threatening to put me in a *casket*. And the call before I went down, the American with the same question: *what did I know*?' He looked at Alison. 'He makes this crap up for a living, that's what you're thinking. But what about Mrs Jamal? And look who's in charge again.'

'Her flat's on his patch,' Alison said.

'And how long's he been there? Three months I heard. Transferred about the same time she lodged her application to have her son declared dead. Now I don't like to accuse a fellow believer of a mortal sin, but it does start to make you wonder.'

'He had nothing to do with Mrs Jamal's death,' Alison snapped.

'I'm sure you're an intelligent woman, Mrs Trent, but even an ex-copper should have learned that evil bastards don't always go around in black hats.' He nodded to the newsletter he'd dropped on the table. 'I couldn't help noticing that you and he get a mention in the church news there—'

Alison marched across the room, snatched her coat from the peg and thumped out of the office.

McAvoy picked up the newsletter, turned to an inside page and handed it to Jenny. 'Adult baptism's a wonderful thing, but it kind of takes the shine off . . .'

He pointed to the notices section. Mrs Alison Trent was

listed as one of five new members of the Body of Christ baptized the previous Sunday. She had two sponsors – the adult equivalent of godparents – one of whom was named as Mr David Pironi.

McAvoy said, 'It's pretty low, even by his standards. How'd he pull that off? She hasn't got a terminal illness or something, has she?'

'No,' Jenny said, 'just some family troubles.'

They talked in Jenny's office. McAvoy said a long-running trial he was involved with had been adjourned for the day because the judge had to conduct an all-day sentencing hearing: eight members of a paedophile ring each claiming they were tricked into it by the others. Thinking about Mrs Jamal had kept him awake most of the night. It was deep in the small hours, when he was running low on cigarettes, that he had started to put the pieces together. He'd called an old contact inside the police who'd told him about Pironi's recent transfer to New Bridewell. The same detective had also tipped him off about Pironi's church-going – he'd been at it since his wife died, apparently, still fitting up and whoring on week-days like he always had, but born again afresh every Sunday.

Speaking with McAvoy like this, businesslike, across a desk, Jenny's doubts about him began to recede. He was measured, logical and always gave a self-aware smile after he'd lapsed into hyperbole. She didn't feel he was pulling conspiracies from the air: like her, he was simply trying to arrange the pieces into an order that made sense. After she had gone with him to see Madog, Jenny had been almost convinced by Alison's insistence that he was inventing evidence to further his own agenda and prise his way back into the solicitors' profession. Looking him in the eye, she couldn't believe it. How did Alison's theory fit with Mrs Jamal's death? Would she argue that McAvoy was involved, that

he'd persecuted her with late-night phone calls? And for what
– merely to discredit Pironi?

No. The man now leaning towards her open window
smoking a cigarette was no monster. He was too edgy, too
weathered and grooved by life, too obviously worn down by
conscience to be a psychopath of the kind Alison imagined.
Ruthless people had charm; McAvoy had warmth. It was of
an erratic and slightly hazardous kind, a naked flame which
guttered then flared, but she could feel it burning in him
nonetheless. She was convinced that his passion for justice,
or his brand of it at least, was real and heartfelt.

Jenny showed him the list of Toyotas Alison had produced
and the ones she had circled. He ran through them with the
criminal lawyer's eye. If you were going to spirit someone
away, you wouldn't do it in a privately registered car, he
said. You'd most likely hire a vehicle using false documents,
a trail you could cover. On the list there were only two cars
registered to hire companies. One was in Cwmbran, south
Wales, the other was thirty miles to the north in the small
city of Hereford on the English side of the border.

Jenny reached for the phone, intending to call them.

McAvoy said, 'Do you think that's a good idea? You never
know who's listening.'

Jenny said, 'You're right. I'll pay them a visit.'

It was time to draw the meeting to a close. McAvoy met
her gaze as she tried to find a tactful way of saying so.

Before she spoke, he said, 'If I didn't want to upset your
officer any more I'd ask if I could come along for the ride.'

'You think I need my hand held?'

'Mrs Jamal could have done with it.'

Jenny tried not to let the shudder she felt pass through her
show on her face.

# SIXTEEN

McAVOY SMOKED AND DOZED DURING the hour-long journey to the former coal-mining town of Cwmbran. Once or twice Jenny tried to make conversation, but he barely responded. With eyes half-closed, he stared out at the grey landscape, the ever-present drizzle turning to sleet as they headed deeper into south Wales.

She asked if there was something on his mind. He responded with a moody and disconcerting 'Mmm.' His mood was impenetrable.

The car-rental franchise was on the edge of town, on an industrial estate in sight of evenly sloped hills which had been fashioned from the slag heaps formed when the former mines turned the earth inside out. McAvoy woke as she pulled up, and followed her inside. There were no customers, only a fleshy desk clerk chewing a sandwich. He wiped crumbs from his mouth as they came through the door. McAvoy ignored his corporate hello and fetched himself a free cup of coffee from the machine while Jenny dealt with business.

She produced one of her calling cards and told the clerk she needed to know who, if anyone, was renting the Toyota on the night of 28 June 2002. The clerk said he didn't have access to those kind of records. It was a matter for head office in Cardiff. He searched his computer for the right number to call and said he didn't hold out much hope –

the company only kept their vehicles for a year, two at the most.

From behind her, Jenny heard McAvoy say, 'The fuck's that got to do with it?'

'I beg your pardon, sir?'

'What's how long you keep the cars got to do with your records? You keep them for the tax man. Where are they?'

Jenny saw the clerk waver as he measured McAvoy up.

'There's no need to swear.'

McAvoy strolled over to the counter, set down his coffee and glanced at him with red, puffy eyes. Jenny felt her stomach turn over.

'I do apologize,' McAvoy said. 'The company I keep in my profession sometimes causes me to use inappropriate and intemperate language. Please ignore my earlier outburst.'

Cringing, Jenny lowered her eyes in embarrassment. The clerk turned warily back to his screen. McAvoy sipped his coffee, throwing him a malevolent glance.

'Here's the number, ma'am,' the clerk said, warily. 'Oh-one-two-nine-oh—'

McAvoy interrupted. 'The paper records, the forms you sign when you hire a car – where do you store those?'

The clerk glanced at Jenny, who said, 'It's OK, I'll call the number.'

'What's through there?' McAvoy said, pointing to the door at the back of the office. 'It's where you keep the files, right? VAT man comes, that's where he goes to check you're being straight with your paperwork.'

'I'm not authorized to release those documents, sir.'

'What you said was, you don't have *access*,' McAvoy said quietly, but with a murderer's menace. 'That's not quite true, is it, son?'

The clerk wiped a bead of sweat from his upper lip, his eyes flicking to the phone on the counter.

McAvoy said to Jenny, 'There you go. No need to go round the houses,' picked up his coffee and strolled outside.

Jenny and the clerk looked at each other. He was waiting for her lead now.

Jenny said, 'I think it might be easier if you just fetched me the records for those dates.'

He snatched a key from a drawer and disappeared into the back office. While he rummaged in filing cabinets she looked over her shoulder and saw McAvoy strolling over to the pond and aquatic supplies outlet opposite. He stopped to help a young woman who was struggling through the door with a baby in a buggy and unwieldy shopping bags. He said something that made her laugh, then bent down and tickled the child's cheek.

The clerk reappeared with several sheets of paper. He said, 'If you want I can copy them for you. It went out on the 24th for a two-week hire to the Fairleas Nursing Home – signed contract and credit-card slip. Anything else you want to see?'

Jenny flicked through the faded documents. 'No. That's fine.'

She swung out of the estate with a screech of tyres and headed out of town. McAvoy sat impassively in the passenger seat, taking in the view. Gaps had appeared in the clouds and beyond the rows of identical modern houses there was a pretty dusting of snow on the hilltops.

Jenny accelerated angrily out of a roundabout, pushed the Golf up to seventy in third and slammed straight across into fifth. The car lurched as she mistimed the clutch. McAvoy rocked forward in his seat but said nothing.

'Is that how you always behave?' Jenny said.

'You were going to let him fob you off to some hopeless shite in customer services.'

'How did this happen? You shouldn't even be here.'

'What's more important?' McAvoy said. 'Getting to the truth of this thing or upsetting some guy who couldn't care less?'

'I'm a *coroner*, I can't behave like that.'

'You think he's never heard the f word?'

'For God's sake – you were intimidating him. And undermining me.'

'You were doing pretty well at that yourself.'

'You've got no business interfering with my investigation. If you can't understand that, you can get out of the car now.'

'You're going to make me walk home?'

'You can freeze to death for all I care.'

McAvoy shrugged, then peered sideways at her as if he were arriving at a judgement.

'What?' she barked.

'You need to calm down, Jenny. You're a bag of nerves.'

'Oh, really?'

'I saw that when you were sitting outside that hall, all huddled up like the whole thing was nothing to do with you ... I thought, there's someone who's had the confidence knocked out of her.'

Jenny said, 'If I want your opinion, I'll ask for it.'

McAvoy said, 'Why don't you get the tears out now? Clear the air between us.'

'Fuck you.'

Anger was one emotion that kept tears at bay. She held onto it throughout the drive across country to Hereford. McAvoy sat silent and unnervingly still, squinting out at the patchwork fields. His shifting moods frightened her. He reminded her of some of the more sinister wife-batterers she had confronted across courtrooms in her former career: men who flipped from charm to violence and back again without warning. Their hapless partners always said the same thing:

*when he's in a good mood he's the nicest man in the world.*
She cursed herself for ever having let him come with her.

Hereford was a city, more of a market town, that she'd
visited occasionally over the years and seen degenerate from
charming and unspoiled to paved-over, litter-strewn and
leached of its character by chain stores in its historic centre
and US-style retail barns on its margins. It was yet another
casualty of the same small minds that had systematically
wrecked most British towns. Only the thousand-year-old
cathedral and handful of surrounding streets had maintained
their character, but the philistines were slowly claiming them
too: a pizza chain had taken over the Victorian post office
and tacky shops with cheap plastic signs had replaced once
dignified family-run businesses.

The car-hire firm was an ageing cabin and area of hard-
standing in a former railway goods yard, hidden behind a
row of electrical and home-improvement warehouses. It was
a rare survivor in this barren landscape: St Owen's Vehicle
Hire established 1962, the sign announced. Opposite was a
noisy backstreet mechanic's cluttered with dismantled vehicles and stacks of spent tyres. To the right was a carpentry
shop. A handful of workers on their break stood outside it,
gathered around a fire they'd lit in an oil drum and stamp-
ing their feet against the piercing cold. It reminded Jenny
of places from her own small-town childhood: the smell of
damp bricks, engine grease and wood smoke.

'I suppose you won't be wanting me,' McAvoy said.

'What do you think?' She climbed out of the car and
walked over to the office.

A young man of no more than twenty, dressed in a cheap
suit and tie, was tapping on a grubby computer keyboard
behind the counter. The air was heavy with the smell of
ageing lino and fumes from an elderly gas heater.

Jenny showed him her card and politely explained the

nature of her inquiry. He wasn't the quickest, and she doubted he'd ever heard of a coroner, but he was eager to help.

'I've only been here since Christmas,' he said, 'so I don't remember that particular car. I could call the boss on his mobile.'

Jenny said, 'Don't you have the records here?'

'Not the paper ones. The boss takes them home with him.'

'What about your computer – you log everything on there, right?'

'Yeah . . .'

'Let's have a look, shall we?' She smiled in a way that she hoped might encourage him to cooperate. He started to hit the filthy keys. A column of data appeared on the screen of the old-fashioned monitor.

'OK . . . here's the Toyota. We got rid of it in '05.' Jenny turned and glanced apprehensively out of the window. McAvoy was no longer in the passenger seat. Feeling a stab of alarm, she glanced left and right, then saw him strolling towards the carpenters' brazier, raising a hand in greeting to the two men still standing there.

'It's June '02 you're after, isn't it?'

'That's right.' She turned back to the young man, who was dragging his finger down the screen making a line in the dust. 'It was out from the 20th to the 23rd, and didn't go out again until 6 July.'

'You're sure?'

'That's what it says. Look . . .' He swivelled the screen towards her.

He was right. There was no record of the car being hired on that date.

'Oh well,' she said, disappointed. 'Thanks for trying. Maybe you can give me your boss's number anyway.'

McAvoy was strolling back towards her as she stepped out of the office. It was only three p.m. and already the light was fading. Sparks jumped out of the oil drum and carried past him on the sharp breeze.

'All right?' he said, suppressing a smile.

Jenny headed for the car. 'It wasn't hired out on those dates. We checked the computer records.'

'D'you ask him if they do deals for cash?'

'He's just a kid. I've got the boss's number.' She climbed into the driver's seat.

McAvoy caught hold of the door as she went to close it. 'If you were going to hire a car to snatch someone, would you want to leave a paper trail? Look at this place. A few hundred quid in notes – are you telling me they'd say no?'

'I'll speak to the owner. Can you let go? I'm getting cold.'

He jammed his knee against the door, wedging it open. 'And say what – do you remember a cash job eight years ago?'

'What do you suggest?'

'That you try a bit harder, Mrs Cooper. Jesus.'

Exasperated, Jenny said, 'I think we've had this conversation already.'

'Listen – those boys over there are Latvians. They've seen a guy with a ponytail come to rent a car once or twice. Mid-forties or thereabouts. Comes over in an old Mark 1 Land Rover and has it seen to in that garage. Had an aluminium hard top made for it last autumn – one of the Lats is an arc welder by trade, helped the mechanic get it done.'

Jenny sighed. 'Do they know the man's name?'

'Not a clue.' McAvoy gave an innocent smile. 'All I'm suggesting is a polite inquiry.'

'Fine. But I'll be the one making it.' She climbed out of the car. 'Don't you dare follow me.'

She returned to the office to find the young man coming off a call. He looked surprised and slightly disconcerted by her reappearance.

Jenny said, 'Help me out here – you have a customer, a man in his forties with a ponytail. Drives an old Land Rover. Do you know who I mean?'

He shook his head. 'No . . .'

She came up close to the counter, giving him the smile. 'This is just between you and me, all right – do some customers pay in cash to hire a vehicle, no records, no paperwork?'

'Not from me,' he said with a shrug. 'Can't speak for the boss.'

She tried again, 'I really need to know about this man with the ponytail. Are you certain you haven't seen him?'

'I've only been working here six weeks.'

'I'll believe you,' Jenny said. 'You'd better give me the boss's address.'

McAvoy was sitting on the bonnet, blowing into his hands and looking across the yard through the open front of the mechanic's workshop.

Jenny said, 'He's new here. I'll have to talk to the owner.'

McAvoy said, 'Why don't you try over there? That guy'll know him – spent a week working on his vehicle. Makes more sense than approaching a man you're asking to incriminate himself.'

She glanced over at the garage. The mechanic, a big man with heavily muscled arms, was working on the exhaust of a vehicle sitting up on an overhead ramp. 'Stay here.'

She stepped between puddles on the rough gravel, water seeping through the soles of her shoes. She made it to the concrete forecourt and approached the doorway. She'd never been sure of the etiquette in these places – should she wait for him to come to her or call out?

She knew from the glance he'd cast as she headed over that he'd seen her, but he let her stand there getting colder while he continued to wind off another bolt.

'Hello,' she called out, competing with a radio that was pumping out non-stop nineties techno.

Only when he was good and ready did he turn slightly and look her over. 'What can I do for you?'

'My name's Jenny Cooper. I'm the Severn Vale District Coroner. I'm trying to locate one of your customers. Have you got a moment?'

The mechanic slotted the spanner into a long pocket on the leg of his overalls and ducked out from under the ramp, wiping oil-stained hands on the backs of his thighs. He was tall, six-three at least, and broad as a bull across the shoulders.

Jenny told him politely about the man with the ponytail who owned a Mark 1 Land Rover.

The mechanic's eyes flicked towards the carpentry shop as he worked out who had sent her here.

'I would appreciate your assistance. He could be an important witness.'

He slowly shook his massive head. 'Don't know who you mean.'

'You made something for him last autumn . . . a cover . . .' Jenny said, out of her depth talking to mechanics. 'One of the Latvian guys over there helped you.'

'Not me,' he said, and turned back towards the ramp.

Jenny said, 'Excuse me. I'm not sure you realize how serious this is. I could call you as a witness.'

'Go ahead.' He fetched out his spanner and went back to work.

'Then you can expect a summons. I'll see you in court on Monday morning,' she threatened feebly and to no effect.

'Hey, big fella.' She turned to see McAvoy coming across the gravel at a jog. 'You ought to know who it is you're protecting.'

Jenny gave him a look that pleaded for him to stay away.

He held up his hands, 'Relax.' He called out to the mechanic, 'This ponytail guy's a nonce. Likes to spray paint on little kiddies.'

The big man turned round.

'That's right. I don't know about you, but I wouldn't want to have people like that known to be my friends. The way people talk—'

Jenny said, 'Please, Alec, for Christ's sake.'

Ignoring her, McAvoy stepped over to the ramp and pressed the button that released the hydraulics. The mechanic darted out from underneath as it started down, the spanner in his hand, 'The fuck are you doing?'

'Getting your attention.' McAvoy took a step forward. 'Forget about a pick-up truck – hell will rain down on you, my friend, if you don't try to be a little more helpful . . .'

The mechanic tightened his grip on the spanner. Jenny watched, open-mouthed. The muscles in her throat contracted in panic.

'A little girl of six years old, that's who he preyed on. You want someone like that going about?' McAvoy moved forward another half step, inches away from the taller, much heftier man, 'Or do you want to do the decent thing?'

Jenny watched, disbelieving, as the mechanic met McAvoy's eyes, raised the spanner a fraction ready to strike, weighed the odds, then slowly lowered it, lifting his chin defiantly as he took a step back. Without saying a word he crossed to the messy shelf – a plank laid across stacks of tyres – that served as his office, tore off a scrap of paper and scratched on it with a stub of pencil. He handed the note to Jenny then disappeared into the back of the building. He'd written: *Chris Tathum, Capel Farm, Peterchurch.*

They sat in stationary traffic outside what had once been a cattle market. Their damp coats were steaming up the windows, making Jenny feel increasingly claustrophobic. She wanted to take a pill but didn't dare in front of McAvoy: she already felt as if she had no secrets from him, as if he had an unnatural ability to detect her weaknesses and work his way into them.

He broke the silence which had persisted since they'd left the garage. 'You don't want to pay this man a visit now you're out here?'

'I'm not a detective,' Jenny said flatly.

'But you'll have to ask him to make a statement saying where he was that night.'

'I'll send my officer.'

They crept forward several feet. The lights ahead flicked back to red.

'If you ask me, you should show your face, let him know you mean business. Politely, of course.'

Jenny tapped her thumbs nervously on the wheel, keeping her eyes fixed on the road ahead, fighting the feeling that the sides of the car were closing in on her.

'If you don't,' McAvoy said, 'he might just slip through your fingers. Those Latvian guys have seen him a few times. The boy in the car-rental place will already have called his boss, the mechanic might even have tipped him off, we don't know. If it were any other case, you might say to yourself the police can always help me out, but I doubt that's an option here.'

'What's it to you anyway?' Jenny said. 'Why this case? You're not even getting paid for it.'

He nodded towards the distant tower of the cathedral, poking above the faux city wall surrounding a supermarket on the far side of the lights. 'Same reason they built that – seems like the right thing to do.'

'The spirit moved you, huh?'

'If you like.'

Jenny said, 'Why do I feel cynical?'

'Why wouldn't you – a man with my history?'

'Well, there you are. You can see why I'm not about to drive you out to say hello to Mr Tathum.'

McAvoy wiped his window with his cuff. 'You know, Jenny, I don't believe it's me you're frightened of, or Tathum – whoever he may be. I think the person who scares the living shit out of you is you.' He looked at her sideways across his shoulder, studying her face with a quizzical frown. 'I followed that case you did last year, the kid who died in custody. That must've taken some guts. And you know what I believe?'

Jenny closed her eyes and shook her head. He'd done it again, cut right through her.

'That we find ourselves in these situations for a reason. I bet you learned something about yourself. Took on those principalities and powers without even thinking. I'll bet it's only afterwards you thought to be scared.'

'Not quite true.'

'What I'm saying is you know as well as I do what it is to be moved. It's not comfortable. The first time you're swept up on the wave. Each time after that you tend to have a choice.'

The address was that of a small stone farmhouse in the shadow of the Black Mountains. From the village of Peterchurch they threaded along three miles of narrow lane, which dissolved into a further half mile of rough track. It was fully dark by the time Jenny pulled up at the gate to an untidy yard littered with tools and building materials. The house, which looked like two cottages joined together, was in the process of being renovated. One half looked inhabited and had lights in the downstairs windows, the other was still a roofless shell. She made McAvoy promise, swear on the Holy Mother herself, that he would stay in the car. He told her to please herself and reclined his seat a touch, settling back for a nap.

She lifted the latch on the heavy gate and picked her way across the pot-holed yard by the light of a miniature torch on her key fob, passing the elderly Land Rover with its smart new aluminium hard top. Before raising the heavy iron knocker on the front door she looked back at her Golf to check: in the darkness McAvoy was invisible. He'd better stay that way.

A man dressed in jeans and a paint-spattered sweatshirt answered. Dogs barked excitedly from behind an inner door. He was the right age, but his skull was shaved in a tight crew cut. He looked fit and muscular, an outdoors man. More nervous than she had expected, Jenny asked him if he was Christopher Tathum. He confirmed that he was, with no trace of anxiety or apprehension, she noticed, just a man living out in the country doing up a house.

She felt guilty saying it, her heart in her throat, but regretfully told him that his name had arisen as a possible witness in a case she was investigating.

'Really? What case is that?' he said. 'I don't think I know anyone who's died recently.' His voice was educated but not overly so. It had a quality Jenny found familiar but couldn't place. His eyes were intelligent, his expression patient but questioning.

The words tripped out of her mouth without conscious thought. 'Two young Asian men went missing from Bristol in late June 2002. We have a sighting of them in the back seat of a vehicle we believe you may have been renting at the time.'

Tathum smiled, nonplussed. 'Where did you get that from?'

'I'm afraid I can't tell you at the moment. What I need is for you to give a statement saying where you were at the time, 28 June to be precise.'

He seemed amused. 'And if I can't remember?'

'Have a think. See what comes back to you.' She offered him the last business card in her wallet. 'Maybe you could set it down in the form of a signed letter and fax it through to my office over the weekend? Or I can send my officer over to take a statement if you'd prefer.'

He peered at the card by the light of the dim bulb in the open porch in which they were standing. 'I don't know anything about any Asians. I'm a builder.'

'Was that your job at the time, sir?'

'I thought you wanted me to write a letter.' There was a hint of threat in his expression now, his facial muscles tightening into a defensive mask.

Jenny said, 'If you could. Thank you.' She stepped away from the door and started across the yard.

Tathum said, 'Hold on a minute. What is it I'm being accused of here?'

She stopped and glanced back. 'You're not being accused of anything. A coroner's inquest merely pieces together facts and events surrounding a death, or in this case a presumed death.'

'I know nothing about your case. You're wasting your time.'

'Then that's what you should write. Set down where you were working, who you were with, and I can discount you from my inquiries. Goodnight, Mr Tathum.'

She turned back towards the gate.

'You come all the way out here and won't even tell me what I'm meant to have done?'

An instinct told her not to stop.

'Hey, lady. I'm talking to you.' She heard his footsteps coming after her.

She wheeled round to face him. Away from the lights of the house, he was nothing more than an angry shadow.

'It's very simple, Mr Tathum, I'm just asking you to account for your whereabouts on a particular night: 28 June 2002.'

'You know what?' He stepped closer. Jenny moved back and found herself pressed against the gate.

'Mr Tathum—'

Where was McAvoy now she needed him?

Tathum glared at her and seemed to swallow the abuse he was ready to hurl at her. She flinched at a sudden movement of his head towards hers, but there was no contact, only a violent jolt to her nerves. He marched back to the house. She fumbled for the latch on the gate, made it through and tumbled into the car.

When she'd got her breath, McAvoy said, 'That was more like it.'

It was McAvoy's idea to pull over at the pub. If she hadn't been desperate to swallow a pill she would have put up more resistance. She retreated to the sanctuary of a draughty ladies' room and thanked God for the opportunity to medicate herself. She had got it down to a fine art: just enough to soothe her nerves without making her dopey. She had asked him for tonic water and had drunk most of the contents of the glass before she realized the feeling of well-being spreading through her wasn't only due to the log fire in the inglenook or the relief of having escaped her encounter with Tathum unscathed. There was vodka in it. Six months of sobriety up in smoke. She should have told him, but part of her thought: *what the hell? I've been longing to feel this good. Where's the harm in just one drink?* Instead, she sipped the rest of it slowly, telling herself it would hardly touch her that way. Like McAvoy said, she didn't want to go through life frightened. Having a drink was part of learning to handle herself again.

He was funny and contagious, sensitive and witty. He told her stories about his courtroom adventures that made her laugh until she cried, and tales of the tragic characters he'd met in prison that moved her to tears. And the more he drank, the warmer and more poetic he became. She began to see the complex layers of his contradictory character and to understand his moral code: his acceptance of people, both good and bad, with equal humanity because 'ultimately we're all God's creatures'. In her mildly intoxicated state she found him a beguiling mixture of humility and creativity, of wilful independence and thoughtful submission. His guiding philosophy as a lawyer, he said, had always been, 'Judge not, that ye be not judged.' It didn't mean – as most people thought – that judging others was sinful, but that all who cast judgement would one day be judged, and by far more demanding laws than any contrived by man.

'And that's where I find my grain of solace,' he said, his fingers cradling his tumbler a whisker away from hers. 'I've done some wicked things in my life, mixed with some truly evil men in this fallen world, but I've never doubted for a moment that I'll be judged as harshly as the next.'

'Do you think you'll get through the strait gate?' Jenny said, with a smile.

'I'd like to think I might squeak it . . . who knows?' He sipped his whisky, his gaze drifting inwards.

Jenny watched him, wondering what he was thinking, what sins he was hoping this crusade might wash away.

She was tempted to ask, but something stopped her. She didn't want to know, didn't want to be forced into judgement. She was learning from him, that was enough, drawing down some yet to be defined wisdom.

From deep in his reverie, McAvoy said, 'Do you think those kids really were terrorists?'

Jenny said, 'Does it matter?'

'What's done in the dark must always come to the light,' McAvoy said. He tipped back the rest of his whisky. 'We should be going.'

# SEVENTEEN

'MUM . . . YOU OK?'

Jenny rose out of a leaden, dreamless sleep, her limbs too heavy to move. Ross's anxious voice was coming from the foot of the bed.

'Mum?'

'Mmm?' she said, turning her eyes away from the shaft of light streaming through the partially opened curtains.

'I thought you might be ill . . .'

Something felt wrong, constricted. Barely awake, she tried to move to a sitting position and realized she was dressed in her skirt and suit jacket.

'You weren't well when you came home last night,' Ross said. 'I didn't know what was wrong.'

She blinked, her vision slowly coming to focus. Her sleepy gaze wandered around the room. She saw her shoes lying near the door, her handbag on the floor at the side of the bed, the contents – including her two bottles of pills – spilling out on the rug.

'How are you feeling?'

'Fine . . . just tired. What time is it?'

'Just gone nine. It's all right, it's Saturday.'

He glanced down at the pills then back at her with the same questioning eyes he'd had as a young child. 'What happened?'

She didn't have a clue. Didn't remember going to bed or even arriving home. A dim memory surfaced of driving out of Bristol on the motorway, jerking awake at the sound of a rumble strip under her tyres, a loud horn sounding behind her . . .

'I'll be right down,' she said weakly. 'Just give me a moment.'

She moved to the edge of the bed and swung her legs out onto the floor to prove the point. Unconvinced, Ross withdrew and went downstairs.

'You could make some coffee,' Jenny called after him.

It took several minutes under a cool shower to get any life back into her muscles. As the blood started to flow, the previous evening's events gradually drifted back to her. She remembered driving back from the pub to Bristol feeling fine. She and McAvoy were laughing and listening to music. Nearing the city, she'd become drowsy – that would be the alcohol combining with her beta blocker, slowing her heart. She had dropped him off outside his office. He told her to look after herself, then reached out and brushed her cheek with his hand. There had been a moment when he might have leaned forward and kissed her, but he did it with a look instead. She relived a feeling of near elation as she drove back through Clifton, crystal white fairy lights glittering on trees outside the cafés and boutiques like star dust. Then it went hazy . . . drooping at the wheel . . . crossing the Severn Bridge . . . her shoulder dragging against the wall as she climbed the stairs, Ross following behind her.

She was back in her bedroom pulling on a sweater over her blouse when she noticed the notebook, her journal, lying open on the floor at the foot of the bed where Ross had been standing. She stooped down and snatched it up, her heart in her throat. She had written yesterday's date in an erratic hand, and three scrawled lines:

> *I don't know what happened tonight. That man . . . he does something to me. I don't even find him attractive – he's so tired and used up. But when he looks in my eyes I know he's not afraid of anything. What does it mean? Why him? Why now? It's as if*

The last 'f' trickled off down the page leaving the thought forever incomplete.

She stuffed the journal into the drawer at the foot of her wardrobe, her cheeks flushed with embarrassment and shame.

Ross called up the stairs. 'What do you want for breakfast?'

'Toast is fine. I'm coming now.' She took a deep breath and told herself not to panic. He hadn't seen the journal. He'd been too concerned about her to notice it. He'd probably spotted the pills, but she could explain those – stress of the divorce, new career; the medication a temporary help in easing the strain. Everyone took them at some point in their life. He'd understand.

He'd made toast and coffee and set out cups and plates on the small fold-out table, only big enough for two, which took up most of the floor space in the tiny kitchen. He was showered and shaved and wearing clean clothes – unheard of on a weekend.

She put on a bright smile. 'Anything planned for today?'

He shook his head. 'Karen's away with her mum.'

'I've got to work tomorrow so I thought maybe we could go for a walk, drive over to the Beacons as it's sunny.'

Ross poured her some coffee. 'Don't you think you'd better rest?'

'It was a long week,' Jenny said, 'that's all. The mother of the boy who disappeared died on Thursday—'

'I read about it in the paper.'

'Oh?'

'This case is a big deal. It's been on the news and everything.'

'I try not to listen. They never get their facts straight.' She tried to sound light-hearted and fell short.

'Are you sure you're up to it?' Ross said, in the scathing way only a teenager can. 'You seem pretty stressed to me, crashing out in your clothes.'

'I fell asleep reading. Don't you ever do that?'

'God, do you have to be so touchy all the time?'

'I'm sorry if I'm not Julie-bloody-Andrews.'

'Why do you always over-react?'

'Can we just have breakfast without arguing?' She grabbed a piece of toast and stabbed her knife into the butter. It slipped out of her fingers. She picked it up and fumbled it again. She gave up and forced her hands into her lap, tears pricking the backs of her eyes.

'What's wrong with you?' Ross said.

'Nothing.' She sniffed. *Damn.* Why did she have to fold now?

His irritation melted into concern.

'What are all those pills for?'

'They're just to help me cope . . . It's taken me a while to get over the divorce.'

'But you were ill before you got divorced.'

'I wasn't—'

'Then why were you seeing a psychiatrist?'

'Who told you that?' she said, as if he'd been fed a lie.

'I heard you and Dad arguing about it.'

It took all Jenny's effort not to break down. 'I'm better

now. Everything's changed. I've got a new life. It just takes a while to adjust.'

He was having none of it. 'Why can't you just tell me the truth for once? Steve doesn't think you're better. I know he doesn't.'

'What's he been saying?'

'Nothing specific. I can just tell from the way he talks about you.'

'Ross, please, you have to believe me. Yes, I was very unhappy for a time, but I'd been with your father since I was twenty, barely older than you are now. Being on your own takes some getting used to.' She forced in a breath, somehow managing to keep the tears at bay. 'It's all getting better now. I've got a great job, you . . .' She reached across the table and took his hand. 'You don't know how much that means to me.'

'No pressure then,' he said sarcastically.

'No. There isn't. Honestly.' She let go, realizing how oppressive and guilt-making she must feel to him, but at the same time filled with the selfish need for his reassurance. 'All I want is for you to feel free, but cared for. Your father and I both—'

He recoiled in embarrassment. 'Yeah, all right.'

Jenny allowed herself to smile. They'd made connection. 'I was serious about the two of us going out together. How about it?'

'Whatever you like,' Ross said, and took a mouthful of toast.

Jenny knew the expression he was trying to hide from her behind his mask of macho indifference. In all its essential elements his face hadn't changed since he was a toddler. He felt reassured, comforted in the way he had when he'd run to her with scraped knees needing a hug.

'Do you have to keep looking at me?'

'I'm not—'

The phone rang in the sitting room.

'I'll get it,' Ross said, and went to answer, eager to break the tension.

He came back with the receiver and handed it to her. 'For you. Andy someone.'

*Andy*? She had a mental blank. 'Hello . . . ?'

'Mrs Cooper. Andy Kerr, sorry to call you on a weekend – your officer gave me your number.'

'Is this about the Jane Doe?'

'I'm not sure . . . I came into work this morning to catch up. I still had the dosimeter kicking around my office. I was playing around with it waiting for my computer to boot up when I realized it was still picking something up. I took it over to the fridge thinking there might still be traces from the body when it started going crazy . . .' He paused, sounding as if he scarcely believed what he was about to say. 'Mrs Jamal's body is giving off radiation. Whatever the source is, it's pushing out nearly fifty milliSieverts an hour.'

Jenny felt as if the room had been suddenly shaken by an unexpected tremor. *Radiation*? She was baffled.

'I don't understand the measurements,' she said, 'What does it mean?'

'Put it this way,' Andy Kerr said, 'background radiation is two milliSieverts per *year*. Five hundred milliSieverts is usually considered very bad for your health. We're not talking sudden death, but we are talking dangerous levels.'

'Where could it have come from?'

'No idea. I've got someone from radiology on the way. I'm hoping she might come up with some answers. I thought you might want to be here.'

'Have you told the police?'

'Shouldn't we get the facts straight first?'

'I'll be right down.'

Jenny promised she'd only be an hour or two, but Ross said wearily that he'd learned to multiply her time estimates by three. Forget going out, he'd rather be dropped in Bristol, where he could meet up with friends.

He told her to let him out near Bristol docks. She watched him saunter off towards the coffee shops and bars where she suspected he and his friends liked to mingle. Seventy-five weekends until he was gone. How many of those would they spend together? A handful if she was lucky.

She tried McAvoy's mobile number twice during the fifteen-minute drive to the Vale hospital. Each time she reached his answerphone, and each time she froze when it came to leaving a message. She could no longer deny that in a deeply confusing and incomplete way she was attracted to him, but it wasn't shyness that stopped her, it was a vague and unsettling sense that whatever awaited her would be complicated enough without his unpredictable presence. And, if she were brutally honest with herself, she remained suspicious. There was still something about him, the bit that by his own admission remained wholly unredeemed, that she didn't trust.

A stiff female figure swaddled in an anorak and gloves was waiting outside the mortuary entrance. It was Alison. Jenny could sense her mood of martyred disapproval at twenty yards.

'Good morning, Alison.'

'On your own, are you, Mrs Cooper?' she replied sharply.

'Yes.'

'I was half-expecting you to be with Mr McAvoy – as you and he seem to have become so friendly.'

'I know you've got a history, but I think he may have

helped me make a breakthrough. I tracked down the man who was driving the Toyota, the one who paid Madog a visit. Have you managed to take his statement yet?'

'Yes,' Alison said curtly. 'But helpful or not, I've known you long enough to say this, Mrs Cooper – that man's using his charm to get the better of you. He's got mischief in mind, I know it.'

Jenny could have pointed out that Alison was hardly objective when it came to her good-looking former boss or her confidant and baptismal sponsor, DI Dave Pironi, but her more humane instincts told her to hold back. This was her officer's way of saying that she was concerned, and Jenny appreciated it. Now didn't feel like a good time to have to manage without her.

'I'm under no illusions,' Jenny said. 'The next time I see him will be in court. That's a promise.' She pushed the buzzer.

Andy Kerr came along the corridor to meet them, dressed in a radiographer's apron, surgical mask and cap.

'I can't let you go any further,' he said, holding up his hands. 'We've found hazardous levels. Sonia's got some kit up there that should help identify the source. Undertakers are on the way with a lead-lined coffin.'

Jenny craned past him to see a young woman dressed in a similar outfit to his. She was kneeling on the floor tapping on a laptop. It was hooked up to some equipment housed in boxes that resembled photographer's cases.

'Could she have been poisoned?' Jenny said.

Andy said, 'Come through here. It's one room which isn't giving a reading.' He pushed through the swing doors into the empty autopsy room. Jenny and Alison followed.

Andy pulled off his mask and ripped at the Velcro tabs on his apron. The beach club T-shirt he was wearing underneath was soaked through with sweat. 'Sonia says she's found radioactive particles on the surface of the skin. They're beta emitters, which starts to narrow it down. She also found a particle in the nasal passage. It's early days, but her initial impression was that Mrs Jamal has been in an environment where she's come into contact with a radioactive substance.'

'Such as?' Alison asked.

'There are some medical and commercial applications for these radionuclides – iodine 129 is used to treat thyroid complaints – but it's more likely she's been exposed to low- or medium-level nuclear waste.'

Jenny said, 'How likely is that?'

'Beats me,' Andy said. He pulled his dosimeter from his pocket – a small yellow gadget about the size of a pager – and switched it on. He waved it in Jenny and Alison's direction and checked the digital readout. 'You're both clear.'

Sonia Cane was a Ghanaian woman who wore a permanent frown. Having finished her work at the fridge she scrubbed down in the autopsy room while reeling off a list of urgent tasks. The Health Protection Agency would have to be informed immediately. Their radiation team would oversee the clean-up of the mortuary and the storage and eventual disposal of the body. Until the building was clear of contamination it would be sealed off and no bodies would be allowed to come or go. The levels of radiation were high enough to make this a significant incident.

'Do you have any idea where this came from?' Jenny asked her.

'No, but I can tell you what the substance is. There'll be more detailed tests, but I'm pretty certain it's caesium 137. Tiny amounts – no more than specks of dust – but from a potent source.'

'What's that when it's at home?' Alison said, saving Jenny from revealing her ignorance.

'A by-product of the nuclear industry,' Sonia said. 'It results directly from the fission of uranium. You'd also find it where there'd been a nuclear explosion—'

Jenny interrupted, 'This woman worked in a clothes shop.'

Sonia said, 'I find it as puzzling as you . . . If she worked at a nuclear power plant you could understand it.' At a loss, she shook her head. 'You read about terrorists trying to get hold of this stuff to make dirty bombs. It doesn't make any sense.'

'Do you know when she was contaminated?' Andy said.

'Very recently – the particle in the nose can't have been lodged there for more than a few days, even hours before death. The natural processes would have expelled it.'

'And this contamination was on her skin, right?' Jenny said. 'Her body was found naked.'

'I'm not sufficiently expert to tell you whether or not she was clothed or not when she was exposed,' Sonia said. 'We'd have to bring in specialists.'

Jenny's mind raced through a number of equally baffling possibilities. None of them seemed credible. All of them pointed to Amira Jamal having a far more complex connection with her son's disappearance than Jenny could ever have imagined.

'We'd better inform the police,' Alison said.

Andy reached for the phone on the wall.

Jenny stopped him. 'Hold on. I'd like to go to her flat first. It's only a few minutes away.'

Sonia said, 'This is a radiological incident. We're under a legal duty—'

'I know. But let's find out how big the incident is first, shall we? Could you come with us?'

Sonia and Andy traded an uncertain glance.

'He can make the call in half an hour. Meanwhile I'm

gathering evidence for my inquest into her son's death – I'll explain on the way. Bring whatever you need to take measurements, but we'll have to be quick.'

Alison held fire until they were marching back out across the car park. Sonia, following behind, was on the phone offloading the day's domestic duties to an evidently disgruntled husband.

Alison said, 'Would you mind telling me what you think you're doing, Mrs Cooper? We have a duty to report this incident immediately.'

'It was you who told me that the Security Services put pressure on the police to shut down their investigation in Nazim and Rafi's disappearances before they wanted to.'

'I told you there was talk, that's all,' Alison said defensively.

'That's not how I remember it . . . Look, I know Pironi's your friend—'

'He did everything he could.'

'He could have resigned.'

'Why are you bringing him into this?'

'Why wouldn't I? He's part of it.'

'He's a decent man.'

'That's not what I'm hearing.'

'Oh, from McAvoy—'

Jenny stopped abruptly next to her car. 'You may trust a man who allowed himself to be silenced. I don't, and I'm the one running this inquiry. So which horse are you going to ride?'

Alison met her with a flinty glare as Sonia's arrival brought their exchange to an unresolved end.

'Your call,' Jenny said.

Jenny drove Sonia the three miles to Mrs Jamal's flat in her Golf, repeatedly checking her mirrors for Alison's Peugeot.

There was no sign of it. She felt an unexpected pang of sadness verging on betrayal. Relations with Alison had always been bumpy, but until this week she had never truly doubted her loyalty. In the space of a few days it appeared to have all but dissolved.

It took three long blasts on the doorbell to rouse the irritable Mr Aldis, the caretaker, who growled over the intercom that he didn't work on weekends so could they kindly get lost. Jenny responded with another extended ring which finally drew the hefty, bulldog-faced Mrs Aldis hobbling to the front door on a single crutch. She shoved a set of keys at Jenny telling her to help herself, then limped back indoors.

Sonia Cane produced a sensitive dosimeter the size of a small cellphone. It was fitted with a Geiger-Muller counter, she explained, and was able to differentiate between different categories of radiation. She held it discreetly in her hand so as not to alarm any passing residents and took a reading in the front hall. There was an electronic crackle – each blip an electron firing through the dosimeter's sensors like a microscopic shotgun pellet. It was a similar reading to that she'd found on Mrs Jamal's body – fifty milliSieverts. It petered out towards the stairs, but spiked alarmingly to eighty when they entered the lift.

'We're going to have to get this building cleared,' Sonia said anxiously.

'Five minutes,' Jenny said. 'Let's just sweep the flat.'

Sonia moved quickly, not wanting to take a fraction more radiation than she had to. The trail cooled to twenty-five milliSieverts along the stretch of landing between the lift and the front door of Mrs Jamal's apartment; once inside the front door the dosimeter erupted like dry twigs on a bonfire.

'Je-sus,' Sonia said, poking the meter around the living-room door. 'Ninety-three.'

Jenny pointed to where Mrs Jamal's clothes and the whisky bottle had been found. 'She was sitting just about there.'

Sonia hastened into the room, pointed the meter at the spot, then swiftly drew it in a circle around her. She stepped towards one of the two armchairs and swept the meter over it.

'A hundred and ten.' She headed for the door. 'That's enough. We're going.'

Sonia was reluctantly persuaded to sweep the remaining four landings of the building before reaching for her phone, but found only slightly higher than background levels. It confirmed that the trail led from the front door directly to Mrs Jamal's flat. The fact that the fabric of an armchair had the highest reading suggested that someone or something contaminated had come into direct contact with it. It was only a matter of a few particles – a faint dusting, Sonia called it – but it screamed to Jenny that in her final hours Mrs Jamal had had a visitor.

Sonia refused to take the lift and hurried ahead down the stairs, making a call to the Health Protection Agency. Within the hour the building would be evacuated and sealed off. A team of operatives in post-apocalyptic white overalls would search for and suck up every last radioactive crumb. The neighbourhood would never have witnessed a more incongruous sight.

Descending the penultimate flight of steps, Jenny heard voices in the lobby below. She turned the corner to see Alison standing on the doorstep of the caretaker's flat talking to Mrs Aldis. Sonia was already outside the building, phone pressed to her ear as, with much gesticulating, she explained the situation to an incredulous official at the Health Protection Agency.

Leaning on her crutch, Mrs Aldis nodded gruffly towards the lift. Jenny heard her say, 'Tall fella, slim.'

'Colour?'

'White. Fiftyish, I'd say. Baseball cap on. Shoved straight past me. No sorry or nothing.'

Alison said, 'Did you tell the police this?'

'I wasn't here, was I? I was on my way to hospital to have my knee seen to.'

'At what time?'

'Must've been about one-ish, maybe a few minutes after.' Mrs Aldis noticed Jenny. 'You remembered to lock up, love? There's no way my husband's going up there today. Lazy sod. It'd take a bomb to get him off that sofa when the football's on.'

Jenny said, 'You might be in luck.'

They sat for a while in Alison's car, a few moments of peace before the air would be split by the scream of sirens. Jenny resisted any temptation to discuss her officer's decision to step away from her friend and fellow churchgoer, DI Pironi. She was simply grateful that she had. She hated to admit it, but it was a childlike gratitude: there was something of the mother substitute in her relationship with Alison. What did that say about her? She heard McAvoy's voice: *there's someone who's had the confidence knocked out of her*.

'I'll take a statement later,' Alison said quietly. 'The man who came out of the lift sounded rather like the one Dani James saw in the student halls all those years ago.'

'White . . . I don't know why, I was expecting her to say he was Asian.'

'We don't know he was connected with Mrs Jamal. He could have been anyone,' Alison said, but with no conviction.

After a moment of silence, Jenny said, 'Anna Rose Crosby worked at Maybury power station. Our missing Jane Doe had a thyroid tumour . . .'

'You can't start building castles in the air, Mrs Cooper. Best start with what we know.'

Then came the first one. A squad car screamed up behind them and screeched to a halt outside the block. Sonia Cane rushed to meet the two constables who scrambled out.

Alison said, 'She may never get another one like this. We'll leave her to enjoy the limelight, shall we?'

'Why not?' Jenny said. 'And talking of which, I think Monday might be a little soon to start taking evidence again, don't you?'

'Whatever you think's best, Mrs Cooper.'

The day had taken on a dreamlike quality, its moods shifting as swiftly as the restless sky. She used the last of her phone's battery dialling Ross's number, only to reach him for a few short seconds in which he announced he was staying at his father's for the rest of the weekend, and could she drop his things off on her way to work on Monday?

Deflated and dejected, Jenny drove home. The roads were eerily quiet as the sun sank towards the hilltops, briefly casting the Wye valley in a light of almost angelic clarity. For a brief moment the whole of life seemed to stop and be held in stark relief. She was a mere onlooker to the series of baffling tableaux which made up her present existence: a son disillusioned by her weakness; a disturbing and erratic man to whom she felt a visceral attraction; a case that, as much as she tried to ignore the fact, touched her darkest fears; and the latest bizarre composition in the city that lay a mere river's span behind her – a trail of radiation that led to the naked corpse of a woman whose final call for help she had ignored. She should have felt guilty, horrified that she'd taken McAvoy's call in preference to Mrs Jamal's, but in this moment of stillness she felt almost a selfish sense of relief. It was as if everything that had been ominous and unseen had briefly surfaced and shown itself. Mrs Jamal's killer – Jenny had convinced herself that was who the spectre in the baseball cap had been – was one and the same demon who had visited on the night of Nazim and Rafi's vanishing. Eight years ago he had left only scratch marks on the door frames; this time he'd left a smear of hell itself.

Evil now had a form if not a face.

There was no time to reflect or elaborate on her theories; the phone calls came relentlessly for the rest of the afternoon. Andy Kerr, the undertakers, various functionaries from the Health Protection Agency, DI Pironi and even Gillian Golder managed to obtain her supposedly ex-directory number. All wanted information she didn't have and none of them believed her when she claimed ignorance. Both Pironi and Golder sounded close to desperate for any lead to the source of the radiation; both seemed convinced she was keeping critical evidence to herself. She told them about Mrs Aldis and the man in the baseball cap, rationalizing that in doing so she had fulfilled her duty, but made no mention of either Madog or Tathum. They belonged to the past and that, she told herself, was still her exclusive territory.

Between calls Jenny sat at her desk, trying to work out her next moves. She had already gone far beyond the accepted bounds of coronial practice by behaving like a detective, but her gut told her there were questions that would never be answered merely by examining witnesses in court. The stolen Jane Doe had an early-stage thyroid tumour possibly caused by exposure to low-level radiation; the missing Anna Rose worked in the nuclear industry; Nazim Jamal had been a physicist. It was more than just wishful thinking, there *had* to be a connection.

The phone interrupted her thoughts for what felt like the fiftieth time. Jenny answered with a weary hello.

Steve said, 'That good, hey? Busy?'

Jenny's mood lifted. 'What did you have in mind?'

Steve said, 'I'd like to talk.'

The Apple Tree was quiet for a Saturday. Steve was a lone figure sitting next to the iron brazier on the flagstone patio. The snap of the fire and the rush of the nearby stream making its final descent to the Wye were the only sounds in the damp, chilly night.

'Can you stand it out here?' Steve said as she climbed the uneven steps.

'I like it,' Jenny said and took a seat next to him on one of the three rustic benches arranged around the fire. It was throwing out a good heat, but she was glad of her thick wool sweater and the waxed jacket which made her look like a farmer's wife.

Steve touched his roll-up cigarette to a lick of flame and took a draw. 'Got you a Virgin Mary.' He handed her a glass.

'Thanks.' She took an alcohol-free sip. 'God, it's boring being virtuous.' She reached for his tobacco tin. 'Am I allowed one sin?'

'As many as you like.' He gazed into the flames.

Clumsily rolling a cigarette she said, 'I'd tell you what kind of week I've had, but I'm not sure I'd believe it myself.'

'Ross told me some of it,' he said, as if from a far distance.

'You've been talking to him a lot . . .' Jenny replied, fishing.

'Here and there.' He blew out a thin trail of smoke. 'He worries about you.'

She licked the paper and performed the final roll. Not bad. She poked it though the iron slats of the brazier to catch a light.

'He really does,' Steve said.

'What can I say? I do my best . . . Is this what you wanted to talk about?'

'No. You mostly.'

'What about me?'

He held his cigarette hesitantly in front of his lips.

'*What?*' she insisted.

'The other night when we were in bed . . . it was as if you weren't there. And it's not the first time.' He turned and held her gaze. 'You don't feel the same way any more.'

'That's not true.'

'You hardly call me.'

'I'm a working mother.'

'And I go to an office, too . . . I'm not the same, am I?'

'The same what?'

'The fantasy. The guy with no chains.'

Wounded, Jenny said, 'I think you're confusing me with your ex-girlfriend. If you remember, I encouraged you to go back and qualify.'

'I really didn't want to argue, Jenny.' His head sank towards his knees. 'I just want to know what's going on with us, what you're expecting.'

She drew hard on her cigarette until the hot smoke scorched her mouth. 'I'm sorry if I seem that way. It's probably the pills my shrink put me on. I'll be off them soon.'

'Didn't I used to make you happy?'

She felt her legs twitching nervously. A shiver passed through her, physical sensations taking the place of thoughts. 'You know what I am, Steve. I try to keep the parts of me I'm trying to deal with separate, but sometimes they escape from the box.'

'You know you can talk to me all you like. I wish you would.'

'It doesn't work like that. That's not what I need from you.'

'Can you tell me what you do need?'

*To touch me, hold me, reassure me, give me a place to hide* ... The words tripped out of her mind but stumbled and fell somewhere short of her mouth. All she could manage was to shake her head.

Steve said, 'Do you love me? Or just the idea of me.'

'You're not leaving?'

'I need to know what the future is, I need to know how you feel. A girl at work asked me if I was with anyone the other day. For a moment I didn't know what to say.'

'Was she pretty?'

'For God's sake, Jenny.' For once he was closer to tears than she was. 'You've got to stop being afraid. Letting yourself feel loved is a gamble, don't I know it, but you won't even try.'

'I ... I do ... I try all time.' The words sounded empty even to her.

Steve said, 'I've been thinking more about your dream – the part of you that died. Why would you have it again now? When we got together I watched you come alive. You smiled and laughed and lost yourself. And then it was as if you felt too guilty to let yourself be free again.' He tossed his cigarette end onto the fire and drew his palms back across his face. 'What I'm trying to say is, sometimes being faced with a choice is the best way to get bounced out of a rut.'

He stood then leaned down and kissed her lightly on the forehead. 'Think about it. Give me a call.'

He disappeared down the steps and into the night.

# EIGHTEEN

JENNY HAD SUFFERED MANY INSULTS from many men over the years, but no one had accused her of being lifeless in bed. True, she'd allowed herself to think about someone else during sex, but she'd done that many times with her ex-husband and even in the midst of their acrimonious split David had had the good grace to say that he had few complaints about the physical side of their marriage.

Studying her face in the mirror she did detect a certain absence, a dullness in her eyes, a lack of vitality in her features. She felt sure these changes had occurred since she had been on her latest regime of medication. Yes, the malaise Steve had detected was partly existential, but she could see in her own reflection that it was partly physical too. The pills had been a useful support at her low points, they'd staved off the melancholy and anxiety which forced their way in when her mind wasn't absorbed with work, but they'd blunted her edge, diluted her passion.

Steve was right: part of her had died, the part that wasn't afraid to feel the rush of life.

It was time for a new strategy; to cut loose. The deadening drugs must go. Across the wet grass and into the dark stream with Dr Allen's poisons. She'd rather live raw and true, be like McAvoy – a force of nature, a raging gale or a barely moving breeze depending on how the spirit moved her.

And if she faltered, a glass of something nice or a tranquillizer or two couldn't do any harm.

She checked in the bottom drawer of the oak chest where she kept her special things – silk underwear, white cotton gloves with delicate pearl buttons, a pair of stockings she had worn only once – and dug down to the bubble-wrapped package she'd stashed there months before, when she'd vowed that the single container was for life-saving purposes only. She slit the sticky tape with nail scissors and released the small brown bottle. Xanax 2mg. Contents 60. A reassuring rattle. She unscrewed the lid and pulled out the plug of cotton wool just to make sure.

She had her parachute. Now she could jump.

The phone woke her shortly before seven a.m. on Sunday morning. Jenny went downstairs, turned the ringer to mute and had breakfast in peace. She had no intention of answering any calls today. She had nothing to say to anyone until she had some more answers. Two cups of strong coffee took away her sluggishness. She felt more exposed without Dr Allen's pills; a small hard kernel of fear sat stubbornly between her throat and diaphragm, but there was also an energy she wasn't accustomed to. A sense of excitement, of unleashed emotion. The day felt fresh and full of possibility.

She arrived outside the Crosbys' home in Cheltenham shortly after nine. It stood in a terrace of identical regency townhouses, distinguished from one another only by the varying designs of their intricate wrought-iron porches and balconies. Built with the first flush of serious colonial money to reach the hands of the merchant classes, these stuccoed streets in the heart of the town were an idealized vision of what it was to be English and civilized. Even on a dull February morning the buildings seemed to shine.

It was Mrs Crosby who answered the door, her hair still slightly rumpled, though she'd had time since Jenny's call half an hour before to dress and, judging from the smell, burn some toast. She took her through to an elegant, unfussy drawing room that matched tasteful contemporary sofas with an antique chandelier. The paintings were modern abstract, the huge decorative mirror above the white marble fireplace was tarnished with age. Eight-feet-high windows looked out over a mini Italianate garden.

Jenny said, 'It's lovely. So light.'

Mrs Crosby offered a sad smile and glanced up at the door as her husband entered, hair still wet from the shower, his irritation at being stirred so early on a Sunday morning written across his unsmiling face.

'Found a body, have you?' he said, taking a seat next to his wife.

'No. There's no body, nothing to suggest she's dead.'

Husband and wife exchanged a look of relief tinged with a sense of anti-climax.

'This may sound odd,' Jenny said, 'but the reason I need to speak to you is that a small trace of radioactive material was found on the body of woman connected to another case I'm investigating. You might have read about it – Nazim Jamal.'

Mrs Crosby looked puzzled.

'I've read reports,' her husband said, abruptly. 'What's this got to do with Anna Rose?'

'Maybe nothing. I don't know. Let me explain.' She gave them the bare bones: a brief history of Nazim and Rafi's disappearance, Mrs Jamal's campaign, her bizarre death and the traces of caesium 137 that could only have originated in a nuclear power plant. She told them that, from what she'd managed to find on the internet, the main source of black market radioactive material was the former Eastern bloc, but Anna Rose's job at Maybury presented her with a coincidence that needed at least to be discounted.

Mr and Mrs Crosby listened in silence, exchanging the occasional fretful glance. Jenny sensed she had touched on something, but finished her exposition before asking if it brought anything to mind.

There was a pregnant pause. Mrs Crosby spoke first. 'You didn't know that Anna Rose studied physics at Bristol?'

'No—'

'She graduated last summer,' Mr Crosby said.

'I see . . .'

The three of them sat in silence for a long moment.

Jenny said, 'When did she go missing, exactly?'

Mr Crosby said, 'We spoke to her on the phone on the night of Monday, 11 January. She was at work on the Tuesday, but didn't arrive on the Wednesday.'

'Where was she on the Tuesday night?'

'In her flat, we think. The bed looked slept in. Her boyfriend called her mid-evening. Everything seemed fine.'

'Did she take anything with her?'

Mrs Crosby said, 'It looked like she'd packed a bag. Her wallet and passport were gone. She took five hundred pounds from an ATM near her flat at seven-thirty on the Wednesday morning.'

'Has there been any activity on the account since?'

'No,' Mr Crosby said definitely. 'And no record of her leaving the country that we can find.'

Jenny said, 'Was there any indication that anything was wrong?'

'It was a complete bolt from the blue,' Mrs Crosby said. 'She seemed perfectly happy. She had a good job, a new boyfriend—' She stopped mid-sentence and glanced at her husband, who seemed to have been struck by the same thought. She let him take over.

'We think she might have been seeing an Asian chap last year,' he said, as if it was a source of great shame. 'My wife was visiting one day last October and saw him leaving her flat. She said he was just a friend, but ... you know. One has an instinct.'

'Do you know who he was?'

'Salim something, I think. She never mentioned a surname.'

'What did he look like?'

Mr Crosby turned to his wife, who said, 'Mid-twenties, a little older than Anna Rose. Perfectly respectable,' adding apologetically, 'quite good-looking, really.'

Mr Crosby said, 'Christ, I knew we should have said something. What the hell has she got herself mixed up in?'

Mrs Crosby put a calming hand on her husband's back. 'I don't think it was still going on. She was really taken with Mike. They met at work.'

'At Maybury?'

'Yes ... He was her first line manager, her boss, I suppose. She started a two-year training programme last September – the graduate programme.'

'This Asian friend, do you know anything more? Was he involved politically in any way?'

'I've no idea,' Mr Crosby said. 'I've never heard Anna Rose talk politics in her life.'

'What are her interests?'

'Having a good time, as far as I could make out,' he said. 'Stunned us both completely when she went straight into a job. She only took physics because she thought there would be less competition getting onto the course.'

'Did she do well?'

'Not particularly,' Mrs Crosby said. 'A 2:2. She was lucky

to get on the graduate scheme at all. She'd always talked about going off travelling for a year.'

'Her looks probably helped,' her husband said. 'Men would do anything for her.'

Jenny glanced at the few tasteful black and white family photographs arranged on a polished walnut bureau. Anna Rose in her late teens had shoulder-length blonde hair and a twinkling, mischievous smile that spelled trouble. She was more elemental, less refined than her adoptive parents.

Jenny said, 'How did she end up in this job? It sounds almost out of character.'

Mr Crosby shrugged, seemingly at a loss to explain it other than as just another of his daughter's many surprises. His wife said, 'She got on very well with one of her tutors – Dr Levin. I had the impression that she pushed Anna Rose in that direction. Pulled a few strings, probably, but Anna Rose would never have admitted to taking someone else's help.'

'She was very independent?'

'Oh yes,' Mr Crosby said. 'And headstrong. It didn't matter how wrong she was, she was always right.' His tone suggested he'd already made up his mind about what had happened: his feisty, naive daughter, too good-looking for her own good, had got involved with some damn-fool foreigner. If she wasn't already dead, she was certainly beyond any help they could offer.

Mrs Crosby said, 'Does this mean there will be a criminal investigation?'

'Of course there will,' her husband snapped. 'It's bloody obvious. She's up to her eyes in something.'

'You don't know that, Alan,' she protested, pained by his anger.

'You know how impressionable she is. She's been like it since she was small.' He turned to Jenny. 'I'll be honest with you, Mrs Cooper – we were amazed she survived her teens. Expelled from two good schools, God knows how many unsuitable boys. She was always getting into trouble.'

Mrs Crosby, succumbing to tears, said, 'That's not fair—'

Jenny said, 'I've no reason to talk to the police at the moment. But I would like to look around your daughter's flat, and also talk to Mike Stevens.'

Jenny left the Crosbys' home with a set of keys to Anna Rose's flat and Mike Stevens's mobile number. She called him from her car, hoping to meet him later that morning, but he answered from a hotel room in the Lake District. He was on a week-long business trip to the nuclear reprocessing plant at nearby Sellafield. There was nothing to be gained from staying at home, he said: Anna Rose's parents had followed up every one of her friends and acquaintances they knew, who were far more than he did. They had only been together for a little short of three months.

Jenny said, 'I know this is going to sound a little strange, Mr Stevens, but would Anna Rose have had any access to radioactive material, caesium 137 for example?'

She was met by what she interpreted as a stunned silence. When Mike Stevens found his voice, he said, 'Why would you ask that?'

'It's just that traces of that substance have turned up in another case I'm investigating.'

'A *death*?'

Jenny said, 'Don't panic. There's no connection with Anna Rose apart from the caesium. I just need to know if any could have escaped from your plant.'

'God, no. Do you know anything about the nuclear industry? Everything's dealt with by robots.'

'You're saying it's impossible for her to have got hold of such a substance?'

'You'd have as much chance. What is this? What's she meant to have done?'

'Nothing. It's probably just two unconnected events. One more question – what do you know about an Asian friend of hers called Salim?'

'Never heard of him.'

'Her mother saw him leaving her flat last October.'

'Where the hell is all this coming from? Anna Rose doesn't have a friend called Salim. She was seeing me last October.'

'Sorry to have troubled you, Mr Stevens. Mr or Mrs Crosby will fill you in. Try not to worry.'

'Hey—'

She hung up and dialled Alison's home number. It rang seven times before she answered with a cautious hello.

'I thought you might be at church,' Jenny said.

Alison ignored the comment. 'You're alive then, Mrs Cooper. Half of Bristol's trying to get hold of you. Everyone thinks you know something.'

'Not yet, but I'm working on it. Has it hit the news yet? I haven't heard anything.'

'Not a squeak. There must be some sort of blackout.'

'I don't know if that's frightening or reassuring. I need to get hold of a dosimeter.'

'A what?'

'Andy Kerr's number will do.'

Andy took her call from what sounded like a gym with bad pop music and weights clanking in the background. There was obviously no girlfriend to keep him occupied on a Sunday morning. He still had the dosimeter in his lab coat pocket, he said, but the entire mortuary building had been sealed off while it was being decontaminated. He wasn't expecting to be allowed back in before mid-week. He would have called Sonia Cane, but he'd heard she was writing a report complaining that he'd acted improperly in not informing the Health Protection Agency immediately he discovered radiation on Mrs Jamal's body.

'What's she frightened of?' Jenny said.

'Same thing as me – getting sacked. I've already been told not to discuss it with anyone, not even you, apparently.'

'I won't tell. So where can I get a dosimeter?'

'Today?'

'It'd be helpful.'

Andy sighed. 'I'll make some calls.'

Jenny picked up the badge dosimeter from the junior radiographer working the Sunday shift at the Vale. He didn't ask any questions and Jenny didn't offer any explanations. He had a queue of casualties waiting, and in his line of work the badge was a standard and unremarkable piece of equipment. It was nowhere near as sophisticated as Sonia's handheld device: a small piece of photographic film contained in a credit-card-sized badge with a colour key. When exposed to radiation the film would turn a steadily darker shade of green.

It was less than a fifteen-minute drive to Anna Rose's flat in a new build not far from Parkway station on the north-west edge of the city. An area punctuated by business parks, industrial estates and arterial roads, it was charmless but convenient for the motorway, and less than twelve miles to Maybury. The block was a three-storey building wedged into a far corner of the estate. Every inch of narrow roadway was lined with parked cars. There wasn't a space to be had, so Jenny left her car blocking a turning circle.

There were two keys on the ring the Crosbys had given her. The first opened the door to the confined communal hallway, the second unlocked the door to Anna Rose's flat. Jenny checked the dosimeter: it remained the lightest shade of green.

She entered a small, conspicuously orderly one-bedroom apartment. The door opened straight from the outside landing into a kitchen-cum-living room furnished with a few items of simple modern furniture. A window looked out over a fenced-off area of scrub that had been cleared for development which had never happened. The dosimeter remained unchanged. She moved around the room, glancing over a shelf unit laden with university text books, opened drawers, checked the bathroom and thoroughly searched the tiny bedroom, poking the dosimeter into every corner, but it stuck stubbornly at *no hazard*.

She was both relieved and disappointed, and a little weary. She sat down on one of the two chairs at the small pine dining table and took stock. It was what she hadn't found that was most interesting. There was no suitcase or rucksack, no computer, camera or mobile phone. No wallet or toothbrush. There were empty hangers in the wardrobe, only a few pairs of socks and underwear in the chest of drawers. There were no signs of forced entry at the front door. The pile of mail on the kitchen counter and the few items she had picked up from the mat were unremarkable – bills or junk. Unlike Nazim and Rafi, it seemed that Anna Rose had packed and left deliberately.

Jenny tried to avoid the temptation to speculate, but she had an instinct she couldn't ignore, a sixth sense that told her this room belonged to someone who was alive, still in the game. It didn't smell dead; the atmosphere was disturbed but not leaden.

She scanned the room one last time for any hint of a clue. There was nothing. No notebooks, no scraps of paper, no rubbish in the bin. Virtually no trace of Anna Rose except her textbooks and a number of paperbacks lined up on the shelf beneath them. Jenny glanced at the titles: all light, slightly risqué fiction aimed at young women and a couple of trashy celebrity biographies. Anna Rose might be intelligent, but she couldn't be called cultured. It seemed odd to Jenny that a bright young woman would have no intellectual curiosity beyond her narrow subject, yet the syndrome felt somehow familiar. She turned her attention to a framed poster – the only object approaching a piece of art in the flat. She had barely noticed it before: from a distance it looked like a crude cartoon rendering of the Mona Lisa. Up close it was a collage of hundreds of photos of a younger, barely clad Britney Spears striking provocative poses. It was clever, Jenny thought, and imagined it appealing both to the scientist and the party girl in Anna Rose: sexy and serious at the same time. She was reminded of her visit to Sarah Levin's home: the young academic who spent her days with her head in particle theory but came home at night to MTV and glossy magazines. They struck an attitude, these young women: took a whole lot of things for granted Jenny's generation never had, but felt strangely shallow and unformed for it. What did they believe in? What then did they have to fall back on in times of crisis?

She checked the dosimeter one last time and locked the apartment door behind her. The radiation trail had gone cold, but she left the building certain of her next move.

There was no reply to the doorbell at Sarah Levin's apartment. Jenny waited outside in her car for over an hour and tried to order the theories invading her mind into a series of credible possibilities. Given that each one had to begin with the theft of radioactive material, it wasn't easy.

It had started to rain and she was feeling both tired and in need of a pill when a powder blue Fiat 500 pulled into a space across the street. Sarah Levin jumped out carrying several upmarket carrier bags and headed for her front door. Jenny beat her to it, intercepting her on the pavement.

'Dr Levin – I need to ask you some more questions.'

The young woman was surprised and affronted.

'Now? Are you joking? I'm only calling home for five minutes and then I'm on my way out again.'

She made for the front door. Jenny pursued her.

'It's about Anna Rose Crosby. I understand you knew her well.'

Sarah Levin stopped and turned, irritated.

'I've got friends who are lawyers – they couldn't believe that you came to my house. What do you think you're doing?'

'She's missing.'

'I heard.'

'Do you know why that might be?'

'Why would I know? I was her tutor, not her friend. I really have to get on.' She fished her keys from her pocket.

Jenny said, 'Her family were very surprised she got on the graduate scheme at Maybury. They said you might have pulled strings for her.'

Sarah Levin sighed theatrically and flicked back her long blonde hair. 'I write references for all my students. I have no idea what any of this is about, and as you don't seem inclined to tell me, we'll leave it there, shall we?'

Jenny was about to hit her with the whole story – Mrs Jamal, the caesium 137, all of it – but an instinct told her to hold fire. There was panic in Sarah Levin's defiant expression, and anger. Jenny had her denial and if need be she could use it against her later.

Calmly, Jenny said, 'You seemed rather alarmed when I mentioned her name.'

'That wouldn't have anything to do with me being door-stepped?'

'You have no idea what might have caused her to disappear?'

'This is ridiculous. None at all.'

'When were you last in contact?'

'I don't know. Last summer.'

'You'd say that on oath?'

'I'm sorry, Mrs whoever-you-are, I've had enough of this. You can ask me for a written statement, but you can't interrogate me out in the street. I'm not stupid.'

She went through the door and pushed it hard shut behind her. Her scent hung briefly in the air. If Anna Rose was pretty, Sarah Levin was beautiful. It wasn't simply her looks, it was chemical. Not a man or a woman would pass her without glancing back either in lust or envy. From the photographs she had seen of him, Jenny assumed that Nazim had had something of that quality, too. He was certainly better looking that Sarah Levin's current partner. She could imagine Nazim falling hopelessly in love with her, no matter what religious principles might have stood in his way. And for a girl who could have had anyone, he must have been one of the more interesting propositions.

Jenny hurried back to the car and pulled out her phone.

'Alison, it's me.'

'I know, Mrs Cooper. I can tell from the ring,'

'There was no radiation at Anna Rose's flat.'

'Oh. Is that surprising?'

Jenny disregarded the sarcastic tone. 'I've just spoken to Sarah Levin again. I've had a thought – can you get hold of her medical records?'

'What, without her consent?'

'Yes.'

Somewhere in the background Alison's husband called out for her over the sound of a yapping dog. She shouted at him to hold on, then returned impatiently to the conversation.

'Isn't that a bit irregular, Mrs Cooper? Aren't you meant to ask the witness?'

'Sod the protocol, just get them.'

*

Jenny had driven across the city and was staring out through a streaky windscreen at a foggy dual carriageway when it occurred to her that there was one other person who linked both Anna Rose and Nazim Jamal: the gawky Professor Rhydian Brightman. She knew little about how universities worked, but thought it safe to assume that in a closed institution professional relationships would be intense and not much would go unnoticed by colleagues. Brightman must have discussed the inquest with Sarah Levin, if only out of concern for the reputation of his department. He must have heard about Anna Rose, and if strings had been pulled on her behalf, it was more than likely he had done some of the tugging.

She pulled into a filling station just short of the M4 motorway and made some more calls. Eventually she tracked down a porter in one of the halls of residence, who relished telling her it was more than his job was worth to give out the private number of a member of staff. Jenny lost patience and told him that unless he called back with it in five minutes he could expect a visit from the police.

It was Brightman himself who returned her call and asked tentatively how he could help. Jenny apologized for disturbing his weekend and asked if they could meet.

'What is it you want to know, Mrs Cooper? I really have no light to shed on what happened to those two young men.'

Jenny said, 'Nazim Jamal's mother was found dead on Thursday.'

'Oh. Poor woman.'

Jenny paused, weighing her next move. What the hell, why not hit him with it? He'd hear it sooner or later. 'It seems she may have had a visitor shortly before her death. And there were traces of caesium 137 on her body. The block of flats where she lived has been evacuated.'

He was silent for a moment. 'Well, I really don't know what to say . . .'

Jenny said, 'I've only a few questions. It won't take long.'

'Maybe it's best if you come to my office.'

Professor Brightman was waiting for her on the steps outside the physics department dressed in a scruffy anorak and carrying a battered leather briefcase. Making awkward small talk, Jenny followed him through cold, deserted corridors to his office: a tiny, cluttered room on the second floor overlooking the street. Clearing her a chair, he apologized for the temperature – economies meant that the heating was turned off on Sundays. They sat on either side of the desk in their coats. Jenny could barely feel her toes.

Agitated, Brightman pushed his thick glasses up his nose. 'Do you mind if I ask what manner of conversation this is, Mrs Cooper? My employers would normally expect me to inform them if I were being questioned by the authorities.'

'You're not under any suspicion, Professor. You can tell them anything you wish.'

He tapped his fingers anxiously on the desk. 'I'd rather this remained between us for now, if you don't mind. Obviously, if you need me to make an official statement—'

'Let's take it a step at a time, shall we? What brings me here today is a more recent student of yours – Anna Rose Crosby.'

'I remember her. You're not going to tell me—'

'No. All we know is that she's missing. The only reason I'm interested in her is because she works in the nuclear industry, and, as I told you, Mrs Jamal's body shows signs of radioactive contamination.'

Brightman frowned, perplexed. 'Caesium 137? You're sure?'

'The Health Protection Agency confirmed it. One hundred and ten milliSieverts.'

He shook his head in bewilderment. 'How on earth? Why?'

'I've no idea. But with Anna Rose having been missing for ten days, her connection with this department makes this an obvious line of inquiry, I'm sure you'll agree.'

'I hardly knew her, not personally – I only supervise post-grads these days – but she was a perfectly ordinary student as far as I know. Caesium 137 . . . ? We don't have anything like that here. I don't know if you know how—'

'I've got some idea. It's not the sort of thing you'd find lying around a university. Am I right?'

'Correct. Minute quantities for specific experiments, maybe, but very tightly controlled. There's not been any here.'

'Anna Rose Crosby was on the graduate-training pro-gramme at Maybury. Does that surprise you?'

'Not particularly. She was an average student from what I recall.'

'I meant more from the point of view of her character.'

'Really, I couldn't comment. Dr Levin would have more of an opinion.'

'I tried, but she's not inclined to help.'

'Oh,' Brightman said guardedly. 'You've already spoken to her?'

'Anna Rose Crosby's mother says that Dr Levin helped her daughter get the job. She formed the impression she used her influence.'

'I suppose she may have contacts. We do have the occa-sional industry presentation for the students.'

'You seem uncertain.'

'No . . . I'm just thinking about what you said. Dr Levin is still quite junior in the department. I can't see that she would have much influence to exert. And it's not really how we do things here.'

Jenny studied his face. He seemed genuinely confounded and troubled at the direction her questions were taking. He didn't strike her as a man who would lie convincingly. He was a scatty academic, unworldly to the bone. There were stains on his anorak, and signs of frequent shaving injuries on his neck. She could imagine him misreading people, failing to notice all manner of things happening right under his nose, but she couldn't see him orchestrating anything underhand.

'Anna Rose's parents think she may have had an Asian boyfriend last year. Salim someone. Ring any bells?'

He shook his head. 'Sorry. As I explained, I'm really not the person to ask.'

'Perhaps you could check with one of your colleagues who might have been closer to her, Dr Levin, even.'

'Yes . . . Yes, of course,' he said distractedly, his mind clearly racing ahead to the possible scandals that might engulf him.

Jenny hesitated, feeling sympathy for him. He seemed helpless; plainly he wasn't a political creature. She could imagine junior colleagues eagerly manoeuvring to lever him out of his untidy office at the slightest suggestion of mismanagement.

She struck a softer tone, moved by an urge to make him less anxious. 'Could I ask you something purely in your professional capacity?'

'Of course.'

'All I know about caesium 137 so far is that it's dangerous, that it's a by-product of the nuclear industry and there's a lot of it near Chernobyl. What could it be used for, exactly?'

'You're right to mention Russia,' he said, in rapid, animated staccato. 'That's where most of the illegally held substance is suspected of having originated – impoverished Soviet scientists making a few dollars in the early nineties. Yes, from what I've read in the popular press it's the material of choice for a dirty bomb. A small amount at the heart of a conventional device would scatter over a city on the wind, rendering it uninhabitable for decades. Dreadful.'

'I see.' A clearer picture began to form in her distinctly unscientific mind. She'd had a vague idea that it might be used for poisoning, or even in a localized bomb, but had never conceived of a target as vast as an entire city.

They looked at each other across the unruly stacks of books and papers, and for the first time Jenny understood the true depths of his concern.

'Do you have any idea how Mrs Jamal came to be contaminated?' he asked. 'I can't think of anything more worrying for the anti-terrorist people.'

'No,' Jenny said. 'But a man was sighted at the scene. Tall, white, slim, around fifty years old. He bears some resemblance to a figure seen leaving the hall of residence where Nazim Jamal was living on the night he disappeared.'

Brightman gazed into space. 'I remember the police mentioning someone like that at the time. One of the students claimed to have seen him.'

'Her name's Dani James. She gave evidence at the opening of my inquest last week. She also claims to have slept with Nazim during the week before.'

'I saw a press report . . .' His voice trailed off as he tried to make sense of these disjointed fragments.

Jenny said, 'There's a hint that Nazim might have been seeing another girl at the end of his first term; someone well spoken. I don't suppose you're able to say if that was Dr Levin?'

Brightman swivelled his eyes towards her. 'I beg your pardon?'

'I just wondered if she and Nazim had been an item?'

'What gives you reason to ask that?' His pupils, dilated with surprise, were grossly magnified by his thick glasses.

Jenny said, 'His mother accidentally took a phone call from a girl. It's a long shot, but whoever she is might still know something about him we don't.'

Brightman swallowed uncomfortably.

She'd hit on something, she could tell.

'As a matter of fact I did once see them together,' he said. He cleared his throat. 'The reason I remember is that I was asked this question once before – in late 2002 it must have been – by Mrs Jamal's solicitor, I think it was.'

Jenny's heart started to race. 'Alec McAvoy?'

Brightman frowned. 'Yes – Scottish.'

'He asked you if you thought Nazim and Sarah Levin had had a relationship?'

'He did,' he said, guiltily. 'And all I could remember was the one incident. It was in the lab along this corridor. One gets used to it among students . . .'

Jenny could barely speak. 'What did you tell McAvoy?'

'That I walked in on them. They stepped apart as if they'd been kissing. I remember they both looked rather flustered.'

'Have you ever spoken to Dr Levin about this?'

'It's not the sort of thing that comes up,' he said, adding defensively, 'She's very able. She went to Harvard on a Stevenson and came back with the most superb references.' His expression was almost tortured. 'Sarah wouldn't be mixed up with anything untoward. It's unthinkable.'

Jenny took a breath. 'If you don't mind, I'd like you to make a statement.'

Her body was burning; she no longer felt the cold.

# NINETEEN

PEOPLE HAD ALWAYS REMARKED ON how calmly Jenny accepted bad news. While others succumbed to tears at the announcement of a sudden death or unexpected tragedy, her outward response was invariably the opposite. An unnatural serenity would descend, her eyes would remain stubbornly dry as the emotional ones gravitated towards her seeking reassurance. She had such profound perspective, they would say, she was such a steadying presence. For many years she had believed that she did in fact possess a unique immunity to grief; that she was simply stronger than most. It took until her thirty-ninth year and her 'episode' (she had always refused to call it a breakdown) to realize the truth. Dr Travis, the kindly psychiatrist who had patiently and confidentially nursed her through the acutely painful months that followed, had helped her to understand that beyond a certain threshold her emotions internalized, failing to break the surface. They existed, powerfully so, but were confined to a strongroom somewhere deep in her subconscious. The trick was to open the door inch by inch to let the stored-up trauma – whatever that was – seep out to be processed. But try as she might, she hadn't yet found the key.

Alec McAvoy had deceived her. He had known all along that there had been something between Sarah Levin and Nazim, but he hadn't told her. Why? He had come to her inquest, sought her out when she was alone and quoted poetry to her.

Who was he, this crooked lawyer and convict who knew how to reach inside and touch her, this man, who, like no one else, made her feel that she wasn't alone? What did he want from her? Could Alison be right – was he hijacking her inquest in the hope of salvaging a wrecked career? Or were his motives even darker than that?

She didn't know. She couldn't know. Her instincts had dried up, her responses dulled. The rage and fury and betrayal that should have poured out of her were locked deep inside, leaving her nothing to cleave to except a flimsy layer of logic. Was he angel or devil? Floating in limbo, she had no means of knowing.

With the dry sliver of consciousness left to her, she resolved to retreat to solid ground. She would trust only her intellect, resist all speculation and conduct her inquest strictly by the rules. Her mistake had been to allow that precious rational part of her that withstood every assault to be undermined. Dig deep enough foundations, Dr Travis had told her, and you might shake, but you'll never fall down.

Winding the final mile up the lane to Melin Bach she became aware that forty minutes and twenty miles had passed in an instant. The fears and imaginings that often plagued her during these dark journeys home had dissolved. Her eyes followed the headlights and her mind turned as dispassionately as a clockwork mechanism as she planned her strategy. She would schedule the inquest to resume mid-week. She would issue witness summonses first thing in the morning and prepare detailed cross-examinations that would tease out every flaw in the evidence. She would make no judgements and reach no conclusions other than those precisely justified by what she heard. She would place herself beyond influence or criticism and deliver justice according to the law. That was how to build foundations and win back the confidence that, McAvoy had so effortlessly and astutely observed, had been knocked out of her.

She indulged herself in a moment of defiance: perhaps, unwittingly, he had made her stronger.

The lights in the cottage were on, the front path lit up by the powerful halogen lamp she'd had installed for the winter. And there was a dark blue BMW parked outside in the lane. She recognized it at once: it belonged to David, her ex-husband.

As she drew close and pulled up, he stepped out from the driver's seat. He looked even slimmer and fitter than the last time she had seen him over three months ago. He wore chinos and a T-shirt beneath a snug lambs-wool v-neck. Forty-seven years old and his hair was still its natural deep brown, his face sufficiently lined to lend him gravitas but the boyishness still lingering in his features. And somehow he managed his feat of agelessness despite working fifteen-hour days as a cardiac surgeon. There was no justice in his getting better looking as she slowly faded. He strolled forward to meet her as she climbed out of her car, his bearing as casually arrogant as ever.

'Jenny. We wondered where you were.' He looked at her in that way of his that said everything about her would inevitably prove mildly amusing.

'I switched my phone off – people pester me at the week-end.' She glanced up at the house and saw Ross pass the uncurtained landing window. 'I thought he was staying with you tonight.'

'He is . . .' He offered a more placatory smile. 'But he's decided he'd like to extend it for a while.'

'He's what? How long for? What have you been saying to him?' She heard the brittleness in her voice.

'Calm down, Jenny. I didn't come here for any sort of confrontation, quite the opposite. It's cold out here. Why don't we go inside?'

He motioned towards the gate. She stood her ground.

'When did he decide this? I thought he was happy here. He's got his girlfriend down the road—'

'He sees her at college.'

'The whole idea was to keep him out of the city. He hasn't touched drugs since he's been with me.'

'He's grown up a lot since last summer. I probably notice it more since I'm seeing less of him.'

'How did this happen? What's prompted it?'

'Can't we talk about this calmly?'

'I'm perfectly calm, David.'

'You're shaking.'

Jenny closed her eyes, telling herself not to react.

'All I'm asking,' she said with enforced restraint, 'is for you to tell me what's changed. You must have spoken to him.'

'Do you really want to have this conversation out here?'

'Wherever you want.'

She strode up the path.

David said, 'Do you want me to come in or not?'

'It might be an idea, as you're proposing to take my son away.'

The front door was ajar. She shoved it open and went straight through into the sitting room, wrenching off her coat and throwing it over a chair. David followed hesitantly.

'It sounds like he's upstairs,' Jenny said. 'You'd better shut the door.'

She remained standing, arms crossed, waiting for an

explanation. David glanced around the room with its stone-flag floor, low beams and draughty windows, his expression saying: *no wonder he doesn't want to stay.*

'Well?' Jenny said.

David stepped over to the sofa and perched dubiously on the arm as if it might give way beneath him. 'I'll be honest with you, Jenny. He's concerned about you. He thinks you might have too much pressure on you to worry about looking after him as well.'

'He said that?'

'Yes.'

'Because I don't have dinner on the table every evening at six? You work even longer hours that I do.'

'I do have Deborah.'

'She's got a career, too.'

'She's just gone part-time.'

'Has she? Did you give her any choice in the matter?'

David rode the punch with a hint of a wry smile. 'Actually, it's her decision. I was going to tell you – she's pregnant.'

'Oh . . . I see.' She felt numb. 'I suppose I should say congratulations.'

'Thank you. It wasn't exactly planned.'

Jenny didn't respond. Desperate as she had been to escape from David at the end of their marriage, part of her still resented the presence of another woman in his life. The fact that Deborah was still in her twenties, attractive and sweetly compliant made it all the more galling.

'I didn't mean to surprise you with that today,' he said with a trace of apology.

'No need to feel guilty on my account.'

But he did. She could see it in the heaviness that had settled around his eyes.

In the brief silence that followed Ross's footsteps moved across the creaking boards in the room above. Drawers opened and closed, the wardrobe door slammed: the sounds of hasty packing.

'I assume you would prefer me to be honest?' David said.

She resisted further sarcasm. How would dishonesty ever be preferable? It was always his way to make the wounds he inflicted feel self-imposed. She presumed it was a technique he had learned in his practice, his instinctive method of distancing himself from his patients' suffering and not infrequent deaths.

David braced himself. 'He doesn't think you can cope, Jenny. He's not being selfish, it makes him feel a burden. And if he stays and sees you struggling, it makes him feel even guiltier.'

'What makes him think I'm struggling? I love having him here . . . I thought we were getting on fine.'

'There's never any food in the house.'

'That's not true—'

'It's not a judgement. I wouldn't do any better by myself.'

'Why isn't he telling me this? We'll get a delivery.'

David sighed and drew a hand around his sinewy neck. 'Christ, Jenny, you're not well enough to be looking after someone else.'

'What do you know? I'm fine.'

'He told me about the other night, the state you came home in.'

'I was just tired.'

'He had to help you into bed. You don't even remember, do you? What happened? Did you take too many pills?'

The feeling retreated from her hands and feet. Each breath became a conscious effort as her nervous system began a systematic shutdown.

'It was late, that's all.'

'What are you doing, Jenny? Are you getting help? You may not believe it, but I do worry about you.'

'I see someone.'

'Good. These things can be overcome. I've colleagues who assure me—'

'You discuss me with your colleagues?'

'In the past . . .'

Her look arrested his lie.

'Only in the strictest confidence. Of course I want to know what more can be done for you.'

'To hear you talk, you wouldn't think I held down a responsible job, conducted inquests, consoled grieving families—'

'I know you do. But just holding it down isn't enough, is it? You've nothing to prove to me, Jenny, and money isn't an issue. I just want you to be right. So does Ross.'

'And this is your way of helping me along?'

'Sorting out other people's problems won't fix your own.'

Above them a door closed. Ross's footsteps sounded on the stairs.

'Give up my career as well as everything else, is that what you're suggesting?'

'Please don't be like that. You know what's right, I know you do. And our son has problems of his own to work through. He needs security.'

Ross reached the bottom of the stairs.

'We're in here,' Jenny said, as brightly as she could manage without sounding hysterical.

The latch lifted. He looked in, pale and awkward.

'Hi, Mum.' He glanced to his father.

'It's OK, Ross. We've had a chat.'

Jenny forced a smile. Words wouldn't come.

'We'll sort something out with weekends and what have you,' David said, more to Ross than Jenny. He got to his feet. 'We ought to hit the road. I'm sure you've got work to do.'

Ross looked at the floor. 'I'll see you.'

'Soon, I hope,' Jenny said.

He nodded, hair flopping over his eyes.

David moved towards the door placing a fatherly hand on Ross's shoulder. 'We can see ourselves out.'

Their footsteps retreated swiftly down the path. The boot clunked, the engine fired and David sped off down the hill, leaving a silence as absolute as the blackness of the night.

Jenny lowered herself into an upright chair and sat quite still, wishing she could feel the shame that should have accompanied the images playing through her mind: waking in her clothes, the pills spilled across the floor, the incoherent scrawl in her journal lying open at the foot of the bed. He would have read it, of course, if only for a clue as to why his mother had arrived home staggering, unable even to make it to her own bed. He would know about a man called McAvoy, her guilt, her lust, her ghosts. He wouldn't tell his father of course; that would only double his confusion at having a semi-lunatic for a mother. He would keep it to himself.

And the worst of it was David was right. She wasn't fit to nurture an adolescent with troubles of his own. She'd deluded herself into thinking that Ross had straightened himself out under her roof, when in fact his relative calm was due to her drama constantly upstaging his own. She hadn't given him space, she had stifled him.

It felt indecent to think in terms of irony, but she remembered what her late mother, who had abandoned her own family while Jenny was still at school, had once said when she had first talked of divorcing David – that children fared better with unhappy parents together than happy ones apart. How she had railed against that thought. How she had resented the notion that a woman oppressed and miserable could do better for her child. Another of her mother's axioms forged from bitter experience: a woman who leaves home, leaves everything. Perhaps she was right after all. She had experienced nothing to disprove it, nor for that matter had Mrs Jamal.

The telephone rang with a suddenness that jarred her nerves. She answered with a clipped hello but was met with an electronic voice informing her that she had messages on her answer service. Dumbly, she obeyed its request to play them.

There were eight. DI Pironi had called twice, first to stress that events at Mrs Jamal's flat were strictly a police matter, and second to emphasize that the investigation into the source of the radiation was secret. The press had been told that the white-suited operatives who had descended on the apartment block were searching for further forensic evidence. There were two calls from local journalists fishing for information, one from Gillian Golder asking abruptly for Jenny to call at her earliest convenience, and two from Simon Moreton, the senior official at the Ministry of Justice with responsibility for coroners. In the polite, faux-friendly manner he adopted with his wayward charges, he asked her to call 'on a matter of importance', leaving his home number. The last message was from Steve, asking how she was, and saying he'd like to come over if she was around.

With blunt fingers she punched in his number, not sure why, or what she would say to him. He answered on the second ring.

'It's me. You left a message,' she said.

'Yeah. Look, I . . . I shouldn't have left it like that the other night.' There was a quiet urgency in his voice, as if he had been on tenterhooks waiting for her call.

'Right,' she said distantly.

'I've been going through some things myself, you know . . .'

'Uh huh.'

A pause. He sighed, impatient with himself. 'What I was saying to you – about choices – it cuts both ways. I've been hiding away for ten years trying to avoid the issue.'

She knew she was meant to say something meaningful, meant to react to the subtext, but she couldn't fathom what it was. 'What issue?' she said.

'Commitment,' Steve said. 'What I stand for. What I feel.'

'I see.'

'I need to speak to you, Jenny. There's something you should know.'

'Steve, I'm very tired . . .'

'Jenny—'

'David took Ross away.'

'Oh. You're by yourself?'

'I'm no good to you right now. Don't come over . . . I need to sleep.'

'Jenny . . .'

'Please, don't.' She set down the receiver and felt only relief.

She was tempted to destroy her journal, to throw it into the grate and reduce it to ashes. She carried it from her study to the hearth and reached for the matches, but was seized by an overwhelming curiosity to read her last entry, to glimpse into the madness that had brought the world crashing around her ears.

*I don't know what happened tonight. That man . . . he does something to me. I don't even find him attractive – he's so tired and used up. But when he looks in my eyes I know he's not afraid of anything. What does it mean? Why him? Why now? It's as if*

She had a partial recollection of writing it, of sitting at her study desk seized with a sense of profundity which she couldn't transfer to the page. A nervous tap at the door. Ross had come in and told her it was late. She'd clasped the journal to her chest as he urged her up the stairs . . . Her shoulder had grazed the wall, she'd faltered, the climb too steep. And there her memory faded to black.

She snapped the notebook shut with a pang of self-disgust, but could only stare at the matches. She could hear Dr Travis back in the early days, warning her to rein in her imagination and not to let instability tempt her into believing nonsense, or finding connections where none existed. 'Stick to terra firma,' he had said, 'even the tiniest piece of land is better than all at sea.' For the recent casualty it was sound advice, but there had to be a time to move on, to strike out to new territory.

*It's as if* . . . It came to her now. She reached for a pen, turned back to the page and completed the sentence: . . . *he's come to tell me something I need to know.*

It was nearly midnight. She took the journal upstairs and hid it in her special drawer. As she climbed into bed and huddled against the cold, she realized that something had changed. For the first time in hours she felt a flicker of sensation, of fear and anger, and a hint, the faintest suggestion of excitement.

# TWENTY

She dressed in the black two-piece she normally reserved for formal occasions: an ivory silk blouse, a plain silver necklace and narrow, elegant shoes that squeezed her toes, dabbed perfume on her wrists and put on her best black cashmere coat. She swallowed a Xanax, checked her make-up and set out along the valley through drifting mist.

As she cleared the Severn Bridge she called the office number, knowing Alison would not yet have arrived, and left a message saying that she had a stop to make on her way in. She switched off the phone and tossed it into her bag. She drove past her usual exit, continued on to the next and headed towards the city centre and the Law Courts.

Outside on the steps tired lawyers and a cluster of slouching, hooded young men with their sulking, pinched-faced girl-friends smoked cigarettes and avoided each others' eyes. She picked her way through them, drawing stares, and pushed through the doors into the atrium, thankful that no one had spat at her. She cleared the security check and scanned the noisy crush of lawyers, clients, witnesses and court ushers. If it had been a County Court every other face would have been familiar, but she had never practised criminal law and the Crown Court – where criminal cases were tried – was an alien and daunting world to her.

She skirted through the crowd and looked into the steamy,

crowded cafeteria but couldn't see McAvoy's face. She would have glanced into the solicitors' room but shyness held her back. Instead, she stood in line at the reception desk until, after a ten-minute wait, the heavy-set girl behind the desk came off the phone for long enough to bark out an announcement over the tannoy: 'Would Mr McAvoy of O'Donnagh and Drew please come to reception immediately.'

She hovered self-consciously by the desk, watching the barristers and their clients arguing and horse-trading. There was an atmosphere of barely suppressed anger: the air was filled with expletives and the police officers who passed through walked quickly, eyes fixed on the ground. Near to where she was standing a young woman suddenly wailed then swore violently at a lawyer who had delivered bad news. Two other girls held her back as she lashed out at him. She struggled, wrenched free and had dug her nails into his face before a court usher and an elderly constable came to the man's rescue. He stood dabbing incredulously at his bleeding cheek with a crumpled handkerchief as his ungrateful client was dragged away.

'It wouldn't be you taking an honest man from his work, Mrs Cooper?'

She looked round from the commotion to see McAvoy approaching, carrying an untidy bundle of papers under his arm.

'I've a man downstairs with his life in my hands – the barrister's proving himself a useless shite – so I can't be long.'

'Is there somewhere we can talk in private?' she said. 'A conference room?'

'At this time of the morning? You'll be lucky.'

'There's a café over the road.'

'I've a bail application in ten minutes. Fella'll have my guts on the floor if we don't spring him – he's got a plane to catch

282

at lunchtime.' He glanced around the atrium then motioned her to follow him. 'Let's see what we can do.'

Jenny followed him through the shifting crowd that smelled of poor homes and stale sweat and into a small, empty courtroom. The advocates' benches were piled high with thick files and textbooks, suggesting a long-running trial was in progress.

McAvoy glanced up at the clock above the door. 'We've got five minutes.'

She'd prepared a speech which she'd spent the entire journey into town reciting. She was Her Majesty's Coroner, she was going to say, a judicial officer charged with a grave and serious task, and he had not only interrupted her investigation, he had misled her. He had failed to tell her that eight years ago he had discovered facts about Nazim Jamal that could have a material bearing on the case. If he didn't explain himself he would be fortunate not be charged with attempting to pervert the course of justice for a second time in his dubious career.

She steeled herself, but was torn from her moorings by a rush of anger. 'Who the hell do you think you are, McAvoy? What the fuck are you playing at? You spoke to Brightman eight years ago. You *knew* about Sarah Levin and Nazim.'

The smile faded. He glanced to the door, then looked back at her with a convict's eyes.

'There's nothing to know.'

'He saw them together. This teenage jihadi was screwing a white girl who was the only person to say anything about him going abroad.' She felt her face glowing with rage.

McAvoy shrugged. 'The boy was a hypocrite, or he got lucky. What of it? Hadn't his poor mother suffered enough? She was a very conservative woman.'

'His mother's *dead*.'

'I'm as shocked as you are.'

She took a step towards him. 'Why did you lie to me?'

'I told you. He was all she had. Why not let her believe he was the only woman he'd ever loved?'

'You *bastard*.'

She went to hit him. McAvoy dropped his papers, caught her wrist and gripped it hard.

'Are you crazy?'

'Fuck you.'

As if by reflex, she grabbed a ballpoint from the desk to her right, swung her arm wildly and stabbed it hard into the side of his shoulder. McAvoy exclaimed in pain, releasing her wrist as he clutched at his shoulder.

'*Je-sus*.'

Jenny stepped backwards, breathing hard, the pen still gripped tight in her left hand. McAvoy looked up at her, jaw clenched. He flicked out a hand, smacking her smartly across the face and sending her tumbling back against the rail of the dock. She caught hold of it and pulled herself upright, more stunned than hurt. She turned to see him straightening, catching his breath. She flinched, expecting another blow, but he stooped and gathered his scattered papers from the floor.

Holding a hand to her stinging cheek, she watched him sifting and checking the disordered documents as if she wasn't there, grimacing at the pain in his shoulder. There was something obsessive, pathetic almost, in the way he fussed over them.

'I shocked you, didn't I?' Jenny said, feeling a pulse of adrenalin coursing through her veins. 'You weren't expecting that.'

'I think you shocked yourself,' he said, without looking up.

'I knew you'd be an unrepentant liar.'

'You know what you are? A danger to yourself.'

284

'And what are you? A coward? Are you frightened I'm going to have you put in jail?'

McAvoy shuffled his papers against the surface of the desk and turned to face her. 'And why would you do that?'

'For trying to hijack my inquest. Trying to use it to reinstate your tawdry career. I can't imagine how humiliating it must be going from big-shot partner to outdoor clerk.'

'At least I never cracked in court,' he said. 'No one could ever say I flinched.'

Jenny had wondered when he would reveal the fact he'd dug the dirt and use her past against her. It was a relief. She could see him for what he was now.

'You lied with a straight face – is that the best you can say about yourself?'

'I've never lied to you. I tried to push you towards the truth.'

'Oh, really?'

'I gave you leads, evidence you wouldn't have got anywhere else. I got you Madog and Tathum.'

'How can I trust you? How do I know Madog is for real? He could just be another one you've bought.'

'You're the coroner, Mrs Cooper. Work it out. I've got a hearing to get to.'

As he stepped past her, Jenny said, 'You look terrified.'

He paused at the door and looked back at her. 'Maybe if you'd been a stronger woman I might have found a little more courage, but you're really quite a fragile flower, aren't you, Jenny? Damaged, I'd say. So why don't you let yourself off the hook. You're out of your depth.'

'You're full of shit.'

McAvoy said, 'I'm sorry. I made a mistake upsetting you. And as you said, Mrs Jamal's gone, so what does it matter any more?' He smiled faintly and turned to go.

Jenny said, 'You still haven't explained why you hid things from me.'

He hesitated a second time, then dipped his head. He addressed his quiet words to the door. 'I drink, Jenny. It eases my burden but it makes me trust others even less than myself. I look at people I've known for years and they change before my eyes.'

'What were you *thinking*? What do you *want* from me?'

'It's of no interest to you.'

'Try me.'

He shook his head.

'Tell me, Alec. Let *yourself* off the hook.'

A pause. 'Proof, I suppose . . .'

'Of what?'

'That He hasn't completely got me yet.'

'Who?'

'The author of all this sadness.'

'You're not making sense.'

'No . . .' He glanced back at her briefly with pale, red-rimmed eyes. 'What happened at her flat? I heard there were men in white suits there all weekend.'

She hesitated. 'Something was found on her body, a substance.'

'You trust them? Who knows what dirty tricks they'd play. She was a very inconvenient woman, Mrs Jamal.'

'I'm not sure who to trust.'

He nodded with a heavy sadness. 'Maybe you are better off out of it. If they'll bury the truth, they won't worry about burying you.'

He pushed out into a busy corridor.

'Alec—' Jenny called out after him, but he was gone.

McAvoy's expression lodged behind her eyes like a vision of a drowning man. She was left with the unsettling feeling that she had got barely to the threshold of something; that he had darker secrets to tell but had spared her for fear of dragging her down with him. She had gone to him hoping to exorcise one ghost, but had come away pursued by several. She should have felt shock or humiliation at her behaviour – no better than the girl lashing out at her lawyer – but the sense of disjuncture she felt was overwhelming. Her mind, body and emotions seemed to occupy three separate spheres that were tugging apart.

Alison looked up from her desk as she entered and spoke in an urgent whisper.

'There you are, Mrs Cooper. Mr Moreton's here to see you. I sent him through.'

'Moreton? What does he want?'

'He wouldn't say. He's been waiting nearly an hour.' There was a definite note of censure in her voice.

'I was busy.'

'Wait till you see what's come in over the weekend.' Alison pointed to a thick pile of fresh death reports.

'I'll get to them later.'

Jenny braced herself and went through to her office.

Moreton set down his newspaper and greeted her warmly, but with a certain reserve. 'Jenny. How lovely to see you again.'

He extended a hand.

'Simon.'

'It's been far too long. When was it, August?'

'It must have been.' Jenny had done her best to forget the summer drinks party the Ministry had held in the Middle Temple Hall. Moreton had drunk too much cheap champagne – as had she – and made a clumsily veiled pass, mentioning several times that his wife was in France with the children. Unluckily for him, it was chiefly the mention of his family which had stopped her from being tempted.

'You didn't get my phone messages?' he said.

'I was out until late last night,' she said, taking off her coat.

'Never mind. I'm always glad of the excuse.' He flashed a flirtatious smile and settled back in his seat.

'I can guess what brings you here.' She pulled her chair away from her desk, placing it at an informal angle. 'I presume you've heard about Mrs Jamal?'

'That would be something of an understatement even by civil service standards. I kept Gillian Golder and her people at bay – didn't want to put you under any undue stress – but blind panic wouldn't be a misdescription of their current state.'

'Do they have any theories about where the caesium came from?'

'Theories, yes; suspects, none at all. I believe they've pulled a few people in, including one of your witnesses.'

'Anwar Ali?'

'Sounds familiar. But I don't get the impression they're making any ground.' He shrugged and looked expectantly to her for a contribution.

'I suppose they're assuming that whoever contaminated her had something to do with her son – a terrorist cell perhaps.'

'I'm sure that's the thrust of it.'

'Do they think it was murder?'

'It's being considered.'

'All I know is that she had become convinced she was being watched. She reported it to the police. And around the time she died the caretaker's wife saw a suspicious man in the lobby of the building who pushed past her. My officer spoke to her; she'll have given a statement to the police too.'

'Yes, I had a bit of a briefing yesterday, got the general gist.' He tapped the arms of his chair with his fingers, a sign that he was being forced unwillingly to the point. 'Look, I know all about the sanctity of a coroner's inquest, but they are rather hoping that any evidence you might have would be shared.'

'I don't have any.'

'I understand you adjourned your inquest to pursue further lines of inquiry.'

McAvoy's parting words echoed back to her. She could mention Sarah Levin, Anna Rose, Madog and Tathum, but where would that leave her inquiry? They'd get to her witnesses first and contaminate them like they had Mrs Jamal. *Christ*, she was thinking like McAvoy now. Why not tell just tell him everything, hand over responsibility?

'Well?' Moreton said gingerly. 'Did they yield anything?'

'No.' Her denial emerged without conscious thought.

Moreton was disappointed. 'That's not exactly right, is it, Jenny? You've been sniffing after a car. Your officer's taken a statement from a witness.'

'You've been interrogating my officer? You've no right to do that. My inquiries are carried out in the strictest confidence.'

He spread his hands in a gesture of innocence. 'I'm afraid in a situation like this the rules have to bend a little – surely you of all people understand that.'

Defiantly, Jenny said, 'If you've been sent to mine me for information ahead of my inquest, you can forget it. Gillian Golder and her people can sit in the public gallery like anyone else.'

'In any normal case I could see your point, but there's someone running about out there with radioactive material. Who knows what they might be doing? Certainly not waiting to be caught out by your inquest.'

'I have no information to offer on Amira Jamal's death other than what I've told you. Anyway, it's a police matter.

All I'm concerned with is finding out what happened to her son.'

'I must say, I'm very disappointed, Jenny. In this of all cases, I was hoping for a rather more cooperative attitude. We are all in this struggle together.'

'I know it's frustrating for your friends to have to accept there are some doors they can't simply kick down when they choose, but this is one of them. I don't just have the right, Simon; I have a legal duty to carry out a thorough and *independent* inquiry. I don't even know what you're thinking of coming here like this. You should be fighting my corner, not theirs.'

Moreton nodded patiently as if her outburst had gone some way to persuading him. 'I'll level with you, Jenny. MI5 think there's an argument for seeking a warrant to search these premises under the Terrorism Act. They'd have done it yesterday, but I persuaded them you'd voluntarily offer up anything that could possibly be of use.'

'They'd do the same for me, would they? They won't even release their files from 2002.'

'I could suggest they go some way to accommodating that request.'

Jenny could have picked up the telephone and hurled it into his gutless poor-me smile, but she held tight and suppressed her fury. It wasn't just that the Security Services, a branch of the executive, was trying make a coroner into a puppet; a man whose job it was to defend the principle of judicial independence was doing his utmost to destroy it. All the fashionable talk of friendly cooperation across the branches of state meant only one thing: all power to the most powerful. Tyranny.

Looking into Moreton's weak face with its superficial charm, any lingering doubts were dispelled.

'If I don't do my job as it's meant to be done, Simon, there is no rule of law. All that's left is what's convenient, which is fine until you're branded the inconvenient one. Mrs Jamal wasn't convenient, nor was properly investigating her son's death. I'm certainly not convenient, but if you were in a tight spot, I bet you'd rather have me on your side.'

With a note of regret, Moreton said, 'If only all aspects of your character inspired such confidence.'

'I'm resuming my inquest on Wednesday. And it's not going to end until I've found out what happened to Nazim Jamal.'

To his credit, Moreton knew when he was beaten. He offered no threats or inducements, no warnings of retribution: Jenny had faced him down and won. With a limp handshake and a polite goodbye to Alison he left with nothing more than the name and occupation of Frank Madog.

Emboldened by her victory, Jenny stepped out into reception and followed the sounds of clinking crockery to the kitchenette. Alison glanced up guiltily from her ritual tea-making.

'Can I get you anything, Mrs Cooper?'

'You told Moreton about Madog.'

'He didn't give me any choice. He said I had to.'

'Had to what?'

'Tell him what more we'd found.'

'Did he say what would happen if you didn't?'

'I'm sorry, Mrs Cooper, but who am I to contradict him?'

'You could have waited for me.'

'He wouldn't let me. He insisted. He said there would be implications.'

'He threatened you?'

'Not exactly.'

'Did he say why he wanted this information?'

'No . . .'

'You just gave it up without a struggle.'

'It wasn't like that. He said that the Security Services had spoken to him. They'd told him Nazim Jamal and Rafi Hassan were involved with terrorists. They think the same ones might even have killed Mrs Jamal.'

'Did he offer any evidence for this?'

'Maybe if you'd been here—?'

'What else did you tell him?' Jenny snapped, cutting her off.

'Nothing. I didn't even mention Dr Levin's medical records.'

'So you didn't trust him *that* much?'

'I'm not a lawyer. I didn't know what to think.'

'Who else have you been speaking to – Dave Pironi?'

'Of course not.'

'It's a reasonable question. You pray with him.'

Alison's defensiveness hardened to anger. 'With respect, Mrs Cooper, that's my private business and nothing to do with you.'

'It is if it affects my investigation. Have you ever stopped to think that he might be using you? For all I know he was personally involved in whatever happened to Nazim Jamal. Isn't it a coincidence that when it comes back to light he casts himself as your spiritual mentor?'

'You don't know what you're talking about.'

'I know about your daughter.'

Alison froze and stared at her. 'Really? And what exactly do you think you know about my daughter, Mrs Cooper?'

'I've heard you on the phone to your husband. She's living with another woman. What's Pironi told you – that she can be healed by the power of prayer?'

'I'll tell you about my daughter,' Alison said. 'When she was seventeen years old, a young man forced himself on her. You can call it rape, if you like. For two years she would hardly leave the house. And even then she wouldn't be alone in a room with another man, even her father. And Dave Pironi didn't seek me out. I went to him. I'd seen him lose his wife to cancer and cope with his son being out in Afghanistan; I wanted to know what he'd got that I hadn't. It may not suit your way of seeing the world, but you of all people should know that the truth isn't always what you'd like it to be.'

The kettle clicked off as it came to the boil. With trembling hands Alison poured water over her tea bag and doused it with milk. 'I got your copies of Dr Levin's records, by the way. She was diagnosed with chlamydia in April 2002. Too late, poor girl. She lost her fallopian tubes to it.'

# TWENTY-ONE

'WHERE WERE YOU WHEN THIS blackout happened?'

'In my office . . .'

'You became unconscious?'

'Not quite. My heart started racing. It wouldn't stop. I couldn't breathe, couldn't move, not for half an hour or more.'

'And then you called me?'

'Yes.'

'And then?'

'I took some pills and carried on working.'

'What pills?'

Jenny paused and briefly considered lying but couldn't summon the energy to face the cross-examination that would inevitably follow. 'Xanax.'

Dr Allen's registered no surprise. He simply made a note. 'In addition to your other medication?'

'No . . . I stopped taking that several days ago.'

'For any particular reason?'

Jenny faltered. 'I thought it would make me more effective, give me some passion back.'

He nodded with no hint of judgement. 'Did it work?'

'I suppose it heightened everything.'

'Did you experience mood swings?'

'I'm not sure.'

'Erratic behaviour?'

She cast her mind back over the past several days. 'I felt driven. Less inhibited . . . but anxious, on edge.'

'Yes, you would have done.' He gave her a look as if to say he was sorry he hadn't been there to intervene.

If I was him I'd be furious, Jenny thought. I certainly wouldn't have come running all the way from Cardiff to Chepstow because an irresponsible woman had deliberately ditched her medication. But that's precisely what he had done, and not for the first time. She felt ashamed of herself. Her stupidity seemed all the more unforgivable in his benign, unruffled presence.

'Tell me what was going on just before the attack,' Dr Allen said.

Jenny cringed. 'I argued with my officer. She'd given out information I thought she shouldn't have . . . and then I accused her of something.' Her voice deserted her.

'What?'

Jenny forced the saliva pooling in her mouth down her throat.

Dr Allen smiled calmly. 'Take your time.'

'She had an issue with her daughter . . . She's been preoccupied with it. I was annoyed that it was affecting her work, but it turned out I'd misread it all. I'd leapt to the wrong conclusions . . . I hurt her badly.'

'Do you want to tell me what the issue was?'

'Not particularly.'

'I think you should, Jenny. It might help.'

She rolled her head from side to side trying to release the tightness in the back of her neck.

'Try,' he said, coaxing gently.

'It's not what it was about, it's the fact I got it so wrong. I was so sure of myself . . . It's why I stopped the pills, to get the certainty back, the fire . . . I felt so *deceived*.'

He noted down her answer. 'Are you going to tell me or not?'

Jenny let out an angry sigh. 'Her daughter's a lesbian. She's been praying with a man at a church for her to be healed. He's a detective I don't happen to trust. I said this man was using and misleading her. But it turns out the reason her daughter is living with a woman is because when she was a teenager she was raped. And the detective's had more than his share of suffering too.' She dug her nails into the arms of her chair. 'God, I feel so much better.'

Ignoring her sarcasm, Dr Allen looked up from his notes and regarded her thoughtfully. 'You hurt her and, what's worse, you felt deceived into hurting her?'

'It was just an incident. It was probably coming off the pills. It's not as if you hadn't warned me.'

'Now you're avoiding the issue.'

'I'm not avoiding anything. I came straight here.'

'Then if you want my help, you'll let me offer it.' It was first time she'd heard him issue anything like a rebuke. He continued in this sterner vein. 'You practised family law for fifteen years, is that correct?'

'Yes.'

'You represented the local authority, taking vulnerable children into care.'

'Mostly.'

He flipped back through the pages of his notebook. 'Yes, here we are. And the first time you had a full-blown anxiety attack was in a courtroom. You were reading out a medical report . . . Can you remember anything about the case?'

'I could hardly forget it.' She felt her heart beat faster. She closed her eyes and took a breath, fixed her mind on a vision of a Mediterranean sunset. It helped a little, but not much. 'There was an eight-year-old boy, Owen Patrick Lindsey. I'd dealt with his case off and on for two years. His mother wasn't coping so we took him into care. Most kids are glad to be out of a chaotic home, but he kept trying to escape and get back. I went against the social worker's advice and chose not to contest his mother's application to have him returned to her. The first weekend he was at home she got drunk and threw a pan of scalding water over him . . . It was a report from the burns unit I was reading out.'

Dr Allen scribbled rapidly. Still writing, he said, 'And you went from the vulnerable to the dead – dead people beyond help, or your ability to harm them, at least.'

'Hmm. Maybe.'

He lifted his pen from the page and fixed her with a look of intense interest. 'You don't like hurting people, do you, Jenny? In fact, I'd say you'd do almost anything to avoid causing pain.'

'I don't make a very good job of it.'

'When you've spoken of your ex-husband it's always of his arrogance, the offhand way he treats you and his patients. Yes, I remember: you once said it infuriates you how little he's affected by what you see as the damage he causes.'

'A heartless heart surgeon. Work that one out.'

'Perhaps he's just reconciled to a basic fact of life. You can't live without causing some pain. And we do tend to marry people with qualities we lack.'

'I despise his attitude.'

'But you try to mimic it. It's not a submissive, motherly woman I see sitting in that chair twice a month.'

'A moment ago you were saying I couldn't bear to hurt people.'

'Your defensiveness tells me I'm onto something. People's emotional responses break down when they can no longer bear the burden they are consciously or subconsciously placing on themselves. Believe me, it's becoming obvious you have an overwhelming sense of responsibility for things beyond your ability to control.'

'Is this a eureka moment? It doesn't feel like it.'

'The dream you mentioned last time – the children vanishing into thin air. Nothing, not a thing you could do to help them. It terrified you.'

'I can't fault your logic,' Jenny said drily.

'And the other image that haunts you: the crack opening up in the corner of your childhood bedroom; the monstrous, unseen presence in a secret room behind it. It's the realm beyond your control where the horrors happen.'

Jenny let out a heavy sigh. She had lost the ability to be excited by potential revelations.

Dr Allen continued undaunted. 'What have you been writing about in your journal?'

'Hardly anything.'

'Really?'

Just the mention of it consumed her with yet another more powerful wave of shame. There was no question of confessing to him that Ross had found it. She couldn't even deal with the thought herself. She parried him with a partial truth. 'Mostly stuff about wanting to feel real again, connect with myself.'

'To find what you haven't got.' He presented it as a statement, an answer that neatly completed his theory.

Jenny felt a sense of disappointment, of having been here so many times before. Dr Travis had had at least half a dozen big ideas that had come to nothing.

'We're going to try regression.'

'Again?' Jenny said, failing to conceal her cynicism.

'Please, go with me,' he insisted urgently. 'It's for your own good.'

She was taken aback. In eight months of consultations he'd maintained an unbroken mask of passivity. This was something new.

'Close your eyes, feel yourself sinking into the chair . . .'

She forced her eyes shut and unwillingly submitted to the well-worn routine. He talked her down through the gradual stages of physical relaxation. Feet, ankles and legs grew heavy, hands, arms, head, chest, then abdomen, and lastly internal organs. As she sank deeper, Dr Allen's voice became fainter, more remote, until it was little more than a distant echo in the comforting darkness that was her envelope of safety between sleeping and waking.

She wanted to slip quietly under.

'Stay with me, Jenny,' Dr Allen said. 'You're perfectly safe. Nothing can happen to you here. I want you to go back to where we've been before. You're a child upstairs in your bedroom, playing by yourself. You hear the banging on the front door, the raised voices – it's your grandfather. He's shouting, screaming.'

Jenny's body gave an involuntary twitch.

'Tell me what he's shouting.'

'I can't . . . I can't hear.'

'You can't hear the words?'

'No.'

'Are there other voices?'

A pause. Jenny's eyes moved sideways under their closed lids.

'It's a woman . . . sobbing, wailing . . . my mother.'

'Is she saying anything?'

'She's crying out, "No, no—." She keeps saying it . . . over and over.'

'Then what?'

Jenny shook her head. 'It just goes on and on.'

'What about the men? What are they saying?'

'They've gone quiet. It's just my mother . . . It's just her crying. Her voice carrying up the stairs.'

'How are you feeling about this? What are you doing?'

'I just want to get away . . . I want to go, get out of there.'

'Why?'

'I don't know . . . I just want to go.'

'What are you frightened of?'

Tears squeezed out of the corners of her eyes. 'I can't . . . It's nothing to do with me. It's not my fault.'

'What's not your fault?'

'The screaming . . . I can't stand it.'

'Why would it be your fault?'

'I don't want this . . . I hate it here . . . I *hate* it. I just want to go.'

'Where do want to go, Jenny? Tell me where you'd go.'

'There isn't anywhere . . . They'd see me . . . There's nowhere . . . I can't even go to . . .' Her body convulsed as violently as if she touched an electric wire. She bolted back to consciousness, staring into space with wide, blank eyes.

Dr Allen gave her a moment. 'You couldn't even go where?'

Jenny blinked. 'Katy's,' she said, with a rising inflection, as if the name was unfamiliar.

Dr Allen tugged a Kleenex from the box on his desk and handed it to her. Jenny dried her eyes feeling oddly empty, neither calm nor anxious.

'Who's Katy?'

'I've no idea.' She sniffed back the tears and shivered.

'A sister, relation, friend?'

Jenny glanced upwards. 'God, I don't know. Not a sister . . .' Dr Allen was staring intently at her face. 'What?'

'Your grandfather came with bad news that made your

mother wail. You said it wasn't your *fault*. Were you referring to whatever it was he told her?'

'I can't say . . .' She shook her head. 'The moment I'm awake it hardly seems real . . . I could even be making it up.'

'You've got a name: Katy. I want you to find out what that means.'

'I told you—'

'Please, do what I say. I'm going to make it a condition of you coming back here. You're going to do something positive for yourself. Next time I want to hear about your research.' He turned to his notebook and wrote the instruction down.

'You're getting impatient with me, aren't you?' Jenny said.

'Not at all. You're just in need of a push. You're also going to stick to the medication this time.' He reached for his prescription pad. 'I don't suppose there's any chance of you easing off at work?'

'Not unless you section me.'

'When you're abrasive it suggests to me you're feeling delicate. If you must carry on as normal, just be on your guard. Try to avoid emotional responses.' He tapped his temple with his finger. 'You'll always make your best judgements up here.'

She collected the drugs from the dispensary and swallowed her first dose in the ladies' room. They were both new brands to her: one blue, one red, like jelly beans. The world they led her to was less colourful. They took away her excitement and any sense of danger. Her attention was held by the immediate and the mundane: the instruments on the dashboard of her car, the squeak when she touched the brakes. She was aware of her emotions, but they were pale reflections of what she'd experienced during the last two days. She turned her thoughts to her inquest and without any conscious effort they lined up in logical order as a neat list of tasks waiting to be performed: jurors to be telephoned, witnesses to be summoned, law to be researched. Dr Allen had given her the mind of a bureaucrat.

The sensation was short-lived. She wasn't yet halfway home when her phone beeped, signalling a message. She glanced at the lit-up screen: Call me. Urgent. Alec.

A jolt went through her. Dr Allen's parting words rang like a warning bell in her head. She should ignore him, see him only once: in the witness box. Her finger hovered over the call button but reception faded and vanished, saving her from the decision. She had the ten minutes until she arrived home to sober up and get a grip.

As she pulled into the cart track at the side of the house she had worked out a strategy: call Alison and tell her to take any message from McAvoy. Tell him the inquest would resume on Wednesday morning and request that he attend to give evidence. Keep it all businesslike and at arm's length. She could deal with the feelings he had stirred in her afterwards. She would have something by which to judge him then, a clearer insight into his motivations.

She reached over to the glove box to get the torch she used to navigate the ten yards along the path to the front door. She found it and was searching for the switch when the car lit up. Startled, she looked up to see a tall, male figure beneath the halogen lamp that automatically triggered on approaching the porch. He was featureless with the bright light behind him, but the silhouette was unmistakable: the long dark coat, the scarf, the unruly wisps of hair. He raised a hand in a tentative wave that acknowledged her alarm. Arrested by the drugs her heart held steady, but a fierce heat spread across her chest and neck and prickled across her lips as fear blazed another pathway to the surface.

'It's only me,' he called out. 'It's Alec. It's OK.'

She thought about driving off and hoping he'd vanish, but she knew he wouldn't. He was the kind who'd walk all night and go days without sleep; he had a prisoner's patience and a madman's will.

She left her keys in the ignition and stepped out into the biting air, holding the torch defensively in front of her as she stepped around the car.

She stopped by the passenger door, still some twenty feet between them. 'What are you doing here?'

'I've got some information.'

She swept the torch beam over him. He was in a suit and tie, clean shoes.

'I meant what are you doing *here*?'

'My car packed up. I caught a cab.'

'Are you going to stand there talking bullshit or answer my question?'

Jenny aimed the beam of light at his face. McAvoy shielded his eyes.

'I didn't want to speak to you on the phone . . . I found out who Tathum was working for when those two boys disappeared.'

'You spent forty quid on a cab to tell me that?'

'I didn't mean to scare you. I'll go if you want me to . . . It's just . . .' He looked down, ran his hands distractedly through his hair. She heard him exhale wearily. 'The truth? These are dark waters, Jenny. I'm not sure how deep in you want to get. I thought it better to tell you here, away from everything. You can make your own decision. No public pressure.'

She slowly lowered the beam away from his face, responding to the sincerity in his voice. If he had wanted to hurt her, he could have run straight over or jumped out of the shadows. He wouldn't have sent her a text, left a trail.

'All right,' she said. 'I'd better hear it.'

She unlocked the front door and led him into the sitting room. Straight to business, she sat at the small dining table and motioned to the chair opposite. No offer of drinks. Even in forgiving light McAvoy looked tired. Dark shadows haunted his eyes. His face was drawn, his thick stubble grey in patches. He knotted his fingers and leaned forward in a way which suggested he had agonized long and hard, and arrived at a painful decision.

'Remember Billy Dean, the private investigator?' McAvoy said. 'His son took over the business. I gave him a call after our visit to Mr Tathum last week, asked him what he could dig up. He got back to me first thing this morning, just before you turned up.' He gave a strained smile. 'In 2002 Tathum was registered self-employed. He declared an income of sixty-five thousand pounds and his bank records show it came in the form of three payments from the same account. That account was in the name of Maitland Ltd, a private security contractor with a registered office in Broad Street, Hereford.'

'Where did he get hold of that?'

'He's got someone in the tax office, I expect. His dad always made most of his money from divorce. Anyway, until the year before Tathum was receiving his pay cheque from the army. Mid-thirties – I guess he must have done his time.'

'What do you know about Maitland?'

'According to their website they're close-protection specialists. Hereford's the home town for the SAS, so I'd guess that's where they draw their personnel from. I gather it's something of a local tradition: the ex-special servicemen cross the road and make their fortunes in the private sector.'

'What would Maitland want with Nazim and Rafi?'

'They're just being paid to perform a service. If you're asking me to speculate, I'd say they provided a snatch squad. But for whom . . . who knows? Could be the kids were terrorist suspects who were spirited away to God knows where. Or they could have been agents whose cover was blown, in which case they'll be living happily in condos in Australia.'

Jenny said, 'Why tell me now? Why not save it for the inquest? You know how risky it is for me to talk to a witness. Anyone could turn around and say my inquiry was tainted and have it overturned.'

'Well, there's the thing, Jenny – neither of us knows where each other stands, not truly.' He fixed her with a sad, searching look. 'I've seen and done enough wicked things in my span to know not to lead you to this lightly. British citizens disappeared by their own state – is that ever going to be allowed to be exposed? Call me a hoary old cynic, but I'd say another life or two would weigh lightly in the balance.'

'But?' She knew there was a but, that the flame that still burned in his eyes wouldn't be extinguished that easily.

'You're not cut from the regular cloth, are you?' McAvoy's worn-out face creased into a smile. 'I've got a shoulder so sore I've hardly been able to lift a drink all day.'

Unrepentant, Jenny said, 'That was for lying to me. And for what it's worth, I think you still are.'

There was a pause. McAvoy lowered his head. 'It's a funny thing, Jenny: I made a fine career out of telling other people's lies for them. The other side were always the bigger sinners. Even when I was caught out and put away, all the virtue was with me. But this case . . . I've fixed trials, I've bought and sold witnesses, I've helped murderers walk free and drunk their good health with a clear conscience, but this one *fucking* case.' He shook his head and turned his gaze away from her. 'And then you turned up like the Angel of Desire . . . like a sorceress . . . what's a spent force like me meant to do with that?'

Jenny inwardly reeled. The breath left her lungs. The visceral part of her willed him to touch her, to make the slightest contact so he could feel his charge and let it happen.

She knew he could feel the change in her, read what was written in her face.

'You're a temptation, that's what you are,' McAvoy said. 'A sweet and beautiful temptation as dark and damned as I am. I can't even touch your hand for fear—'

'Of what?' Jenny said.

He shook his head again. 'Let's talk about something else.' He swallowed and pushed himself on. 'Dr Sarah Levin – she's a beautiful girl, I understand. She was eighteen years old at the time. She would have been spoken to, I'm sure of that. Wherever Nazim and Rafi went they would have been interrogated, questioned within an inch of their lives. It's no coincidence she was the one who spoke to the police – she wouldn't have had any choice. I guessed as much eight years ago. Should it be dragged out of her now? Does she have to be destroyed too? How much damage is enough?'

'Why would she be on your conscience?'

'She was a blameless child. Why wouldn't she be?'

'Don't you think you're idealizing her?'

'Compared with me, she's the Blessed Virgin herself.'

Jenny said, 'What about the man who telephoned you, the American?'

'I've no idea, except that whoever took those boys hounded Mrs Jamal to death, even if they didn't physically kill her.'

'You don't even know the whole story,' Jenny said, feeling an irrational compulsion to share her burden. 'There were traces of radiation in her flat and on her body. Caesium 137.' As soon as she'd said it, she knew it was too much. She stopped herself from mentioning Anna Rose.

'To make it look like terrorists,' McAvoy said. 'Dirty bastards. At least regular criminals only kill their own. You wouldn't find a man above the gutter to hurt an old woman. Only godless government and mad mothers can tar a man's soul that black.'

Jenny made a faint noise that was almost a laugh.

'What?' McAvoy said.

'The way you talk.'

'How do you make sense of things?'

'I don't.'

'You should try poetry, or scripture, both preferably. You seem like you could do with it.'

'When I came to court, I didn't mean to hurt you . . . I don't know what possessed me.'

'There's a question . . .'

The faint smile, the longing behind the eyes. The grizzled face masking a spirit that was already inside her, touching her, knowing things about her she didn't know herself.

'Tell me you're for real, Alec,' Jenny said. 'Swear that you're not using me or being paid.'

'What words can I say that are worth their weight? I came here to tell you that you're not alone, that's all . . .' He held her gaze. It seemed to take every ounce of strength. 'And that I know I scare the hell out of you, but if it's any comfort the feeling's mutual.'

He pushed up from his chair and made for the door.

'You're not going?' Jenny said.

'I better had, don't you think?'

'Can I drive you?'

'I'll be just fine.' He lifted the latch, then paused. For a moment Jenny thought he might turn back, sweep round and break the unbearable tension between them, let their bottled-up forces explode.

Without allowing himself to look at her, he said, 'When this case is over, can I see you again?'

'Yes . . . yes, we must.'

'Goodnight, Jenny.' Then, with a hint of a smile, 'I'll see you in court.'

McAvoy let himself out, closing the door gently behind him.

She tugged back the corner of the curtain and watched him walk down the path. She remained at the window until long after he had gone, willing him to come back, even though she knew he wouldn't.

There was mail to sort, food to cook, messages on the machine including a plaintive request from Steve for her to call, saying there was something he needed to say, but she could think of nothing except McAvoy. He'd gone with a promise to return, but left a deep sense of incompleteness behind him. It was as if he'd come to make a confession and stalled. The atmosphere in the cottage hung heavy with it: there was something Alec McAvoy had yet to tell her, and it was weighing on his conscience. She could tell.

Jenny woke, palpitating, as abruptly as if she'd been kicked in the ribs. There was no dream lingering, just a sense of having been disturbed by a threatening sound. She imagined footsteps on the flags outside, a man's breath. She lay still and alert for more than twenty minutes, flinching at every faint creak and groan of the old house. But whatever phantom it was that had disturbed her had retreated to its hiding place. Nothing stirred except the breeze. As her eyelids grew heavy she thought of Ross, and of David sleeping soundly next to his happy, pregnant girlfriend, and wondered what she had done to be driven out onto such a lonely limb. 'I think you'd do almost anything to avoid causing pain,' Dr Allen had said to her, and on the same day that she'd picked

up a pen – *the irony* – and thrust it into McAvoy's shoulder
. . . McAvoy. Looking at him was like looking into a mirror
and seeing her dark shadow looking back. That was it, that
was the thrill: the sense that in knowing him she might truly
know herself.

# TWENTY-TWO

JENNY CLIMBED OUT OF BED before six with a pressing sense of urgency. The inquest was due to resume in twenty-four hours and there were vital decisions to be made. Hurrying a shower, she felt a pang of guilt at the almost intimate moment she'd shared with McAvoy and the fact that thinking about him was crowding out thoughts of her son. What kind of mother was she? Recognizing the signs of rising anxiety – tingling fingertips and a pounding heart – she rushed down to the freezing kitchen wrapped in a towel and swallowed her two jelly beans with the dregs of a week-old carton of orange juice. She felt like an addict forcing down the vinegary liquid. The new pills were like magic: by the time she had dried and dressed she was at the helm. Mrs Jenny Cooper, coroner, with important business to attend to.

She ate a breakfast of stale cereal at her desk in the study while she searched for Maitland's website. She found it in the online Yellow Pages and clicked through to a largely anonymous yet somehow exclusive-feeling site which presented the minimum of information. The registered office was a Hereford address, which accorded with what McAvoy had told her. The MD was listed as Colonel Marcus Maitland. The company's chief areas of expertise were listed as 'foreign and domestic close protection, operational assessments and security planning, and strategic security services'.

The explanation was limited and the jargon dense and oblique: it could have been describing an investment consultancy. There was no mention of former special servicemen or mercenaries.

Only McAvoy's word connected the company to Tathum, but even if the link were fictitious, even if Madog's story about the black Toyota was a fantasy or a red herring, she felt obliged to call Colonel Maitland as a witness, if only to disprove the allegations once and for all.

Jenny printed off a pro-forma witness summons and completed it by hand, requesting Maitland to attend her inquest on Wednesday, 10 February. It was unreasonably short notice, but it would flush him out and make him pay attention if nothing else. Rather than trust a courier to collect a signature on delivery she decided it was safer to take it herself. Reluctant witnesses were apt to claim the summons had never arrived. She wanted no arguments: if Maitland or Tathum refused to comply she would have them committed to prison for contempt. There weren't many perks to being a coroner, but the power to bring to heel those who normally thought themselves above the law was one of them.

It was shortly after eight and barely light when she drove into Hereford and parked in a quiet street a short distance from Maitland's office in the city centre. There was no reply when she rang the buzzer to the first-floor suite and no sign of lights in the window. Faced with a choice between killing time in the coffee shop four doors along or the cathedral opposite, Jenny turned up her coat collar and crossed the road.

The choir was rehearsing in the vast, resonant interior. It smelt of incense, cold stone and polished oak. Great iron coke stoves gave out an inadequate but welcome heat. She drifted along the nave, past the transepts and into the Lady Chapel and sat, for no conscious reason, in one of the rows of chairs facing the altar, at the side of which, guarding the sacrament, an eternal flame flickered.

In the stillness, an image of Mrs Jamal returned to her; the pain in her face as she talked of her missing son. Jenny imagined her final thoughts being of reuniting with him, of seeing him again wherever souls go. It was a comforting notion, but not one she could sustain. The building in which she sat was built as much through fear of hell and damnation as it was out of the love of God. She seldom prayed except in desperation or self-pity, but something moved her. Words sprang from nowhere.

She pleaded for the souls of Amira and Nazim Jamal and Rafi Hassan. 'Please God, don't let them be lost.'

The reception area was sleek and expensively furnished with tasteful original art and cream leather sofas. It belonged in central London, not a rural backwater. The receptionist was no more than twenty-five, pretty, and spoke with a crisp, educated voice without a trace of local accent.

'How can I help you?' she asked.

Despite being dressed in her best suit and coat Jenny felt clumsy and inelegant next to the girl. She handed over one of her business cards. 'Jenny Cooper, Severn Vale District Coroner. Is Colonel Maitland in? I'd like to speak to him.'

'No,' the girl said, sensing danger. 'He's out of the office today, I'm afraid.'

'Tomorrow?'

'I think he may be back.' The second lie was less assured than the first.

Jenny reached into her coat pocket and brought out the envelope containing the summons and a form of receipt.

'This is what's called "personal service". This is a witness summons for him to attend my inquest tomorrow. I've even included the taxi fare – it's a legal requirement. If he really can't attend he can contact my office today to make further arrangements. If I could just ask you to sign the receipt?'

'Well, I—'

Jenny pre-empted her evasion. 'If you don't, you'll become a witness to the fact that I've served the document –' Jenny checked her watch – 'at eight forty-two a.m. on Tuesday, 9 February, and you'll be coming to court with or without him.'

She passed the girl a pen. She looked at it for a moment, then took it and hurriedly scribbled her signature on the receipt. It was illegible.

'If you could print it as well.'

She did as she was told, reddening with either anger or embarrassment, Jenny couldn't tell. As she completed the task, Jenny said, 'One last thing, I just need to confirm the up-to-date address for your employee, Mr Christopher Tathum.'

The girl's eyes flicked uncertainly to her computer.

'You're going to tell me you can't give out private addresses, right?'

'Yes,' the girl stammered.

'Technically I could force you, but let's do it this way – I'll tell you what it is, you tell me if I'm wrong.'

Jenny repeated Tathum's address. The girl hesitated for a moment, then tapped on her keyboard. Sideways on, Jenny saw a list of addresses scroll up.

'Anything to say?' Jenny said.

She shook her head.

'Good. You'll make sure Colonel Maitland gets his letter this morning, won't you?'

Jenny drove back to Bristol with a weight lifted from her shoulders. McAvoy hadn't lied to her. Tathum *was* employed by Maitland and if needs be she had a witness who could be persuaded to confirm it. There were many obstacles to be overcome in court, but for the first time in days she felt she was standing on something approaching solid ground. She trusted McAvoy again, and was beginning to trust herself.

She arrived at her office feeling big enough to deal with Alison and ready to heal the jagged edges. Since her painful faux pas the previous day they'd hardly spoken, except to exchange a few words as Jenny had hurried out to her emergency appointment with Dr Allen. She braced herself for a frosty reception and prepared a conciliatory speech.

'Good morning, Mrs Cooper,' Alison said with pointed formality as Jenny entered.

She noticed the room was unnaturally tidy: the magazines on the table were neatly arranged, there were fresh flowers in a vase, the inspirational messages had been removed. It felt . . . sanitized.

'Good morning, Alison,' Jenny said with a note of contrition and took her mail – stacked in size order – from the tray on her desk.

'You got to your son on time, did you?'

It took Jenny a moment to recall the excuse she'd muttered as she bolted from the office an hour earlier than usual.

'Yes, thank you. Just.'

She flicked through the envelopes bracing herself to make an apology. If she left it any longer it would become impossible: they would pass the whole day in frigid silence.

'Look, Alison, I'm sorry for what I said yesterday . . . I had no business mentioning your daughter, or passing judgement on your personal life. I was angry with Simon Moreton, not with you. He had no right to ask for confidential information.'

'Apology accepted, Mrs Cooper,' Alison said, her eyes fixed firmly on the desk.

'You didn't have to take the cards down.'

'They're not appropriate in the workplace. They wouldn't be tolerated in the police. Not nowadays.'

'Whatever you think best.'

There was an awkward silence, neither sure how to end their exchange.

'I know I fly off the handle sometimes, but we both know I wouldn't get very far without you.'

Jenny offered a smile. Alison's jaw remained rigid with tension.

'I may have made a fool of myself over Harry Marshall,' Alison said, referring to the former coroner, her ex-boss, 'but it's different with David. Not that there's anything improper between us,' she added hurriedly. 'I've seen him go through some of the most trying situations a person can face. He's not a liar, Mrs Cooper. He's doing his duty.'

'I respect that, of course, but the coroner's duty is different from a policeman's. No one else seems to get it, but my duty, my *legal* duty, is to do whatever it takes to get to the truth no matter who would rather I didn't. Until the Lord Chancellor picks up the phone to tell me I'm fired, I have to keep on digging.'

Alison nodded, but without conviction. She was still a dutiful detective at heart. Legal distinctions and high ideals weren't for her. She preferred the comfort of belonging to a powerful tribe and was fearful of being out on her own. But she kept Jenny's feet on the ground, which is why they were still together after eight often turbulent months. Jenny had come to need her like a tree needs roots.

Alison said, 'There's a message from that woman at MI5. She wants you to call. I expect it's about the report from the Health Protection Agency – it came last night.' She handed Jenny a print-out of a document headed, 'Radiological Assessment'. It was stamped 'Highly Confidential'.

Jenny turned to the final paragraphs:

*The caesium 137 particles taken from the address were chiefly concentrated in the fabric of an armchair. Several particles were also found in the common parts of the building and on the skin of the deceased, Mrs Amira Jamal, notably on her lower back and buttocks. It is safe and indeed logical to conclude that the deceased was contaminated through contact with the armchair in the period shortly before death. It is not possible, however, to say for how long the particles had been present on the armchair or in the building. Circumstantial evidence suggests a recent contamination: there were no traces of contamination in either the vacuum cleaner in Mrs Jamal's premises or in that used by the caretaker of the building in the common parts.*

*In conclusion, it is suggested that contamination occurred at some time during the days immediately preceding Mrs Jamal's death.*

Alison said, 'If it's any comfort, the police haven't got a clue. They're guessing it was someone her son was mixed up with. Some of them are even saying it might have been him coming out of the woodwork. There are all sorts of wild ideas flying about.'

'On an armchair? It's as if someone who was already contaminated sat on it,' Jenny said.

'Imagine if it was Nazim,' Alison said. 'That would have shocked her – seeing him back from the grave.'

Jenny shook her head. 'No. That doesn't make any sense.'

'Why not? There's no proof he's dead. All we've got are two contradictory sightings of him alive and heading in different directions. He might even have come back to shut his mother up. They don't care about life, these jihadis – if you die a martyr's death, you and seventy of your relations get a free pass to paradise anyway.'

Jenny could tell Alison had been in the thick of the police-canteen gossip and had soaked it up. And as usual the police had concocted theories to suit their prejudices: an all-Asian affair with a matricide thrown in would absolve them entirely; no need to feel guilty for caving in to the Security Services and letting two young men vanish into thin air.

Jenny said, 'You haven't mentioned Madog's statement to anyone?'

'Of course not, Mrs Cooper,' Alison said, affronted. 'I do talk to my ex-colleagues, but I'm not indiscreet.'

'I wasn't suggesting—'

'I know you're putting a lot of store by him, but I really shouldn't, if I were you.'

'I haven't told you everything yet. There's a chain of evidence building—'

'Before you do tell me, there's probably something you ought to know – about Alec McAvoy.'

'Oh?' Jenny felt her hackles rise but resisted the urge to snap back. It would be better not to tell Alison about the Maitland connection before court. The last thing she wanted was her best evidence leaking to the police and Security Services before it had been heard.

'Just so you're clear what kind of man he is,' Alison said. 'He's been part of the team defending Marek Stich. He's the Czech fellow who shot a young traffic policeman dead last October. I don't know if you heard the news yesterday?'

'I try to avoid it.'

'Stich got off. It's not that surprising – all they had was a couple of ID witnesses who only saw him further down the street driving away from the scene. The thing is, there was a car which had stopped behind Stich's. According to another witness the driver was a woman who must have seen it all. CID never tracked her down, but last night they had an anonymous call. An emotional female caller said Stich pulled the trigger – she watched him do it. She was going to give a statement, but later that afternoon she was approached by a man with a Scottish accent who stopped her outside the gates of her son's school. He told her that if she said a word she'd lose her child. This was in front of him, mind you, an eight-year-old boy.'

Another apocryphal story to explain away CID's failure, was Jenny's immediate thought. How they must have hated to see a troublesome lawyer they thought they'd seen off for good return to humiliate them.

'I'm sure it'll be looked into,' Jenny said, seeking to avoid another confrontation.

'It's what I told you, Mrs Cooper. He fixes witnesses – finds them or shuts them up – that's all he knows.'

Avoiding the issue, Jenny said, 'Talking of witnesses, are we on track for tomorrow?'

Alison pushed a list across the desk towards her. It contained the names of Detective Sergeant Angus Watkins, the officer who had examined Nazim and Rafi's rooms for signs of forced entry; DI Pironi; David Skene, one of the MI5 agents attached to the initial inquiry; Donovan; Madog; Tathum; Sarah Levin; Professor Brightman; McAvoy; Hugh Rees, the owner of the car rental firm in Hereford; and a name she didn't recognize – Elizabeth Murray.

Alison said, 'She's the old lady who thinks she saw the Toyota. You asked me to see if she was still around. She is. I took a statement from her on my way home last night. She's eighty-six, but still game.'

She passed Jenny another piece of paper containing a few brief sentences in which Mrs Murray said little more than that she had seen a stationary black car with two men inside. Reading it through, Jenny tried and failed to recall asking Alison to trace the witness. She wondered what else she might have forgotten or missed . . . It was McAvoy again, absorbing all her attention, even when she wasn't aware of it. And Alison knew: she could see it in the wary, concerned way she was looking at her, registering her mental slip. Her detective's instinct was telling her that Jenny's mind had been skewed, that she was in danger of favouring the mad and illogical, of ignoring obvious truth because a corrupt and dishonest man had fascinated her.

Alison said, 'I do understand, Mrs Cooper. I know what it's like to be impressed with someone. Look at me and Harry Marshall . . . The ideal man is always the one you could never have. That's the whole point. It's a fantasy – what you think you want.'

She had seen straight through her. She was right, it was a fantasy. Just as Alison had dreamed of Harry leading her to a gentler, finer world, Jenny imagined McAvoy, a man who had been to darker places than she had ever imagined, slaying her monsters at a single stroke.

Lying to herself as much as to Alison, Jenny said, 'Don't worry. I could never have feelings for him. The man's a wreck.'

Alison gave a faint, only partially convinced smile. 'I'm glad to hear it.'

Leaving Alison with instructions to double-check witnesses, ensure jurors had fail-safe transport and to take care of the myriad administrative tasks all other categories of court would have a battery of staff to attend to, Jenny retreated to her office to make the call to Gillian Golder.

'Jenny, finally. I was beginning to wonder if *you'd* disappeared.' It was meant as a joke, but came out gracelessly.

'You must have spoken to Simon Moreton,' Jenny replied. 'I told him all I know, which isn't much.'

'That's the problem in a nutshell,' Golder said. 'We're all rather groping in the dark and not sure what we might find.'

Jenny didn't like the 'we'. It sounded ominous.

Anticipating what she expected would come next, Jenny said, 'If you're concerned about my inquest trespassing on the criminal investigation into Mrs Jamal's death, I can assure you it won't. I'm only interested in what happened eight years ago.'

'But can we be sure the two events are entirely separate?'

'I have no reason to delay any further, Miss Golder. Your organization and the police gave up on the criminal inquiry years ago.'

'Let's live in the real world for a moment, shall we, Jenny? My service and the police are desperately looking for the source of illegally held radioactive material. And one of the chief suspects is the subject of your inquest.'

'You have evidence that Nazim's alive?'

'We'd rather the whole issue stayed out of the news until we find the son of a bitch we're looking for. Even if you don't mention Mrs Jamal, the media are going to be all over it. If anything's going to drive him or whoever it is further under, that will.'

'I don't see that at all,' Jenny said. 'What I see is you trying to save yourself from potential embarrassment. It was your service who let the trail go cold. It may have suited your purposes at the time – boosting the argument for war and all of that – but I wouldn't be fit to hold this office if I let that sway me.'

Icily, Gillian Golder said, 'Believe it or not, we're not as unreasonable as you seem to think. I'm sure we could find a way to stop your inquest if we really wanted to, but perhaps we can agree on a reasonable compromise.'

Golder paused, waiting for Jenny to step willingly into her trap. She remained silent.

'This is what we propose: rule seventeen of the Coroner's Rules enables a coroner to hold an inquest in camera if it's in the interests of national security. I don't know what evidence you intend to call, but Nazim Jamal and Rafi Hassan were suspected by us of having extremist sympathies. In the light of the fact that Mrs Jamal died in circumstances which suggest she came into contact with a substance which can only be of interest or use to a terrorist, we think there's a compelling argument, if not a necessity, for your inquest to be held in secret.'

'I can see why you'd like that,' Jenny said, 'but I think you may have forgotten some of the basic principles of justice.'

'Let me put it this way, Mrs Cooper,' Golder said. 'We have lawyers briefed and ready to go the High Court this afternoon to seek an injunction that will ensure rule seventeen is correctly applied.'

Jenny felt the dead hand pressing on her. She had no doubt that Golder was serious and that the government lawyers would hint to a well-chosen judge that evidence of a highly sensitive nature – the significance of which a mere provincial coroner would not understand – might emerge to threaten national security. The judge, already used to closed hearings in terrorist cases, and inured to the denial of once inviolable liberties, such as the right to silence and a prisoner's right to know the evidence against him, would have no problem with gagging a coroner. Jenny could fight all she liked, but it was a battle she would never win. She could appeal to Simon Moreton at the Ministry, but even if he could be persuaded to protest on her behalf he would be swept aside by his superiors. All that was left was for her to salvage what she could from the wreckage.

Jenny chanced her luck one last time. 'There wouldn't be any need to exclude the public if I were to impose reporting restrictions.'

'In the days before the internet, perhaps, but I'm afraid

that wouldn't be sufficient,' Golder said. 'We can allow immediate family to attend, but on the strict understanding that they mustn't communicate any part of the evidence.'

'I could tell you to go to hell.'

'You could, but that wouldn't help anyone, would it?'

# TWENTY-THREE

ZACHARIAH JAMAL WAS AN ARRESTINGLY dignified man in his mid-fifties and bore an uncanny resemblance to his son. Strikingly handsome, he shared the same fine features and raven black hair. Jenny could see at once why he parted company with his late ex-wife. He was self-contained, composed, the polar opposite of effusive and emotional. He sat alone at one end of the three rows of seats behind the lawyers, which the previous week had been filled with news-hungry journalists and the militant members of the British Society for Islamic Change.

Jenny had contacted him shortly after her last conversation with Gillian Golder and informed him of developments. She had asked him if he would like her to defy the request and fight for a full public hearing. He had answered unequivocally: no. She had ventured to ask him if he had any insight into what had led to his ex-wife's death. 'She was not a stable woman in recent years,' was all he had said. He had sounded so remote and removed that Jenny hadn't expected him to attend the hearing. However, according to Alison he was waiting out-side the hall when she arrived shortly after eight a.m. Seeing him in the flesh, Jenny realized she had misread him over the telephone. The grief behind his stoical mask was palpable. Remarried with a second family he would have had few chances to mourn his first-born son. This was his opportunity.

Out of courtesy she had also called Mr and Mrs Hassan to tell them they would be welcome to attend. Mr Hassan told her flatly that they would not be present, reporters or not. There had been barely suppressed anger in his voice which Jenny read as guilt. Mr Hassan blamed himself for his son's fate. If only he hadn't fought with him that Christmas vacation, if only he'd been more attentive . . . She felt sure he and his wife would have liked to be there, but even after eight years they simply couldn't face it.

Sitting at the head of an echoing village hall more accustomed to hosting dances and produce shows, she felt an almost unbearable sense of responsibility.

The morning had already proved traumatic. Jenny had arrived to find more than a dozen uniformed policemen surrounding the hall's entrance. Their sergeant said he had been ordered to prevent journalists and members of the public from gaining access to the resumed inquest. Jenny had been remonstrating with him when several vanloads of BRISIC supporters arrived and angry, hostile scenes developed. While incredulous local residents looked on, name-calling and slogan-chanting tipped into violence. Punches were thrown at police officers, who eagerly responded with truncheons and pepper spray. Temporarily blinded and screaming in agony, several protesters were arrested and driven away. Most of the rest were dispersed. Only after Jenny had threatened the sergeant with multiple lawsuits if he didn't comply, did he allow a remaining handful to mount a symbolic vigil.

Many of the witnesses had arrived in the thick of the disturbance. Flanked by police, Alison had managed to shepherd them through to a side entrance. They were now corralled in a small committee room separated from the hall by a single door. Maitland and Tathum had yet to show their faces, but to Jenny's surprise all the others had answered their sum-monses, including McAvoy.

Aside from Mr Jamal, the only other observer to the proceedings was Alun Rhys, Golder's man in the field, tucked away at the end of a row at the back. She would have been within her rights to exclude him – the hearing was in camera and he had no legal right to be present – but an instinct told her to let him be. She wanted to read his face, to see when it registered surprise, alarm or even approval.

Extremely grateful for Dr Allen's new medication, which was successfully holding her anxiety in check, she turned to the lawyers. Yusuf Khan, the solicitor representing BRISIC, was anxious to speak first.

'Ma'am, I must protest most strongly at your decision to conduct this inquest in camera. The law clearly states that all coroner's inquests are to be held in public unless it is against the interests of national security to do so. Those I represent can only conclude that it is their presence that you wish to avoid.'

'Not at all, Mr Khan,' Jenny interjected. 'Obviously, you'll respect the reporting restrictions which have also been placed on this hearing, so I can tell you without fear of it being repeated that I have made my order directly at the request of the Security Services.' She glanced at Rhys. 'What it is they fear, what evidence they anticipate will affect the safety of the realm, they have not seen fit to tell me. However, I decided that it was preferable to proceed under these circum-stances than not at all.'

'But this is preposterous,' Khan said. 'A coroner cannot be dictated to. This is an independent court, not a political tribunal.'

'As we're in camera I can again speak to you candidly and say that I entirely agree.'

Rhys's face hardened in disapproval.

Jenny continued. 'I'm more than happy for you to shout your objection from the rooftops, but if I let your supporters in now I can guarantee this inquest will not be allowed to proceed. It's not what either of us think is right or just, but I suggest you save your energy for the witnesses.'

Unappeased, Khan jabbed his finger in the air. 'I am serving notice now: my clients will fight through every court and do whatever it takes to make the transcript of these proceedings public. There is no such thing as justice conducted in secret.'

The two barristers, Fraser Havilland for the chief constable, and Martha Denton QC for the Director General of the Security Services, appeared vaguely bored and unimpressed with Khan's performance. Trevor Collins, the unassuming and undistinguished solicitor representing Mrs Jamal's estate, was the only lawyer to nod in agreement.

Jenny said, 'Thank you, Mr Khan,' and glancing at Alun Rhys added, 'I'm sure if nothing affecting national security does arise your wish will be granted.'

Rhys was poker-faced. It occurred to Jenny that he was strangely emasculated: an observer to secret proceedings with no further sanctions to apply.

She turned to the jury and thanked them for their patience during the week they had been adjourned. So as not to alert Rhys or any of the lawyers to what they might hear, she explained in deliberately vague terms that the delay had been necessary to pursue further lines of inquiry, with the result that they would be hearing from several new witnesses. Unimpressed, the jurors responded with impatient looks.

As Jenny turned to Alison to request she bring in the first witness, Fraser Havilland rose abruptly to his feet.

'Ma'am, before we proceed to evidence, my learned friend

Miss Denton and I would be grateful if you would furnish us with a list of who these witnesses may be, and, dare I suggest it, copies of their statements. It is customary practice in a modern coroner's inquest.'

Sitting beside him, Martha Denton fixed Jenny with an impassive stare.

Sure of her ground, Jenny said, 'Customary perhaps, Mr Havilland, but not obligatory. I suggest you take a look at *R. v. H.M. Coroner for Lincolnshire ex parte Hay* (1999). Disclosure of documents to counsel, even witness statements, is a matter in the coroner's discretion.' She turned to the jury. 'A coroner's inquest is not a trial; it is an inquiry on behalf of the Crown. The lawyers representing the interested persons are merely here to assist, and are granted the right to ask questions. They cannot *require* me to produce anything.'

'With respect, ma'am,' Havilland persisted, 'the 2003 *Bentley* case did stress that it is preferable for a coroner to release witness lists, especially in complex cases.'

'You're not easily satisfied, are you, Mr Havilland? Not only are we sitting in camera, but your and Miss Denton's clients now wish to know exactly what evidence this inquiry is going to call. I think that's called wanting to have your cake and eat it.'

Several of the jurors smiled.

Havilland remained po-faced. 'It's called good practice, ma'am.'

'I'm amenable but no pushover, Mr Havilland,' Jenny said, feeling a swell of anger which she struggled to dampen. 'You'll get what you've a right to, no more.'

Havilland thought about retaliating. He was pre-empted by his instructing solicitor, who tugged at his sleeve and whispered to him to back down. 'Very well, ma'am,' Havilland said, and resumed his seat.

Martha Denton's deadpan gaze didn't waver. She was studying Jenny's face, probing for her weaknesses, biding her time.

Elizabeth Murray was the first witness to make her way from the committee room to sit at the small table on Jenny's left which served as a witness box. The eighty-six-year-old was frail and stooped but walked determinedly and unaided. Wearing a smart navy suit, her hair set for the occasion, she was determined to make the most of her moment in the spotlight. She read the oath clearly and solemnly. No one doubted she intended to tell the truth.

'Mrs Murray,' Jenny said, 'do you have any reason to remember the night of 28 June 2002?'

'I do,' she said adamantly. 'There was a large black car parked outside my house all evening, with two men in the front seats. The longer they were there the more suspicious I became. At about ten-thirty p.m. I decided to call the police. I'd just picked up the telephone when I heard the engine start up. I went to the window and saw they'd moved off.'

'What sort of car was is it, do you remember?'

'A people carrier, I think you call it.'

'And did you call the police?'

'No, I didn't think it was worth bothering them.'

'But you had a visit later in the year?' Jenny prompted.

'That's right. A man knocked on my door in the December as I recall. He said he was representing the family of a young man who'd last been seen leaving a property further along my road that night. He was going from house to house trying to find witnesses. I told him about the car.'

'You remembered the precise date you saw it, even after six months had elapsed?'

'Yes. It was the last Friday in June. It must have been something about the two men – it just seemed to stick.'

'What about them?'

'They looked threatening somehow. I could see the one in the driver's seat quite clearly. He was stocky with a shaved head.'

'What about the passenger?'

'I didn't get a good look at him. I think he might have had longer hair.'

Jenny noticed Alun Rhys making a note – this seemed to be news to him.

Jenny said, 'Did you see in which direction the car went when it moved off?'

'The way it was facing – to the right.'

Jenny indicated to Alison, who distributed copies of a large-scale map to the jurors and lawyers. It showed Marlowes Road, the street where both Mrs Murray and Anwar Ali had lived at the time. Mrs Murray confirmed that she lived at number 102 on the south side of the street. Anwar Ali's flat, where he hosted the halaqah, was approximately two hundred yards to the west of her house on the north side at number 35. The stop at which Nazim and Jamal would have caught the bus back to campus was thirty yards to the west of her house on the south side. Mrs Murray confirmed that an east-bound bus would have passed the parked car as it left the stop; however, when she was asked if a bus had indeed come past shortly before the car pulled off, she couldn't remember.

'Could you see how many people were in the car as it drove away?' Jenny asked.

'No. I was out of sight of the window at that point,' Mrs Murray said.

'And apart from the private investigator, has anyone else asked you about the events of that night?'

'Never.'

'You've never had a detective knock on your door?'

'No.'

Neither Fraser Havilland or Martha Denton had any questions for the witness. Trevor Collins also declined to cross-examine. Khan, who had grown increasingly excited during her testimony, grilled her for several minutes attempting to extract any identifying detail of the mysterious occupants of the car. Elizabeth Murray did her best, though she said little that Jenny hadn't already gleaned. After fifteen minutes of fruitlessly repeating the same questions, Khan sat down disappointed. He'd had a taste of conspiracy and was hungry for more.

Detective Sergeant Watkins (retired) was the next in the witness box. A grey-haired man who looked older than his fifty-seven years, his beer drinker's stomach sagged over the waistband of his suit trousers. He read the oath card with the tired resignation of a long-serving officer for whom the world could offer few more surprises.

'Mr Watkins, you made a statement on 3 July 2002 following your inspection of the rooms of Nazim Jamal and Rafi Hassan. Have you read that recently?'

'Yes. Your officer gave me a copy.' Watkins spoke in a thick Bristol accent, and nodded to Alison in recognition.

'Do you recall making those inspections?'

'Vaguely. I'd been on the obbo with DI Pironi, so he asked me to pop over when we'd had word the boys had gone missing.'

Jenny referred to his statement. 'And you found signs of forced entry. Laptops and mobiles were missing from both rooms, but other valuable items such as an MP3 player in Rafi Hassan's room were still there.'

'Yes, ma'am.'

'What did that indicate to you?'

Watkins breathed out heavily through closed lips, making a noise like a weary old carthorse. 'Could have been a break-in, I suppose, but the impressions on the door frames were the same on both rooms. It was a bit of a coincidence. Could be they were trying to make it look as if the doors had been forced.'

'On the day you wrote your statement you had no idea what had happened to the two boys – the witness who claims to have seen them on the London train didn't come forward until 20 July.'

'That's right.'

'So what was the police response to your discoveries?'

'I gave my statement to the DI, that was it.'

'Detective Inspector Pironi?'

'Yes.'

'You weren't asked to investigate a potential break-in?'

'No, ma'am.'

'Were you aware that on 8 July another student living in Manor Hall, Miss Dani James, gave a statement saying she'd seen a man in man in a puffy anorak and baseball cap leaving Manor Hall quickly on 28 June at around midnight – the evening the boys went missing?'

'A couple of colleagues and myself had been going round the halls speaking to the students, so I'd heard it mentioned.'

'What steps were taken to find this man?'

Watkins shook his head. 'I couldn't tell you, ma'am. It wasn't much of a description, so I don't suppose very many.'

'Enlighten me, Mr Watkins, was there a sense that this was a major investigation? Were you concerned for the where-abouts of these two young men?'

'As far as I knew there'd been no crime as such. Of course, we knew they'd been keeping bad company if you like – we probably thought it was more likely they'd hopped off somewhere.'

'Did you form that opinion, or was it suggested to you?'

'I think DI Pironi might've said it. We were still on the obbo like, seeing who was coming and going down at the mosque and at Anwar Ali's place.'

'When you say "bad company", what exactly did you think Nazim Jamal and Rafi Hassan had been exposed to?'

Watkins shrugged. 'The DI would have been the one reading the intelligence reports. My colleagues and I were just keeping a note of the movements.'

'Did you believe you were observing potential criminals?'

'Yes. Especially at that time. We didn't know what might go off.'

'All the more strange, then, that there wasn't a major manhunt.'

With a half-smile and a glance at Alison, Watkins said, 'I'll leave that one to the DI, I think. I was just one of the foot soldiers.'

Not content, Jenny pressed him. 'What reason were you given for there not being a more concerted effort to find them?'

'I wasn't, ma'am.' He hesitated. 'I don't think it's any secret that MI5 got involved, but I never had anything to do with them.'

Jenny reached for the file containing the police observation logs. She turned to the page she had already flagged. 'Were you on observation in Marlowes Road on the night of 28 June?'

'No, ma'am.'

'There's an entry saying: "Subjects NJ and RH seen leaving 35 Marlowes Road 10.22 p.m. Subjects walk off in easterly direction towards bus stop." It's not initialled.'

'Not on the transcript, maybe – there would have been initials on the handwritten originals.'

'Long since destroyed, I suppose.'

'I wouldn't know, ma'am. You'd have to ask the DI.'

'I will.' Jenny had many questions for Pironi. 'Thank you, Mr Watkins. Wait there, please.'

Fraser Havilland rose with a look of weary sympathy for the witness. 'Mr Watkins, when an adult is reported missing and there is no immediate evidence of any criminal activity surrounding their disappearance, what is the usual police response?'

'There's very little we can do.'

Havilland gave the jury a patient, *isn't it obvious* look as he asked his next question: 'And was there evidence of such a crime?'

Watkins shook his head. 'No signs of violence.'

'So you might say your response was unusually thorough?'

'I'd say so, yes.'

'That's all.' Havilland glanced sympathetically at the jury as if to say that Watkins's entire spell in the witness box had been an unnecessary waste of everybody's time.

Martha Denton once again didn't deign to ask any questions, but this time Collins got his nod in before Khan, and the quiet solicitor, more at home conveyancing than cross-examining, rose nervously to his feet.

'Mr Watkins,' Collins said, swallowing his words, then coughing nervously. 'Your statement describing the damage to the door frames of the two boys' student rooms wasn't released to my client, the late Mrs Jamal, until nearly a year afterwards, and then only when her then solicitor requested it. Why was that?'

'I wouldn't know, sir.'

Collins tugged awkwardly at the flaps of his jacket pockets, 'That damage could have been interpreted as evidence of violence,' he said, as a statement rather than as a question. 'Why on earth wasn't a full-scale investigation launched?'

'It was, sir.'

'None that was worth the name. There were no forensic tests done on the room, no dusting for fingerprints.'

'It was a missing persons, not a criminal investigation. They're two different things.'

'You seemed very uninterested in the whereabouts of two young men you had spent months observing going to and from supposedly seditious political meetings.'

'Like I said, I just did what I was asked.'

'Which, it seems, was not to try too hard,' Collins said with a forthrightness which seemed to take the other lawyers by surprise. He raised his voice even louder. 'You and your colleagues were ordered not to look for Nazim Jamal and Rafi Hassan. That's the unpalatable truth, isn't it, Mr Watkins?'

Watkins glanced uneasily at the jury. 'Those are your words, sir, not mine.'

'You have no answer – is that it, Mr Watkins? Would you have been satisfied with the police response if it had been your son or daughter who had gone missing?'

Watkins looked to Jenny, hoping to be rescued.

'It's a perfectly proper question,' Jenny said.

After a pause, in which Watkins seem to toy with the idea of going off message, he said, 'I was a detective sergeant, sir. An NCO. You're better off asking those questions of the officers.'

Fraser Havilland and Martha Denton traded a glance and went into a huddle with their instructing solicitors. The two legal teams were planning something in concert.

Khan shook his head, giving Watkins a look of undisguised disdain when Jenny invited him to cross-examine. The witness he wanted was DI Pironi. Jenny wanted him, too, but he could wait for the moment. There were others she needed to hear from first.

'You may stand down, Mr Watkins.' She turned to Alison. 'Simon Donovan, please.'

Donovan came to the witness box for the second time. He looked jaded; what little muscle tone there had once been had gone from his plump face, which sagged unhealthily from his cheek and jawbones.

'You're still under oath, Mr Donovan,' Jenny said. 'I've just a few questions to clear up following your testimony last week.' She turned back through her longhand note of the evidence and found her verbatim record of his testimony. 'You told us that you reported your sighting of the two young Asian men on the London train on the 29 June because you recognized their faces from newspaper reports.'

'That's right.'

'You went on to say that the police came round – I presume to your home – with a selection of photographs, from which you identified Nazim Jamal and Rafi Hassan.'

'I did.'

Jenny noticed Zachariah Jamal looking intently at Donovan.

'And this was prompted by your concern that they might have been involved in illegal activity.'

'Yes, ma'am.'

Jenny paused and studied Donovan carefully. He clasped and unclasped his hands.

'What was your occupation at the time, Mr Donovan?'

'I was a chartered accountant, ma'am.'

'In private practice?'

'Yes.'

'From April of that year were you under investigation for offences of fraud?'

Khan and Collins exchanged a look. Havilland and Denton appeared unmoved: Havilland engrossed in another document, Denton patiently taking a note.

'I was questioned by police, ma'am,' Donovan said, 'but completely exonerated. No only that, I gave evidence against several of my clients and a former business associate, who as it turned out were guilty of fraud.' His answer was pre-rehearsed but confidently delivered. Jenny noticed his eyes dart towards Havilland as if he were subconsciously seeking approval.

Jenny said, 'Do you recall whether you were questioned by police as a suspect between 29 June and 20 July, the date on which you gave your statement?'

'I don't recall exact dates, but there's a good chance.'

'I won't sidestep the issue, Mr Donovan: did you strike a deal with the police over the issue of the fraud charges? Was giving a statement saying you'd seen Nazim Jamal and Rafi Hassan part of it?'

Havilland got indignantly to his feet. 'Ma'am, as counsel for the chief of the police force in question, I really must object to this line of questioning unless it's backed up by credible evidence.'

'Evidence will be called which explains the question Mr Havilland. You'll just have to be patient.'

'Ma'am, purely in the interests of fairness I must remind you of your absolute duty of impartiality. This line of questioning does sound suspiciously like a cross-examination mounted by an advocate making a partial case. That is not the manner in which a coroner is expected to conduct an inquiry.'

'I can assure you, Mr Havilland, I have no intention of compromising my impartiality,' Jenny snapped. 'If you'd kindly let me continue.'

Havilland gave way reluctantly, heaving a theatrical sigh as he sat.

'Mr Donovan,' Jenny said, 'please give a straight answer –

did the police suggest you make the statement identifying Nazim Jamal and Rafi Hassan?'

'No,' Donovan replied, with almost too much force to be convincing.

'Then do you have any proof that you took this train journey – a credit-card statement perhaps?'

'I paid cash.'

'And for the ticket to the football match you were heading to?'

'That was cash, too.'

'Were you travelling with anyone who could verify your account?'

'No.'

'There must be someone who could substantiate your story?'

'You could try my ex-wife,' Donovan said, hoping to raise a smile from the jury.

Jenny tried again to shake his account by suggesting that he may have been tempted to come forward with the intention of gaining credit with the police at a time when he was facing charges, but he denied everything. His statement had been the spontaneous gesture of a concerned citizen, he insisted. That's all there was to it.

Havilland decided not to dignify Jenny's insinuations with any further inquiry, and Martha Denton again followed suit. Khan reprised his attack of the week before, implying that Donovan couldn't tell one Asian face from another, but the jury seemed visibly irritated by Khan's barracking tone: the more he railed, the harder their expressions became. Jenny was slowly learning about British juries: it didn't matter if their skins were black, white, brown or any combination, they had an instinctive dislike of sentiment. It was a paradox but, in a culture obsessed with the public parading of every shade of self-indulgent emotion, inside a courtroom the instinct to reject all overt displays of passion still held firm.

When Khan had finally run out of breath, Collins rose to ask a question of his own.

Quietly, and nervously twiddling a pen between his fingers, he said, 'Are you asking us to believe, Mr Donovan, that it never occurred to you that identifying two potential terrorists – which is what you said you thought they were – might help you in your own case? I can't imagine what sort of solicitor was advising you if it didn't.'

Donovan hesitated a fraction too long to appear completely honest. 'I can't say I had that thought before I gave the statement, no. My solicitor might have said something afterwards.'

'Yes, I'm sure he or she did,' Collins said, then, as if to himself, added, 'I certainly would have done. Yes, indeed.' He looked down at the floor for a moment, his mouth twitching as if he was suffering from an unfortunate nervous tic, then looked up again with an unexpected flash of fire. 'And even though you face no charges, even though this hearing is in secret and your words will never be broadcast, you're still not man enough to admit that your statement was extracted from you in return for favours. It was a lie, wasn't it, Mr Donovan?'

The mouse had roared. The jury sat up and paid attention. They watched Donovan closely as he tried to effect a dismissive smile, all the while his thick, fat neck growing a more livid shade of purple.

'No,' Donovan said tightly. 'I saw them. Two Asian lads. It was them. I'm sure it was.'

As he left the witness box and headed gratefully for the exit at the back of the hall, Jenny reminded herself that her job was not simply to pursue the agenda McAvoy had set for her. It was possible that Donovan was largely telling the truth. Perhaps he did see two young men Asian men on the train; they might conceivably have been Nazim and Rafi. She had to keep an open mind.

She took a deep breath. 'Stay calm,' she told herself. 'People are relying on you for the truth. Stay calm for them.'

Dr Sarah Levin managed to look both businesslike and effortlessly glamorous. She declined a religious oath and chose instead to affirm. Jenny imagined McAvoy mocking her. 'Let's see how much of an atheist you are when eternity calls,' he would have said. 'Would you rather have your long-neglected priest or your hairdresser at your bedside?'

'Dr Levin,' Jenny said, pushing the unkind thought from her mind, 'you were a physics student in the same year as Nazim Jamal, weren't you?'

'Yes, I was.'

'You went to lectures and tutorials together?'

'We did.'

'You had a room in Goldney, a different student hall of residence.'

'That's right.'

'And approximately twelve days after he disappeared you gave a statement to the police.'

'Yes.'

'Do you remember what you said?'

'I said that I had overheard him talking to some Asian friends in the canteen about "brothers" who had gone to fight in Afghanistan. Their conversation was about jihadis fighting the British and Americans. Nazim seemed impressed with the idea. Whether he was just showing off or not, I couldn't say.' She shrugged. 'They were very young.'

'When was this incident?'

'Sometime in the summer term, May probably.'

'Did he ever mention to you that he was thinking of going to Afghanistan?'

'No. Never.'

Jenny paused briefly, telling herself to rein in, take her time, tease out the truth.

'Dr Levin, your statement to the police was dated 22 July. That was three weeks after Nazim Jamal and Rafi Hassan's disappearance. What was happening during that period?'

'It was after the end of term. I'd stayed on for a while. Everything had been frantic, but as they quietened down I think I must have remembered overhearing that conversation.'

'Detectives had been speaking to students, had they?'

'There had been a few around, yes. None of them spoke to me directly.'

'I see. And having recalled this conversation, what was in your mind?'

'I suppose I thought telling the police was the responsible thing to do.'

'Did you go to them or did they come to you?'

'There was a notice up in the physics department. I called the number.'

'Of course, by that time Mr Donovan had given his statement to the police and it had been reported in the local press.'

'I was aware of that. It was probably what prompted me.'

Jenny looked hard at Sarah Levin. Her manner was modest, that of a witness trying to do her best, but there was a fragility about her, a tendency to address her answers in the direction of Havilland and Denton rather than the jury, as if she felt the gravitational pull of the authority they represented. Yet she didn't know who they were. She'd hadn't been at court the week before and she had been behind closed doors in the committee room when the introductions were made at the start of the session.

Jenny said, 'How well did you know Nazim Jamal, Dr Levin?'

She thought for a moment before answering. 'Not very.'

'What about in your first term at university. Were you closer to him then?'

Sarah Levin paused, a sadness stole across her face and she lowered her voice slightly. 'I know what you're going to say.'

'You had a relationship with him, didn't you?'

Sarah Levin glanced at Mr Jamal. His expression was set and unreadable.

'Nazim and I had a very brief "relationship", if you can call it that . . . It was our first term, first time away from home . . .'

Jenny glanced at the lawyers. She noticed Khan looking a little bemused by the confession.

'How long did this last?'

'A week or two . . . It wasn't anything serious. You know what it's like when you're a student.'

'I do. But wasn't Nazim going through a religiously ortho-dox phase at the time? He was wearing traditional clothing and growing a beard, wasn't he?'

Uncomfortable, Sarah Levin said, 'I really didn't want to cause any offence to his family, that's why I never mentioned it . . . We were both eighteen. You're not really sure what you believe at that age. You're still searching for your identity.'

'The point I'm making is that he didn't have any scruples about sleeping with you.'

'He didn't seem to have, no.'

'Did he talk to you about his religious beliefs?'

'Only to say that no one should find out. Not his family or his Asian friends ... It was all very illicit. Exciting, I suppose.'

'Did he seem to you to be a religious fanatic?'

'Not at the time. He was certainly observant – he would pray five times a day – but in all other respects he was just a normal young man.'

'Who ended the relationship?'

'He didn't call me over the Christmas vacation. It just sort of petered out.'

'You may or may not know that Nazim had a subsequent brief relationship with another student in your year, Dani James.'

Sarah Levin nodded. 'I heard last week. I had no idea.'

'She thinks she contracted chlamydia from him. Did you have a similar experience?'

Sarah Levin tensed, her shoulders suddenly rigid. A spontaneous reaction, Jenny thought. She groped for a response. 'Is this relevant?'

'It could be. I have had sight of your medical records, Dr Levin . . .'

The witness blinked and reeled from the unexpected blow. 'I was diagnosed with the infection a few months later, yes,' she said, acutely embarrassed. 'Whether it came from Nazim, I couldn't say.'

'Did you mention it to him?'

'No.'

'Were you angry about it?'

'Not in the sense you're suggesting.'

'Dr Levin, did the police know about your previous relationship with Nazim?'

'No. I've never mentioned it to anyone until today.'

'You see the importance of that question, don't you? This isn't a criminal trial, I'm not accusing you of anything, but if, for example, the police had got hold of that information, and if they were trying to prove that he and Rafi Hassan went abroad, they might have come to you and asked if he had ever suggested he might?'

'I know what you're implying, but it's not the case.'

'Did anyone from the Security Services ever speak to or question you?'

'Never.'

Jenny sat back in her chair with the uneasy feeling that something was still missing, that a question remained unanswered. If she had been an advocate she could have grilled Sarah Levin relentlessly on her unlikely lack of malice towards the young man who had wounded her in such an intimate way, but it would have been inappropriate for a coroner, laying her open to accusations of heavy-handedness and bias.

'Could you please tell us, then, whether Nazim ever said anything to you which might have indicated what happened to him.'

Sarah considered her answer carefully. 'It wasn't anything he said at the time, but looking back I can see that he was angry. I'm not even sure he knew what he was angry with. He channelled it into his religion – it gave him a sense of purpose, of specialness perhaps – but he was also intelligent, sensitive . . .'

'Do you believe that he went abroad?'

'I can believe it,' she said. 'It would have seemed like an adventure.'

'Did he ever talk to you about Rafi Hassan?'

'I didn't even know who he was until they both vanished. Nazim never spoke about him. Looking back, I suppose he was leading two very separate lives. I didn't see the other one.'

Jenny ended her examination with her niggling sense of

doubt unresolved. As Havilland rose to confirm with Sarah Levin that all her contact with the police had been at her own initiative, Jenny wrestled with the fact that McAvoy had kept his inkling of an affair between her and Nazim to himself. She didn't buy his explanation that he'd wanted to protect Mrs Jamal from shame and scandal. He had pushed her towards a complex and sinister conspiracy theory and away from the person with whom Nazim had been most intimate. It was as if he didn't want Nazim and Rafi to have gone abroad. He wanted a grand struggle between good and evil; he wanted to place himself on the side of the angels and bid for redemption.

When Havilland had finished polishing the reputation of the police, Martha Denton stood to cross-examine for the first time that day.

'Dr Levin, I'm sure we all understand your motives in not mentioning your intimate association with Nazim Jamal before now, but I'm sure you understand the importance of telling this court everything that could possibly cast light on what became of him.' She spoke with a reassuring softness, without a trace of threat or impatience.

'Absolutely.'

'And, of course, any insight we can gain into his state of mind will help to shore up or indeed weaken the case for him having left the country for political or religious motives.'

'If I could tell you, I would. I don't know what Nazim was thinking.'

'Did he not talk to you about his religious beliefs?'

'Not in any detail. I knew he went to mosque, I saw that he had books on politics and history, but to be honest I wasn't that interested.'

'You didn't get a sense that he was using you?'

'Not really.'

'You sound unsure . . . He was a young radical Muslim

having sex with an unbeliever. That was a very compromising situation for him.'

'I suppose it was.'

'Did he suffer from feelings of guilt?'

Sarah Levin glanced at Mr Jamal, whose face was finally beginning to show signs of strain. After so many years of unanswered questions he was being forced to peer into the troubled mind of his son. 'Yes, I think he probably did, but he was too considerate to share that with me. There was obviously a conflict.'

'A conflict between extremes – was that your impression?'

'He was a passionate person . . . You don't appreciate the full depth of these things at such a young age, but thinking about it now I can see that's what he was.'

'And when he dropped you, did he end all contact?'

'Completely.'

'Why did you think he did that?'

'His religion must have won out . . . I was hurt, but I tried to move on.'

'You've been most helpful, Dr Levin,' Martha Denton said.

As if to demonstrate his own immunity to Sarah Levin's now wounded beauty, Khan proceeded to question her aggressively, seeking to attack the notion that Nazim suppressed sexual passion and transformed it into a zealot's anger, even suggesting that the affair was a figment of her imagination. It was as if the Nazim Jamal he had imagined was beyond corruption, but at the very least – as a direct consequence of his spiritual purity – innocent enough to have been cruelly seduced.

Hearing Sarah Levin's pained replies, it occurred to Jenny for the first time that she may have been genuinely in love with Nazim: the more battered she was by Khan's invective, the more she seemed to expose her hurt. Perhaps she felt responsible for his disappearance; a beautiful and unwitting siren who'd propelled him onto a fatal course.

# TWENTY-FOUR

JENNY WAS PICKING AT A soggy cheese sandwich in the small upstairs room when Alison knocked and delivered the news that their missing witnesses, Tathum and Maitland, had arrived. Maitland had requested to be heard early as he was due out on a flight to the Middle East the next morning. Jenny said she'd get to him that afternoon. She had decided to follow the chain of evidence from Elizabeth Murray's sighting of the Toyota back to Maitland's office before calling McAvoy. Only then would she call Pironi and Skene. The morning's testimony had exposed a number of cracks in the official version of events: she wanted them to be as wide as possible before the detective and the MI5 officer were called to account.

'I've also got a request from Detective Inspector Pironi,' Alison said, a little embarrassed. 'He's asked if Mr McAvoy can wait somewhere other than the committee room – he's behaving oddly, apparently.'

'I can imagine it's rather intense in there,' Jenny said. 'Fine. As long as he's kept away from the hall while the others are giving evidence.'

'Thank you, Mrs Cooper,' Alison said and dithered for a moment as if she wanted to say more.

Jenny gave her a look. 'What is it?'

'Nothing.' Alison turned to the door.

'You've not been speaking to Dave Pironi?'

'No . . . I haven't, honestly.'

'But?'

'I shouldn't be giving you my opinions. He'll give an account of himself. I just hope that worm from MI5 does the same.' She hurried away before Jenny could push her further.

But there was nothing more Jenny needed to know: Alison was convinced that whatever shortcomings there had been in Pironi's investigation were not down to him. Like all good policemen he'd only been obeying orders. He wasn't brave enough to say so in court, so he'd filtered the message back through his old friend. Spineless bastard, Jenny thought, and cowardly with it. Being locked in the same room as McAvoy all morning must have been hell for him, like seeing his conscience in human form.

Madog stuttered through the oath and fidgeted with his glasses as Jenny led him through a few preliminary questions, a number of which she had to repeat. After several attempts she established that he was fifty-nine years old and had worked as a toll collector on the Severn Bridge for twenty-three years.

'I appreciate it's a long time ago, Mr Madog, but can you tell us if you remember witnessing anything unusual on the night of 28 June 2002?'

He glanced apprehensively at the lawyers, then back at Jenny. 'The black car, you mean?'

'If you could just take us through what you have already said in your statement.'

'Well it was late, about eleven at night, like,' he began uncertainly. 'I was in the booth there when a black car pulled up. There were two white fellas in the front and two Asian lads in the back.'

His answer was met with a flurry of whispers amongst the

lawyers. Martha Denton and Havilland turned to confer with their respective solicitors, then briefly formed into a larger, collective huddle. Alun Rhys, however, did not react.

Jenny said, 'What kind of vehicle was it?'

'A big seven-seater type. A Toyota I think. A black one.'

'Can you describe the occupants in any more detail?'

With a little prompting, Madog limped through a description of the crew-cut driver, the man with the ponytail and the two frightened passengers cowering in the back seat. During this, Jenny noticed Mr Jamal's eyes widen in alarm, his resolute composure giving way to an expression of outrage.

Jenny said, 'You collect tolls from hundreds of vehicles every shift. What was it about this one that drew your attention?'

'The driver had an attitude, you know. No please or thank you, virtually snatched the change out of my hand. And one of the lads in the back looked at me in a way I couldn't forget. He had a beard like, but there was something about him – he looked much younger, like a kid.'

'Usher, could you show Mr Madog photographs of Nazim Jamal and Rafi Hassan?'

Alison left her table at the side of the room and took two large photographs across to the witness. He peered at them both before nodding. 'Looks like them.' He pointed to the picture on the left. 'That'd be the one I noticed.'

Alison checked the printed label on the back of the photograph. 'That's Nazim Jamal, ma'am.'

Mr Jamal was looking directly at Jenny now, horrified and expectant, waiting for the pieces to fall into place.

'Did you ever see the occupants of this vehicle again, Mr Madog?'

'I'm afraid I did . . .'

Still, Jenny noticed, Alun Rhys sat tight, showing not the

slightest flicker of surprise. It was as if he knew what was coming next.

'Go on, Mr Madog.'

Battling his failing nerves, Madog managed to recount his encounter with the ponytailed passenger the following Saturday. He told the jury how the man had sprayed paint on his granddaughter's hair, and how he hadn't even looked angry as he was doing it. He showed no feeling at all, Madog said.

'Did you tell the police about this attack on your granddaughter?'

'Didn't dare. I wasn't going to put her at risk, was I?'

'Have you seen this man since?'

Madog shook his head.

Jenny's stomach turned over. She glanced over at Alison, who gave a slight shrug. Madog had been sitting in the same room as Tathum for at least fifteen minutes before he came to the witness box. He must surely have remembered his face, even if he was now shorn of the ponytail. She could call Tathum into the court and ask Madog to identify him, but it presented a huge risk. The higher courts frowned on court-room identifications – the circumstances in which they were made were considered artificial and dangerously pressured – and were prone to ruling them inadmissible. But unless Madog did single Tathum out, a vital link in the chain of evidence would be broken.

She decided to bide her time. She would ask Madog to remain in the hall after stepping down and recall him to the witness box after he'd watched Tathum give evidence.

Jenny invited counsel to cross-examine. Havilland deferred to Martha Denton, who rose to address Madog with a faintly amused smile.

'You claim to remember the details of a single car and its occupants the best part of a decade after the alleged event.'

'Not exactly . . .' he glanced to Jenny. 'A fella asked me about it after, must have been the following July.'

'Oh, really? And who was this?'

'Mr Dean, I think his name was. Said he was a private investigator.'

'An investigator for whom?'

'I can help you there, Miss Denton,' Jenny said. 'Mr Dean was instructed by Mrs Amira Jamal's then solicitor.'

'I see.' Martha Denton's instructing solicitor tugged at her elbow and whispered to her. She smiled, then turned accusingly back to the witness. 'And this solicitor would be Mr Alec McAvoy? A man who in December of 2002 was imprisoned for an offence of attempting to pervert the course of justice? So presumably Mr McAvoy was in prison at the time?'

'I didn't know anything about that,' Madog said.

Wishing she had kept her mouth shut, Jenny said, 'You'll be hearing from Mr McAvoy in due course. You can address that issue with him directly.'

'I certainly will, ma'am. Did this investigator take a written statement from you, Mr Madog?'

'I didn't like to say anything at the time – because of my granddaughter.'

'Why did he come to you of all people?'

'He knew what kind of car he was looking for and that there would have been a couple of Asian lads in it. He wanted to know if any of the toll collectors had seen it.'

'Ah. So he specifically asked you whether you had seen a large black vehicle containing two white men and two Asian youths?'

'He did.'

'Did he pay you, Mr Madog?'

'No. Nothing.'

'And did he suggest the incident with your granddaughter and the paint?'

Madog shook his head firmly. 'I never told him about that.'

'I see. So when did you first recount that alleged incident?'

'Last week, when I was asked to make a statement.'

Martha Denton adopted a puzzled expression. 'Let's be absolutely clear about this, Mr Madog. You claim to have been too frightened to tell the police about a vicious attack on your six-year-old granddaughter, yet you happily talked to a private investigator who turned up out of the blue.'

'Not about my granddaughter. I told you, I didn't mention it.'

Martha Denton stared into space, as if trying and failing to make sense of his answers. Then, with a dismissive shrug and a curt, 'Oh well,' dropped into her seat.

Jenny watched two jurors in the front row exchange a knowing look. Martha Denton had made them feel clever and made Madog look a fool.

Havilland had no questions, content to align himself with Denton's attack. Sensing a breakthrough for his cause, Khan managed to repair some of the damage she had inflicted by establishing that Madog had no credible reason for lying about his sighting, and his subsequent encounter with the ponytailed driver, short of being bribed. Madog insisted he had never taken money and had told only the truth. Not all the jurors appeared convinced.

Collins had no questions for the witness. Madog stepped eagerly from the witness box, keen to escape as quickly as he could.

Halting him in his tracks, Jenny said, 'If you could wait in the hall until the end of the afternoon, Mr Madog – you may be required to answer some further questions.'

Jenny watched for Rhys's reaction. He remained impassive. Smug. She allowed herself a brief indulgent fantasy: perhaps she could still raise sufficient doubt, pose enough awkward questions to lead the jury to a brave decision that would shock him out of his complacency. Although the substance of the evidence would have to remain secret, the jury's verdict could not be suppressed. And a coroner's jury had the unique power to deliver their findings in the form of a narrative. If they decided Nazim and Rafi had been spirited away against their will and that the official investigation had been negligent or deliberately suppressed, they could spell it out.

The eight very unsuspecting men and women, currently suffering varying degrees of boredom and annoyance at having to perform their obscure civic duty, had the power to whip up a storm.

The next witness was David Powell, the proprietor of the vehicle-hire firm Jenny and McAvoy had visited in Hereford. Short and heavy-set, he spoke in a broad borders accent and made no attempt to disguise his impatience at being prised away from his business. He glowered at Jenny with the same suspicious disdain with which she imagined he greeted all officials.

Yes, his firm had owned a black Toyota Previa in June 2002 he said, but his records showed it had been rented from 20 to 23 June and not again until 6 July. It would have been sitting in the yard out front on the 28th. When Jenny suggested that he might have hired it out without keeping a paper record, Powell answered with an adamant no and wouldn't be moved. If the records said it wasn't hired, it wasn't. No argument.

Jenny changed tack. 'You have a regular customer called Mr Christopher Tathum, don't you?'

'Not that regular,' Powell grunted.

'Have you brought details of the cars he's hired?'

He nodded and unfolded a sheet of paper which he produced from his jacket pocket. Alison took it from him and handed it to Jenny. Printed on office stationery, it was a computer-generated list of transactions conducted with *Tathum, C. Mr*. The first was for the hire of an Audi saloon in December 2001. Running her eyes down the list, Jenny saw that Tathum had rented the same vehicle half a dozen times over the next two years, usually for week-long periods. There was only one hire of the Toyota listed: in March 2003.

Jenny said, 'Are you friendly with Mr Tathum?'

'Not particularly.'

'You wouldn't do him any special favours – a cash deal, for example?'

'No.'

Jenny fixed him with a look as she asked her next question. 'Has he or anyone else spoken to you or your staff about this vehicle?'

Avoiding her gaze he muttered, 'No, ma'am.'

It was little to go on, just a hint that he was lying, but it stoked her anger. She couldn't resist making a point for the jury. 'Are you quite sure you've told this court the whole truth, Mr Powell?'

'Quite sure.'

After Khan had probed with a few speculative questions, all of which met with denials, Jenny asked Powell to join Madog in the empty public gallery. It was a piece of theatre – lining up the links in the chain to keep the story vivid in the jurors' minds – but one Jenny felt justified in using. Since Donovan had given his implausible evidence, she'd been fighting a growing suspicion that events were being managed. She had been scrupulous in keeping Elizabeth Murray, Madog, Tathum and Maitland's identities secret until they had reached the witness box, but none of them had raised Alun Rhys to even a moment of visible concern. She needed to push harder. Her chest tightened at the prospect. She had to fight panic with determination.

Tathum took his time walking from the committee room to the witness box. Dressed in a suit and tie, he could have been a business executive. All that gave him away as a former military man was the solid squareness of his shoulders and a certain predatory quality to his narrow gaze. Jenny glanced over at Madog, hoping to detect signs of anxiety: he touched his cheek, scratched his neck. Tiny clues, but not sufficient to reassure her.

Tathum took the Bible and read the oath with the relaxed demeanour she imagined he might have adopted while leaning through Madog's car window. She felt an instinctive and visceral dislike for him, an irrational loathing which she knew would only weaken her if she let it show.

'Mr Tathum,' she said, having confirmed his name and address, 'can you tell the court who you were working for in late June 2002?'

'As far as I can remember, ma'am, no one.'

'Then how were you supporting yourself?'

'I'd left the army the year before. I had a military pension and I did occasional contract work. I still do.'

'What kind of contract work?'

'Close protection is the technical term.' He aimed his explanation at the jury. 'A bodyguard in layman's language.'

He was effortlessly confident, not in the least frightened of the jury knowing who and what he was.

'Who was your main employer during that year?'

'I had several contracts with a company called Maitland Ltd. I was looking after British oil execs in Nigeria and Azerbaijan.'

'Were you armed while carrying out these duties?'

'I wouldn't have been much use if I wasn't.'

Despite her blanket of medication, Jenny's heartbeat picked up and her diaphragm drew tighter. She kicked herself on.

'You had a different hairstyle at that time, didn't you, Mr Tathum? You wore it in a ponytail.'

'I did,' he said without hesitation.

Jenny stalled, his directness had thrown her. 'Let's talk about 28 June of that year. Are you able to say where you were on that day?'

'I was probably at home, what there was of it. I bought a broken-down old farmhouse when I came out of the army and was rebuilding it.' He smiled at the jury. 'It's turned into my life's work.'

They didn't react. There were neither smiles nor frowns, just a vague sense of wariness at Tathum's practised charm.

Jenny steeled herself. 'Two men were seen in the front of a black Toyota people carrier that evening in Marlowes Road, Bristol. The same or a similar vehicle was seen crossing the Severn Bridge at about eleven p.m. The driver was a white man, thickset, with close-cropped hair; the passenger, also white, had a ponytail. There were two young Asian men in the back seat. Were you in that vehicle, Mr Tathum?'

Tathum smiled and shook his head. 'No, I wasn't.'

'On several occasions you have rented cars from Mr Powell's company in Hereford. Were you travelling in one of his vehicles that day?'

'No. I have my own car which I use when I'm not working.'

His denials weren't surprising, but Jenny was rattled by the depth of his confidence. She didn't believe anything she could throw at him would shake it. The jury's questioning expressions told her that they were slowly putting two and two together, but still there was no solid evidence on which they could hang their suspicions.

'On the following Saturday, Mr Madog, the toll collector on the Severn Bridge who noticed the Toyota, says that he was accosted by a man with a ponytail whom he recognized as the driver of that vehicle. This man told Mr Madog that he "hadn't seen him", then proceeded to spray paint into the hair of his six-year-old granddaughter who was sitting in the back seat.' Jenny met Tathum's gaze and felt herself weakening. 'Was that man you?'

He responded with a look of genuine astonishment. 'No, ma'am.'

'Are you able to say where you were on that day?'

'Still at home, I expect.'

All she needed was one thing to implicate him beyond a flimsy chain of circumstantial evidence, one tiny patch of solid ground. Out of the corner of her eye she saw Mr Jamal, his face filled with pent-up anger, willing her on. Now was the moment. She had nothing more to lose. She looked over the heads of the lawyers to Madog.

'Mr Madog,' she said, 'I'm not asking you to perform a formal identification, but can you say if you recognize this witness?'

Startled, Madog flinched, then gave a nervous shake of his head.

'It's very important that you give this proper thought and don't feel at all intimidated, Mr Madog. I'll spell it out: do you recognize this witness as the man whom you allege accosted you and your granddaughter?'

Rising timidly to a hunched, semi-standing position, Madog said, 'No, ma'am . . . That's not him.'

A dreadful familiar numbness crept over her. She continued mechanically, a dispassionate observer. She scarcely absorbed a word of the cross-examinations offered by Havilland then Khan, except to register that Tathum had survived without a blow being landed. Tathum brushed aside every accusation and hectoring question Khan threw at him, and stepped down from the witness box as confidently as he had entered it.

Maitland's evidence took less than ten minutes. A brisk, polite, ex-SAS colonel, he confirmed that he ran a company specializing in the provision of highly trained ex-servicemen as bodyguards and security advisers to wealthy businessmen and foreign governments. Tathum was one such, who had completed three contracts in the year 2002. None of them, he explained with the reassuringly nonchalant tone of a high-ranking officer, involved the escorting of two young Asian university students over the Severn Bridge from Bristol.

It was nearing four o'clock when Maitland strolled out of the hall with Tathum. It was a natural moment to call a halt and take stock of the ruins of the day, but Jenny couldn't bear to send the jury home having made up their minds. It was a gamble, but maybe it was the right time to introduce them to McAvoy. He would be wild, full of extravagant speculation and conjecture, but at least he'd make the jury take notice.

'We'll have Mr McAvoy next, please,' she said to Alison.

Her officer gave her a look as if to say she hoped she knew what she was doing, then made her way to the back of the hall to call him in from the front lobby, to which he'd been banished at lunchtime. After an unnaturally long pause, Alison returned announcing that according to the constable at the front door, McAvoy had left the building an hour ago.

'Oh,' Jenny said, failing to disguise a sudden surge of panic. 'Well, then perhaps we'll call it a day and see if we can't have him back here first thing tomorrow.'

Martha Denton interjected, 'If I could trouble you for a moment, ma'am preferably in the absence of the jury.'

'Is there a matter of law you wish to discuss?'

'It's more of a procedural issue, but nothing that need

concern the jury at this stage. I'm sure they're extremely keen to get away after a long day.'

She was greeted by a ripple of thankful laughter.

'Very well,' Jenny said and reminded the jury not to discuss the case overnight, even with members of their close families. They had begun to gather coats and handbags even before she had finished talking, and bustled eagerly out of the hall with almost indecent haste.

'Yes, Miss Denton?' Jenny said, still trying to accept that McAvoy had deserted her.

Martha Denton produced several copies of a document. Alison brought one forward to Jenny. The rest were distributed among the other lawyers.

Denton said, 'In the interests of clarity, my clients felt that David Skene should make a statement setting out the substance of his evidence. As you'll see, it raises one major legal issue, but my clients are confident about how that should be resolved.'

'Hold on, Miss Denton.'

Jenny skimmed over the brief three-paragraph statement.

*I am David Skene, a former intelligence officer employed by the Security Services. From 2001 until 2004 I was attached to the anti-terrorist team. In early July 2002 I was asked to head a unit to liaise with CID officers in Bristol who were investigating the reported disappearance of two male Asian university students, Nazim Jamal and Rafi Hassan. Jamal and Hassan had been regular attendees at the Al Rahma mosque, which had been under police surveillance following receipt of intelligence suggesting that the resident mullah, Sayeed Faruq, and a number of his close associates including a postgraduate student, Mr Anwar Ali, had been acting as recruiters for the Islamist organization, Hizb-ut-Tahrir.*

*During the following weeks my colleague, Mr Ashok Singh, and I interviewed a number of students and staff at the university as well as members of the missing men's immediate families. We failed to gather any significant evidence to indicate their whereabouts. The CID had more success. In particular, they obtained anecdotal evidence (from a then student, now 'Dr') Sarah Levin that Jamal had been heard in a student canteen glorifying young British radicals who had gone to fight as jihadis in Afghanistan. A member of the public, Mr Simon Donovan, then came forward and claimed to have seen Jamal and Hassan on a London-bound train on the morning of 29 June. While police continued their investigations on the ground, Mr Singh and I were redirected to other duties though we remained in regular contact with Bristol CID.*

*In August 2002 intelligence was received from a trusted human source which corroborated the theory that Jamal and Hassan had indeed left the country with the assistance of a radical Islamic group. This source was considered highly credible and the nature, although not the substance, of the intelligence was passed on to the CID in Bristol. This led to a gradual winding down of the investigation on the ground.*

*The substance of this intelligence remains highly classified.*

Jenny looked up from the document, realizing she had stumbled into a trap from which there would be no escape. A wave of nausea rose up from deep in the well of her stomach.

'Are we going to hear the substance of this intelligence?'

'I hardly think so, ma'am. I'm instructed that the source is still extremely sensitive and that any disclosure could seriously compromise him or her. As I'm sure you are aware, the law is very clear on this issue, but to answer any question you may have, I have prepared a brief submission.'

Martha Denton's instructing solicitor was already handing out copies of authorities back to the 1960s. Jenny's knowledge of the law pertaining to national security and the disclosure of evidence was sketchy at best. Martha Denton proceeded to give her a lesson.

Since the ground-breaking case of *Conway v. Rimmer* (1968), she explained, evidence could be withheld from the court if the Secretary of State was satisfied that it was overwhelmingly in the public interest to do so. Even Jenny knew this much. What she hadn't appreciated, however, was just how wide the definition of 'public interest' had become. The cases were clear: it was now considered in the public interest to protect vulnerable or important intelligence sources and, it seemed, evidence which might be used to identify them.

Denton said, 'Needless to say, the Secretary of State is satisfied that the evidence of our source does indeed pass this test, and a certificate of public interest immunity will be at the court in the morning.'

Jenny flicked hurriedly through the pages of *Jervis* and found a passage which seemed to suggest that coroners, along with other judges, had the right to view evidence which the Secretary of State wished to certify to determine whether it did in fact pass the public interest test. Denton was ready with a further battery of precedents, all of which stated that there were cases in which a 'judicial peep' at the disputed evidence was not even appropriate. This was such a case, Denton insisted: the evidence in question was so sensitive that not even one of Her Majesty's coroners could be trusted to view it. If Jenny refused to agree, the inquest would have to be adjourned and the issue referred to the High Court.

'Let's forget the law for a moment, Miss Denton,' Jenny

said. 'What you're telling me is that there is evidence that Nazim Jamal and Rafi Hassan left the country. Eight years have passed but you have never told the families what this intelligence is, and you still don't intend to.'

'With respect ma'am, the families were told that the evidence pointed to their sons having left the country. But I'm afraid even families aren't necessarily entitled to have access to such sensitive intelligence, particularly the families of suspected extremists.'

Khan could contain his anger no more. 'Ma'am, this is outrageous. You must insist on seeing this so-called intelligence and if it's refused fight through every court until justice is exhausted.' He jabbed an accusing finger at Martha Denton. 'Her clients, the Security Services, are the people who complain that young Asian men are being lured by extremists, and she wonders why. These aren't respectable people, they're secret police. Does she honestly think hiding this information is in the *public interest*? I'll tell you what the public is interested in – fair and open justice.'

'I take your point, Mr Khan,' Jenny said. She needed time to research, to gather arguments as powerful as Martha Denton's. 'I'm going to adjourn and continue this discussion first thing tomorrow.'

Martha Denton refused to be silenced. 'I'm not sure that will be necessary, ma'am. Given that my clients intend to go directly to the High Court should you rule against them, further discussion is, quite frankly, fruitless. Furthermore, as far as I can ascertain, there is no evidence whatsoever that either Jamal or Hassan is in fact dead, certainly none upon which a jury could reasonably be expected to return a verdict.'

Jenny's fraying temper snapped, 'Miss Denton, I made a special application to hold this inquest and it will continue until its conclusion. If, once all the evidence is heard, the jury are not able to reach a verdict, then so be it. In the meantime, I will not and I shall not be dictated to by you or anyone you represent. Do you understand me?'

Martha Denton gave an indifferent shrug. She no longer cared what Jenny thought.

As Denton and Havilland gathered their papers and Khan and Collins approached Mr Jamal to express their outrage, Jenny noticed Alison hovering near the committee-room door. She recognized her officer's expression of guilt-ridden indecision as the one that had been a frequent feature of the traumatic two weeks of their first case together the previous summer. There were good people and bad people in Alison's world, and when the categories blurred it angered and confused her.

Jenny caught her eye and saw that they were both wrestling with the same thought. Hell would freeze over before Skene or any other intelligence office would be persuaded to tell the whole truth to her inquest. But on the other side of the door sat DI Pironi, a career cop with only a handful of years to serve until he collected his pension. Was he decent and brave enough to risk that comfortable future? Would Alison use what little leverage she had to persuade him?

Martha Denton's instructing solicitor made for the committee room. Alison held up her hand to stop him and disappeared briefly behind the door. David Skene emerged seconds later. After several moments Alison followed with a glance towards Jenny and the slightest nod.

It was a place of Pironi's choosing: a small deserted car park leading to an area of woodland invisible from the road. It was dark and already approaching freezing, though with enough light from a milky moon for Jenny to make out two silhouettes in the front seat of Alison's car. For a brief while they seemed to dip their heads in prayer. Jenny thought she saw Pironi's lips moving, his shoulders swaying gently to and fro as he sought God's guidance. Alison placed a comforting hand on his shoulder.

They spoke for nearly twenty minutes. While she waited, Jenny tried several times without success to reach McAvoy. His phone was switched off. She dared to imagine that he might have picked up a lead, that he was out brokering deals and twisting arms, teasing out evidence that he would deliver with an arrogant flourish, sending Martha Denton and Alun Rhys into furious spasms.

She turned at the sound of a car door closing. Pironi hurried the few steps to his vehicle and pulled away swiftly. Alison waited until his tail lights had faded into the night before crossing the ten yards of muddy ground and climbing into Jenny's passenger seat. She was silent for a moment as she composed herself, hands resting on her lap.

She brought the smell of her car with her and a trace of Pironi. Jenny felt like a trespasser on their intimacy.

'He didn't want to give a sworn statement,' Alison said quietly. 'Once you do that you're as good as on oath, and you swear to tell the *whole* truth.'

'He won't do that?'

'He's trying to be true to his principles, Mrs Cooper.'

'What did he think he was going to do in court?'

'He got the impression he wasn't likely to be required.'

'Who told him that?'

'He didn't say exactly . . . Look, he really isn't to blame for any of this. He's being put in an impossible situation. Surely you can see that? It's only the fact he's got such a conscience that brought him out here.'

'Better a late convert than not at all, I suppose.'

'It's not like that. You know it's not.'

Jenny removed the acerbic edge from her voice. 'What did he say?'

'This is all completely off the record, it has to be . . .'

Jenny fought the urge to be facetious. It struck her that Pironi's religious conscience was rather more elastic than his church, let alone his personal saviour, might have liked.

'Fine. Just tell me.'

'He didn't soft-pedal the missing persons inquiry. He did try to find them, but MI5 were pretty certain from the outset that they'd left the country.'

'Was Donovan's sighting genuine?'

'He didn't mention him.'

Jenny drew her own silent conclusion. 'What else?'

Alison sighed. 'He had two officers in a car opposite the halaqah. They definitely didn't see a black Toyota; they wouldn't have been able to see as far as Mrs Murray's house anyway – the road curves round. He sent an officer down to the bus depot, who found the man who would have been driving the bus – he couldn't remember the two boys getting on that night. He did remember them from other nights, though.'

'Did he make a statement?'

'Yes . . . But it went higher up the chain of command. He doesn't know what happened to it.'

'Did any other statements go missing?'

'No. But apparently it was a bit chaotic for a while. MI5 already seemed pretty sure the boys had left the country. They didn't seem too bothered about Dani James's sighting of the man coming out of the halls. Could have been anyone, they said.'

'What did Pironi think?'

'He felt he was being kept in the dark. MI5 asked him to pass anything he had on, but they didn't return the favour, of course. He felt bad for the families mostly, especially Mrs Jamal.'

'Glad to hear it. Any theories about what happened to her?'

'He's being kept well away. Anti-terrorist branch from Scotland Yard have taken it over.'

'I can't say it's getting any clearer. What did he have to say about McAvoy?'

Alison glanced down at her hands. 'He didn't really want to talk about him.'

'You didn't discuss the charges against him?'

'I did try,' Alison said, with a trace of self-pity. 'I don't doubt he acted in good faith. He's not like that.'

'Meaning what – the witness who came forward had been set up? He doesn't believe it's a coincidence it happened when it did, just as McAvoy was starting to dig?'

'I don't know, Mrs Cooper. I honestly don't.'

'I do,' Jenny said.

'There are all sorts of possibilities,' Alison protested. 'Have you ever thought that Mrs Jamal might have informed on her son? Think about it – she tips off the police that she's worried he's involved with extremists and the next thing she knows he's vanished.'

'And eight years later she sprinkles herself with radioactive dust and jumps out of the window?'

'No. Nazim's associates came for her and made it look like suicide.'

'Is that what Pironi believes?'

'It's as good a theory as any.'

They fell into moody silence, Alison nursing her hurt at Pironi's fallibility and Jenny brooding and wishing she had a ready target at which to hurl her anger. It was cheap after-shave she could smell on Alison. Pironi had been sweating it out of his pores as he shot his meagre bolt.

'I should be going,' Alison said.

'Hold on,' Jenny said. 'What was the story with McAvoy this afternoon?'

'He was behaving strangely, apparently. Dave said he started talking to himself, like a drunk, except he didn't smell of alcohol for once. I don't think he would have made much of a witness.'

'What was he saying?'

Alison shook her head. 'Dave tried to talk to him but he couldn't get any sense. He kept muttering something about the devil and an American.'

# TWENTY-FIVE

JENNY WAITED UNTIL ALISON HAD driven out of the car park, then took the jelly beans from her handbag and swallowed a prophylactic dose three hours before they were due to knock her out for the night.

What had happened to McAvoy? He couldn't be going mad. He was stronger than that. He'd made a career out of his resilience to the insanity of others, weaving in and out of the minds of criminals and policemen, playing off their delusions. He couldn't have let her down, not now. His strange behaviour had been a feint, a tactic to unnerve the opposition.

He had mentioned an American. Was it the caller who'd threatened to put him in a casket? Did McAvoy know more about this man than he'd let on? He'd held back on other things, Sarah Levin in particular, and now Jenny thought about it, Levin had an American connection of her own – Professor Brightman had mentioned that she'd been a Stevenson scholar at Harvard. That much could be dismissed as a minor coincidence, but when her relationship with Anna Rose was factored in, it became a solid connection.

There were uncanny similarities between the two young women: like Sarah Levin before her, Anna Rose had had an Asian boyfriend, she too was very beautiful. But there were also significant differences. From what Jenny had learned of her, Anna Rose was a markedly different personality from her mentor. She was feisty and intelligent, but naive and unformed, still in search of herself. Her adoptive parents had been surprised at her gaining a place on the graduate scheme at Maybury, as if they had never conceived of her as a professional woman, as if there had to be a catch. Jenny pictured the Crosbys' faces when she'd first seen them in the morgue: their aura of dread tempered with resignation. Alive or dead, Anna Rose had already seemed lost to them.

And then it came to her. A single face among the many who had been to view the Jane Doe that day. The man was tall, lean, in his fifties, with a tanned, weathered face. She'd noticed his accent: transatlantic. He said he was a businessman whose missing stepdaughter had been travelling in Europe, last seen in Bristol. He'd not flinched as he'd stepped up to the open drawer and looked down on the dead face. She had been intrigued. A mischievous voice in her own head had said, 'He's used to death.'

Jenny flicked on the overhead light and reached for her phone and the tatty address book, spilling frayed pages, in which she had written the Crosbys' home number. She dialled it; there was no reply. She flicked forwards, dropping valuable fragments of paper into the footwell, and found Mike Stevens's number squeezed into a corner of a cardboard divider. After several rings an answer machine activated. She started to leave a message.

'Hello. Mrs Cooper?' his voice cut in abruptly. He sounded agitated.

'Yes. Don't worry, it's not bad news.'

'Right—'

'I was just calling to ask you something. It may sound irrelevant and it most probably is, but do you know if Anna Rose had anything to do with an American, an older man, in his fifties?'

He fell silent.

'Mr Stevens?'

'Do you know who this man is?'

'No . . . do you?'

She heard him breathing, fast and shallow.

'Where are you calling from?'

Mike Stevens lived in a former labourer's cottage at the end of a low, stone-built terrace on the outskirts of Stroud, a gentrified south Gloucestershire market town of the sort with health-food and bespoke kitchen stores. He answered the door on the security chain, getting a clear look at Jenny's face before he would let her in. Immediately she'd crossed the threshold he double-locked it behind them.

'Are you all right?' Jenny said.

He gave a non-committal shrug and motioned her inside.

The front door opened straight onto a snug sitting room furnished with an elderly suite and tasteless patterned carpet.

'I rent the place,' he said by way of apology.

He was wearing the suit trousers and shirt he would have worn to work. Although the house was cold, beads of sweat glinted on his forehead. Jenny kept her coat on and took a seat on the sofa.

Mike sat in a hard-backed chair opposite her, his face tense and drawn. 'What can I do for you?' he said.

Jenny said, 'When you came to the mortuary ten days ago with the Crosbys, there was a man, tall, suit and tie. He was American—'

Mike closed his eyes briefly, then blinked. 'Jesus . . .' It came out in a whisper.

'What?'

He looked at her with wide, frightened eyes.

'What is it, Mike?' Jenny said insistently. 'It's important. It could be connected with an inquest I'm conducting.'

'What inquest? Who died?'

'Two Asian boys disappeared. It was eight years ago. They were both first-year students at Bristol. One of them was studying physics.'

She waited while he sat looking straight through her for a moment, processing this information. Eventually he said, 'Someone came here last night . . . I've spent all day trying to work out where I'd seen him before.'

'The American?'

He nodded and held his head in his hands, fighting off tears.

'What is it, Mike?'

'I woke up in the night . . . I was *woken* . . . with a knee in my chest and a gun at my head.'

It was Jenny's turn to fall silent.

'This man . . . he had an American accent. He said, "Tell me where the fuck she is or you end up in a casket." I said I didn't know . . . He punched me hard, here.' He tugged open his shirt and revealed a violent black bruise that spread across the entire upper portion of his ribs. 'I couldn't breathe. I thought he was going to kill me.'

Jenny thanked God for her pills. A fierce heat broke out across her chest and neck, but she could still think and reason.

'What did he do then?'

'You don't want to know.'

'Tell me. Please.'

He looked away and focused on a spot on the ceiling, gathering strength. 'He held my nose . . . and he urinated in my mouth, until I choked.' His eyes were suddenly shot through with red veins. 'Then he left.'

'Did he say anything more?'

Mike shook his head.

'Have you told anyone?'

'I was going to call the police tonight but I didn't want to use the phone . . . I was trying to figure it out . . . Who the hell is he?'

'I don't know. Let's talk about Anna Rose for a minute. Do you have any idea where she is?'

'No.'

'How was she behaving before she went?'

'She seemed fine, just her usual self . . . a little quiet, maybe.'

'Since when?'

'About a month ago, I suppose.'

'What about this Asian guy her parents saw her with last autumn? Salim someone.'

'He was just a college friend. A post-grad of some sort.'

'You know him?'

'I've asked around.'

'Spoken to him?'

'Left a few messages on his mobile.'

'Do you know where he lives?'

'I tried calling the university. They won't give out personal information.'

'I'll talk to them.' Jenny made a note to call. 'You know I spoke to you before about whether she could have got hold of radioactive material.'

'Yes. What was that about?'

'Long story, but traces of caesium 137 turned up in an apartment in Bristol.' She gave a brief account of Mrs Jamal's struggle to achieve an inquest, and her sudden and violent death. 'It looks like the caesium could have been brought in on someone who was contaminated.'

'Anna Rose spent her entire time in an office. She wouldn't have clearance to go anywhere near anything hazardous.'

'Are you sure?'

'Completely. It's out of the question.'

'You sound angry. Why does that question make you angry?'

'I don't know . . .'

'Yes you do.'

He looked down at the ugly patterned carpet. 'It's not possible, there's so much security . . . But she was so . . .' He trailed off, unwilling to complete the thought.

'So what?'

'So . . . *innocent*, I suppose. And every man in the place fancied her. You couldn't not.'

'Are you saying she played up to it?'

'Occasionally.'

Jenny's mind raced ahead, putting together what he couldn't bring himself to say. 'You're frightened she could have been talked into something, used by someone?'

He shrugged. 'Of course, I've thought about it – I haven't thought about much else.'

'Any theories?'

'I've been hoping she'd call. She said she loved me, I believed her.'

'Do you think she's alive?'

It took him a moment. He said, 'She's been picking up messages, or at least her phone has . . . I'd have told the police only I wanted to speak to her first.'

'Do her parents know?'

A pause. He shook his head.

'Can I have the number?' She rummaged in her bag for her address book. 'Who else has got it?'

'I don't know. It's a phone I gave her on my contract – so we could keep in touch.'

She handed him the pen and watched him print the numbers in an even, meticulous hand. He was dependable, not bad-looking but no prize. She pictured his family as teachers or civil servants, people who lived within tightly drawn, reassuring boundaries. She could understand why Anna Rose might have been attracted to him – he was safe – but the young woman he'd described wouldn't stay for long and he knew it. He'd ridden his luck, even splashed out on an extra phone, but this was the moment at which he was finally being forced to let the fantasy go. Wherever she was, Anna Rose wasn't coming back to him.

Jenny glanced over at a framed photograph hanging on the wall above the television: Mike in lab coat posing with a glass trophy, *Graduate Trainee of the Year 2004*, written at the bottom in gold type. She noticed a now familiar object clipped to his breast pocket.

Jenny said, 'You wouldn't happen to have a dosimeter in the house?'

He looked up abruptly. She saw the alarm in his eyes and knew that she had assumed correctly: he hadn't been to work today. The fustiness in the room was the smell of prolonged confinement.

'You noticed it before you left this morning?' she said. 'He was contaminated . . . and you couldn't go to work because it would have been detected on you. There are radiation monitors everywhere, right?'

He nodded dumbly.

'How bad is it?' Jenny said, feeling a return of the panic she'd experienced in court earlier that day.

'Two hundred milliSieverts . . . it was in his urine.'

Jenny said, 'Should we be here?'

Mike said, 'Downstairs is safe enough. I wouldn't go upstairs . . . I don't know what to do.'

'You've no idea what connection this man might have with Anna Rose?' she said.

'No.'

'You'll have to call the police.'

'I should have done it this morning.'

'You've done nothing wrong. You'll be fine.' She attempted a smile. 'Just do one thing for me – leave it an hour before you make the call. I need to go somewhere and I don't want to be snagged up with the police all night.'

His eyes darted to the telephone sitting on the sideboard. 'An hour?'

Jenny said, 'Please, Mike. I'm going to try to find Anna Rose, OK? I'd like to talk to her before they do.'

'How? Where are you going to go?'

'Do you want to come with me?'

He thought about it for a moment, then shook his head.

'If I get anywhere I'll call you.'

He nodded, seeming a little more confident now he'd settled on a course of action. Jenny knew she had half an hour at the most. He'd last ten minutes before picking up the phone and telling the police everything.

Jenny drove in the direction of the Severn Bridge along minor roads, checking her mirror for phantom pursuers. Heavy rain flecked with sleet pounded the windscreen. She dialled McAvoy's number repeatedly without success. He was switched off. Beyond her reach. She toyed with contacting Alison and asking her to take another statement from Sarah Levin, but an instinct told her it would be futile, that whatever story Sarah had yet to tell would remain locked down until something far bigger gave way.

She waited fifteen minutes in the empty reception area of Chepstow police station for Detective Sergeant Owen Williams to make his way from the pub, from where she had dislodged him with her enigmatic call. He greeted her with a fond, resigned smile as he peeled off his wet coat.

'Mrs Cooper. Never a dull moment with you, is there?'

'I'm sorry. It's just one of those I can't trust with the boys across the water.'

'I can only help if it's on my patch.'

'Elements are.'

'Just so long as I can tick the box.' He checked the time. 'Not going to take long, is it? I haven't stood my round yet.'

'I'll talk quickly.'

She followed him through the security door to his office, a ten-by-ten cubicle lined with steel shelves laden with dusty box files. His computer sat on a separate desk protected by a plastic cover. The machine had the feel of an object which was unveiled on special occasions only. While Williams spread his coat carefully along the radiator, Jenny gave him a potted history of recent developments in her investigation. He hadn't heard about Mrs Jamal's death and was shocked, but not surprised, that he hadn't been informed of the presence of a radioactive substance at the scene: his office was only a dozen miles from the centre of Bristol, but as far as the English police were concerned it might as well have been on the far side of the world. They treated their Welsh colleagues with indifference bordering on contempt, and the feeling was mutual.

He listened quietly, stroking his thick, greying moustache as she summarized the evidence which had led to her search for Anna Rose. He was barely aware of her disappearance, let alone her connection with a nuclear-power plant that stood directly across the estuary from his station.

'Two miles from here that bloody place is,' Williams said. 'And you know where the tide brings the crap that comes out of it – right up the mouth of the Wye on the Welsh side, here. They deny it, of course. Lying bastards.'

'Her boyfriend gave me a mobile number she's been using. He thinks she may have been picking up messages.'

'Where from? There's nothing I can do if she's in England.'

'Think of it this way: the last time Nazim and Rafi were seen they were heading over the bridge into Wales. There's already evidence that would justify a criminal investigation into kidnap, and Anna Rose is a potential witness.'

'I see . . .' He was warming to the idea.

'All I need is for you to get onto the phone company and find out the last known location of that number.'

'How soon do you want it?'

'Now?'

'You're joking? You can't just magic this stuff up, Mrs Cooper. You have to pay. These companies make you sell the farm for an expedited search – it'd be five grand if it's a penny. I can't authorize that sort of money.'

'Well, who can?'

'I could try the Super, but I wouldn't hold your breath.'

'Then we'll put it through my office.'

'Can I have that in writing?'

'You can have it in blood, if you like.'

Williams looked at her with avuncular concern. 'Mrs Cooper, you know I don't mind sticking my neck out for you from time to time, but only as long as we're on the right side of the line. This girl's phone number and her whereabouts could be classed as information connected with an act of terrorism, in which case it's a serious offence not to disclose it to the appropriate authorities.'

'You are the appropriate authority.'

'And I have to obey the protocols – refer it up the chain of command. What I'm saying – can I call you Jenny? – is that, no matter how much I'd love to steal a march on those English crooks, this one can't be a secret.'

'Fine. Just give me a few minutes' head start.'

Tracing the last known position of a mobile phone was a new procedure to Williams. He called several colleagues, conversing exclusively in Welsh, and learned that the phone operators only dealt with such requests when they were made by certain designated senior officers. Yet another phone call yielded the name of a friendly detective inspector in Cardiff whom Williams persuaded, by telling more half-truths than he was comfortable with, to broker the request. Then came fifteen minutes of haggling with a surly official at the mobile network who opened with a demand for £10,000. Williams beat him down to £6,000 at which point the official dug in his heels.

What the hell, Jenny said. There was no way her minuscule budget could cover it, whatever he wanted. She produced her office credit card and prayed the payment would clear. It didn't. Only after another fractious call to Visa and with promises of a personal guarantee was the transaction approved.

After more than an hour of cajoling and persuading, Jenny had the information she wanted. Anna Rose's phone had last been connected to the network forty-eight hours before. It had been located in an area – accurate to within one hundred yards – centring on a section of Hanley Road, at the north end of central Bristol. On that occasion it had been on for less than two minutes. It had also been activated for a similar brief period, at the same location, three days before that.

'I hope it's bloody worth it,' Williams said, as he set down the phone.

'I'll send the bill to Bristol CID,' Jenny said. 'They'll sure as hell want the arrest.'

'Well, give them my love, won't you, Jenny? And, while you're at it, a good hard kick in the nuts.'

It was after ten p.m. by the time Jenny crossed the Severn Bridge, heading for Bristol on the motorway. She fought and failed to suppress the temptation to switch on her own phone to try McAvoy's number one last time. No joy. She was groping for the off switch when it rang. Her heart jumped as she glanced at screen: UNKNOWN CALLER.

'Hello?' The line was faint. She waited on tenterhooks for McAvoy's reply.

'Mrs Cooper? DI Pironi. I've just been talking to Mike Stevens.'

*Shit.*

'About time,' Jenny said.

'Who the hell is this American?'

'You tell me.'

'You've been speaking to McAvoy. He knows.'

'Well, ask him.'

'Where is he?'

'Pass.'

Pironi lost patience. 'You know the penalty for withholding this kind of information.'

'I've withheld nothing. I've already told the police everything I know.'

'Which police?'

'Chepstow.'

'Dear God. What the hell are you playing at, Cooper? I've got the anti-terrorist branch, MI5 and uniform all out looking for Anna Rose Crosby. We could have a dirty bomb maker out there.'

'I'd just about worked that out.'

'If you're holding anything back from me—'

'I'll make you a deal. Whoever finds Anna Rose first, we both get to talk to her.'

'You think either of us is going to be allowed anywhere near her? You're more deluded than I thought.'

Jenny said, 'I sense you're a man with a troubled conscience, Mr Pironi. If you hadn't sat on your hands for eight years, Mrs Jamal might still be with us, Anna Rose Crosby might still be going out to parties. Why don't you do the decent thing and see if we can't both get what we want?'

There was a brief pause, then Pironi said, 'I've reasonable

suspicion that you have withheld information concerning terrorist activity. I advise you to go to the nearest police station and surrender yourself for arrest.'

Jenny said, 'Have they told you to do this – the same high-ups that had you frame McAvoy?'

'You heard what I said.'

'You should think hard about who you're working for. I'm not sure going to church is doing the trick.'

Jenny drove into the zone from which Anna Rose had picked up her messages. Cloaked in sleet, the Victorian buildings that lined Harlowe Road were grimy and soot-stained in the dingy orange street light. She crawled past a parade of shuttered-up low-rent shops, several down-at-heel pubs and a shabby late-night convenience store. She pulled into a side street and hurried back to it, her coat pulled up over her hair.

An elderly Asian man, wearing one cardigan on top of another and fingerless gloves, was watching a Bollywood movie on a tiny TV perched precariously on the tobacco shelf. Fishing in her handbag and producing a dog-eared card, Jenny introduced herself and said she was looking for an attractive young woman he might have seen in the shop recently.

The old man squinted at the rain-smeared print. She gave him a charming smile, aware that many among the Asian community regarded coroners with deep suspicion. Traditional Hindus were opposed to autopsy, as were many Muslims.

'She's a potential witness,' Jenny said. 'A young woman in her early twenties, short blonde hair, intelligent, very pretty – you'd have noticed her.'

The man drew down the corners of his mouth and shook his head.

Jenny said, 'I know for a fact she was in this street two days ago. She might have looked anxious, wary of people.'

It seemed to stir his memory. 'English girl?'

'Yes. Have you seen her?'

'I'm not sure. Maybe. There's bed-and-breakfast places along there.' He gestured eastwards with his thumb. 'A lot of young people use them, mostly foreigners.'

He handed back her card.

'Thanks. I appreciate it.'

He frowned, gave a rattly cough and turned back to the TV.

The first one she arrived at, the Metropole, was a converted Victorian villa with flaking paint and a single bare bulb hanging in the porch. She approached the tatty reception desk, behind which sat a slender woman with premature crow's feet at the side of her eyes, and launched into a description of Anna Rose. The receptionist responded with a blank look, then explained in a heavy East European accent that the hotel's occupants were mostly foreign workers. Jenny noticed that the laminated signs taped to the wall behind the desk were written in Polish. The Metropole was a labourers' flop house. Anna Rose was not their kind of guest.

Freezing water seeped though the soles of her shoes as she dodged the angry traffic and ran up the steps of the Hotel Windsor, which stood opposite. It considered itself upmarket from its neighbours, but its feeble attempts at grandeur made it tackier. The chintz sofas in the lobby were stained and sagging; the fraying carpet was patched with duct tape. Jenny pressed a buzzer on the unmanned counter. A short, fat man with a stained navy waistcoat and matching tie emerged bleary-eyed from a back office. He wore a plastic badge that said, 'Gary, Assistant Manager'. His annoyance at being disturbed faded on seeing a passably attractive woman. He gave her a greasy smile.

'Good evening, madam. What can I do for you?'

Jenny presented the card she'd shown the store keeper and ran through her story. Shifting effortlessly from solicitous to unctuous, Gary said he didn't think any of his guests matched the description.

Jenny detected a note of uncertainty. 'You're sure about that? What about the daytime staff – is there anyone I can call?'

He scratched his head and thought again. 'There has been a girl staying here for a few days, but she had black hair, short, like a crew cut . . .'

'What was her name?'

'Sam, Sarah . . . something like that . . .' He tapped on his computer. 'That's her – Samantha Stevens.'

'Is she still here?'

'She checked out earlier this evening – about an hour ago.'

It figured. If she'd collected her messages tonight, there were bound to have been several from Mike. She would know about the American and that he was coming for her.

'Any idea where she went?'

'I know she caught a cab. I heard her call for it.' He nodded to a payphone screwed to the wall beside the counter.

'Did she have much luggage?'

'Just a rucksack, I think . . . she seemed in a hurry. Is she in some kind of trouble?'

Pretending not to have heard the question, Jenny grabbed the receiver and pressed redial. The call was answered by a controller at PDQ Cabs. Short on patience, Jenny demanded to know where the last fare from the Hotel Windsor had been dropped off. The controller, a hostile woman with a smoker's rasp, claimed the rules forbade her from releasing confidential 'passenger information'.

Jenny said, 'Let me spell it out for you – you don't have a

choice. I've no doubt your office is pretty shitty, but I'm sure it beats a police cell.'

Gary stepped out from behind the counter and gestured for her to give him the receiver. 'Let me —'

Jenny reluctantly gave it up.

'Hey, Julie, my love,' he purred, 'it's Gary. Look, sweetie, I'm with the lady now, trying my best to help. So why don't you tell her what she wants or maybe we'll be recommending a different cab company in future . . .'

Jenny heard the controller give a bad-tempered grunt and tell Gary the fare had been to Marlborough Street bus station in the middle of town.

He came off the phone all smiles and asked if there was anything else he could do to assist, his eyes dipping downwards towards Jenny's breasts.

'No thanks. You've been more than helpful.' She drew her coat across her chest. 'See you around, Gary.'

As she pushed out through the doors she caught his reflection in the glass: he was flicking his tongue at her like a hungry lizard.

# TWENTY-SIX

JENNY DIDN'T NOTICE THE MIDNIGHT blue Lexus sedan tucked in two cars behind her as she gunned towards the city centre. The sleet had given way to big flakes of wet snow that were starting to lie. She was out of screen-washer and the street lights kaleidoscoped through the dirty windscreen. She jostled though the heavy traffic on the Haymarket, narrowly missed a jay-walking drunk, shot the lights and slewed into Marlborough Street.

She pulled up on a double yellow and ran into the bus station. Save for a handful of weary-looking stragglers waiting at a cab rank, the concourse was deserted. The only buses in evidence were parked up for the night. A metal grille was drawn down over the ticket-office window. Jenny hurried between the rows of silent vehicles: there was no sign of a young woman lugging a rucksack.

Fighting off a rising fear that Anna Rose had slipped through her fingers, Jenny headed back towards the timetables. She spotted a man in liveried overalls climbing down from an empty coach with a vacuum cleaner. She hurried towards him, fishing her damp and crumpled card from her coat pocket.

'Excuse me—' Breathless, she handed it to him. 'I'm a coroner. I'm looking for a young woman who would have come through here about half an hour ago. Short black hair. Rucksack.'

The cleaner, a mild West Indian with heavy-lidded eyes and the weary expression of a man resigned to a lifetime of joyless, badly paid work, peered suspiciously at the card.

'Have you seen her?'

Cagy, the cleaner said, 'Don't think so.'

'Have any buses gone out in the last half hour?'

'The London bus would have left at a quarter to.'

Jenny glanced at her watch: nine minutes to eleven.

'Was that the only one?'

'Far as I know.'

'Does it go straight through?'

The cleaner shrugged. 'I never been on it.'

Jenny ran back to her car, her dainty work shoes slipping on the light covering of snow. The feet of her tights were wet, her toes aching with cold. Sliding into the driver's seat she turned the heater on full blast and took off, the back end of the car fish-tailing as she swung away from the kerb. Fifty yards behind her, the stationary Lexus flicked on its headlights and followed.

The main road out of town widened swiftly into the M32 motorway. Jenny pushed up the empty outside lane at eighty miles an hour, cutting virgin tracks through the slush. What would she do even if she did catch the bus? she asked herself. She could follow it all one hundred and twenty miles to London, but what then? Even if Anna Rose was on it, there was no reason why she'd cooperate, and God knows what she was carrying in her backpack. The rational thing would have been to call the police and assert her right to take a statement once Anna Rose was safely in custody. If they were obstructive she could come armed with a High Court order and insist. Cold, wet and painfully tired, it was an attractive proposition. Her phone was right there in her handbag. She could be speaking to Pironi in seconds.

Another more persuasive voice told her not to be seduced,

that she'd never get to speak to Anna Rose if the police got to her first. She'd be pushed out, gagged, and issued with threats of dismissal if she threatened to make trouble. The full might of the terrorist-fighting state would be wheeled out against her.

She thrust her foot down harder. The needle climbed towards ninety.

On the margins of the city she took the east-bound lane and swept in a semi-circle to join the M4. The motorway descended into unlit darkness. Her eyes smarted with the strain of squinting through the smeared arcs of dirt on the windscreen: every oncoming set of lights blinded her to the road in front.

Rigid with tension, she had covered more than fifteen miles when the double-stacked tail lights of an express coach appeared out of the gloom. It was cruising at a steady seventy in the inside lane, filthy fountains spewing from its massive tyres. Keeping the middle lane between them, Jenny drew alongside, trying to distinguish the passengers' faces, but all she could make out through the bus's steamy windows was the flickering of seat-back screens.

The car lit up with strobing light. Startled, Jenny glanced in the mirror. A large, aggressive vehicle inches away from her rear bumper flashed its headlights a second time. Dazzled, she swerved left into the centre lane and caught the full spray from the bus as a Range Rover powered past. Instinctively, she touched the brakes and swung back away from the bus. A horn sounded behind her; another set of lights flashed, forcing her to jerk sharply to the left. She barely saw the Lexus accelerate away as the back end of the Golf flicked out to the right. For a brief moment she was sliding sideways along the carriageway. She wrenched at the wheel, clipped the rear corner of the bus, travelled through a long, slow, graceful one-hundred-and-eighty degrees and came to rest on the hard shoulder, pointing into the traffic. A huge lorry thundered past honking long and loud as it swerved to avoid her front end.

Exhilarated at simply being alive, she snatched at the ignition, brought the engine to life and slammed the stick into first. The front wheels spun in two inches of snow, then caught and lurched erratically forwards. Several tightly bunched cars sped past on the inside lane sounding their horns. Aiming for the gap before the next wall of approaching headlights, Jenny stamped on the accelerator, threw the car sharply left and crunched through the gears past sixty, to seventy to eighty . . .

She sped precariously over the skin of snow for over a mile and caught up with the lorry that had nearly struck her. She edged past and emerged ahead of it to see the distinctive tail lights of the bus up ahead. It was indicating left and exiting onto the slip road of a service station. Jenny swerved across two lanes and made the exit with only feet to spare.

At the crest of a slope she followed signs to the bus and lorry park. The coach had come to a halt in the far right-hand corner of the football-pitch-sized lot. She nursed the Golf across the lying snow, passing rows of trucks parked up for the night, and contemplated the prospect of coming face to face with Anna Rose. What if she refused to talk? Or ran off into the night? Hot needles spread outwards from her chest and down her arms.

She made for the coach's left-hand side. She was no more than thirty yards away when the front passenger door swung back. At the same moment, two figures ran swiftly out of the shadows: wiry, athletic men in black paramilitary overalls and caps. They reached into their jackets as they gained the bus door and burst inside. She stamped on the brakes and slid to a halt, watching the blurred, frenetic movement of bodies behind the misted-up windows. She heard muffled snatches of shrieks and raised voices. A slight, indistinct figure was bundled along the aisle.

It was a glint of reflected light on metal which caught her eye. She looked sharply left and saw his tall, slender silhouette appear from between two goods trailers. He was dressed in jeans and a puffy anorak, a baseball cap pulled down over his forehead, obscuring his face. He stopped at the corner and glanced briefly towards her.

It was him. The American. The man who'd come to the mortuary claiming to be looking for his lost stepdaughter. His attention snapped back to the bus. He raised both hands and took aim as the two men manhandled their prisoner down the steps.

Some reflex made Jenny stamp on the throttle and accelerate towards him. A burst of orange light issued from the barrel of his gun, then another; several more flashes issued from the direction of the bus. The American staggered and reached out a hand to the side of the trailer. Jenny spun past him and slewed to a stop.

Ten yards to her left the two men threw a small, dark-haired female into the back seat of a Range Rover, leaped inside and took off over the kerb, crashing through the thin hedge separating the bus park from the exit road beyond.

The fleet of police cars and unmarked vehicles arrived less than two minutes later. A helicopter followed soon after, illuminating the scene from above with an array of search-lights. The bus park was sealed off. Jenny was rounded up together with the hysterical passengers from the bus and a handful of bewildered truckers. All were frisked and relieved of their mobile phones, cameras and other electrical equipment, before being herded towards the service-station building. Jenny refused to move and was protesting to a uniformed officer that she was one of Her Majesty's coroners on official duty when she saw DI Pironi, with Alison in tow, striding angrily towards her.

'I'll deal with that woman, Officer,' he shouted at the constable, waving his warrant card.

The constable took a reluctant step back.

Pironi erupted. 'Do you think you're bigger than all this? Someone's running around with a dirty bomb and you're playing beat the detectives.'

'I've a legal right to speak to Anna Rose.'

'You have a right to remain silent, Mrs Cooper. Withholding information—'

Jenny shouted over him. 'I saw the American. He was right there.' She pointed to the corner of the trailer. 'He took a shot at those men snatching Anna Rose.'

Pironi fell silent for a moment. 'Where'd he go?'

'He took off just after they did. I think he might have been hit.'

'Stay here.'

Pironi strode over to the corner of the trailer.

'What's his problem?' Jenny said to Alison.

'He's been told to nick you.'

'Who by?'

'There's a question.'

'What's that meant to mean?'

'He doesn't know. It just gets passed down the line.'

'And what are you here for, moral support?'

'I think he needed to talk.'

Pironi marched back towards them. He looked at Alison, then at Jenny, fear and indecision in his eyes. 'Did you get a look at his face?'

'I saw him at the mortuary ten days ago. He claimed to be looking for his missing stepdaughter.'

Pironi looked down at the dirty snow. 'You weren't here. Get lost.'

Jenny said, 'What about my car?'

'Give me the keys. Wait over there.'

She handed them over. 'Are you going to tell me who this man is?'

'We haven't got a fucking clue.'

The events at the service station played repeatedly behind her eyes like a disturbing fragment of rolling news. After all her efforts, they had got to Anna Rose first. And as surely as they had put her beyond reach, they would by now have silenced Sarah Levin. Jenny felt nothing except an absence of sensation. Like her own frustrated inner journey, her inquest had reached the foot of an unscalable cliff.

A thin crust of snow lay on the ground outside Melin Bach. The earlier storm had passed, leaving the air deathly still. The night was as silent as any she'd known. Even the restless timbers of the house had stopped their quiet groaning. There was only the sound of her breath and her footsteps on the flagstones. Huddled in a nightgown and cardigan, she paced restlessly to and fro from the living room to the study groping for any argument or authority that might keep her inquest alive. She was beyond the territory covered by the textbooks. They spoke grandly of a coroner's powers to apply to superior courts for orders for production of witnesses and documents, but they presumed a due process, a system of law that didn't bend to political pressure, impartial judges who looked on all agencies of the state as equal. They didn't provide for tricks, fixes, official denials and deliberate misunderstandings.

It was four a.m. when her mind finally folded. She collapsed into a chair and tried to relax her still-agitated body. There's nothing more to be gained, she told herself. You tried, you did more than any other coroner ever would. Slowly her muscles began to unwind and grow heavy. *Some things are simply beyond your grasp; let yourself off the hook, Jenny.*

Her eyelids began to droop. She rocked forward, meaning to take herself to bed, but instead fell into a doze, then into a deep, defeated sleep.

It felt like only moments later when she was painfully jolted to consciousness by the phone. Disorientated, she reached for the receiver and murmured a croaky hello.

'Jenny? It's Alec.' McAvoy's voice was quiet and sober.

'My God.' Jenny blinked at her watch: it was nearly four-thirty. 'Where the hell did you go?'

'I didn't think you'd get to me today . . . I had things to do.'

Her thoughts came at her in a jumbled rush.

'I need you. You've got to give evidence tomorrow. I need you talk about the American – you know something, don't you?'

'I've plenty to tell you, Jenny. Plenty. I could fill a book with it.' He sounded tired.

'Alec . . . you are all right, aren't you? Pironi told Alison you didn't seem well.'

'Oh. Was this a physical or a spiritual diagnosis?'

'I'm bringing him to court to hear your evidence. There's a chance he could be persuaded to come round, at least as far as to say who made him halt his original investigation. He might even admit that he was ordered to put you away.'

'That'd be the day.'

'I think he's had an attack of conscience. Something happened this evening . . .' She checked herself. 'I'll tell you after you've testified. You will, won't you?'

McAvoy was silent.

'Alec, listen to me, listen. You have to come. I'd begun to think there was no hope, but there is still some, isn't there? . . . Alec?'

'There's always hope.'

'And when this is over, we'll talk?'

'We will. Goodnight, Jenny.'

'Goodnight . . . Alec—' *You didn't tell me why you called* was what she wanted to say, but the line had already gone dead. She could have rung him back, but it would have spoiled the moment. Besides, she knew what he wanted to say, she could feel it: that she wasn't alone. He was with her.

# TWENTY-SEVEN

FROM HER OFFICE ON THE first floor Jenny could hear the protesters chanting outside the hall. The crowd of angry young Asian men had swelled to more than thirty, but they remained outnumbered by the police. Still not a word about the inquest had been published in the papers or broadcast on radio or television. Nor had the snatching of Anna Rose and the exchange of gunfire in a motorway service station made it to the news. As far as the outside world was concerned, none of it had ever happened.

Alison knocked on the door and entered wearing an apologetic expression.

'There's no sign of Mr McAvoy yet, nor Dave Pironi. I've left another message for Dr Levin. She knows she's meant to be here.'

'What about Salim Hussain – did you manage to trace him?'

'I got an address and phone number from the university office. He's not answering. I spoke to his tutor, who says he's missed his last two supervisions.'

'When was the last time he saw him?'

'Nearly three weeks ago.'

Jenny fought back the suspicion that her witnesses were being deliberately withheld from her.

'What do you want to do?' Alison said. 'We should have sat fifteen minutes ago. Miss Denton's getting impatient.'

Jenny drew on her dwindling reserves of strength. Deep tiredness combined with the overwhelming anxiety about everything slipping through her fingers was threatening to overwhelm her medication. Her heart was hammering against her lungs.

'I ought to tell the jury something,' she said, and got up from behind her desk. 'Keep trying McAvoy and Pironi. Who knows? Maybe they're on their way together.'

Alison raised her eyebrows. 'Stranger things have happened.'

Martha Denton rose impatiently as soon as Jenny had taken her seat at the head of the courtroom.

'May we have a word before the jury are brought in, ma'am?'

Jenny could think of no reason to refuse.

Denton produced a document. 'You won't be surprised to hear that the Secretary of State has issued a certificate of public interest immunity covering the intelligence relating to the whereabouts of Nazim Jamal or Rafi Hassan during the time immediately following their disappearance.'

Alison took a copy over to Jenny. She glanced over the impersonal text and noticed that Mr Jamal looked older today, resigned.

Jenny said, 'I suppose if I demand to see this intelligence I'll be refused.'

'If it's any help, ma'am, there is a High Court judge currently sitting in Bristol who can make himself available this afternoon.'

With his appeal-proof judgement already written, Jenny didn't doubt.

'I have several other witnesses to call, Miss Denton. I'll make my decision on this certificate when we've heard their evidence.'

With a look of surprise, Denton said, 'Surely, if you don't intend to challenge this certificate, the correct course would be to direct the jury to return an open verdict sooner rather than later. Mr Skene's statement does at least confirm that the intelligence places the missing men outside the country. It's not concrete evidence, but as far as I can see it is the best evidence that will ever be available.'

'Unless I can see it, it's no evidence at all, Miss Denton,' Jenny said, prompting an approving nod from Khan.

Denton shot straight back. 'Ma'am, although it's a highly unusual occurrence, a coroner's verdict can be overturned and a fresh inquest ordered when the verdict is clearly perverse. And although it may be frustrating, without hearing the content of this intelligence the jury can reach no credible verdict other than an open one.'

Calmly, Jenny said, 'Miss Denton, my jury will deliver a verdict of their choosing when, and only when they have heard all the available evidence. That may or may not include your so-called intelligence.'

Alison appeared at the committee-room door on the right-hand side of the hall and mouthed, 'Dr Levin's here.'

'Bring the jury in, please,' Jenny said. 'And then we'll have Dr Levin back.'

Martha Denton shot a look over her shoulder at Alun Rhys and thumped into her seat. Rhys fixed Jenny with a threatening glare, but there was nothing he could do except sit and watch. The jury filed back to their places and Sarah Levin made her way out from the committee room.

She glanced apprehensively between Jenny and the lawyers as she took her seat in the witness chair.

'You're still under oath,' Jenny said. 'I've asked you to come back to help us with a few background questions that may be of assistance. Has anyone from the police or Security

Services spoken to or made contact with you since you gave evidence yesterday?'

'No.'

'Has anyone told you what you may or may not say in evidence?'

She shook her head.

Jenny was unconvinced, but tried not to let it show. Havilland and Denton would leap at the merest suggestion of bias.

She struck a conciliatory tone. 'You were a Stevenson scholar, weren't you? After graduating, you secured a scholarship to study for your doctorate at Harvard university in the USA.'

'That's right.'

'You were one out of only a dozen or so that year.'

'Yes.'

'Did you have any American connections while you were an undergraduate at Bristol?'

'No,' Levin replied, with a trace of apprehension.

Jenny pressed on. 'A man in his forties was seen leaving Manor Hall at midnight on 28 June – the night Nazim and Rafi disappeared. He was described by Dani James as wearing a blue puffy anorak and a baseball cap. He was carrying a rucksack or holdall. Do you know who that man was?'

'I've no idea.'

'Did you know any American men at the time who met that description?'

'No . . .'

'You don't sound very sure.'

'No, I didn't.'

'Last week a man of a similar description, only several years older, was seen leaving the building where Nazim

Jamal's mother lived, only minutes after she had died. Have you met any fifty-year-old American men lately?'

Martha Denton slapped her hands on the desk in front of her as she sprang to her feet. 'Ma'am, what possible relevance could this have to the events of eight years ago?'

'Miss Denton, I'll remind you that I decide what's relevant, not you.'

'Ma'am, if I'm correctly informed, Mrs Jamal's death is currently the subject of a police investigation. It is only right that I remind you that any speculation in this court regarding it runs the risk of prejudicing the jury and invalidating their verdict.'

'Sit down, Miss Denton. And don't interrupt again.'

Jurors smiled. Martha Denton did as she was told with a venomous glare.

Jenny returned her attention to the witness. 'You haven't answered my question, Dr Levin.'

'I can answer it very well. I don't know a man meeting that description.'

'But you do know Anna Rose Crosby, don't you?'

Alun Rhys sat up sharply.

'Yes . . .' Sarah Levin said tentatively.

'Could you please tell the jury who she is?'

'She is . . . she was a student in my department. She graduated last summer.'

'And you helped get her a job last autumn as a trainee in the nuclear industry.'

'I was her tutor . . . I wrote the usual references.'

'And are you aware that she has been missing for the past fortnight?'

Sarah Levin glanced anxiously at the lawyer's bench. Alun Rhys had left his seat and was crossing the floor of the hall towards them.

'I did know that, yes.'

'Are you aware that last year she became involved with a young Asian man – a postgraduate student at the university – by the name of Salim Hussain?'

'No . . . I didn't know that.'

'And do you have any idea why the same American man might have been looking for her since she's been missing?'

Sarah Levin shook her head, her eyes on Rhys, Denton and Havilland. Their solicitors were hurriedly conferring.

'You've no idea at all, Dr Levin?'

'I told you, no.'

'Really? Would it help prompt your memory if I told you this man seems to have been contaminated with a radioactive substance that you'll doubtless be familiar with—'

Denton interjected. 'Ma'am, I am instructed that this line of questioning has to stop.'

'I've told you already, Miss Denton—'

Rhys leaned over the desk behind her, issued Denton with further orders and hurried from the hall.

Denton stalled, her expression of indignation replaced with one of bewilderment. 'Ma'am. I am instructed to inform you –' she spoke as if she could scarcely believe what she was about to say herself – 'that Dr Levin is a criminal suspect and will be placed under arrest immediately.'

'She's a witness in a lawful inquiry. Anyone who interferes with her giving evidence will be in contempt of court.'

Rhys crashed through the doors at the back of the room flanked by two uniformed police officers, a sergeant and a constable.

'Apologies, ma'am,' the sergeant stammered. 'I've been asked to arrest Dr Sarah Levin.'

'You can wait until she's given evidence or be committed for contempt,' Jenny snapped.

'Do it,' Rhys ordered.

The two police officers marched up to the witness box.

Jenny unleashed her fury at them: 'Don't you dare interfere with the proceedings of this court.'

Behind the emotionless masks of uniformed men obeying orders, the two policemen took hold of a terrified Sarah Levin and led her from the witness box. Rendered speechless with impotent rage, Jenny watched them take her from the hall. As they left, it was DI Pironi who held the door open for them.

'Mr Pironi,' Jenny said, in scarcely more than a whisper, 'are you going to tell me what's going on?'

From the crummy depths of her handbag she fished out the two Xanax tablets covered in fluff and grime which she'd kept – pretending to herself they weren't there – for dire emergencies. She swallowed them both and waited a clear two minutes for them to hit her system before summoning Pironi. Alison traipsed in behind him. Jenny was beyond objecting. No breach of protocol could make the situation any more absurd.

Jenny glared at him. 'Well?'

'I've no idea, Mrs Cooper,' he said, deadpan. 'What just happened in there was nothing to do with me. I think you can pin that one on MI5. And what I've got to tell you is nothing to do with them. Not yet.'

Jenny pressed her hands to her aching head. 'What are you talking about?'

'About an hour ago I had a call from Mr McAvoy . . . He claims to have found the remains of Nazim Jamal and Rafi Hassan. He's given a location in north Herefordshire.' Pironi swallowed. 'And to quote him, he said, "*That black-hearted bastard Tathum held onto it until his last God-forsaken breath.*" '

\*

Pironi called Jenny with the news about Tathum as she and Alison hiked up a steep muddy track. It was located over a mile from the nearest road through a plantation of dense, oppressive pines. His body had been found in an outbuilding at his farm with holes the size of pudding bowls in both his thighs where the shotgun blasts had ripped away the flesh. One side of his face was staved in and his right arm was broken in several places. The weapon was found outside in the yard. McAvoy was being hunted on suspicion of murder. Jenny could think of nothing to say and rang off with a muted, 'Thank you.'

They arrived at the tiny clearing which had been formed by several fallen trees. Jenny and Alison watched in silence as two scene of crime officers gently brushed away the earth to reveal the heel of a shoe, a white shin bone, shreds of semi-decomposed clothing, a wristwatch around a wrist bone. As more soil was removed, the pelvis of a second body gradually emerged, also laid face down. Vertebra by vertebra, the painstaking work uncovered the spine and finally the curve of the skull.

'Jesus Christ,' the sergeant said under his breath, 'look at this.' He pointed a gloved finger at the base of the skull, just above the junction with the spine.

Jenny stooped forward in the fading light to see a neat, round entry wound.

'At least it would have been quick,' Alison said without conviction.

The moment of dispatch might have been, but the preamble would have been protracted. It was a ninety-minute drive from Bristol and a long, lonely trek up the hill to the place of execution.

Something stirred in Jenny: a bitter sense of satisfaction that Tathum had suffered as much, if not more, than his victims. She was glad for what McAvoy had done. She pictured him standing outside the village hall on the very first day of her inquest, his hair tossed in the wind, the lines he had recited:

'Oh, I could kneel all night in prayer, To heal your many ills . . . My Dark Rosaleen.'

She would see him again. She had to.

# TWENTY-EIGHT

IT WAS FRIDAY MORNING. Gillian Golder and Simon Moreton sat alongside Alun Rhys at the reconvened secret inquest. They had come to ensure that the deal stuck. Only after lengthy and ill-tempered negotiations and having secured the personal approval of Mr Jamal and the Hassans, had Jenny grudgingly agreed to the terms: there would be no mention of Anna Rose Crosby or the ongoing investigation surrounding her; neither would there be any mention of Mrs Jamal or the continuing police inquiry into her suspected murder; and finally, as Dr Sarah Levin was in protective custody while she assisted the Security Services with their inquiries, her evidence was to be delivered by way of a statement to be read aloud to the jury. In return Golder had agreed that at the conclusion of the inquest Jenny would be fully briefed on why the secrecy measures had been necessary, and on what had become of Alec McAvoy.

Dr Andy Kerr produced detailed photographs of two complete skeletons, copies of which were shown to the horrified jury. He stated that DNA tests and dental records had confirmed that the remains were those of Nazim Jamal and Rafi Hassan. Both young men had met their deaths in a similar fashion: they had been shot through the base of the skull with a single nine-millimetre bullet. Each had an identical three-inch diameter exit wound on his forehead.

A ballistics expert, Dr Keith Dallas, confirmed that the same firearm had been used to kill both men. Two spent Corbon 115 gram DPX rounds had been recovered from the area near the bodies. These were hollow-tipped bullets designed to expand on impact: Nazim and Rafi's brains would have been quite literally blown out of their skulls.

Neither Denton nor Havilland asked any questions of these witnesses, leaving Collins and Khan to extract every last gruesome detail. When there were no more physical horrors left to be exposed, Alison read Sarah Levin's statement to the jury.

*I am Dr Sarah Elizabeth Levin of 18C Ashwell Road, Bristol. This statement is true to the best of my knowledge and belief and I make it knowing that if it is tendered in evidence I shall be liable to prosecution if I have wilfully stated in it anything I know to be false or do not believe to be true.*

*In October 2001 I was a first-year undergraduate student at Bristol university studying physics. Towards the end of that month I was attending a faculty drinks party when I was approached by an American man who introduced himself as Henry Silverman. Silverman said he was a Professor of Chemistry carrying out confidential research for an Anglo-American defence company. I would estimate he was in his early to mid-forties at the time. He was polite and charming and I was flattered by his attention.*

*Several days later Silverman telephoned me to ask if I could meet him to discuss a 'professional matter'. He said my head of department, Professor Rhydian Brightman, had given him my number. I met him on a Friday evening after lectures in a café near Goldney Hall, where I was living at the time. It was during this meeting that he told me he was also helping to collect intelligence for the American government on British Muslim students suspected of being engaged in extremist activity. He* said he was looking for a 'bright young woman' to work with, and that his employers could help me a great deal. He claimed to have helped other students gain scholarships to top American universities and said he could do the same for me. At that time my education was being funded through loans and I was tempted by the prospect of being able to pay off my debts and study abroad. I told Silverman I would think about it, and met him on one further occasion – at the Hotel du Vin restaurant in central Bristol – before agreeing to work for him.

During our third meeting, this time at a cafe in Whiteladies Road, he told me that he wanted me to pay special attention to Nazim Jamal, one of the students in my year group. He said that Nazim was involved with an organization called Hizb ut-Tahrir and that, along with other students, he was attending a radical mosque. I was told their mullah was a man named Sayeed Faruq, who was suspected of being a recruiting agent for terrorist groups. Silverman claimed that emails had been inter-cepted in which Nazim and a close friend of his – a law student by the name of Rafi Hassan – had discussed ways of 'bringing off a British 9/11'. He admitted that it might just have been a case of young men fantasizing, but emphasized that they both exactly fitted the profile of those al-Qaeda was known to be recruiting. When I asked Silverman why he thought I could get close to Nazim, he replied that he liked to look at pretty blonde girls on the internet. I told Silverman right then that I had no intention of prostituting myself, but he assured me that wasn't what he was asking of me – I was just to try to talk to and befriend him. He offered me £500 in cash and promised there would be more payments as and when I came up with infor-mation.

Getting close to Nazim proved easier than I had anticipated. I teamed up with him during a practical exercise in the lab and struck up a rapport. He wasn't at all how I had expected. He'd been to a good school and it turned out that we had many *interests in common. During the following weeks we worked a lot together and became genuinely fond of each other, although Nazim was uncomfortable about being seen with me in public. During the last week of term, at the beginning of December 2001, he invited me back to his room and we ended up spending the night together.*

*We kept in touch during the vacation and our relationship continued into the following term. By this time I had become extremely attached to Nazim and had almost allowed myself to forget how the relationship had started. But Silverman began calling me in January and pressing me for information. Over the course of the spring term Nazim and I became closer. We spent several nights a week together, although he was very conflicted over this and would get up to pray at dawn, even when I was in the room. He didn't talk much to me about religion or politics, but I could see from the books he read and by checking the sites he visited on the internet that he had become very committed to the Islamist cause. Several times I overheard him talking to Asian friends about Israel and Palestine and the war in Afghanistan. On the few occasions I tried to speak to him about his beliefs, he would invariably change the subject and say that it was irrelevant or that I wouldn't be interested. Increasingly, I got the feeling that he had two lives: one he shared with me, the other with his Asian friends, and he never allowed them to cross. As a result I didn't have much to tell Silverman, who became frustrated by my lack of progress. He started phoning me most days, suggesting ways I could ask more questions. He even said I should talk to Nazim about converting to Islam.*

*I was growing increasingly uncomfortable with the situation, and quite frankly I was looking for a way out when, at the very end of term Nazim announced that he wanted to end our relationship. He wouldn't give any reasons, but he was visibly upset. I remember thinking that it was almost as if he'd been found out and had been ordered to stay away from me.*

I told Silverman what had happened and he was furious. He said he had other information that Nazim and several friends had been discussing an attack on one of the four nuclear power stations along the Severn estuary. They'd been followed one weekend driving to Hinkley Point, then on to Maybury. He ordered me not to take no for an answer. By this time I was really frightened of him and had no one to turn to for help.

At the start of the summer term I tried to get back with Nazim, but he became hostile towards me, telling me to stay away from him. Silverman responded by giving me several miniature listening devices and told me I had to hide them in Nazim's room. That was the one time I did prostitute myself. I went to see him late in the evening and begged him to let me in. We spent the night together, but he made me swear not to tell anyone. The next morning he was in tears: he'd missed his dawn prayers and he blamed me. He said I was a whore and had been sent by the devil to tempt him. He was very emotional and left the room while I got dressed. I was angry with him and disgusted with myself. I locked the door and searched though his papers. I found a pad on which he'd taken down notes at one of his religious meetings and discovered that at the back of it he'd written a list of times and places. I remember the first entry: it was Avonmouth fuel depot. I photographed the page with a miniature digital camera Silverman had given me.

He was delighted with the list and said it was evidence that Nazim and his friends were planning to hijack a fuel tanker and crash it into one of the four power stations. He even speculated that they were planning multiple hijacks and hoping to blow a hole in the side of a reactor. He wanted to know more. I told him the relationship had broken down, but he insisted I get as close to Nazim as I could. No detail was too small – changes in mood, the slightest alteration in appearance – he wanted to know everything.

*I did what I was asked. Throughout June I contacted Silverman nearly every day. I observed Nazim become increasingly distracted and withdrawn. He missed lectures and classes. He wouldn't speak to me or any of the other students. I became concerned and asked Silverman what was going to happen to Nazim. He wouldn't answer. He just told me to keep reporting.*

*By mid-June I had convinced myself that Nazim was genuinely involved in a terrorist conspiracy. Then something happened to change my mind. Out of the blue he stopped me in the corridor – I think it was on the 24th – and said that he was sorry he had behaved so badly towards me. His mood had completely altered: it was the first time I'd seen him smile in weeks. I asked if he was OK. He said he was fine. He touched my hand and then walked away. We never spoke again.*

*On Saturday 29 June 2002 Silverman phoned and arranged to pick me up outside Goldney Hall. He drove me up to Bristol Downs and handed me an envelope containing £5,000. He told me that Nazim and Rafi Hassan had been arrested – he didn't say by whom – and that I wasn't to say a word to anyone. He didn't make any specific threats, but he didn't need to: his manner told me everything I needed to know.*

*About a week later he called again and instructed me to give a statement to the police, saying that I had overheard Nazim talking to Asian friends in the canteen about going to fight in Afghanistan. He told me to keep it short. I didn't dare disobey him.*

*He contacted me once more in late July. He said he was leaving the country to work abroad but that he'd hold good to his promise. In the first term of my third year I was sent an application form to apply for a Stevenson scholarship to Harvard. I was successful: I studied there for three years and gained a doctorate in 2007.*

*I have no knowledge of what happened to Nazim Jamal or Rafi Hassan. From the little that Silverman told me, I formed the impression that they had been arrested by the Security Services. As I became better informed about the political situation, I speculated that they had been taken into custody by the US authorities and removed to a foreign country, but I have no evidence for this.*

*I am now in the protective custody of the British Security Services and make this statement freely, willingly and am receiving no reward or favour in exchange.*

Khan shot to his feet.

'Ma'am,' he said, with an expression of complete incredulity, 'are you honestly proposing that the contents of this statement cannot be reported or made known to anyone outside the immediate families of the deceased? If what Dr Levin says is true, words cannot describe the depth of corruption that this represents.'

Collins, sitting alongside him, nodded in agreement. Havilland shifted uncomfortably in his seat. Martha Denton wore an expression of impassive detachment.

'I'm not proposing anything, Mr Khan. How each of us behaves with a gun pressed to our heads is a matter of individual conscience.'

Khan was defiant. 'I refuse to be silenced. I intend to make the evidence we have heard public by whatever means possible.'

Jenny felt the eyes of Golder, Rhys and Moreton on her. She realized that the wall of silence that had been erected around her proceedings would never be breached. Immediate imprisonment awaited any newspaper editor or broadcaster who disobeyed the order. If Khan wanted to spread the word he would be restricted to megaphone and soapbox or an obscure extra-territorial corner of the internet, where he would compete for attention with the cranks and conspiracy theorists.

'You must do as you see fit, Mr Khan,' Jenny said, and began her summing up to the jury.

A sense of anticlimax greeted the verdict of unlawful killing. There was no sense of a blow being struck for justice, no surge of satisfaction that the truth would now be made known to a waiting world. Rather it was a guilty, furtive moment in which everyone in the room felt as if they had tacitly participated in the concealment of an evil too monstrous and powerful to confront. The uneasy feeling of complicity was completed when Jenny reminded the jury that every last word they had heard must remain absolutely secret, even from their immediate familes.

She couldn't decide whether she had uncovered the truth, or buried it more deeply.

As the jurors shuffled from their seats, she looked across at Mr Jamal. He wiped tears from his cheek, gave her a brief nod of acceptance, and made his way to the back of the hall, where police officers waited to escort him to his car. It was cold comfort, but she sensed he was glad there would be no publicity.

Not so Khan. He burst outside and announced to waiting supporters that their brothers had been murdered by American and British agents. A minor riot broke out. There were scuffles and arrests, cracked heads and screams of pain, but no reporters to witness them.

Jenny met Golder and Rhys in the restaurant at the bird sanctuary. They sat by the window overlooking the pond. The light was fading from a brilliant sky and the flamingos wading in the water gleamed fluorescent pink.

'Do you like birds?' Gillian Golder asked, stirring sweetener into milky tea.

'Most kinds. Don't you?'

'As long as they're not grubby,' Golder said. 'I think all the pigeons in London should be exterminated.'

'I rather admire their tenacity.'

Alun Rhys cut in, 'What do you want to know, Mrs Cooper?'

Jenny sipped her tepid coffee. There was so much she wanted to be told, and she trusted them so little.

'Who is Silverman?'

Golder answered. 'As far as we can ascertain he was an American agent operating outside the usual channels of co-operation. He appeared to have access to our intelligence, but we knew nothing of him or his activities.'

'You're denying all knowledge of him?'

'They were fearful times. The Americans were understand-ably jumpy and we had let the grass grow under our feet rather. Not that that's any justification for summary killing, I grant you.'

Jenny remained sceptical. 'If they thought they'd identified terrorists, why not just hand them over to you or fly them out of the country?'

Golder and Rhys exchanged a look. Golder said, 'We're still working on that. All we have at present is the little Alec McAvoy told us. Apparently Tathum confessed that he and his colleague – since killed in Iraq, if that's any consolation – brought the two boys straight from Bristol to the woods, where they were met by Silverman. He interrogated them for most of the night, extracted nothing except denials, then shot Hassan as an incentive to Jamal. Seemingly it didn't have the desired effect.'

'You're in contact with McAvoy?' Jenny tried not to show her excitement.

'He made a single call to the police. There's been no other communication.'

'Will he be prosecuted?'

The loyal Crown servants exchanged another glance. 'That's a decision that depends on many factors,' Rhys said, 'not least of which is whether he's still alive. The police found a vehicle yesterday which we think may be his.'

'Where?'

'Just along the estuary from here, at Aust, near the bridge.'

Jenny gazed out at the birds and told herself it was a ruse on McAvoy's part. He was buying time, that was all, throwing them off the scent while he worked out his next move. He wouldn't leave her now, he had promised . . .

Golder's harsh, businesslike voice interrupted her thoughts. 'We're informed by the police that he's also wanted in connection with another suspected killing. He recently orchestrated the defence of a Czech nightclub owner by the name of Marek Stich, who shot dead a young traffic policeman but got a miraculous not guilty. Stich's girlfriend went missing shortly before his trial. She was Ukrainian. Apparently CID are working on the theory that hers was the body that was famously stolen from your local mortuary last week.'

'That can't be right . . .'

'I couldn't possibly comment,' Gillian Golder said, 'I suggest you talk to the police.'

He wouldn't. He couldn't have . . . But why else would he have come to view the Jane Doe that day? She remembered now: he had told her a story about a client with a missing daughter which he never repeated again. It was a fiction – his client was Stich. He must have sent McAvoy to identify the corpse that had unkindly washed back up on the tide. But that wasn't illegal, it wasn't complicity, it was just what criminal lawyers did for their clients. McAvoy would have had nothing to do with the murder or with the theft of a body.

'I presume you'd like our thoughts on Mrs Jamal?' Golder interrupted her reverie.

'Yes,' Jenny said, distracted.

'We're assuming Silverman was involved in her death. Our best guess is that the prospect of a public inquest rattled him somewhat. From what we gather he's not the most stable of individuals. We've no concrete evidence that he forced her to strip naked and drink half a bottle of whisky, but it seems as likely an explanation as any.'

'Why? She didn't know anything.'

'She might have known about Dr Levin. She might have approached her, prodded her conscience, got her to talk.'

'But he knew Levin. He could have talked to her directly.'

'We assume he probably did,' Rhys said. 'Disposing of Mrs Jamal was merely a housekeeping exercise, if you like.'

'What about Anna Rose?'

Rhys deferred to Gillian Golder, who considered her words carefully. 'As far as we know, Silverman resurfaced early last year after an extended period in the Middle East. He came back to Sarah Levin, looking for another young woman to work for him.'

'In the same university?'

'That's where he had the contacts,' Golder said. 'But we think his big idea this time was rather different.' She paused for a moment to weigh her words. 'Let's just say that, despite outward appearances, certain of our American cousins still harbour a residual frustration with Britistan, as they like to call us. They think we still need shocking out of what they see as our complacency over the radical elements among our Muslim population. Anna Rose was to be less of an informer and more of an agent provocateur.'

Golder gave Jenny a look as if to say that was as far as she was prepared to go.

Jenny wasn't satisfied. 'He was using her to set up Salim Hussain. She was to pretend she could get hold of the ingredients for a dirty bomb, but they actually came from Silverman. Then what . . . she took fright and ran?'

'You understand that we're not at liberty to disclose.'

'What does Silverman want? What's his agenda? He surely wasn't going to let a radioactive bomb go off?'

I wouldn't have thought so, no, but the propaganda value would have been, well . . . immeasurable. And I'm sure our American colleagues would have been more than happy to advise us on the necessary cleansing measures to prevent any future occurrence.'

'What's happened to him? Have you got him, too?'

Gillian Golder glanced at her watch. 'I'm afraid we have to go.' She gulped a mouthful of tea and stood up from the table. She told Rhys she'd see him outside and headed for the ladies' room.

Faintly embarrassed, Rhys said, 'Regarding Mr McAvoy, you wouldn't know who this might be for, would you? It was found in his car.'

He produced a clear plastic evidence bag from his jacket pocket which contained a folded scrap of lined paper. Written in an elegant cursive hand in ink that might have been spattered by rain or teardrops, were the words, 'My Dark Rosaleen'.

'May I?'

'Of course,' Rhys said, awkwardly. He opened the bag and handed her the note.

She turned away from him, pretending to need the vestiges of daylight afforded by the window to read it. The verses were set out with copybook neatness:

> *Roll forth, my love, like the rushing river,*
> *That sweeps along to the mighty sea;*
> *God will inspire me while I deliver,*
> > *My soul of thee!*

*Tell thou the world, when my bones lie whitening*
*Amid the last homes of youth and eld,*
*That once there was whose veins ran lightning*
    *No eye beheld.*

*Him grant a grave to, ye pitying noble,*
*Deep in your bosoms: there let him dwell.*
*He, too, had tears for all souls in trouble,*
    *Here and in hell.*

'Does it mean anything to you, Mrs Cooper?' Rhys said. 'Mrs Cooper . . . ?'

Throughout Saturday Alison drip-fed Jenny snippets of information gleaned from ex-colleagues in CID. She learned that photographs of Marek Stich's missing girlfriend appeared to match those of the Jane Doe, and that Stich himself had been arrested on suspicion of murder and conspiracy to commit arson. McAvoy was being sought as an accomplice to the 'unlawful concealment, disposal or destruction' of a corpse. There had been no activity on his credit cards or bank account for forty-eight hours and his phone hadn't been used since his final call to Pironi. There were unconfirmed reports of a smartly dressed middle-aged man seen walking along the public walkway at the edge of the Severn Bridge late on Friday morning, but no one had witnessed a suicide. The clever money in CID was still on him turning up in a few weeks' time to cut a deal: immunity from prosecution in exchange for giving evidence against Stich.

But Jenny sensed he had gone; not out of self-pity or despair but willingly to receive his judgement. Just how he had touched her, just what his brief presence in her life had meant she couldn't yet discern, but that she soon would she had no doubt.

# EPILOGUE

JENNY CROSSED THE YARD AT Steve's farm. She found him at work in the vegetable garden behind the barn, a flurry of hungry birds scrapping over the worms and insects he'd turned up in the black earth. He was too absorbed in the physicality of his task to notice her leaning on the rail watching him. He'd dug a whole row before a sixth sense made him glance over his shoulder.

'Jenny, how long have you been there?' He wiped his forehead on the sleeve of his plaid work shirt.

'A while. You looked like you were miles away.'

'I was.' He planted the spade in the soil and wandered over.

'I'm sorry not to have been in touch,' she said. 'You left a message days ago. I got caught up with things at the office.'

'I guessed as much.'

He leaned against the opposite side of the fence, out of touching distance she noticed, squinting against the sharp stabs of winter sunlight. He'd lost weight, the skin drawn tight against his jawbone, a slight hollowness to his eyes. He seemed pensive.

'Ross still with his dad?' Steve said.

'Yes . . . I don't know, maybe he's better off in town for the time being. I'm not much company for him.'

'You said David took him.'

'It was my fault . . . Ross found me in a bit of a state one night. Had to put me to bed.'

Steve picked at a splinter on the weather-worn fence rail. 'You want to talk about it?'

'You must be sick of me coming to you for therapy. It's about time I got a grip on myself.'

He looked up at her. 'Can I say something?'

She nodded.

'It makes you tense having him around. It's as if the responsibility frightens you.'

She shrugged. 'It does. He's my son.'

'What are you frightened off?'

Jenny shook her head, feeling the tightness in her throat that meant she was resisting tears. 'If I knew that . . .'

Steve moved towards her and brushed her face gently with his hand. 'You don't need to get a grip, Jenny, you need to let go.'

'Yeah, right – an emotionally incontinent coroner. That'd inspire confidence.'

'You've got to try . . . And I think you want to.'

He ran his hand through her hair and stroked her neck, grazed her cheek with his lips.

It felt good to be close again, to feel the warmth of his skin.

Jenny said, 'On your message you said there was something you wanted to say.'

'There is . . . but I wasn't expecting . . .'

He closed his eyes, trying to find the words.

'I don't know how you feel,' Steve said, 'whether you want to be with me or . . . but I want to be with you, Jenny. I've spent months trying not to say it, but I have to. I'm in love with you.'

She was shocked. 'You don't mean that.'

'You've got enough to deal with without me saying things

415

I don't mean.' He kissed her lightly on the forehead. 'There, I've said it. Over to you.'

He stepped away and picked up his spade. 'I promised myself I'd finish this section before lunch. Do you want to stay?'

'I'm meant to be going to see my father.'

'Oh . . . I didn't know he was still around.'

'He's in a nursing home in Weston. There's something I need to ask him about the past. Doctor's orders.'

'Then you'd better go . . . But if you're going to turn me down, I'd rather you put me out of my misery now.'

Jenny looked up at the ice blue sky. 'I could come back afterwards.'

'Will you stay?'

'Yes. I'd like that . . . It feels like a day for a new beginning.'


For the previous five years Brian Cooper's life had been an eight-by-ten single room on the second floor of a large pebble-dashed villa a short walk from the sea front. He was only seventy-three years old and physically in robust health, but dementia had struck during his mid-sixties and his second wife, a woman for whom Jenny had never had any affection, took less than a year to dump him in the home and find another man to take her on cheap Mediterranean cruises. There had been plenty of visitors at first, but as Brian's lucid moments became rarer they dried up to a dutiful trickle. Jenny hadn't seen him since Christmas Eve, when he'd thrown his dinner at the television, believing it was his first wife, Jenny's mother, reading the evening news.

The nurse warned her that she might find him a little quiet. He was taking new tablets to help control his increasingly erratic and explosive moods. Jenny felt in no position to criticize.

She tapped on the door and pushed it open.

'Hi, Dad.'

He was sitting in his shirtsleeves, his armchair facing the window which looked out onto the street below. He was clean and shaved, his hair cut neatly.

'Dad? It's Jenny.'

She came to the corner of the bed by his chair and sat down.

'I haven't seen you for a while. How are you?'

His eyes flicked suspiciously towards her; his mouth started to move, but he made no sound. Then, seeming to lose interest, he turned his gaze towards a seagull which had landed on the windowsill clutching a crust of burger bun in its beak. He smiled.

Jenny said, 'You're looking well. How are you feeling?'

There was no answer. There seldom was, but the specialist had told her to keep talking to him like an adult as long as she could bear to. There was always a chance that some of it might be going in, he had said; she would know when he stopped comprehending entirely. Jenny looked for signs of recognition and saw a childlike quality in his face; almost playful as he gazed at the gull tearing at the scrap it had pinned beneath its foot.

'Dad, I need to ask you something. I've been trying to remember some things about when I was little. I thought it would be good to record them for Ross, put them together with some of the old photographs – something he can show his kids one day.'

Brian nodded, as if he understood perfectly well.

She dipped into her handbag and brought out several old Polaroids she'd dug out from a shoebox earlier that morning.

She showed them to him: pictures of her on a swing aged four or five in the back garden of their house, Brian smiling, pushing her with one hand, a cigarette in the other.

'I remember you putting that up. It was a birthday present, wasn't it?'

'Yes, that was your birthday. You were a little smiler. Look at you.' He took the photograph from her and stared at it.

Jenny felt a surge of excitement. 'You remember that?'

'That was the dress my mother made you. She slaved over that, cost her eyesight, she said.'

They were well-worn phrases, words she'd heard a thousand times before, but they'd been prompted by the pictures, not thrown up at random like most of what little he offered these days. She had to strike while she could.

'Oh damn, I must have forgotten to put it in. There was one I found with Katy written on the back. I couldn't think who she was . . .'

'Cousin Katy?'

*Cousin?* Jenny could only think of three first cousins, all of whom were boys.

'Katy's my cousin? You're sure?'

'Jim and Penny's little girl.'

Jim and Penny were Brian's brother and his wife. They only had one child, a son who was ten years younger than Jenny.

'I don't think that can be right, Dad.'

Brian dropped the photograph on the floor. 'You wouldn't get a cup of tea in this place if you were dying of thirst.'

Jenny picked it up. 'I don't remember a Katy. Jim and Penny only had Christopher, didn't they?'

'Oily bastard all dressed up in his suit and tie. Your mother thought he had money. Hah!'

Another familiar, but this time disconnected refrain – he

was referring to the estate agent who had run off with Jenny's mother.

'I'm not talking about Mum now,' Jenny said. 'What happened to Cousin Katy?'

A second gull joined the first on the windowsill and snatched the remainder of the bun from its beak. Brian chuckled.

'Dad, it's important. I need to know.'

His eyes faded and seemed to mist over.

'Dad, please try.'

She took hold of his arm and shook it. He wrenched it away, the muscles in his forearms hard as iron.

'You remember, Smiler,' he said. 'You killed her.'

# ACKNOWLEDGEMENTS

Writing a first book is an act of pure speculation. So what if it doesn't work, you say to yourself; at least I gave it a try. Writing a second, with a deadline to meet and people waiting expectantly for your manuscript, is a different enterprise entirely. Fortunately for me those people have been unfailingly supportive and encouraging. Special thanks go to Greg Hunt, my straight-talking screen-writing agent, who propelled me into writing novels with the unerring assertion that 'no one takes you seriously until you've written a book', and to Zoë Waldie, my literary agent, who has given me nothing but faultlessly sound advice. Huge thanks also to Maria Rejt, my publisher and editor at Macmillan, who has many fine gifts including the rare ability to convey her great wisdom in the subtlest and most respectful of ways, and also to all her friendly and highly professional team.

I would also like to thank my colourful and lively family and extended family, all of whom lend their unconditional support. In particular, my mother and stepfather, writers both, are always there with an understanding of what it takes to return day after day to the lonely task of putting one word after another, and my father, a musician, has consistently proved to me that a level head can rest on artistic shoulders. My wife and sons, daily spectators to the many ups and downs of the writer's life, make everything possible.

Ed Husain's book *The Islamist* (Penguin, London, 2007) was a great help in understanding the mind of the young Muslim radical. It is essential reading for anyone seeking to comprehend how young men raised in the West can be seduced by ugly extremism and also be delivered from it.

Finally, thanks to all those friends and former colleagues in the legal profession upon whom I rely for their experience and anecdotes, especially James McIntyre, who leave me in no doubt that truth is always stranger than fiction.

*If you enjoyed* The Disappeared
*you'll love the next thrilling novel in* M. R. Hall's
Jenny Cooper *series:*

# THE REDEEMED

A man's body is discovered in a churchyard, the sign of the cross carved into his abdomen. Later he is identified as Alan Jacobs, a troubled nurse at a local psychiatric facility. To Jenny Cooper, Severn Vale District Coroner, it seems likely to be an open and shut suicide case, but something tells her to probe a little deeper.

Then enigmatic young priest, Father Lucas Starr, arrives on Jenny's doorstep, entreating her to hold an inquest into the death of Eva Donaldson, a reformed porn actress turned campaigner. A young man has recently been sentenced for Eva's brutal murder, but Father Lucas is convinced of his innocence.

Jenny's investigations into Eva's death lead her to a powerful new religious group: the Mission Church of God, and to those who control it. Meanwhile, Jenny finds herself finally having to confront the demons of her past, which have tormented her for so long. And as her private life threatens to shatter, she is put under intense pressure, from all angles, to cease her investigations. But to Jenny Cooper, whose whole life has been governed by deception, the truth is everything . . .

*I long for scenes where man has never trod –*
*For scenes where woman never smiled or wept –*
*There to abide with my Creator, God,*
*And sleep as I in childhood sweetly slept,*
*Full of high thoughts, unborn. So let me lie, –*
*The grass below; above, the vaulted sky.*

John Clare,
Written in Northampton County Asylum

For the Lord himself will come down from heaven, with a loud command, with the voice of the archangel and with the trumpet call of God, and the dead in Christ will rise first. After that, we who are still alive and are left will be caught up together with them in the clouds to meet the Lord in the air. And so we will be with the Lord forever.

1 Thessalonians 4:16–17

# ONE

JENNY WAS DRINKING cordial by the stream at the end of her overgrown garden, watching a school of tiny brown trout flick this way and that, quick as lightning. It was late June, and the sweet-smelling breeze was warm against her bare legs. Before the telephone intruded, she had managed to lose herself – how long for, she couldn't say – hypnotized by the gently swaying ash trees and the buzz of grasshoppers in the nettles.

A moment of peace. Too good to last.

She walked slowly back across the ankle-high lawn, hoping that whoever was disturbing her on a Sunday morning would give up and leave her to her daydreams. They didn't. She had counted eight rings by the time she stepped through the back door of the cottage onto the cool flags of the tiny kitchen, ten by the time she had lifted the iron latch to the living room that smelled of old oak and soot from the inglenook. It was much colder inside than out. The flesh on her arms tightened into goose bumps as she lifted the receiver. She was a coroner again.

'Oh, you're there, Mrs Cooper.' It was Alison, her officer, with a note of reproach in her voice.

'I was outside.'

'CID just called me. There's a body they think you might want to see while it's still in situ. Looks like a suicide.'

'Is there any particular reason why I should? I can't go every time.'

'You asked them for closer cooperation, this is it.'

'I thought they might do something useful like email a photograph.'

'It's progress, Mrs Cooper. Between you and me, I get the impression you've embarrassed them enough times that they're frightened of you.'

Jenny couldn't imagine frightening anyone. 'I suppose I'd better show willing. Where is it?'

'St Peter's church, Frampton Cotterell.'

'I don't think I know it.'

'You'll like it. It's a lovely spot.'

The Severn Bridge was all but empty of traffic as Jenny crossed the mile-wide river into England. Beneath her, the tide was chasing out to sea at a gallop: the best time to jump if you didn't want to be found; you'd be halfway to Ireland before low water. That's how Alec McAvoy had judged it, over three months ago now. She thought of him each time she crossed, picturing his wispy hair blowing over those moss-green eyes, too young for his face, as he said his final prayers. He hadn't wanted his body fished out and cut open, or for her to see him lying naked in the drawer of a mortuary refrigerator. She told herself it had been a kindness on his part, the last and only thing he could give her.

A forensics van, a single squad car and an unmarked pool vehicle were parked in the quiet road outside the elaborate Gothic church. A skeleton Sunday crew. A handful of teenagers were loitering on the other side of the road, a little blonde girl talking excitedly into her phone, thrilled with the drama of it all. It wasn't even a policeman who had been posted at the churchyard gate, but an overweight community support officer who made a meal of checking Jenny's credentials before letting her through, as if he were doing her a big favour.

The activity was in a far corner beyond the gravestones; an untended triangle that had been left to grow wild. A plain clothes detective glanced up and saw her coming but made no effort to step forwards to greet her, his focus switching immediately back to the body. He watched intently while one man in white overalls positioned a measuring tape and another took photographs.

She made an effort to sound friendly. 'Good morning. Jenny Cooper. Severn Vale District Coroner.'

The detective gave a perfunctory nod.

'Tony Wallace. DI.'

Somewhere in his late forties, slim and fit, he spoke with the clipped abruptness of a man who still entertained ambition. He was wearing what might have been a hand-tailored suit, far smarter than most policemen.

She followed his gaze to the body lying amongst the rye grass and buttercups. It was that of a naked, well-built man in his thirties. His head, which was facing towards them, was shaved to a tight crew cut to disguise his balding temples. He was lying on his back, arms at forty-five degrees to his torso. Carved into his chest and abdomen, stretching all the way down to his groin, was the sign of the cross. By the out-stretched fingers of his right hand Jenny caught the glint of a kitchen knife, the blade no more than four inches long. His skin was waxy yellow and his stomach and face had begun to bloat; bluebottles were gathering on the eyes, lips and genitals.

'Looks like he's been here a few hours,' Jenny said, familiar enough with corpses after a year as coroner not to be shocked by the sight.

'Yesterday evening at the latest, I'd say,' DI Wallace replied.

The men in white overalls nodded their agreement, the larger of the two saying, 'Definitely twelve hours plus – you've only got to look at the colour of his skin.'

'Any idea of the cause of death?'

'Not yet,' Wallace said. 'No obvious signs of injury.'

'Who found him?'

'Couple of kids looking for somewhere to drink their cider. We found his clothes in the bin over there.' He nodded towards the corner of the church.

'Do we know who he is?'

'Not for certain, but a woman who lives a couple of miles down the road reported her husband missing this morning. Sounds like him – Alan Jacobs, thirty-five, senior psychiatric nurse at the Conway Unit.'

Jenny felt a shudder pass through her, a cold, tight feeling around her chest. The Conway Unit was a secure psychiatric facility for the newly sectioned and acutely ill. At the height of her 'episode' she had once spent a single night there. Dr Travis had persuaded her it was for the best, but it was the closest thing to hell on earth she had ever known. Lying awake through the night, believing she might die at any moment, while the woman in the bed next to her screamed at invisible ghosts and demons.

She looked again at the dead man. She could imagine him as a nurse. He was big, like so many of them were, but with gentle hands and a soft face.

'What do you make of the cross?' Wallace asked, his tone softening a little now he could sense she wasn't vying for control.

Jenny shrugged, 'I'd say God was on his mind, or what was left of it.'

Wallace nodded, making no comment, then said, 'I've got a busy week ahead – I persuaded the pathologist to come in and do him straight away. Is that all right with you?'

'Fine,' Jenny said. 'What's this, be nice to the coroner week?'

'You've got yourself a reputation, Mrs Cooper,' DI Wallace said. 'And I'm trying to make super.' He gave her a look, as if to say, *you see my problem?*

Jenny said, 'It's a tough world.'

She had a hectic week in store, too. There'd been a messy construction accident the previous Tuesday which had prompted five separate firms of lawyers to bombard her office with demands for all manner of forensic investigations her puny budget wouldn't stretch to. The inquest, when it came, would last the best part of a month. Two workmen and a site supervisor had been crushed to death in a crane collapse, six others injured. She was already beginning to sense the political pressure to avoid any verdict which might prompt manslaughter charges: the CEO of the lead contractor was a major government donor. Compared with that mess, dealing with a simple suicide would be a holiday.

'Seen enough?' Wallace said.

'For now,' Jenny said, and made her way back across the graveyard, passing two smiling undertaker's assistants carrying a stretcher. One of them beamed at her, not a care in the world.

She drove into the city for a light lunch at a new Italian cafe on the waterfront, sipped her mineral water like a good girl – she'd managed to stay dry since her little slip-up with Alec McAvoy – and headed out to the mortuary at the Vale hospital in time to catch the end of the autopsy.

Dr Andy Kerr was stooped over the steel counter when Jenny entered, picking over a portion of viscera. The radio was playing the same kind of tuneless R&B her teenage son inflicted on her every time they shared a car. Andy – he had somehow persuaded her not to call him Dr Kerr – was creeping reluctantly towards his mid-thirties and trying to turn back the clock. He'd recently added a gold stud to his left ear.

She tried not to look at the corpse which lay open from neck to navel on the autopsy table. 'Hi. Find anything?'

'Hold on . . .' Andy said, concentrating on a delicate task. With a pair of tweezers he lifted something tiny out from what she could now see was the dead man's stomach and placed it in a kidney dish. 'Looks like we might have a cause of death shaping up. He had a belly full of pills.'

'That makes sense. If he's who the police think he is, he was a psychiatric nurse.'

Andy extracted another object, an undigested white tablet, and held it up to the light. 'PB 60. Phenobarbital, probably. Used to treat seizures. Depresses respiration and leads to a fairly painless death. And there's liver inflammation which would be a side-effect of the overdose.'

'An open and shut suicide.'

'More or less.'

'There's something else?' She sneaked a glance and wished she hadn't; the empty rib cage a site from a butcher's window.

'Minor lesions on both forearms,' he looked at her over his mask, 'as if someone had dug their nails in, perhaps.'

'Violently?'

'Hard to say.' Finished with the stomach, he picked it up in both hands and placed it alongside the other major organs he had examined and cut into sections. 'You don't know if the police turned him over? Blood had pooled towards the front of his body but the photos they took at the locus show him on his back.'

'Unlikely. The DI said some kids stumbled across him – maybe it was them?'

'Kids? You think they'd touch a stranger's corpse?' He stepped over to the body with a scalpel and began cutting around the hairline in preparation for peeling the scalp forwards over the face. It was Jenny's cue to leave.

'Keep me posted.'

'Will do.'

She left him alone in the autopsy room, humming along with the radio.

She telephoned DI Wallace as she stepped out into the welcome fresh air, the smell of death clinging stubbornly to her clothes. Wallace listened to Andy's findings and said it sounded as if it would have to remain a police matter, at least until he'd ruled out the possibility of foul play. He informed Jenny that Mrs Jacobs had identified her husband's body from a photograph but had been too emotional to talk. In the meantime he'd been over to the Conway Unit in Clifton and met Alan Jacobs' line manager, a Mrs Deborah Bishop. Jacobs was Senior Staff Nurse in the young persons ward dealing with twelve- to eighteen-year-olds. As far as Bishop had been aware he'd been in good spirits; she had seemed badly shaken at the news.

Jenny said, 'Have you got Mrs Jacobs' address?'

'Thirty-nine Fielding Road, Coalpit Heath,' DI Wallace said after a brief hesitation, the tightness in his voice suggesting that he'd rather she stayed well away from the bereaved until it was her turn.

Jenny's gut told her there was more to his reluctance than protecting his turf. She wondered if Bishop had told him something he hadn't let on. A death, however loosely related to vulnerable teenagers, would have set alarm bells ringing all the way to Whitehall. Senior civil servants in the Department of Health would already be asking questions of their own.

Jenny thanked him for the information and let him know he wouldn't be having it all on his own terms: 'I'll have my officer take Mrs Jacobs through the procedure. Oh, and by the way – did your people alter the position of the body before I arrived?'

'Not to my knowledge. Seen as found.'

'Let me know if you hear different. Dr Kerr thinks it had been rolled over.'

The detective gave a dismissive grunt and rang off.

Jenny waited until early evening before calling on the widow. Technically there was no need for the coroner to disturb the next of kin while the police were still investigating, but she liked to make contact while emotions were still raw and questions had to be thought about before being answered. And there was something about Wallace that had troubled her.

Coalpit Heath was an outlying suburb at the north east of the city. She had resolved not to disturb the household if it was in darkness, but as she drew up opposite number 39 she noticed a crack of light behind the drawn curtains in the downstairs front room.

A woman in her sixties answered the door on the security chain, her face set in a hostile frown. 'What is it now?' The sound of a child's cry carried from somewhere in the house.

Jenny passed a business card through the crack. 'Jenny Cooper. Severn Vale District Coroner. I'd like to speak to Mrs Jacobs.'

The woman held the card out at arm's length trying to make out the print. 'I'm her mother.'

'Would it be all right to have a brief word?'

Sighing, she unhooked the chain and opened the door. 'I'd thought we'd have some peace.'

'I'll be as quick as I can.'

She led Jenny through a short hallway and into a living room that ran straight through into a kitchen. Her daughter, the widow, was lying on a tan leather sofa wearing pyjamas and a towelling gown. In one hand she held a string of rosary beads. A waste basket next to a coffee table was overflowing with used Kleenex.

'Ceri? It's the coroner,' the older woman said quietly. 'Don't worry about Josie. I'll see to her.'

Mrs Jacobs pocketed her beads and lowered her feet to the floor. She was thirty-five or thereabouts, pale with mousy blonde hair in a sensible bob. She attempted a smile with her 'hello', and Jenny saw in her face that she was suffering from shame as much as grief.

'Sorry to disturb you, Mrs Jacobs. I know it's a difficult time.'

'It's all right,' she said with a soft Welsh accent.

Jenny sat on a chair that matched the sofa and glanced around a room that seemed to have been disturbed. The books and DVDs on the shelves by the television were in a jumble. Toys spilled over the edges of a plastic crate.

Embarrassed by the mess, Ceri Jacobs said, 'The police were here most of the afternoon. They went through every-thing. I haven't been able . . .' She swallowed, holding back tears. 'How can I help you?'

'They might have explained that if they don't suspect foul play it's my job to determine your husband's cause of death.'

Mrs Jacobs nodded, and reached for a Kleenex, which she twisted in her fingers.

Were they looking for anything in particular?'

'They said it was routine. I can't remember all the things they took.'

'Computer? Address book?'

She nodded. 'And some of his clothes.' She pressed the tissue to her eyes. 'Ones that hadn't been washed. I don't know what for.'

'Computers are always taken as a matter of course. They'll

check the clothes for third-party DNA,' Jenny said. 'Just in case.'

'No one wanted to kill Alan ... Why would they?' Ceri Jacobs shook her head with an expression of bewildered incomprehension.

'The pathologist found pills in his stomach, Mrs Jacobs. Phenobarbital. It's a barbiturate, something he might have got hold of at the unit.'

Her gaze turned inwards as she seemed to disengage, not yet ready to absorb this information.

'Was he depressed, upset about anything?'

'No, not that he said to me,' she mouthed quietly. 'Work was always difficult, but he loved it. It was his vocation, he always said so.'

'Was he being treated for any psychiatric condition, or had he ever been?'

She shook her head.

'When did you last see him?'

'Yesterday afternoon. He said he'd had a call from the unit saying they had several staff sick and could he cover for the night?'

'Was that unusual?'

'It happens.'

'What time did he leave?'

'About four o'clock.' She reached out for her beads, clinging to them for security. 'I thought he'd be back by midnight. Josie woke me about six and I saw he hadn't been home. I tried to call him but his phone was off ... I don't know why, but I called the office at the unit. They said he hadn't been in, they had all the staff they needed.' Her eyes filled with tears. 'That's when I called the police.' The widow pressed her hands to her face. 'Why? ... What was he thinking of?'

Jenny had tried to train herself not to form judgements on first impressions, yet she couldn't help thinking that Mrs

Jacobs' knowledge of her husband might have been incomplete, to say the least. The house was focused exclusively on their child: framed baby photographs on every surface, nursery school paintings plastering a noticeboard that took up most of the kitchen wall, Ceri's stretchy pyjamas decorated with purple hippos. Alan Jacobs left here each day to work with the city's most mentally disturbed teenagers, a job you could only succeed in by winning their respect and connecting on their level. It was as if his wife had organized her home as a shield against all that; there was nothing of him or his life outside these walls to be seen.

Then she realized her mistake: God featured here, too. The simple oil painting on the wall behind the sofa was an icon – a modern rendering of the Virgin and child – and Ceri wore a silver crucifix around her neck.

'Did the police tell you anything about your husband's body, Mrs Jacobs?'

'I know he was . . .' she could barely bring herself to say it, '. . . naked.'

'And the cross on his torso?'

She shot Jenny a look she wasn't expecting, a flash of steely anger as sharp as a razor. 'What about it?'

'Why might he have done that, assuming it was him?'

'I've no idea.'

'I assume you're a Catholic, was—?'

'No, he wasn't,' she interrupted. 'For most of his life Alan wasn't religious at all; his family had poisoned him against it. But he had begun to change. He was an enquirer at St Joseph's. He'd been every Tuesday night for the last five months.'

'An 'enquirer'?'

'The church runs courses for those who want to learn about the faith.'

'Did he talk to you about it?'

'We talked about everything, Mrs Cooper. We were man and wife.' She stood up from the sofa. 'I'm sorry, my daughter's still crying. I'd like to go to her please.'

'Of course.'

'If you wouldn't mind seeing yourself out?'

Ceri Jacobs left the room.

As Jenny made her way to the front door she felt the coldness of the widow's disapproval follow her to the threshold and beyond. Driving away from the house she was left with an image of Ceri's face, the look she had given her: like an accusation of heresy. She imagined her dead husband mute in the face of her disapproval, enduring his suffering alone.